ABOUT THE AUTHOR

Mark Ellis lives in London and has been a barrister, corporate executive and entrepreneur. *Stalin's Gold* is the second in his Frank Merlin series. *Princes Gate* is the first.

STALIN'S
GOLD

Also by this author

Princes Gate

STALIN'S
GOLD

A FRANK MERLIN NOVEL

MARK ELLIS

Matador
9 Priory Business Park
Kibworth Beauchamp
Leicestershire LE8 0RX, UK
Tel: (+44) 116 279 2299
Fax: (+44) 116 279 2277
Email: books@troubador.co.uk
Web: www.troubador.co.uk/matador

ISBN 978 1783062 461 (paperback)
978 1783062 478 (hardback)

British Library Cataloguing in Publication Data.
A catalogue record for this book is available from the British Library.

Typeset by Troubador Publishing Ltd
Printed and bound in the UK by TJ International, Padstow, Cornwall

Matador is an imprint of Troubador Publishing Ltd

To Victoria, Kate, Claudia and Alexander

ACKNOWLEDGEMENTS

Many thanks again are due in particular to Jon Thurley and Patricia Preece for their advice and great help in pulling this book together. Also thanks to the readers of early drafts for comments and advice: Mair Ellis, my mother, who sadly died just before the publication of this book and who was my great fan in all things, Kate Ellis, Keith Ross, John Harrington and Geoff Barclay. Thank you to Victoria for editing help and to all my family for their support. Special thanks are due to my good friends, Gregg Berman and Norman Lang, who have done so much to help with the promotion of my work in the USA and have been great sources of encouragement. Audrey Manning yet again coped brilliantly with the deciphering and typing of the many drafts. Thank you Audrey. Last, but not least, thank you to all at Troubador Publishing Ltd who helped with the production of this book.

PROLOGUE

Moscow, December 1938

Lavrentiy Pavlovich Beria was not used to feeling intimidated. It was rather his job in life to intimidate others. Some might say that "intimidate" was quite a polite word for what he did. One month ago he had been appointed head of the NKVD, the state security service, by his Georgian compatriot, Josef Vissarionovich Dzhugashvili, otherwise known as Stalin. In this position it was his task to hunt down, terrorise, torture and, more often than not, exterminate the enemies of the state. Since, in the mind of his boss, this category of "enemies of the state" often appeared to embrace the majority of the Russian population, this was no easy task. However, as when he had run Georgia with blood-soaked efficiency, he approached it with ruthless determination. A powerful, self-confident and brilliant man nevertheless, as he sat in the leather armchair beside Stalin's surprisingly modest desk, Beria was feeling intimidated. Through the window he could see the snow beginning to fall in large, fluffy flakes down towards the courtyard. The roofs of the Kremlin already carried a thick layer of snow from yesterday's blizzard. He removed his thick-lensed spectacles and gave them a wipe with his red handkerchief, then rose and walked around the room in an attempt to relieve his anxiety. Pausing at a bookcase, he pulled out a heavy volume of Shakespeare's plays, which fell open at a passage from Macbeth.

"Found anything interesting?" The soft voice with its still thick Georgian accent made Beria jump and the book fell from his hand. "Now then, Lavrentiy Pavlovich, be careful there. That is one of the first Russian translations of Mr Shakespeare. It is worth a rouble or two."

Josef Stalin emerged fully from the side door through which he had gained access to the room and bent down to pick up the book, which was still open at the page Beria had been reading. "Ah, what have we here! 'There's daggers in men's smiles. The near in blood, the nearer bloody!' How true, don't you think? An important thing for men like us to remember. Duncan was not wary enough of those close to him and got himself killed. A mistake we shall not make, my friend, eh?"

Stalin smiled broadly, dislodging a few remaining specks of breakfast from his thick moustache, and patted Beria gently on his shining bald head. "Come."

As Beria went back to his chair, Stalin sat down at his desk, lit a pipe, then removed a folder from a drawer. "Gold, Lavrentiy. Do you know what I'm talking about?"

Unfortunately, Beria did. "The Spanish consignment?"

"Indeed so. Your predecessor, the Poisonous Dwarf, made little progress in this regard. I am hoping you will do better."

The Poisonous Dwarf, otherwise known as Nikolas Yezhov, had been eased aside by Stalin a few months earlier and had entered that black limbo land of disfavour, which seldom ended happily.

"I am just familiarising myself with the papers, Comrade Stalin."

"You may think, Lavrentiy, that in the scheme of things the loss of this gold might be of little account. When you consider that the bullion equivalent of at least five hundred million dollars ended up in our coffers, the loss of five or ten million dollars here or there might seem irrelevant. That, Lavrentiy Pavlovich, is not how I view things."

"No, sir. The theft of such an amount cannot be ignored."

"I want it back. Is that clear? And I want those responsible to pay the penalty – a particularly unpleasant penalty, understood?"

"Yes, sir."

Stalin sucked on his pipe and nodded. "Very good. And Lavrentiy?"

Beria could feel a trickle of sweat running down the back of his neck into his collar. "Sir?"

"People always seem to let me down in the end. You won't, will you?"

"No, sir."

The wind whistled outside as Beria closed the door.

CHAPTER 1

Sunday, September 1, 1940

In his dream he was lying on a bed. There was someone lying next to him. He wasn't sure who it was. It might be his wife. His dead wife. Or it might be someone else. He was in a room with white walls. The ceiling was white too or was it pale blue? There was a buzzing sound. Flies were walking on or flying to the ceiling. Their droning noise was soothing. A window was open somewhere and a pleasant warm breeze was blowing over his face. He felt something on his arm. A little pressure and then his arm was being shaken.

"Come on, Frank." He could hear a soft female voice. A voice with an accent. *An attractive accent*, he thought. "Come on, Frank, we'll miss the train." His eyes slowly opened to reveal a clear blue sky above. Someone was giggling and stroking his shoulder. "Oh, Frank."

He came fully to his senses and the soft comfort of the mattress in his dream gave way to the uncomfortable reality of Brighton's pebbled beach. He could still hear the droning noise above him, but it was the drone of aeroplanes rather than insects, very high above. He wasn't as well up on aircraft recognition as his sergeant, but he thought that they were Hurricanes and, as some of the planes were engaged in an elaborate dance around each other, he presumed he was seeing Messerschmitts as well. Suddenly, one of the fighters banked away from the others and started to drop through the sky. A trail of smoke followed it as its descent picked up pace. He sat up and watched in fascination as the aircraft pursued its deadly downward spiral into the sea. It disappeared some way out from the beach and he saw no parachute. "Let's hope that's one of theirs, eh, Sonia?" He rubbed the sleep from his eyes before rising stiffly to his feet.

His companion was a pretty girl in her mid-twenties. Her hair was still wet from her last swim half an hour or so before. Detective Chief Inspector Frank Merlin himself had not been in the water. He had joined Sonia on this seaside expedition at short notice when he'd realised he wasn't going to get anywhere with the backlog of paperwork he'd hoped to get to grips with. The task facing him the following day was too distracting. On the spur of the moment, he'd left Scotland Yard, grabbed a taxi and hurried round to Sonia's place in Marylebone. They quickly decided on a seaside outing and she threw her swimsuit and a couple of towels into her shopping bag and jumped into the taxi. Merlin knew there was a train for the Sussex coast at 10.35 and he hadn't wanted to waste any time going back to his place for his swimming trunks. In fact, he hadn't been sure that he still had any trunks. He'd had a black swimsuit a few years ago, but he doubted it had survived his various moves.

And so he stood on Brighton beach in the clothes he had worn to work early in the morning. He had taken off his dark-brown suit jacket and his tie, and was wearing a short-sleeved shirt, but all of that only provided slight relief in the baking heat of the day. It was well into the eighties, although it had just gone six. Their train was at 6.40 and Sonia was right to hurry him. It was a good half-hour walk to the station from where they were on the beach.

It had been a blissful day. Merlin hadn't had a proper day off work for four weeks and he'd really needed one. In Sonia's company, he'd managed to forget almost all about his work at the Yard. They had a jolly lunch at a pub on the seafront and then had gone for a long walk through the Brighton Lanes. After looking in the windows of the antique shops, they had enjoyed some ice-cream cornets and Sonia had laughed as Merlin's had dribbled onto his trousers. Then they'd found their spot on the beach. With much laughter, Sonia had manoeuvred herself into her swimsuit behind a towel held for her by Merlin, who averted his eyes. When she had discarded the towel and stood in her bright green swimsuit, Merlin had caught his breath. How had he been so lucky as to snare this beautiful creature? Sonia Sieczko was Polish, the daughter of a Jewish mother and a Catholic father. She had shining, auburn hair, which just reached her shoulders, large, blue eyes, a neat, straight nose and a full mouth. A few freckles were scattered charmingly around her cheeks. She was of medium height, perhaps five or six inches shorter than Merlin, who was just over six feet tall, and had a full figure, which her green swimsuit displayed to great advantage. As she carefully picked her way, giggling happily, over the pebbles on the way to the sea, Merlin sighed with pleasure. She shouted to Merlin as she splashed around in the waves and he clumsily made his way towards her, removed his shoes and socks, rolled up his trousers and paddled cheerfully at the water's edge.

Frank Merlin had a heavy caseload of his own and in addition supervised the work of several other officers. As the ranks of those Metropolitan policemen dealing with domestic crime had been steadily depleted during 1940 in consequence of the demands of the war, so Merlin's free time had diminished to almost nothing. Thank God Sonia Sieczko had come into his life to provide some relief.

"Come on, Frank. We'll be late."

Merlin stared out to sea briefly and then up at the sky where he saw that the British and German fighters appeared to be disengaging from their dogfight. Several planes headed rapidly back across the Channel while the rest turned and disappeared in the opposite direction. "Yes, alright, Sonia. I was having a very peaceful dream, you know, when you so rudely interrupted me."

As Sonia smiled, her pert little nose crinkled disarmingly. "Come on now, Mr Policeman. I have work to go to tomorrow, as do you."

"Yes, of course, my darling, neither of us can afford to miss the train."

Sonia smoothed out the creases in her white summer dress

as she rose to her feet. She gave her left hand to Merlin and pulled him towards her. As she did so, he felt a stab of pain from the wound in his right shoulder, which reminded him of his miserable task the following morning.

"Are you alright, Frank?"

"Yes, thanks. Just a little ache."

"Sorry, my darling, I should have realised."

Merlin shrugged and picked up Sonia's bag and they scrunched their way over the pebbles to the pavement and joined the chattering throng of Londoners making their way to the railway station. By the pier, a Punch and Judy man was packing up his pitch. His face was bright red, whether through exertion or sunburn or a bit of both, Merlin could not tell. As the Punch and Judy man paused to mop perspiration from his forehead, he caught sight of Sonia and winked at Merlin. A welcome gust of sea-breeze blew across Merlin's face. Another gust of wind rustled through a bucket of children's celluloid windmills next to the partly dismantled booth. The pier was still crowded and noisy and the predominant sound seemed to be that of crying children. It had no doubt been a long, hot, tiring day for many. They crossed the street, half-running as they looked up at the clock opposite the pier chiming the half-hour and reached the station with a minute to spare, but the press of people was so great that it was another ten minutes before the train got under way. Merlin ran down the platform holding Sonia's hand and was lucky enough to find an empty compartment in the first of the second-class carriages they entered. By the time the train got under way, their compartment was full. A young couple with two exhausted toddlers sat opposite them and a soldier and his sweetheart next to them. Within a few minutes, as the train gently chugged its way through the beautiful, slowly darkening Sussex countryside, Sonia was dozing with her head against the window and her hand in his. She woke briefly as the train jolted to a stop at the first station and repositioned her head on Merlin's shoulder and he smiled as he breathed in the sweet salty smell of her hair. Within another fifteen minutes, all in the compartment had succumbed to that particularly pleasurable sleep brought on by a day at the seaside. No one stirred until they reached Victoria, even when the guard noisily stretched past everyone to pull down the blackout blinds.

★ ★ ★

They had a long wait for a taxi at the station and it was gone ten when they got back to Sonia's place, a tiny little pink mews house just off Baker Street. Since the girl who had shared the rent with her had left a couple of months before, it had become a little too expensive for Sonia and Merlin had insisted on helping her out with a contribution.

As they got out of the cab, they could see that the lights were on behind the blackout curtains. Sonia smiled. "It must be Jan." Sonia turned her key in the door and they entered the small living room. A tall, lean, young man was sprawled out in a dressing gown on the sofa. He seemed to be asleep but, as Merlin closed the door, one of the man's eyes cracked open.

"Sonia. Is that you?" Jan jumped suddenly to his feet and brushed some crumbs from his pyjama jacket. A half-eaten tomato sandwich lay on the small table in front of him. He leaned over to kiss Sonia on the cheek.

"This is Frank Merlin. Frank, my brother Jan."

The men shook hands. "So you are the policeman. Very pleased to meet you, sir. I have heard much about you from Sonia."

Merlin extricated his hand with difficulty from Jan Sieczko's firm grasp and nodded his head. "Yes, likewise. And I've heard all about you, Mr Sieczko. Good to meet you too."

"Please, call me Jan. And may I call you Frank? After all, you're almost one of the family now."

The two men remained on their feet, smiling awkwardly at each other, while Sonia cleared Jan's sandwich from the table and went into the kitchen to put the kettle on to boil.

5

Jan Sieczko was darker in complexion than his sister. He had a mop of reddish-brown hair, a matching neat moustache, deep-set eyes and a broad, engaging smile. Merlin noticed a vivid red mark on his right hand as Jan reached out to offer him a cigarette. As Merlin declined, Jan looked down at his hand. "It's nothing. I had an accident working on the plane. I'd like to say that it was a war wound, but it's not. They've not allowed us to do anything yet."

The two men sat down opposite each other and Jan Sieczko took a long draw on his cigarette. "And so, Frank, what have you and my beautiful little sister been up to today?"

"We had a day at the seaside. Brighton. Ever been?"

Jan shook his head. "No. Unless you count flying over it as being there. Well. A lovely day for the seaside."

"Yes. And you? Have you had a pleasant day?"

Jan stretched out languidly on the sofa and blew a smoke ring. "Very good, Frank. I have a couple of days' leave and I came up to town from Northolt at lunchtime with a friend. We had drinks at a pub near here then we went for a long walk. Today was my first chance to have tourist look at London, so we did sights, you know, Big Ben, the Houses of Parliament, Trafalgar Square and so on. We had a nice meal at a place my friend knows. Then my friend, Ziggy, went off to meet someone and I came here for a little nap. That was my day, Frank, perhaps not so nice as yours, but not so bad, eh?"

Sonia came from the kitchen carrying a tray with a pot of tea, cups and saucers and biscuits and sat down happily next to her brother. "He's a good-looking man, my brother, Frank. Don't you think?"

Now that they were sitting next to each other, Merlin could see the resemblance more clearly. He noticed that Jan had a few of Sonia's freckles and their smiling mouths were almost a perfect match. Merlin knew from Sonia that Jan Sieczko was a pilot in the Kosciuszko Squadron of the Royal Air Force. Sonia had left Poland before the war began, but Jan had stayed and had fought valiantly with his comrades in the Polish Air Force as Hitler's forces overran his country. When all was lost he had made his way to Romania and then, by a circuitous route through the Balkans, to Britain. Scores of Polish airmen had made a similar journey. In the summer, after some misgivings, the powers that be had gradually realised how valuable these battle-hardened pilots could be to Britain's own war effort. At the beginning of August, just in time for the start of what soon became known as the Battle of Britain, the officers of the new RAF Squadron 303, a squadron made up almost entirely of Poles, arrived for the first time at their base in Northolt on the western edges of London. Merlin felt he should make some comment about the courage of Jan and his comrades, but could not phrase the appropriate words.

"So, Jan. You're staying until tomorrow night?"

Jan stubbed out his cigarette in an ashtray and put his arms around Sonia. "Yes, my lovely sister. I have to report back at seven o'clock tomorrow night. I have almost another full day of freedom. What shall we do?"

"I'm afraid I won't be able to do much, Jan. I have to go to work tomorrow."

Jan made a face and groaned. He said something in Polish, which Merlin took to be a request for her to take the day off. Sonia shook her head.

"Ah, poor me. Well, I'll have to make my own entertainment then. I asked Ziggy to come round. Perhaps he will be up for some fun and games." He shrugged at Merlin then looked back at his sister. "I think perhaps I am being the, how do you say it, the gooseberry here. I think I will go to bed. Please excuse me."

Merlin rose. "No, no, it's alright. I should be going really." He suddenly felt very, very tired. "Well, very nice to meet you, Jan. I hope you have another good day tomorrow. And best of luck when you get back to the squadron."

The men shook hands again. Sonia put down her cup of tea and followed Merlin to the door. "It was a lovely day, Frank, thank you." They kissed gently and Merlin rested his hands lightly on Sonia's shoulders. "It was perfect, darling, just perfect."

Sonia looked at him shyly from under her eyelashes. "You don't have to go, you know." Sonia ruffled Merlin's smooth black hair and then traced her finger down over his high forehead, his patrician nose and over the lips of his generous mouth. As she stroked his chin, Merlin's stubble rasped against her touch. She stared into his warm, green eyes and then caressed his cheek. "You are a beautiful man, Frank. But you are working too hard. Look here. These lines under your eyes are growing and you are too thin. I will have to feed you up. We must try some nice Polish stew with much potato. I will have to see if Jan can use his charms to get me some good meat from the base. He managed it a few weeks ago, but you didn't get to taste any as you were too busy." Sonia sighed and kissed Merlin's neck. "Please stay, Frank."

Merlin hugged Sonia tight. "I'm sorry, I can't. I have something to do very early tomorrow morning. Something not very nice. We'll try and get together during the week. I'll call you on Wednesday. Alright?"

Sonia nodded. The two embraced for a few seconds more and then pulled apart and Merlin slipped through the doorway into the dark. As the door closed behind him he looked up. The stars shone brightly in a clear sky. He couldn't see or hear any aeroplanes above, but, as he came out of the mews onto the main street, he saw a red glow in the southern sky.

CHAPTER 2

Monday, September 2

Merlin walked slowly down the corridor behind the Governor and his assistant. Two uniformed warders followed him. There was a faint smell of urine mingled with the smell of cooking – was it boiled cabbage or something else? Merlin was happy for his mind to wander and think about anything other than what he was about to witness.

The small party turned a corner and then climbed some stairs. At the top was another corridor, which they followed to its end. Faint early morning light permeated through a prison window high above them as they entered a room on the left. Merlin couldn't understand why he had agreed to do this. He'd been dog-tired at the end of a long day and he just hadn't been able to resist the Assistant Commissioner's browbeating – "Of course you should be present, Frank. You were the chief investigating police officer and you brought this disgusting man to justice. I think you owe it to the victims to see the penalty being paid, not to mention to yourself – after all, the man did shoot you!"

Merlin couldn't see how the dead victims could feel any better for his attendance in Wormwood Scrubs this morning and he himself had no particular desire for personal revenge, but there he was. And so he took up his position on one side of the room next to the Governor. It was ten minutes to six. In front of him the infamous Albert Pierrepoint and his assistant fiddled with the noose of thick rope that hung down in the centre of the room. Someone had told Merlin that Pierrepoint's assistant was his own son. *A funny sort of family business if that was the case*, he thought, as the assistant knelt down to check that all was in order with the trapdoor.

The Governor pulled a watch from his waistcoat pocket. "Should be here now," he whispered to no one in particular.

One of the two warders, who had taken up position by the door, stepped into the corridor briefly and then returned. "Coming now, sir."

Merlin could hear the sound of footsteps echoing outside and suddenly four men entered. Merlin's eyes were naturally drawn straight to the man who was at the centre of the proceedings. Flying Officer Peter Harrison seemed to have shrunk a little during his stay in prison. Merlin had not seen him for a month. His head was closely cropped and thus the long cowlick of fair hair he had used to cover his incipient baldness was gone. Without his curls, his ears stuck out even more prominently than they had before. In his grey prison overalls he struck a sorry figure compared with the debonair, confident, smartly uniformed man about town whom Merlin had first encountered.

Flying Officer Harrison had been convicted in July at the Old Bailey of four murders. All the murders had followed a similar pattern. Harrison had picked up a prostitute on the London streets or in a pub, had engaged in sex with her in some back alley and had then slit her throat. The murders had taken place between February and May. Through a combination of good police work and luck, Harrison had been arrested at his base in Kent in June. In attempting to escape he had fired his service revolver and hit Merlin in the shoulder. It could have been a lot worse as the bone was only slightly chipped, but it still caused him some pain. Harrison had been a cocky little chap through the trial proceedings, but little of that spirit remained as Pierrepoint motioned to Harrison's two accompanying prison officers to bring the man forward. The other man who'd arrived with Harrison was the prison padre, who now opened his bible and began reading.

"Ashes to ashes, dust to dust."

Harrison's motive for the murders was still unclear. He

had come from an apparently warm and loving family in Tunbridge Wells. His father owned a grocer's shop in which his son had happily worked with his parents and his two sisters during the school holidays. He had benefited from a good grammar school education and after taking his school certificate had started out as a clerk in a medium-sized stockbroking firm in the City of London. Joining the forces at the outset of the war, he had swiftly risen to a responsible ground staff job at Biggin Hill. Medical evidence at the trial hinted at some strain in his relationship with his mother, but no convincing reason was given for the killings. Merlin inclined to the simple view that Harrison was evil and committed the murders because he enjoyed doing so. In any event, whatever his motive had been, Harrison stood before him now within seconds of paying the ultimate penalty.

Everything happened very quickly. The padre completed his prayers and the Governor asked Harrison if he had anything to say. Harrison shook his head jerkily and then in a swift movement Pierrepoint pulled a hood over Harrison's head. For a few seconds the only sound was the faint rustling of Harrison's urine trickling from his trousers onto the wooden planks of the trapdoor as his self-control left him. Pierrepoint stood back, pulled a lever and the trapdoor opened. Despite himself, Merlin joined the others in looking down through the trapdoor at the jerking and twitching form below. The stench of Harrison's soiled trousers floated up. Merlin closed his eyes, took a deep breath and walked out of the room.

★ ★ ★

Merlin leaned out of the open window in his office at Scotland Yard, looked down at the Thames twinkling beneath him and took a deep breath of the smoggy London air. He still couldn't rid his nostrils of the smell of the gallows room. Returning to his desk, he fell heavily into his chair and looked vacantly around the office. The décor remained the same – the white walls, the Swiss cuckoo clock, his beloved pair of Van Gogh prints, the large map of London, the picture of a 1924 police football team featuring a young F Merlin, centre half, the brightly patterned Persian rugs enlivening the standard issue linoleum floor. To the left of the frosted glass office door was his Goya print of a firing squad somewhere, probably Spain. This seemed particularly apposite to his morning's early appointment.

The door opened. "So how was it, sir?"

"It was bloody awful, as you'd expect, Sergeant. That's the last one of those I'm going to even if I end up arresting Adolf himself and he's up for the chop."

Detective Sergeant Samuel Bridges, a tall man with a burly rugby player's build, bright blond hair, red cheeks and a countenance that was almost incapable of being other than cheerful, thought it prudent to postpone further conversation for the moment and left Merlin alone in his room. He returned ten minutes later with a cup of tea and found his boss staring quietly out of the window. Merlin's office gave him a good view of the river and of the London County Council building opposite. A number of barrage balloons were spaced out at regular intervals along the river, as Merlin could see as he leaned again out of the open window and extended his gaze to St Paul's and the City beyond.

Bridges deposited the cup and saucer on the only available space on the crowded desk to which Merlin now returned.

"Thank you, Sergeant."

Merlin noticed a new pile of files, which his sergeant must have placed next to the old stack of files heaped on his desk. He groaned and sat down. "Anything happening?"

"Plenty, sir, but nothing urgently requiring your personal attention." Bridges looked meaningfully at Merlin's desk.

"You mean that I might like to get on with reading all this bumf you've dumped on my desk?"

"Well, sir, it might be wise to take this opportunity to clear the decks. Everyone's out and about dealing with their various jobs and you might find today relatively, um, uninterrupted."

"I came in yesterday to try and catch up, but I wasn't up to it." Merlin leaned back in his chair and hoisted his feet onto the desk. He steepled his hands in front of him and blew on them. In days past when his boss adopted this habitual pose, Bridges had been able to take note of which of his boss' shoes had a hole in it. Today, however, as for the past few months, Merlin's shoes were properly intact. *That girl taking him in hand*, Bridges noted again to himself.

"Something funny, Sergeant?"

"No, sir, no."

"Thinking of your beloved, perhaps? And how is Iris? What is it now, four months to go?"

"Nearer three, sir. If all goes well, that is."

"I'm sure it will, Sam." Merlin swung his legs down and pulled his chair closer to the desk. "Now, when you say I might find this day 'relatively uninterrupted', as you put it, you are not taking into account possible interruptions from airborne visitors, I presume?"

"No, sir. Well, who's to know when that's going to get going."

"Indeed, Sergeant, who's to know."

German bombers had been attacking Britain since August 13th, or "Eagle Day" as Hermann Goering had designated it according to the Assistant Commissioner. From that Monday morning throughout August, hundreds of German bombers supported by swarms of fighter planes had crossed the Channel every day to attack airfields, aircraft factories and radar installations mostly in southern England. The London suburbs had been hit heavily, but, with one exception, central London had remained unscathed – on the Saturday of the week before, August 24th, the East End had been hit by bombs and a number of fires had broken out.

As Merlin stared out of his window at another sunny, warm day, both he and Bridges knew that this situation was unlikely to obtain for much longer. After the August 24th bombing, which Jack Stewart, Merlin's friend in the Auxiliary

Fire Service, said was probably accidental, the RAF had launched retaliatory raids on Berlin. While everyone agreed that central London was going to be a target sooner or later, these raids suggested it would be sooner.

Merlin took off his jacket. "Very well, Sergeant. You might as well leave me alone to get on with it. Off you go. No doubt you've got paperwork to attend to as well."

"Yes, sir."

Frank Merlin was a lean six-footer with a full head of jet-black hair. Piercing green eyes complemented a narrow aristocratic nose and a full and generous mouth, and he had seldom encountered a woman who failed to admire his charms. He was no lothario though, unlike his friend Jack Stewart. Despite the odd wrinkle, he looked younger than his forty-three years. Born to a Spanish exile father and an East End mother, he was brought up in a Limehouse chandlery store with his younger brother and sister. From his father he had acquired, amongst other things, a love of history and poetry. He had fought bravely in the Great War, survived and joined the police on his return, rising steadily through the ranks. A brief, loving marriage had been ended by the leukaemia that killed his wife, Alice. At the beginning of 1940 he had attempted to join up for this new Great War, but had been thwarted by his superiors.

Merlin picked up the nearest file. When the war had started, almost a year before, Frank Merlin had been in charge of the Yard's Violent Crimes Unit. As the year passed and the ranks of the Yard had been depleted by officers joining the forces, being seconded to Special Branch or other specialist government units, or otherwise being siphoned off from domestic crime duties to assist in the war effort, Merlin's responsibilities had become more diversified. Effectively his "Violent Crime" Unit had become an "Any Serious Crime" Unit. The file he'd picked up concerned a non-violent crime. It was immaculately neat and Merlin knew without looking at the name on top of the front cover that it was the work of

Inspector Peter Johnson. For several weeks, Johnson had been investigating a racket that was becoming increasingly common in wartime Britain. A deluge of forged ration books and identity cards was flooding through London and Merlin had given Johnson the task of stemming the flow. Johnson had succeeded in identifying several different gangs and had made a number of arrests. Merlin had in his hands the latest report on his investigation, in which Johnson reported that although there was still a good deal of false documentation circulating, the flood of new documentation had been reduced to a trickle by the arrests, for the present at least. There were still forgers out there, but Johnson felt he'd got most of the big players. Merlin was pleased. He'd had the Assistant Commissioner on his back about this for quite a while. He made a note in pencil on the file for it to be forwarded straightaway to the A.C.

The next file concerned the spate of violent robberies in Paddington. His eyes were beginning to strain at the small print and he opened one of the drawers in his desk. Sonia had noticed him reading a newspaper the other day with the print only a few inches away from his eyes. He had not wanted to admit to any failing, but Sonia had been insistent and he'd slipped away one lunch hour the previous week to visit an optician. A mild case of presbyopia had been diagnosed and he had walked away with a pair of not particularly attractive, heavy-rimmed spectacles. Merlin did not think himself a vain man and was surprised to find that he was damned if he was going to reveal the existence of these reading glasses to his colleagues. He kept his eye on the door as he furtively withdrew the glasses from the desk and put them on. It was a lot better, he admitted to himself, as the letters immediately loomed larger on the page. His brow furrowed as he concentrated and began to read.

★ ★ ★

The heavily powdered jowls of Sonia Sieczko's customer quivered as she shook her head. "No, no, my dear. That's simply not my colour. I told you that earlier when you brought out one of the other dresses. I'm looking for a pale lavender. That's really a purple. That's not what I want. What else is there?"

Sonia picked up the dress and struggled hard to hide her irritation as she walked away to put the dress on the large pile of other dresses that had proved unsatisfactory to Lady Theobald. Her ladyship had arrived at Sonia's station about three quarters of an hour ago and had looked Sonia up and down carefully before introducing herself.

"I am Lady Theobald. Whatever has happened to the other girl who used to be here, what's her name, Miss Lewis? Where is she?"

Lady Theobald was a plump lady of advancing years. On her head she wore a vast feathery confection of a hat, which loomed threateningly over Sonia, who smiled nervously. She hadn't met a "Lady" before and wasn't quite sure how to address her.

"Well, come on, girl, speak up."

"Miss Lewis has got married, er, madam, and has left Swan and Edgar. I am the new girl at this station. My name is Sieczko, Miss Sieczko."

"Miss Seek-what? Foreigner, are you? Thought you had a funny accent. Well, what's your Christian name? Perhaps I'll be able to pronounce that." Lady Theobald glowered at Sonia as if she had committed a doubly unpardonable offence by first replacing Miss Lewis and then by being a foreigner.

"Sonia, madam."

"Well, Sonia. Your superiors will no doubt tell you that I am a long-standing and much cherished customer of this establishment, so look smart as I have an important luncheon in an hour's time and I don't want to dilly-dally."

Sonia moved to another rack of dresses and rummaged through them. Her first day in the ladies' clothing department was not going very well. She had been notified a week before of her promotion from the ladies' accessories department and had been given some pointers on her new job by Miss Lewis before

16

she had left on Friday. Miss Lewis had warned her that she would have to handle a few awkward old battleaxes from time to time, but Sonia felt it was particularly bad luck to have one on her very first morning. She rummaged along the rack some more and found yet another dress that she thought might be the right colour. She lifted it out and confirmed that it was the right size. With a sinking heart, she returned to Lady Theobald.

"At last, yes, that's it. That's the colour. Now, let me try it on. Hurry up, girl, or I'm going to be late. Ah, there is the changing room, is it not?"

Her ladyship's ample rear disappeared behind the curtain of one of the booths. After a few minutes of grunts and sighs, Lady Theobald emerged and faced one of the full-length mirrors. "Zip me up, if you please. Ah, yes, that's it. The right colour and a perfect fit. I'll have this. It's lovely. In fact, I think I'll wear it to my luncheon. Hurry up, girl. Wrap up my other dress and charge my account, won't you?"

Sonia watched her customer preen herself in the mirror as she packaged up the green dress that she had arrived in. Green, purple or lavender, Sonia didn't think there was any colour that was Lady Theobald's colour. And in her opinion the dress hung down from Lady Theobald's cylindrical body like a sack. But why complain? The customer was happy and that was all that counted, she thought, as she watched her ladyship waddle contentedly to the row of lifts on the other side of the salesroom. She looked up at the clock on the wall on her right. A quarter to one. At one she could take her lunch break and she was looking forward to some fresh air. The store was airless and very warm, and either the stuffiness or Lady Theobald or both had given her a headache. After re-hanging the rejected dresses, she walked over to Miss Hetherington, the kindly, elegant, slim woman who was in charge of the floor and obtained her consent to take lunch. She hurried down the staff stairs and made her way to one of the Piccadilly exits. As she emerged into the street, she heard someone shout in Polish.

17

"Sonia. Wait, it's me."

She turned and saw her brother's smiling face.

"What luck. I might have missed you. I thought I'd get here earlier and catch you inside, but I lost my way a little. It's your lunch hour, yes?"

Sonia's headache disappeared as she surveyed her handsome brother. She'd not seen him in his uniform before. On his two other brief visits he'd been in civvies and last night he'd been dressed for bed. He wore his air force hat jauntily to one side and looked, as he always had since he was a small boy, as if he had been up to mischief.

"Well, what shall it be? I just walked past the Ritz. Shall we eat there?"

"Don't be silly. It's a lovely day. You can share my sandwiches with me in the park. Look, I found some Polish sausage in a shop the other day. Come on. Follow me."

Jan Sieczko put his arms around his sister and gave her a big hug. "Very well, my little sister. Lead on."

Sonia took Jan's hand and pulled him through a gap in the traffic to the other side of Piccadilly. They walked past St James's Church, Hatchards, Fortnum & Mason and the Ritz and arrived at St James's Park. The park was crowded. All of the deckchairs seemed to be occupied and Sonia led Jan some way into the park until they eventually found a relatively peaceful and shady spot of grass. Jan took off his jacket and laid it down on the ground.

"Oh, no, Jan. You don't want to dirty your uniform."

Jan put his hands on his sister's shoulders and pushed down firmly. Sonia giggled and allowed herself to be seated. Jan dropped down beside her and began hungrily devouring the sandwich that Sonia gave to him while Sonia ate hers a little more delicately and watched her brother eyeing up the more attractive of the passers-by.

"See anything you like?"

Jan chuckled. "And what if I do? I need to make the best of my leave time. After all, this might be my last chance."

Sonia's face darkened. "Don't speak like that."

Jan stretched out to stroke his sister's cheek. "I am sorry, Sonia. Don't worry. I am a survivor and will remain one. Look what I've survived already."

Sonia knew that Jan had been in the thick of things in Poland when the German blitzkrieg had arrived. He'd been shot down twice, but had sustained only minor injuries. At one point a German patrol had captured him, but he had made his escape and then had found his way out of Poland. He had hooked up with his squadron a month or so before the Battle of Britain had begun. She knew that the squadron had been kept in reserve and that he was champing at the bit to get some action. She reached up to clasp the hand on her cheek and stroked it tenderly. She kissed the vivid burn-marks carefully. Jan flinched.

"I'm sorry, did I hurt you?"

"No, no. It hurts all the time. But it will be healed soon. It's because of the burns that I was given the leave." Jan stared up at the sky, whose azure clarity was punctuated by a few wispy white clouds.

"It doesn't look like it now, but things are getting very hot up there – I hope our superiors allow the Kosciuszko to play its part."

Sonia kissed Jan on the cheek. She didn't know whether it was good for him to talk about his flying or for him to forget about it, however briefly, and in her uncertainty she asked no questions.

Jan looked at a pretty nurse who was passing, pushing a baby in a chair. She lowered her head demurely in response to his frank look of appreciation. Jan's gaze passed over her head. "Ah, I see there's some sort of mobile café there. Would you like a drink?"

"A glass of orange squash would be nice. They'll let you bring it over here."

Jan jumped up and ran off and returned rapidly with two glasses of squash. As he sat down, he spilled some of his own glass onto his trousers. "Ah, clumsy old me. Na zdrowie!"

Jan had been renowned for his physical awkwardness as a child and it had been something of a surprise to Sonia and their parents that he had become a pilot, let alone such an apparently excellent one. "Different type of coordination," he had said without elaboration when Sonia had mentioned it on his last visit.

"And so, the policeman, he seems a pleasant fellow. Good-looking too. Is it love?"

Sonia's cheeks reddened. "Maybe, I don't know. He is a very kind man, I think. He has been a little sad also. I like to think that I cheer him up a little."

"And why is he sad?"

"His wife died before the war and I think it has taken him some time to get over it."

"How did she die?"

"I don't know. He doesn't really talk about it and I don't like to pry."

"Hmm." Jan waved his hand at a wasp hovering over his now empty glass. "And will he go to war?"

"No. At least, I think not. He is a little old, but he wanted to join up. His superior said no. Told him he was too important to the police. He did fight in the last war and he is forty-three, and I think he is a very good policeman, so it is perhaps not so surprising. He is upset about it though."

"You do not think that perhaps he is a little too old for you?"

Sonia wrinkled her nose at Jan. "No, I do not. Fifteen or twenty years' difference in age is nothing between a man and a woman, provided the man is the older."

"Oh. Why so? You mean I can't find myself a little widow in her forties to keep me warm? Why not?"

Sonia pushed Jan's shoulder playfully. "Oh, shut up, you idiot."

Two air force officers walked past and Jan nodded to them. "Czechs. I met one of them at Northolt the other day. There are quite a crowd of Czech flyers, not as many as the Poles, but still a good number. And they know how to fly too."

Sonia nodded. It was almost time to get back to work. She lay back and stretched out her arms and basked in the sun. Her brother did likewise. "Five more minutes, then I must return to the shop."

"Hmm."

"Where's your friend Ziggy today? I thought you were going to get together with him again."

"I was. He was meant to call on me at your place this morning. I told him nine o'clock. I waited till ten and there was no sign so I gave up on him. He is a funny chap."

Sonia raised herself on an elbow. "How so?"

"He seems to have a bee in his bonnet about something. He's got a real temper too and watch out if he takes against you, I'd say. I'm not aware of anyone picking on him, although there are a couple of officers he dislikes intensely. He's an obsessive sort of man. But he's a very brave pilot and a good drinking companion and that's all that matters to me."

Sonia rose to her feet. "Well. I really must go now. Are you staying here?"

Jan sat up and watched a group of young office girls walk by. "You know, I think I might."

Sonia punched him lightly on the shoulder and then leaned down to kiss him. "You are going back to the base tonight?"

"Yes, I'm afraid so. I'll get my bag from your place in a couple of hours. Do you want me to leave the spare key somewhere or shall I keep it?"

"Oh, keep it, that's alright."

"You don't think your policeman might need it?"

Sonia punched his shoulder again. Then her eyes suddenly filled with tears. "Please take care. You don't have to be too heroic, you know." Jan laughed and rose to hug her. She walked away briskly and his eyes lingered on her until she disappeared from sight at the park gate.

CHAPTER 3

Merlin woke in his Chelsea flat at just after 4am. It wasn't the noise of aircraft or guns that woke him, as it had the night before, but the pain in his shoulder. The foreign radio station he had found just before he went to sleep was still broadcasting and he recognised the lilting voice of one of his favourite singers, Charles Trenet. He got up, put on the new black slippers Sonia had bought him and padded to the small kitchen at the other end of the apartment. Returning to his bed ten minutes later with a steaming hot cup of cocoa, he retrieved from under his sheets the book he had been reading before he fell asleep. It was part of the small library of Spanish books left to Merlin by his father, which had travelled around with him for years in a battered old trunk. He didn't have much time to read, but when he did he often delved into this collection, sometimes reading books for the third or fourth time, pleased to find that his command of the Spanish language remained as fluent as ever. The book now in his hand was a particular favourite. *The Conquest of New Spain* was the story of Hernan Cortes' defeat of the Aztec Empire in the 1520s, written by one of his soldiers, Bernal Diaz del Castillo. Merlin was fascinated by this tale of adventure, bravery and cruelty at a time when the Spanish Empire was at its height. He turned to the page he had fallen asleep at five or so hours ago, in which the great Montezuma, Emperor of the Aztecs, was taken prisoner by Cortes and read on, enthralled, until his alarm clock rang to tell him that it was time to get up and make his way to the Yard.

★ ★ ★

The Assistant Commissioner had been just about to drop off when the piercing whine of the all-clear siren roused him. Edward Gatehouse was sitting at the bottom end of a long, polished, cherry wood table in an enormous meeting room in the Home Office. From a full-length portrait opposite him, the stalwart bulldog features of the current Prime Minister, represented in a previous incarnation of his as Home Secretary, glared down at him in rebuke. He shouldn't have had the Burgundy with his lunch. That was a definite mistake. He rustled the papers in front of him and cleared his throat loudly to confirm that he was fully alert. At the other end of the table and at its head, the Home Secretary, Sir John Anderson, was attempting to make himself heard above the noise. Since he himself spoke in a monotonous drone, he was not being particularly successful. Eventually, the siren stopped. The Home Secretary paused and looked at the ceiling as if that had been the source of the noise that had been so presumptuous as to interrupt him. "Did everyone hear that or shall I repeat myself?"

A general muttering noise from the assembly encouraged Sir John to repeat himself.

"I was saying that now we have heard the reports from the representatives of the AFS, the ARP, the LDV and the WVS*, I would like to turn to a particularly unsavoury subject. Assistant Commissioner Gatehouse is here to represent the Commissioner and the Metropolitan Police Force. Assistant Commissioner, the floor is yours."

A.C. Gatehouse sent a silent prayer of thanks to the Supreme Being for activating the siren just before his turn arrived and stood up. Facing him around the table was a group made up of nineteen men and one woman. Some of the men were uniformed and some were not. The non-uniformed men were all sombrely dressed, none more so than the sepulchral figure at the head of the table. The lady wore a

---

*Auxiliary Fire Service, Air Raid Precaution, Local Defence Volunteers (Home Guard) and Women's Voluntary Service

black dress, enlivened by a bright red flower in her buttonhole, the only spot of colour in view.

The A.C. began reading. His report principally consisted of a list of statistics, most of which had been supplied by the local forces of the city's outer suburbs, concerning the bombing attacks to date on London. Much of this was a duplication of information already provided in the earlier reports made to the meeting, but his audience listened quietly, without comment. In due course, the A.C. arrived at the final passage of his report. "And now let me turn to the reported incidence of looting so far recorded by our officers."

Sir John Anderson rapped his pencil on the table and raised his eyebrow.

"Yes, listen to this everyone. This is shocking. Most shocking."

"Bexleyheath reports eight looting incidents of which officers were made aware in respect of which four arrests have been made to date. Bromley reports ten incidents with three arrests. Croydon twelve incidents, four arrests..." He carried on to the bottom of his list and then concluded. "Of course, gentlemen and lady." He nodded with a toothy smile to the representative of the WVS. "These are reported incidents. No doubt there have been other unreported incidents."

"Indeed, indeed, Assistant Commissioner Gatehouse, thank you, thank you, please resume your seat." The Home Secretary removed his pince-nez and surveyed the table. "Would you credit it? In all our planning for the Hun's inevitable air attack on us, I don't believe we ever anticipated this problem."

A young civil servant to Anderson's left whispered something to him. "Well, yes, Mr Craig here reminds me that the possibility of looting was mentioned in one of our earlier planning documents, but I am not afraid to admit that I, for one, never placed much stress or weight on it. I never believed that it would be anything other than a very minor concern, but look where we are. We have only had a few weeks of bombing and look at the numbers of reported incidents in the Assistant

Commissioner's list. I am quite shocked at what our countrymen are capable of. Quite shocked! And if this is what's happening when places like Bromley are being attacked, think what it will be like when the centre of London is attacked. I daren't think about what will happen in the City of London, the Docks, the West End."

The Home Secretary's shock was echoed by a variety of exclamations from around the table.

"Well, Assistant Commissioner, what are your plans to deal with this outrageous behaviour?"

The A.C. was not expecting the subject matter to be thrown back to him so quickly and had taken the opportunity to tinker with his wing-collar, which was causing him some discomfort. Withdrawing his finger swiftly from inside the collar, he stared back down the table enquiringly at Anderson. "I'm sorry, Home Secretary, I didn't quite catch you."

"What plans do you have, Gatehouse, for dealing with the looting? We are looking up in the skies at German bombers every day. We are within days, perhaps minutes, of being attacked here right at the heart of the Empire. With so many incidents in the suburbs, clearly this problem is likely to be rife here in the centre. What plans have you prepared to counter the looters? We would all like to receive the benefit of the Metropolitan Force's thoughts on this issue."

★ ★ ★

"Thank God for that, Sergeant. And don't bring me any more for a few days at least."

Sergeant Bridges hurried out with the last file and Merlin exhaled with relief. He had cleared the decks again, for the moment, and could look forward to a relaxed evening with Sonia. As well as completing all his administrative tasks, he had wrapped up the nasty Chelsea knife attack, which he and Bridges had been looking into since early August, and had got far enough down the line on the string of recent Hatton Garden burglaries to be able to pass the case on to a subordinate. It was half past five and he was thinking that for once he would be able to make an early night of it, when the phone rang and he was summoned upstairs.

"Ah, Merlin, come in."

Merlin's heart sank for the second time as he entered the A.C.'s office. It had sunk for the first when the voice on the phone had proved to be that of the A.C.'s prim, blue-stockinged secretary, Miss Stimpson. Now it sank again because the A.C.'s cheeks were flushed bright red. Very occasionally this was a sign only of an excellent lunch. More frequently it reflected the fact of the A.C.'s temper not being at its best.

"Sit down, please."

Merlin did as he was bid and watched the A.C. pace back and forth in front of windows that had the same view as his own office windows save for being one storey higher. The A.C. scratched his neck and attempted to adjust his collar. His cheeks flushed even brighter. Eventually, he sat down at his desk and stared at Merlin. "Well, Chief Inspector."

"Yes, sir."

"Looting. What are we doing about it?"

"Sir?"

"Looting. What's our plan for handling it?"

"Well, sir. I haven't really given it much thought."

The A.C. slapped his right hand on his desktop. "Well, that's the problem, isn't it? No one seems to have thought about it!"

Merlin shifted uncomfortably in his chair. The A.C.'s office windows were closed and it was very warm. "May I ask, sir, why you are interrogating me about this matter?"

The A.C. grimaced, momentarily displaying his unwholesome array of speckled brown teeth. "Why am I interrogating you about this matter? Because it is a matter of extreme importance and I would expect you, as my best officer, to have developed some plans in respect of, of, er, this matter!" Insofar as was possible, the A.C. flushed a little more.

Merlin could feel his own temper rising. In addition to the workload that he had carried all year he was also required to involve himself in making plans to counter looting? This was getting ridiculous. When Merlin became angry his skin usually lost colour, in contrast to the A.C. "I have given no specific thought to looting, save to consider it as a possible occurrence when the German bombing campaign commenced and to anticipate it being something requiring rigorous policing if it happened, sir. You may have noticed that I and my team have been rather busy of late. Insofar as specific planning as regards combating looting goes, I was, or rather am, under the impression that coping with this, together with all the other likely consequences of bombing raids, was a matter for the civil defence authorities rather than my humble little unit. Sir."

The A.C.'s beady little eyes bore into Merlin. He cleared his throat and began to say something then thought better of it. He looked up at the ceiling and when his eyes returned to Merlin the shading on his cheeks had lightened to a rosy pink. "Alright, Frank. Perhaps I was a little unfair. I was just put on the spot today at a meeting at the Home Office. The figures on looting to date were a surprise to everyone and that desiccated calculating machine of a Home Secretary had a go at me in front of a large and powerful audience on this subject, and I suppose I'm taking it out on you in turn. I apologise."

Merlin realised with amusement that, dreadful as the war was, it was capable of some unexpected beneficial side-effects. For example, he doubted very much that in peacetime the two words "I apologise" would ever have issued forth together from the A.C.'s mouth. As the colour receded from the A.C.'s cheeks, it returned to Merlin's. "Well, sir. Thank you. But why on earth are you, or rather we in the force, being taken to task on this issue? I would have thought that the civil defence planners would have been thinking about this for ages."

"Apparently not. A patriotic belief in the goodness of human nature in this country perhaps? A bit of wishful thinking maybe."

"But you and I know, sir, that the war has already been a

godsend to the British criminal classes – and not just to the already established criminals, but to a whole new range of crooks and spivs. Looting was always bound to be a problem."

"Quite, Frank. In any event, we are now required to do some thinking on how to combat it. But we can't do it alone. We need to work closely in particular with the AFS and the other civil defence authorities, particularly those responsible for the heavy-rescue men and demolition squads. I think we need to get some sort of coordinating committee going and we have to do it without delay. The bombs are going to be falling around here pretty soon."

Merlin looked at his watch. It was a quarter past six and he had arranged to meet Sonia at the Lyons Corner House in the Strand at seven. "So what is it you want from me, sir? I'm not really much of a one for sitting on committees, if that's what you were thinking."

"No, no, Frank. I can't afford to have you tied down in this. But I was thinking perhaps someone else in your team? And it wouldn't be just meetings. There'd be some action, I think."

"I'll give some thought to it overnight, sir."

"Thanks, Frank."

"If you don't mind, sir. I have an appointment now and—"

The A.C. waved his hands and offered Merlin another display of teeth. "Yes, yes. Off you go. I hope it's an appointment involving pleasure, Frank. You deserve it. I shall see you tomorrow."

★ ★ ★

They had left the bedside light in Sonia's bedroom on this time. The lampshade was bright red and their perspiring bodies had glistened in scarlet hues as they had entangled their bodies in the act of love. The light was still on and Merlin gazed contentedly at the bare shoulder poking out above the sheet. Sonia had fallen asleep almost immediately after, but

Merlin's mind was buzzing. They had met in the winter, but after an old-fashioned courtship and then Merlin's injury this was only the fourth time they had made love and Sonia was the first woman he had been with since his wife had died almost exactly two years before. The first time had been hurried and unsatisfactory. They had both been very nervous and Merlin had felt as if he'd never done it before. He'd also felt guilty wondering what Alice would have thought. The second and third times had not been much better, but this night, things had clicked. For the first time, Sonia had insisted on the light. "I want to see your face, Frank, your beautiful face." Any lurking anxiety or guilt had been thrust back to the depths of his subconscious as he'd watched Sonia slip out of her clothes. She had laughed with hands on hips as she jutted out her pert, high breasts. Her skin shimmered in the ruddy glow. This time they had also taken the wise precaution of drinking some alcohol – all they had drunk before was hot tea. They'd shared a very nice bottle of wine and Merlin had taken a whisky nightcap. Enough to help loosen inhibitions without undermining performance. However it came about, it had been beautiful. Alice had always told him he was a gentle and generous lover and he hoped he'd retained the knack. He reached carefully across Sonia and turned out the light. He lay back with his arms behind his head. The image of Hernan Cortes, as depicted on the cover of the Castillo book, drifted into his mind. A great man, of course, someone for a Spaniard to be proud of, and what an amount of treasure he had amassed for Spain; but a very cruel man as well. There was another book he must get hold of – the new Hemingway set in Civil War Spain. He had read that it was due out shortly. *For Whom the Bell Rings* or something like that. His eyes closed as the first wave of drowsiness hit him and the distant sound of throbbing aircraft engines at last faded away.

CHAPTER 4

Thursday, September 5

The Count had promised his wife that he would be home by six. She had invited some people for drinks and was anxious for him to be there. She was a good hostess, but a nervous one. The meeting, however, had gone on too long and as he looked grimly down Pall Mall, he realised that he would be lucky to get back by seven o'clock. It was a sweltering evening and for some reason London seemed to be momentarily devoid of taxis. The Count had assumed he'd find one immediately he came out of the Club, but he had been waiting a good twenty minutes. The uniformed doorman, who had been looking apologetically at the Count and the now large crowd of other taxi-seekers gathered on the pavement, again stepped into the road and waved his arms frantically, then lowered them and shrugged. "Sorry, gents. It's an occupied one. You might all be better advised to walk up to Green Park tube. I don't know what's up. It just happens sometimes. Change of shift or whatever."

The Count had been the first to emerge from the Royal Automobile Club into this taxi-drought and so was at the head of the queue. If he'd been at the end of the queue, he would have had no compunction about following the doorman's advice, but it would be particularly galling to give up his position, walk off and then see a taxi arriving. He would wait.

Ten minutes later, his patience was rewarded and he climbed up wearily into the cab. "Hampstead, please, driver."

"Righto, guv."

Count Adam Tarkowski was a small man in his late fifties. The removal of his homburg hat revealed a short outcrop of silvery hair crowning an appropriately aristocratic-looking head. The face was long and spare and deep, hollowed eyes looked out over a prominent Roman nose. The Count pursed his thin lips as he looked at his watch again. "Hmm. More likely seven-thirty," he muttered to himself. "Well, she'll just have to get on with it by herself."

The Count had back problems and leaned forward carefully to open his large brown briefcase. He withdrew a copy of *The Times* and browsed through it. It made bleak reading. He looked for stories about Poland, but couldn't see any. He didn't need to as he knew well enough what was going on. Since the German invasion a year before, Poland had been partitioned. A brief period of Polish independence had been ended yet again and, as in the previous century, Germany and Russia had carved the country up. Russia had taken most of the eastern part of the country and Germany had taken the centre and the west. Warsaw was no longer the capital of Poland, but the administrative centre for the German province of Galicia.

His country had once more been wiped from the map. Furthermore, the occupying powers had waged a vicious war on its inhabitants. Intellectuals, members of the political and military classes, and many other ordinary Poles had been purged ruthlessly as the twin totalitarian masters of Europe imposed their grip. The Jews were having a bad time of it too, but that was only to be expected.

Count Tarkowski thought of his two younger brothers. Where were they now? One had been in the army and one in the air force. He checked regularly on the lists of Polish officers who were reported to have arrived in England. The flow of escapees had been particularly strong after the fall of France, but had now reduced to a trickle, and neither name had yet shown up. Were they prisoners or were they dead? What of their families? And what of Maria's family? Her brothers? What of Karol? He sighed and ran his hand over his thinning hair.

31

His mind turned to the problem at the office, which had caused him endless trouble. What should he do? Replacing the newspaper in his briefcase with a sigh, he took out the papers that had been submitted to the meeting. At the top of the small pile was the text of the rallying cry that the general had given. Sikorski had had a long meeting with Mr Churchill, who had told him, "We shall conquer together or we shall die together." Poland would rise again like a phoenix from the ashes. Britain would provide General Sikorski and the Polish government in exile with all necessary support. Utmost efforts would be made to supply the Polish forces in Britain with whatever they required. And so on. The Count hoped the general's optimism would be rewarded, but he couldn't help thinking that a Britain on the brink of its own precipice was not very well positioned to fulfil its promises.

He stared gloomily out of the taxi window. Baker Street gave way to St John's Wood and then Swiss Cottage, where the traffic was particularly thick. It was indeed just past seven-thirty when the Count got out of the cab and paid the driver. He turned to face the large, rambling, old Victorian house that they had been lucky enough to find. All of a sudden his mood improved as he appreciated again how fortunate he and his wife had been to escape from the hell of their homeland to this new life in London, despite the many problems they faced.

★ ★ ★

As the Count was just about to put his key in the front door, he turned to see a young man in uniform appear from nowhere and hurry up to the cab, which was still standing by the kerb. The Count couldn't see his face as he jumped into the back seat, but there seemed to be something familiar about him. The cab drove off and the Count opened his door, crossed the threshold and deposited his hat on the stand and his briefcase on the table in the hall. He stood briefly outside the drawing room door and listened to the clink of glasses and the murmur of polite conversation. He took a breath and pushed the door open. The room was full and the Count was aware of familiar faces intermingled with some unfamiliar ones. His wife had said she was going to invite members of the Polish exile community to meet some of their new neighbours. At the far end of the room, his wife's beautiful face bobbed in to view. She was smiling happily and evidently hadn't missed him. He walked up to her and kissed her on the cheek. "I am sorry, my darling, but the cabinet meeting just went on forever."

Maria Tarkowski was ten years younger than her husband and could have passed for a woman twenty years younger. She wore her jet-black hair in a short bob and had a Mediterranean look about her, although she had been born and bred in Krakow of good Polish stock. "Never mind, Adam. You are here now." She had been chatting merrily to an elderly lady and, switching from Polish to English, she introduced her husband.

"This is my husband, Miss Davidson. Miss Davidson is one of our neighbours, Adam. She is a romantic novelist. A very good one, so I am told." His wife glided off to another old lady nearby. Miss Davidson, who wore an ornate black dress, which the Count guessed might have done service at cocktail parties fifty years ago, simpered. "Well, I don't know about that. Are you much of a reader, Count Tarkowski?"

"Yes. Well, I don't have much time at present, but back in Poland I have, or perhaps I should say I had, a fine old library. I collected old books amongst other things."

"You don't say. Well, as I was just saying to your charming wife…"

Out of the corner of one eye, the Count became aware of someone waving a hand at him from the other side of the room. As his eyes focused, his heart missed a beat. Miss Davidson was telling him something about her latest novel, but he wasn't taking it in. Why on earth had his wife invited that madman Russian? The maid passed with a tray of drinks and he reached out for a vodka. Miss Davidson's babble seemed to have stopped and she was now looking enquiringly at him.

"I'm sorry, I didn't quite catch that."

"I was just wondering if you read Dickens, Count. I find him…"

At this point he felt a large hand fall heavily on his shoulder. "Na zdrowie, my friend. How goes it?" The Count smiled apologetically at Miss Davidson and turned reluctantly to face a burly, bearded bear of a man. "Voronov. Kak dela? How are you?"

The bear responded by grasping the Count around the shoulders and enveloping him in a great hug. The overpowering aroma of vodka and pickled onions made the Count's nostrils twitch. "Prekvasno, Adam, Spasibo. I am in fine fettle. It has been a long time."

★ ★ ★

Jan Sieczko had been spitting tacks when he got back to base on Monday evening. After waiting around fully kitted up for days in the suffocating late August heat, the squadron had finally gone into action on the very day he'd gone on leave. What made matters worse was that after some frantic activity the day he had been away, the following two had been quiet. He had got into the air, but had not engaged the enemy. He had hoped today would be different, but it was already evening and he'd still not found any action. He looked to his right at the five other Hurricanes. They looked magnificent against the deepening blue of the sky. The sun would set in about an hour, he thought. He was flying as the wingman in Squadron Leader Kellett's A Flight. They had scrambled in the late afternoon on reports of German bombing formations over Hampshire, but they had found nothing in their sweeping reconnaissance of southern England and now Jan could hear Kellett's voice crackling over the radio to suggest that they call it a day. The squadron had begun to swing round on a northerly bearing when Jan saw the bombers. On the northeast horizon a fluffy white bank of cumuli had appeared from nowhere and they were slowly emerging from this cloud cover. By the time the formation was out of the clouds, Kellett's group had realigned itself yet again to face the approaching enemy.

"Dorniers. About fifty or sixty, I think."

Kellett's voice crackled again over the radio. "I can't make out the size of the fighter screen. Can anyone?"

Jan thought he could see about ten Messerschmitt 109s, but there must be more. "Twenty or so, I think."

Miro's voice burst excitedly through the static. "Now we shall have some fun, my friends!" Jan saw Miro waggle his wings to signal his keen anticipation.

"Now, gentlemen. Keep to English please and remember – no grandstanding. Yellow 2! Wait for my order to engage."

They were about two miles distant and closing rapidly. Jan could make out the rest of the Messerschmitts now. His heart began to pound as Kellett signalled for the aircraft to climb. The descending sun behind his left shoulder glinted and sparkled on the glass of his instrument panel. The sky above stretched away to infinity. They levelled off and now he felt his stomach clench. Jan closed his eyes and said a quick prayer. When he opened them the squadron was almost in position. The Hurricanes were flying a quarter mile or so above the bombers and their protective screen of fighters.

"Good luck, everybody. Just pick your targets and go get 'em!"

Kellett's Red Section dived down out of the sun and within seconds two 109s were plummeting earthwards.

Jan was in the Yellow Section with Miro and Jerzy. The three Hurricanes followed close behind the Red Section, broke through the fighter cordon and targeted the leaders of the bomber formation. Golden streams of tracer bullets from one bomber's gun turret flew just past the left of his cockpit and then the right. Jan hunched forward with his finger poised on the gun button. He pressed and a shower of bright lights burst in front of him. He pulled his stick and banked away over the Dornier and he just had time to notice the black smoke pouring from the bomber's engines before he became aware of the 109 on his tail. He veered to the right, down and then to the left. He felt the tremor of a nearby explosion and his radio crackled to life. "That's one you owe me, Jan. First drink is on you when we get down."

Jan glanced to his right and saw what moments before had been his chasing Messerschmitt spiralling down towards the Surrey countryside. He waved at Miro, who waggled his wings back. Another 109 raced in front of him, chased by one of Red Section, which was in turn being pursued by another German plane. Jan followed and fixed the Messerschmitt in his sights. The stick rattled in front of him as the four fighters plunged beneath the bombers. His prey's fuselage now filled the circle of his sights and he pressed the button. Red and yellow flames jumped from the 109's right wing and the fighter wobbled briefly before tailing away. A moment later the Red Section plane, he thought it must be the Squadron Leader himself, nailed his own target.

"Thank you, Yellow 3. Well done." Jan followed the Squadron Leader, who wheeled to his right and headed back up to the bombers. As they were climbing, a 109 peeled off from the bomber formation and headed away from the action. Jan saw a small puff of grey smoke coming from the engine and then another.

"Looks like he's in trouble, Yellow 3. Why don't you put him out of his misery?"

"Roger, sir."

The 109 was flying down into the sun, which was just beginning to touch the horizon. Jan was briefly dazzled by the glare and when he looked again the 109 was nowhere to be seen. Then he became aware of the Messerschmitt descending behind him with its guns blazing. Whatever the reason for the smoke, it wasn't yet restricting the 109's manoeuvrability.

Jan pointed the Hurricane towards the sky and narrowly avoided the tracer bursts. As he rose he twisted and turned and then put the plane into a dive, aiming directly at the 109. As the German tried to pull away to the right, Jan's gunburst hit him right in the middle of the fuselage. Jan could see that the pilot himself had been hit. Jan drew closer and saw blood pouring down his face. He was still alive though and turned towards Jan, smiled bleakly and ran a finger across his throat before the plane began to corkscrew away towards the ground.

Jan looked at his fuel gauge and realised he only had just enough to get back to base. He scanned the skies for his squadron, but could see nothing. "Red 1, Red 1. Am returning to base. Fuel low. Over." There was no reply.

Jan swept the Hurricane round and set a course for Northolt. His first sortie over English soil and quite a successful one at that! The heat of the action had quickly cured his churning stomach and his heart now returned to its normal rhythm. He suddenly felt ravenously hungry. It was good to be alive!

★ ★ ★

"Three pints of bitter, please." Jan tried to make himself heard above the raucous clamour of the room. The landlord leaned forward cupping his ear with his hand and Jan repeated his order. Shouting, excited Polish voices drowned his words again and Jan pointed at the beer of a nearby customer and held up three fingers. The landlord nodded his understanding and drew the foaming dark liquid into three tankards.

Jan pushed his way through to join Miro and Jerzy at the corner table, which some admiring locals had vacated for them. The inhabitants of Northolt had quickly got used to the boisterous but polite and charming Poles, who had suddenly arrived in their midst. News of the initial success of the Kosciuszko Squadron that week had quickly spread and the customers of the Orchard Inn were proud to make room for them.

He deposited the beers and Miro and Jerzy clinked their glasses with his and they drank. "Well, Jan, you are blooded in England now." Miro Kubicki was a dark, stocky man with an unkempt head of thick, black hair. The most notable feature of his face was the thick pair of lips which detracted from what would otherwise have been very good looks. He grunted sardonically and lit a cigarette, which he left dangling from the left corner of his mouth. "Jasne. Of course, I wouldn't be able to say that to you in person if I hadn't saved your backside up there, eh?"

"Oh shut up, Miro. And you wouldn't be able to say anything if I hadn't come to your aid on Sunday. So don't go on about it." Jerzy Kowalski was the oldest of the three men at thirty-one, but looked as though he should still be in school. He was tall and slim with delicate almost feminine features. However, those who interpreted his looks as indicative of physical weakness were wrong. As a teenager he had been a champion boxer in his native Warsaw and he had proved himself capable of looking after himself many times, both on the ground and in the sky. A small scar under his right eye remained as a souvenir of one of his encounters.

Miro puckered his lips, then laughed. "Only teasing, Jerzy. So come on, Jan, how many kills are you claiming?"

Jan wiped some froth from his lips. "Three, I think. There was that bomber at the beginning. I know I hit it, but I didn't see what happened to it after. Did you?"

Miro nodded. "It went down."

"Unless, of course, you hit it too and you're claiming it."

"No, no. I went after another one when I saw you attack. I got that one and the 109 I saved you from." Miro grinned at Jerzy. "I'm claiming two. I had a couple of near misses and one I'm not sure about. Maybe I should claim that one. I don't know."

Jan spilled some beer in his excitement. "Well then, I'll claim the bomber, then there were two 109s, one that was on the Squadron Leader's tail and then the one that broke off from the pack. So I'm claiming three. How about you, Jerzy?"

"Only two, I'm afraid. One bomber and one 109. I thought I'd get another, but I missed out. For some reason my Hurricane felt a little sluggish today. I've asked the ground crew to have a very close look at it. Anyway, that's seven kills for the Yellow Section. Not so bad. And here's to you, Jan, the winner for the day." Jerzy raised his glass to Jan. "And what was the overall count, do you know?"

"Kellett told me that Red Section had six. So that's thirteen in total for A Flight. And apparently B Flight had some action over the Thames Estuary and brought down five, so eighteen in total for the squadron." Miro raised his right hand to his forehead and aimed a salute at the crowd of other Polish pilots mulling around near the bar.

Jerzy helped himself to one of Miro's cigarettes from a packet on the table.

"Hey, Kowalski, I've only got a couple of packets of Polish cigarettes left. Go and get some Woodbines from the bar, will you?"

Jerzy winked at Jan. He lit up and blew a perfect circle of smoke into the air above his head before asking, "Any sign of Ziggy yet?"

Miro shrugged and shook his head. Jan sighed. "I can't imagine what's happened. I know he's a bit of an odd character, but I can't…"

A middle-aged officer with immaculately Brylcreemed dark hair and a bushy moustache arrived at the table, placed his pint on the table and banged his pipe against one of the table legs. "There you all are. Very well done, gentlemen. I think you all performed admirably today. Admirably. And you, Sieczko, you saved my bacon. I am most grateful. Most grateful."

Squadron Leader Kellett patted Jan on the back. Although the Kosciuszko Squadron was made up of Polish pilots, the RAF had insisted that the squadron be under the overall command of a British Officer. Stanley Kellett, a career Air

Force Officer, was that man. There had been some difficult moments, but the Poles had grown rapidly to respect Kellett and Kellett in turn was learning rapidly to respect his pilots' flying skills.

Kellett's pilots reverted to English. "We were just wondering about Ziggy, sir. Any news?"

"No, Kubicki. I haven't heard anything. I can't believe he's gone AWOL, but if I don't hear anything by tomorrow, I'm going to have to list him as such. It's very worrying. Remind me, Sieczko, you were with him at the weekend, weren't you?"

"Yes, sir. We went sightseeing in London on Sunday. In the evening, after dinner, he went off to meet someone. I went back to my sister's place. He was meant to meet up with me on Monday morning, but as you know didn't show."

"Hmm." Kellett stroked his moustache thoughtfully.

"Well, you know, if there's no sign of him tomorrow, I suppose it's a matter for the police. Doesn't look that good though, does it? We're just getting going here with you chaps and we have to report a Polish desertion. Won't do a lot for our image, will it?"

Jan finished his beer. "Sir, I have… or rather my sister has a good friend in the police, at Scotland Yard in fact. Perhaps he would be able to look into it discreetly. I can't believe Ziggy has deserted. Something must have happened to him."

"Good idea. If we don't find Pilot Officer Kilinski back with us tomorrow, you get your policeman on the case, Sieczko. And now, gentlemen, I haven't got your stamina you know, I'm off to bed. I think we're going to have another busy day tomorrow."

CHAPTER 5

Friday, September 6

It seemed to Merlin that the air-raid sirens had been going off constantly for the past twenty-four hours. He had stayed put in his flat, but had been up and down all night. Having finished his Spanish history book, he couldn't decide on a new book to read. Perhaps he'd managed an hour of sleep all told. He'd pulled back the black-out curtain from time to time and watched the dancing searchlights playing back and forth in the sky. He'd heard the almost constant drone of planes in the distance, but still central London, or at least his part of it, seemed to be unscathed. The anti-aircraft guns had pounded away, but again they were muffled and far off. At about 3am he'd put his mac over his pyjamas and wandered down to the Embankment. Judging by the glow he had seen in the east and south, he had guessed that the docks and the southern suburbs were taking the brunt of the attack again.

The early morning news bulletin on the Home Programme confirmed this. The damage was substantial but confined to a small number of dock installations. There was limited residential damage. In his usual cut-glass tones Alvar Lidell described the events of the evening, modified a little as Merlin knew for morale purposes, but fundamentally accurate.

Was this the beginning of the end? All sorts of scaremongering had arisen about the likely impact of an all-out German bombing attack. If the worst were to be believed, London's entire population would be wiped out by Christmas. Merlin didn't think it would be that bad, but he knew that it would be bad.

★ ★ ★

41

Peter Johnson was waiting outside his door when Merlin got to the Yard. "Come on in, Peter. Take a seat."

Detective Inspector Johnson was a well turned out young man in his late twenties. He had dark, heavily oiled hair and a narrow, angular face. He had for a while affected a small moustache whose unfortunate resemblance to that of the German Fuhrer had brought down the A.C.'s wrath and its ordered removal. Johnson still regularly stroked his upper lip in fond remembrance. His slightly nervous and self-effacing manner masked a sharp, incisive brain and a courageous heart. Johnson withdrew a small notebook and pencil from inside his suit jacket and looked expectantly at Merlin.

"I've read your report on the forgers. Well done."

"Thank you, sir. There is still more work to be done though." Johnson spoke in a soft Geordie accent which Merlin found mellifluous.

"Yes, I know, but you've broken the back of the job and I'd like you to pass it over to Verey now."

Johnson twiddled his pencil and raised a concerned eyebrow. "Very well, sir."

"I've got something else for you. A 'Gatehouse' special, shall we call it?"

Johnson winced.

"No, I shouldn't joke about it, I suppose. It's important work and I think you're well suited to it."

A siren wailed from somewhere on the other side of the river. Both men looked briefly out of the window. "Things are about to get very unpleasant, Peter. Very unpleasant."

Johnson frowned. "I sent Dora up to Newcastle last week. She complained, but I thought she'd be safer with my parents." Johnson had got married in June to his childhood sweetheart.

"Get on alright, do they, Dora and your parents?"

"Yes, sir. Dora's family lived in the same street as us when we were kids. Her parents died young and mine have always been very close to her, so that's alright. She didn't want to leave me, but I insisted."

"I'm sure you did the right thing." Merlin had already suggested on more than one occasion to Sonia that he try and get her employment somewhere outside London, but she had laughed at him. "What could I do in the country, Frank? You want me to be a milkmaid or something. No, I'll take my chances here, with you."

Merlin drew himself back to the present. "What we're concerned about now is the subject of looting. Since the German bombing campaign began in August, there has been a much greater incidence of looting reported than was anticipated. Quite naturally the powers that be are worried that if looting is rife in places like Croydon and Bromley, what will the impact be in central London as the bombing attacks accelerate? If there's an epidemic of looting in London, in other words, how do we manage it?"

"And how do we, sir?"

"I don't yet know. But sitting as we are in the centre of Whitehall, you can perhaps guess the first stage of how we work out how to manage the problem."

Johnson nodded his head slowly. "Well, sir, let me see – would that be to establish a committee?" His Geordie origins betrayed themselves distinctly in his slow and unsympathetic enunciation of the last word.

"Bueno, Peter. A committee. And, yes, I would like you to represent the Yard on this committee."

Johnson shifted uncomfortably in his seat. "I'm not really cut out for administrative work, sir. Is there no one else you can—"

"Inspector, you are my best officer. We may view the workings of Whitehall with distaste and frankly I cannot understand why the civil defence people have not planned more actively for this problem, but there it is. This is an important issue and we are on the front line with the various other authorities. We need to cooperate closely with them and combat the problem very effectively. If it's any comfort, Peter, I think this will be a lot more than paper-pushing. We need to establish an efficient unit to act against looters and you can be in the driving seat in doing that. That means there could be plenty of action for you."

"I'm sorry, sir. You know I'll do anything you want and in the proper spirit. If I have to sit on a committee, so be it. I suppose my lack of enthusiasm reflects the problem itself – who'd have thought that in the dire circumstances we are in, we'd have British people behaving in this disgusting way."

"Disgusting it certainly is. Let's hope that things don't get as bad as these initial figures indicate."

"Yes, sir. Well, what's next?"

"I'll have to make a few phone calls and speak to the A.C. again. Come and see me this afternoon – and thanks."

Johnson rose and put his pencil and notebook away. With a smile he reached over the desk to shake Merlin's extended hand.

★ ★ ★

Jack Stewart plunged his hand into the bucket and splashed his face. He pulled a shabby handkerchief out of his trouser pocket, dunked it in the water and wiped some of the black soot from his eyes. The acrid smell of burning chemicals mingled with the stink of his own sweat and he raised an arm to cover his nostrils. He had been on duty for over twenty-four hours and was on his last legs. He looked over at the rest of his squad. Some men were stretched horizontal on a small patch of scrub ground and the others were leaning exhausted against the pump. They had managed to get the main fire under control by mid-morning, but had been kept busy by small isolated outbreaks, which had continued to occur with annoying regularity. It had been an hour, though, since they had had to deal with one of these incidents and Stewart had decided that they had finished the job.

He sat down carefully between two puddles and rummaged in his pockets for a cigarette. The thick, black smoke, which had swirled around them for hours, had finally dispersed and he could look up at the bright morning sky. In the distance, on the other side of the river in Rotherhithe, he saw a couple of small fires blazing away. He looked up again and watched a single fighter, flying at great altitude, creep slowly across his line of vision. British or German, he didn't care. He felt his eyelids drooping and, with a supreme effort, shook his head and climbed to his feet. "Alright, you lazy buggers. Rise and shine. Let's get the fuck out of here. We've done enough for today."

Despite his argumentative and recalcitrant nature, acquired as a matter of course during a poverty-stricken Gorbals childhood, Stewart had achieved rapid promotion in the Fire Service and was the senior officer in charge of the Chelsea station. His membership of the Communist Party had been held against him when he'd attempted to enlist and all three forces had rejected him. None had given him a good reason, but he knew that his politics must be to blame. At least he'd been sure that that was the case until he'd been accepted by the AFS. Perhaps they were just less choosy in the AFS, though whether the armed forces had any right to be choosy in current circumstances was highly debatable.

From the day he had started his service he had questioned everything. The lack of action during the first months of the war had allowed Stewart plenty of time to think and to pick holes in the system. He'd got up the noses of his superiors in his first station, not only because of his bolshy nature, but also because of his conspicuous success with the female sex, whom he pursued vigorously in the many idle hours. He'd been transferred to the Chelsea station where he was initially just as unpopular. In June, however, a new head of station had come in and he was a Scot of a very different pedigree to Stewart. Archibald Steele had recently inherited a Highland baronetcy, fifty thousand acres and a substantial banking fortune. Nevertheless, he regarded Stewart's foibles with tolerance and some amusement. He recognised that Stewart was ferociously intelligent and clear thinking. As the service was increasingly called into action during the summer months to assist other forces in the suburbs, he realised also that Stewart was fearless and a leader. So when Sir Archibald Steele was asked to take up a more senior role in the AFS hierarchy, he spent little time thinking about his replacement. Eyebrows were raised as rumours of Stewart's awkwardness had circulated beyond his stations, but Steele was insistent. And so Stewart had been in charge of his station for one week when the Blitz on London really seemed to have begun in earnest.

"Come on. Let's do a quick roll-call before we get home. Line up here, men." Stewart cast an eye down the line. And then looked again. "Where the hell is Evans? Cooper, you were with him last time I looked."

Cooper, a grizzled veteran of the regular Fire Brigade who'd come into the service from retirement, wiped a smear of dirt from his cheek. "He came out safely with me from the warehouse. I think he wandered off down to the wharf. Maybe he's gone for a swim!"

Stewart laughed half-heartedly. "Yes. Very funny. Alright. Let's get all our equipment together. I'll just have a quick look for him over there. Cooper, you supervise please."

Stewart stepped gingerly over some smouldering timber embers and walked towards the river. He spotted Evans sitting on the edge of the deck with his legs dangling over the water. "Oi. Evans. What the hell are you doing?"

Evans, a serious-looking man in his thirties, turned to see Stewart approaching him and hurriedly jumped to his feet. He ran a hand through his sparse hair then put his helmet back on. "I'm sorry, Mr Stewart. I was in a bit of a daze after getting out of the warehouse. I suppose I came over here because I'd get a little cooler. Is there more firefighting to be done?"

"No, no. It's just that we're finished here now and we need to pack up and get back to Chelsea. I was worried that we might have lost you."

"I'm afraid I lost myself for a moment. I was thinking about

Charles Dickens. *Our Mutual Friend* to be precise. This area of London features significantly in that book. Have you read it?"

Stewart had compensated in part for the deficiencies of his Glasgow education by becoming extremely well read. He had read all of Dickens. "Aye, I've read it. Gaffer Hexam and Roger Riderhood. They were in business fishing out dead bodies in these reaches of the Thames, were they not? Have you seen any dead bodies to fish out?"

"Thankfully not, Mr Stewart. Plenty of dead wood, but no dead people, although I daresay that there'll be an abundance of those shortly."

"Now, now, Mr Evans. Let's not get defeatist."

"I'm not being defeatist, Mr Stewart. I'm being a realist."

Stewart nodded back towards the smouldering building and the rest of their squad. "Come on, let's go."

As they walked back Evans hummed a tune which seemed vaguely familiar to Stewart.

"Handel?"

"Yes, well done, Mr Stewart. From the music for the Royal Fireworks. Appropriate for our task, I think. You know, there is a strange beauty to all this."

Stewart jumped over a large slick of oily water. Evans directed his path around it. "Beauty, you say, Mr Evans. How so?"

"Well, when the inferno was at its height last night, I was just wondering what Turner would have made of it. He loved those fiery colours. 'The Fighting Temeraire' and all that. Do you know that painting?"

Stewart's latterday self-education had not yet embraced much of the visual arts. Evans, he knew, was or had been some sort of art historian from whom he would be happy to learn. "Can't say I do."

"It's a wonderful painting of an old ship-of-the line being burned at sea. You must see it, except..."

"Except what?"

"Well, you won't be able to see it for the duration. It's gone off for safety to the country with the rest of the Tate collection. I have several books on Turner. I'd be happy to bring them into the station if you are interested?"

"I would, yes. Perhaps tomorrow. But for now let's concentrate on getting back to Chelsea. Go over there and help the others, please."

Evans joined Cooper in loading a hose. Stewart saw a gaggle of ARP wardens approaching and went to talk to them about securing the area. Away to the south, the wail of another siren pierced the London air.

★ ★ ★

A long queue stretched around the eastern and southern edges of Leicester Square. A shorter queue lined up along the northern edge.

"Well, that decides it. It's *Rebecca* not *Gone With The Wind*. Do you agree, Claire?"

Detective Constable Tommy Cole adjusted his salmon-pink tie nervously. This was his third date with Claire Robinson. The first one had been as long ago as February, but he had been sent in March on a training course in connection with his move to CID and had only returned to duty at the Yard in July. Fortunately, no one else had taken the opportunity to move in on her and a second date a week ago when Claire had returned from leave had gone very well. Nevertheless, he couldn't help feeling that his aspirations were far above his station. He came from a very ordinary working-class background. His father was a fitter in a factory in Wembley. Tommy had gone into the police straight from school and somehow or other landed on his feet at the Yard. WPC Robinson was Assistant Commissioner Gatehouse's niece. Before graduating from Hendon Police College she had been to public school and her family owned a large country manor in Hampshire as well as a large house in the suburbs. She was also extremely attractive with strawberry blonde hair cut short, twinkling brown eyes, a sweet button nose beneath which lay a charming little beauty spot, and a full and welcoming mouth. She was a jolly girl, who almost always seemed to be smiling. She was also quite tall and leggy. Cole liked tall and leggy girls. All in all, she was perfect, he thought, but he couldn't quite see what she saw in him. Cole was also tall, 6'2" to be precise. His mother said he was lean and trim – he thought he was too skinny. He would like to be at least a stone heavier and to that end he had recently purchased a muscle-building book by Charles Atlas, and had got hold of some Indian clubs and dumbbells on the cheap from a friend of his dad. To match his body he had a long, thin face. He had broken his nose when he had fallen in a cross-country race a year before and when he looked at his face in the mirror he missed his old nose. His large, blue eyes were alright, he supposed, although one seemed to be a little lower than the other and his mouth seemed to have shrunk a little since he was a teenager. Well, whatever the deficiencies of his face, Claire Robinson seemed to find it acceptable. She had even kissed it on their last outing, on the cheek not the lips, but nevertheless…

"I love Laurence Olivier, Tommy. You know that. I always wanted to see this film tonight."

"Righto."

They joined the end of the queue. An old, peg-legged man was singing 'It's a long way to Tipperary' and shuffling along the line. Claire Robinson put tuppence in the hat he held out and put her hand on Cole's arm. "Mr Merlin seemed rather cheerful in the office today, Tommy. Didn't you think so?"

"I didn't see him today. Sergeant Bridges sent me to Earl's Court to check out some suspicious goings on."

"Suspicious goings on. That sounds exciting!"

"Well, it wasn't. Some old biddy said that she was sure her next-door neighbours were German spies. Said she could hear them speaking German and operating a radio transmitter."

"And were they?"

"Well, they were speaking something like German and

49

they had a radio, but that's about it. They were a nice, old, Jewish couple speaking Yiddish to each other – Yiddish sounds like German, you know. They were in their seventies and had escaped here from Hungary. I told the old biddy there was nothing to worry about, but she kept on ranting at me and I had to threaten her with arrest if she didn't pipe down."

"So did that take all day?"

"No, after I finished sorting that one out, the sergeant asked me to go and investigate a supposed sabotage attempt at Chelsea power station."

"And?"

"Nothing. Just a quarrel between two engineers that had got out of hand."

Claire smiled sympathetically. "Oh, well. Anyway, Mr Merlin asked me into the office to ask me to research something for him."

"What?"

"He wanted me to dig out some files on the First World War. Wanted to know whether there was any looting when the Germans bombed us."

"I didn't know that they did bomb us."

"Yes, well, my knowledge about it was not what it should be. They had Zeppelins then and they did a bit of damage in the East End. Nothing like what we're facing now, I'm sure, but there was damage and people died."

"Did they? And was there any looting?"

"A little."

"Well. Who'd think it. So I suppose he's worrying about what's going to happen now."

"Yes. But he seems like a new man to me. I know he's got an awful lot on his plate, but he seems really happy for the first time since I've known him."

"Well, it's that girl, isn't it?"

"He has a girl? I didn't know."

"Yes, that Polish girl, Sonia. You know? The one he met during that American embassy case."

Claire frowned at Cole. "Tommy Cole. A juicy bit of gossip like that and you don't let on. I suppose everyone knows apart from me?"

"Well, I don't think your uncle knows."

They had reached the top of the queue and Cole paid for their tickets. They entered the foyer. "Hmm. Well, good for Mr Merlin anyway. He deserves a bit of happiness." Claire laughed and pecked Cole's cheek as they went through the curtains into the cinema. "As do we, Tommy."

CHAPTER 6

Saturday, September 7

"Hello, Sam, keeping you busy at the old cop-shop, are they?" Sam Bridges muttered these words to himself as he and his pregnant wife waited patiently at the front door in the heat of the late afternoon. As sure as the sun would rise in the morning, he knew that these would be his father-in-law's words of greeting. Frederick Brown was a man of regular customs and habits. He had spent his entire working life in the army, ending up as a Regimental Sergeant Major. "Order, conformity, regularity – that's what makes the British Empire great, mark my words, Sam. Regularity in all things – from bowel movements to meal times to shoe polishing, that's what supported our great imperial adventure. Forget all the fancy stuff – regularity, Sam, regularity!"

The door to the small cottage creaked open. "Hello, Sam, keeping you busy at the old cop-shop, are they? And there you are, my darling Iris. Looks like my grandson is going to be a big, strapping boy. Need a lorry to get her down here, Sam?"

Iris wiped her forehead with a handkerchief. "Oh, shut up, Dad, and let us in. It's boiling out here."

"Come on in then. I'll put the kettle on." Fred Brown was a solid brick of a man, with a ruddy complexion and a ramrod-straight back and, although well in his sixties, Sam guessed that he would be quite as capable of carrying out his full regimental duties now as when he had retired ten years before. Fred Brown liked his son-in-law very much.

"Peas in a pod, we are, Sam. My old Maudie, she always said that girls like to marry men like their fathers, just as boys like to marry girls like their mothers. Well, I can't speak for boys, only having had Iris, but I reckon she was right about girls. Eh, Sam?"

And indeed, Sam Bridges could have passed for a younger Fred Brown. Excepting the hair, of course. Sam had a shock of fair hair and Fred's, prior to its reduction to a closely cropped, greyish stubble, had been jet-black. Fred Brown scraped his fingers over the stubble as he waited for the kettle to boil.

"If I'd known you were coming, I'd have got some biscuits in. I could do you both a cheese sandwich. How about that? Or if you hang about for a bit, I could get us some fish and chips from the shop on the corner for tea? What do you say?"

"No thanks, Dad. We just thought we'd pop down and see if you were alright. It's such a lovely day and we thought we'd hop on the bus and have a cup of tea with you."

"Well, that's lovely of you both. You can see that the bombs haven't got me yet. Shall we sit in the garden?"

Iris dabbed at her forehead with the handkerchief again.

"Too hot for you, dear? That's unlike you. You always liked the heat as a child. Just like your old dad. Maudie couldn't stand it, but I've always loved it. In India, the men used to call me 'Devil Brown' because—"

"Yes, we know, Dad. I still like the heat, but it's not such a wonderful thing when you're almost seven months pregnant." Two small beads of sweat evaded the handkerchief and slid down Iris' left cheek. Sam thought that pregnancy had made her even more beautiful. Her curly brown perm now framed a slightly fuller face than it had at the beginning of the year. There was the slightest hint of a double chin, but Sam found this charming. In fact, he found everything about her charming – her sparkling, oval, green eyes, her high cheekbones, her neat nose and her small, determined mouth.

"Well, yes, of course. But I can move the garden table and chairs into the shade, dear."

"Oh, alright."

Thirty minutes later the three of them were sitting with their empty teacups in Fred Brown's neat little garden, relaxing under the cloudless Tooting sky. The cottage was at the end of a long street of terraced two-up two-downs. It was the only detached property, a fact in which Fred took much pride, and it backed on to some old fields where allotments were kept. A small gate at the end of the garden led into these fields and to his own nearby allotment. As they relaxed in the garden, they could hear birds singing and chickens clucking. They could as well have been in deepest Kent or Sussex countryside as a fifty-minute bus ride from Big Ben. Sam and his father-in-law were stretched out in deckchairs in the small area of garden that still had some sun. Iris sat at the table in the cool shadow of the house with her feet on a chair. They had tried to avoid talking about the war as such discussions usually sent Fred Brown's blood pressure haywire. They had heard that Fred had not slept much in the past week with all the night activity, but, as he reminded them, he could get by with a minimum of sleep as he'd learned in the army. Discussion had moved on to the naming of his grandson.

"It might well be a girl, Dad. Don't count your chickens."

"Poppycock, Iris. It's going to be a boy. I know it. Aren't I right, Sam? Now what do you think about Winston? No, I suppose you're right. Everyone and their uncle will be calling their kids Winston, I suppose. Then again, if things don't go so well perhaps we'll have to call him Adolf, eh?"

Iris steered the conversation away from names to her father's domestic arrangements. Before she had become pregnant she had come down every week from Battersea to see to her father's cleaning and washing, but her father had insisted on her dropping this when he'd learned that a baby was on the way. He'd found someone down the street who was prepared to do for him for a modest fee. Mrs Hammond, a sprightly little widow whom Fred found pleasant company.

"She doesn't have designs on you, Dad, does she?"

Fred spluttered the remains of his tea on his trousers. "Of course not. She's just a nice little old lady, that's all."

A comfortable silence settled on them. A horse neighed

somewhere in the fields. There was the sound of male laughter from one of the allotments. Sam noticed that both Fred and Iris' heads were beginning to nod. A bee was buzzing around his outstretched legs and another flitted around between Fred and Iris. Sam looked at his watch. Half an hour and they ought to be getting back. He was on duty tomorrow and he wanted an early night. He closed his eyes. The bees carried on buzzing and Sam dozed off for a few seconds. The image of a baby came to mind. A baby with a cigar in its mouth. Winston Bridges. Hmm. Sam jerked awake. The drone of the bees had been superseded by a louder buzz and he looked up and blinked to see that the sky was filled with metal. What seemed like hundreds of planes jostled for space from one corner of the sky to the other. Sam focused his eyes and now saw a massive central core of larger aircraft, surrounded by crowds of smaller ones. The giant flotilla was heading north towards central London. This was on a different scale to the previous raids – it must be the big one – the long-awaited, major attack on the heart of the nation. The siren started to wail. *A bit late in the day for that*, Sam thought. He saw his wife and her father staring up with open mouths and looked back up to see a new formation of bombers blotting out the few available patches of clear sky.

"Come on, you two. Where's the nearest shelter, Fred?"

Fred was still staring up in amazement. "Look. There are our boys. Go on. Get the bastards." Iris grabbed his arm and pulled him towards the house.

They watched as waves of British fighters surged up into the sky and tore into the deadly storm cloud of German bombers. They saw some bombers and fighters spiralling down, but the vast bulk of the invaders continued inexorably on their way. A loud crashing sound came from the nearby fields and they were suddenly showered with sods of earth.

Sam shouted at the others, "Let's get in!"

As they closed the kitchen door, Fred pointed towards the hall. He pulled open a door under the stairs and touched a light switch. "It's too late to get to the shelter. Come down into the cellar. I've made it quite cosy. We'll be alright there. Come on, Iris, give me your hand." They made their way down the stairs. Two mattresses had been crammed into the cramped space. An old camp-burner, a relic of Fred's army days, together with a teapot, a packet of PG Tips and some mugs rested on an upturned old crate. A book of Sherlock Holmes stories, a couple of faded issues of *Picture Post* and a copy of *The Thirty-Nine Steps* lay on one of the mattresses. Sam also noticed a bucket discreetly positioned behind the crate.

Another explosion thudded nearby and the cellar door above them clattered open and Sam jumped up the stairs to lock it.

"Alright, love?" Iris' hands were shaking and Sam helped her down onto the mattresses. Fred reached out and patted her stomach. "The young lad's got his first taste of action already. He's going to be a soldier and a fine one at that."

Iris smiled weakly. "I hope to God there are no wars for him or anyone to fight in after this one."

They settled down for the duration. There were two more heavy explosions in the first hour, but mostly they could hear the dull thump of distant bombardment. By the time the all clear sounded at seven, Sam had read two Sherlock Holmes stories and drunk two cups of tea and Iris and Fred were both asleep. He climbed the stairs to enter the hall and pushed through the front door into the street. A house at the far end of the terrace was burning, but everything else seemed normal. He walked back through the house out into the garden and then through the gate, past the allotments and into the open fields. He thought he would be able to get the clearest view of the London skyline from the middle of one of the fields. Until he got there, he didn't turn to look back. When he did, he saw vast billowing clouds of black smoke covering most of the horizon. *All of London must be on fire*, he thought. He stared, his mind a blank, for a moment or two, then came to his senses. *It's best to leave Iris with her dad*, he thought. For some reason the garish music hall image of Max Miller came to his mind. Yes, the centre of town seemed to be top of the bill today and the southern suburbs were just the supporting acts. He'd have to get back to Battersea though – he needed to know whether they had a home to go back to. He felt a firm push from behind and jumped. He turned to find one of the small ponies someone kept in the fields. He put his hand onto the animal's head and stroked it. He could feel it shaking.

"You and me both, mate. You and me both."

★ ★ ★

Maksim tried very hard to keep his hand still as he poured more brandy into his employer's glass. The fact that dinner had been served to the accompaniment of the racket from Germany's largest bombing attack by far on the English capital seemed not to have disturbed Kyril Voronov at all. He had laughed and joked all night. Although most of the bombs appeared to be falling far to the east, they had heard plenty of explosions much closer to home. A neighbour had knocked on the door a little earlier to warn Maksim that Pont Street had been hit by a cluster of bombs. Pont Street was a mere five-minute walk from Voronov's palatial house off Eaton Square. When Maksim had told him this, Voronov had only laughed louder. But then everyone knew that Kyril Voronov was a madman. No one but a madman would call Stalin an ignorant Georgian sheepshagger to his face. Everyone wondered how he had been able to survive that, but he had, as he had survived many other things – the revolution, many battles, the numerous purges. He had survived all those things and had somehow accumulated a large fortune as well. Very few knew how he had managed this, but Maksim was one of them. He had been with Voronov for nearly twenty years. He had seen the distasteful favours Voronov had done, the horse-trading, the wheeling and dealing, the torture, the murder. Call Voronov mad? Maksim himself was the maddest to stick by this ogre.

But then again, things hadn't been so bad recently – a calm, quiet, comfortable period for him at least, until the bloody Germans had decided to bomb the hell out of London.

Another nearby explosion rattled the windows. Maksim jumped and spilled some brandy on the table.

"You idiot, Maksim! What's wrong with you?"

"Do you not think, Kyril Ivanovitch, that we should make our way to the shelter now or at least to the cellar. That sounded very close."

"Bulls' bollocks, Maksim. That was a long way away. By God, we've been through a lot worse than this and survived. And remember, Kyril was born lucky – nothing ever hurts Kyril, does it, my dear?"

Madame Anna Voronov finished her glass of Chateau Yquem and smiled weakly. "Yes, dear. Nothing ever hurts you – just those around you."

Voronov tugged at his thick, grey beard and laughed again. "In this instance, my dear, I think you have it wrong – if a bomb doesn't hurt me then it won't hurt those next to me, will it – eh, Misha? What do you say?"

"You are right as always, my friend. When are you ever wrong?" Misha Trubetskoi, Voronov's assistant and partner in all things, grabbed the brandy bottle from Maksim, poured himself a glass and then poured another, which he passed to Maksim. "Have a slug of this, for God's sake. This will calm you down. Sometimes I wonder how you've lasted all this time with Kyril. Surely you should have a stronger constitution by now? Or perhaps you'd prefer one of my specials, eh?" Trubetskoi produced a hip flask from inside his jacket and waved it menacingly in Maksim's face.

Voronov chuckled. "Leave him alone, Misha. He's my lucky talisman, he is. He's always been a worryguts, but I can't get rid of him now. We've been through too much together. Eh, Maksim?"

Maksim shook his head in resignation and wandered off to the corner of the room with his drink. His work was over now and there was nothing to stop him going down to the cellar himself. But it was true. Voronov was somehow protected by a higher power. It was safer to be near him, as he had said. After all that he had been through, no bomb was going to fall on Kyril Voronov.

CHAPTER 7

Sunday, September 8

September 8th. Merlin's mother's birthday. She had been gone for almost ten years now. What would she make of all this? She had always hated the Germans after his dad had established himself as a freak statistic by becoming one of the very small number of London inhabitants killed by Zeppelin bombs in the Great War. Well, being killed by a bomb in this war was not going to make you a freak statistic. Merlin looked up at what he could only describe as the skeleton of the Chelsea house. Loose fragments of wallpaper in one of the upstairs bedrooms flapped pathetically back and forth. It was raining for the first time in a long time. A thin stream of water ran down from the middle of what remained of the buckled upstairs. Rescue-workers were carefully removing the stones.

"Need a hand?"

"No, mate, it's alright. Best to move along though. The rest of this could fall down at any minute."

Merlin nodded. A young boy in shorts came out of the front door of the next house, which was somehow completely intact. He had a bright red bike with him which he wheeled over. Merlin winked at him and the boy managed a weak smile back. "That's Betty's house."

"Is it? Did she…" He could see that the boy was trying hard not to look at the rescue-workers. He looked across the street and then back at Merlin. He started to mount his bike, but stopped. Inexorably his eyes moved to the mound of rubble that had been the lower floor of Betty's house. Suddenly one of the rescuers shouted. "Watch it. I think there's…"

The men carefully removed some bricks and something

white appeared, poking out of the rubble. It was a child's hand. Merlin shuddered.

The little boy dropped his bicycle and burst into tears. Merlin knelt down and embraced the child who buried his face in the policeman's chest and sobbed uncontrollably. "There, there, son." It was inadequate, but what else could he say?

★ ★ ★

Sonia opened the door and threw her arms around him. "Frank, you're alright?"

"Yes, I'm fine."

Sonia had gone to see Jan at Northolt the previous day and Merlin had been particularly anxious. Sonia was very careless about going to the shelters in a raid. "What will be will be" was her motto. "If my name is on the bomb, so be it. Kismet is the word, isn't it?" Stupid girl.

They stood at her doorway happily embracing for a moment before Sonia pulled him through the door.

Sonia had finally got hold of Merlin just before midnight on Saturday to let him know that she was safe in Northolt and to make sure that the bombs hadn't got him. She had seen Jan for a quick sandwich at the base before his squadron took to the air. Someone told her about the particularly heavy bombing and she'd thought of getting back to London to find Merlin, but she had promised to see Jan later. She had found a telephone kiosk on the base and had been ringing Merlin's flat on and off all night. When she did get him, she had exploded with frustration. "How was I meant to know that you'd gone to Scotland Yard, you stupid man? I've been trying you for ages!" Having grabbed a couple of hours sleep in a chair in the canteen, she had caught the milk-train in the morning and had been waiting impatiently for hours.

They sat down on the sofa and kissed, gently at first, then more urgently. Suddenly, Sonia pulled away. "Now then, Mr

Policeman, hold your horse a minute. I have something for you here. It's from Jan."

Merlin opened the envelope that Sonia passed to him. "It's in Polish."

"I am to translate it for you. He's not confident in his written English. Here goes:

'Dear Frank, I am giving this letter to Sonia for you as I am very concerned about my friend, Ziggy. His full name, or maybe I should say the name he goes by here, is Zygmunt Kilinski. We fought together against the Germans in the Polish Air Force and then escaped together through Romania so that we could fight again in England. He is a very brave man and a very good pilot. The weekend when I came to London and met you, I spent some time with Ziggy. We had some fun and a few drinks, but I could tell that Ziggy's heart was not really in it. He mentioned a few times that there was someone he had to see if he could that weekend. At the end of our meal together on the Sunday, he found a telephone, made a call and then announced that he was going off to meet an old Polish friend. He clearly did not want me to join him, just patted me on the back and told me he'd be round at Sonia's in the morning at nine. He never turned up. I left a note, but Sonia tells me the note was untouched where I'd left it when she got home in the evening. He was due back on duty with me on Tuesday, but did not appear there and he's been missing all week.'"

The sound of a backfiring car nearby interrupted Sonia, who paused, went into the kitchen, and reappeared with a glass of water. She took a couple of sips then resumed.

"'The Squadron Leader has been very good in allowing me to ask you to investigate before posting him as a deserter. I would be very grateful if you or one of your officers could look into it. I am aware that I have not given you much to go on, but if you could make it out to Northolt, perhaps his belongings or some of his colleagues might be able to give you some clues. Obviously we are very busy here as you must be in town. It goes without saying that we shall defeat these

German bastards, English and Polish fighting together! I have given your name to Squadron Leader Kellett and I have written his telephone number at the bottom of this letter. Please call him if you can to arrange a visit. It is hard to predict the pattern of German bombing, but I think they favour the night at the moment, so the morning might be best. The Squadron Leader will have the best idea no doubt.

Jan Sieczko

P.S. Please look…' Oh, I'm not going to read that."

"Why not? What does he say?"

"Oh, he just mentions something silly about you and me and wants you to make sure the bombs don't get me!"

"Silly, how do you mean?"

"Never you mind. Anyway, that's his letter. What do you think?"

"I am very sorry Jan's friend has disappeared. With luck it's nothing sinister, but as your countrymen are fighting so hard for us, if one gets into trouble, they certainly deserve our help. I'll have to sort out things at the Yard though. Gatehouse will need to know if I'm opening an investigation and he might want me to get a junior officer involved. I'll try and swing it though."

Sonia kissed him on the mouth. "Thank you, Frank."

"Now, where were we?"

★ ★ ★

Jack Stewart fell exhausted onto the cot bed. For the first time his team had been kept busy on their home patch. They had received urgent messages for help from the East End, but they had their hands full in Chelsea. With the activity of Friday night in the East India Dock and yesterday's goings on around Cadogan Square, he hadn't slept for forty-eight hours. He wouldn't be on his cot now if he hadn't been ordered by a superior officer to take a break. "They're bound to keep on coming today, perhaps in greater numbers, so it won't do us any good if you're a complete basket case. Get a couple of hours at least. We'll try and rotate your men with the men from Battersea, although they've not had a very easy time of it either. Go on, off with you."

As Stewart lay on the cot he could hear the radio in one of the other rooms. The newsreader said that there had been casualties overnight, but implied they were not great. Stewart knew the truth was much worse than that. Hundreds had died at least and he'd guess that thousands had been injured. Someone turned the radio off. Stewart's eyes closed, but he couldn't sleep. His mind was filled with the images of the night. He had seen many terrible things, but the worst must be the woman and the baby. She was waving at him from the fourth-storey window of a house just off Sloane Street. The fire had taken a firm hold and the floors below were engulfed in flames. The woman had been shouting something, but he couldn't make out a word through the bedlam of the droning planes, the explosions, the multifarious noises of the fire and the roar of the hoses. He shook his head and cupped his hand to his ear. Some of his men were attempting to put up a ladder, but the heat was too intense for them to get close enough. He could see the flames leaping higher around the window and then there was a crack as some of the roof disintegrated. He saw that the woman was holding a baby out from the window. She was going to let the baby go and wanted someone to catch it. Stewart shouted over to his men.

"Forget the ladder. She's going to jump. Get the—" There was another crack and another part of the roof crumbled. An explosion of smoke and flames filled the space where the woman had been. Then he saw them, mother and child, flames streaming from the woman's nightdress as they tumbled through the air into oblivion.

He opened his eyes and reached beneath the cot. He scrabbled around until he found the Johnny Walker. He took a long pull on the bottle. The warm, amber liquid burned his dry throat, but served its purpose. Within seconds Jack Stewart fell asleep.

★ ★ ★

Saturday night had produced some excellent pickings, there was no doubt. Jake dropped the sack carefully on the ground and rummaged in his trouser pockets for the key to the lock-up. Of course, you needed good nerves for this sort of business and good nerves were what he and Billy had. They had done much better than when they'd been traipsing round the suburbs. Tooting and Bexleyheath weren't exciting locations for their activities, though they'd come across some nice jewellery and the odd interesting-looking painting.

"Come on, Jakie, get a move on. This is bloody heavy."

"Well, there's nothing to stop you putting your sack down too while I get this bloody thing open, is there?" Ash spilled onto Billy's shoes from the almost spent cigarette precariously attached to Jake's lips. Billy grunted, but kept hold of the sack, which was slung over his shoulder. Finally, Jake found the key in his back pocket and fumbled in the dark to insert the key and open the padlock. He pushed at the door, which creaked open stiffly. As Billy pushed in behind him, he reached out for the light switch.

Their journey to Shepherd's Bush from Chelsea had not been without incident. The engine of Billy's old Austin had overheated as they were coming along Holland Park Avenue and they'd had to leave the car and walk the last mile. A copper had stopped them and almost given them both heart attacks. However, he hadn't asked them what they were doing or what was in the sacks, but had pleasantly enquired whether they needed any help. Having turned down this kind offer, they had almost been run over by a speeding fire engine as they crossed over from Shepherd's Bush Green into Wood Lane.

Never mind. They were safe now. Billy began to empty his

sack while Jake lit up another cigarette. "Let's have a look then."

Billy pulled out a finely gilded carriage clock.

"Eighteenth century, I think. Very nice. Want a fag?"

Billy shook his head and removed a small painting in an ornate frame.

"Another eighteenth century piece, I think, Billy. Or perhaps early nineteenth. Very soothing. A riverside scene out of town. Could be the Thames. Or perhaps it's French?"

A steady flow of valuable objects followed the picture onto the dingy floor. Jake started unloading his sack as well. Fine pieces of porcelain, which the men had taken the time to wrap in newspaper before setting out on their journey from Chelsea, some miniature portraits, silverware, another landscape painting, ancient leather-bound volumes, candlesticks – all in all, a particularly good haul.

The two men sat down on the floor and laughed. "It's a damn sight better when the Germans bomb Chelsea than when they bomb the Isle of Dogs, eh?"

"Watch where you're dropping that bloody ash, Jake. We don't want to damage anything. He should give us a bloody good price for this lot."

"Yeah. Well, let's not hang around too long. There'll be plenty more pickings tonight from the sound of those planes."

Billy nodded and the two men rose to their feet. They picked up the various valuable objects from the ground, carried them over to the back of the lock-up and loaded them carefully into some empty tea crates. Then they pushed the crates under cover of a large green tarpaulin, which already concealed several other full crates.

As they came out into the yard, a dog barked. They made their way to the street and saw a cluster of incendiaries falling not so far away. The sky to the east was aglow. They hurried on.

★ ★ ★

Count Tarkowski was holding his nose. He and his wife had

been down in the Belsize Park tube shelter for some five hours. They had found a corner spot and had made themselves reasonably comfortable with the blankets that they had brought with them, but as the hours had gone by the shelter had filled up and they had been hemmed in by the press of bodies. The stink of sweat, urine and other bodily fluids had become almost overpowering. To his immediate right was a very fat mother with a screaming baby and two out-of-control toddlers. To his left, next to his wife, an old man in some sort of uniform he did not recognise lay snoring away, alternating this with a regular breaking of wind. In front of him, a well-dressed couple tried to comfort their teenage daughter, who was having hysterics and who had vomited at least twice. A few yards away was the tube railway line and when he had stood up briefly to stretch his legs a while back, he had seen a gang of rats massing in a corner. A couple of them had somehow made their way up to the platform and he watched them darting between prostrate bodies, fortunately away from where he and his wife were.

He sat up and attempted yet again to read his book. He had read Sienkiewicz's great trilogy about seventeenth-century Poland many times. *With Fire and Sword*, the first volume, told the story of the Polish Commonwealth's resistance to a great Cossack uprising. He removed his hand from his nose and pointed the torch. Hard as he concentrated, the words floated meaninglessly in front of his eyes. He looked over at his wife, who amazingly was fast asleep. He wished he'd brought a sleeping draught with him. In the distance he heard raised voices as someone squabbled with someone else about encroaching on his space and others told them to pipe down.

He wondered for the hundredth time whether he should have moved everything. It should have been safe in the office, but then was it really safe in his house? And then there was that young maniac pestering him about it and Voronov hovering around. The one helpful thing the Germans might do would be for them to land a bomb neatly on them both.

That would make life a little easier. The uniformed man farted particularly loudly and Tarkowski turned away. He closed his eyes and forced himself to think of something pleasant. He pictured the estate near Bialystok. There was a small stream running down from the Bialowieza Forest into the fields. He remembered bathing naked in it with his brothers. One day, two pretty, young peasant girls from one of the villages had come upon them. His younger brothers had laughed unconcerned, but he had been shy and had rushed to hide behind some bushes. One of the girls had come and tried to pull him out. He had resisted and then she had smiled and lifted her dress above her head and beckoned to him. Ah yes, that had been very pleasant. His eyelids drooped and sleep came.

★ ★ ★

Merlin decided to get back to his own place that night, despite Sonia's entreaties to stay. His shoulder was giving him gyp again and if he was going to have a sleepless night, he preferred to have it somewhere where his tossing and turning wasn't going to ruin Sonia's night as well. Feeling a little weary from his pleasurable exertions, he decided to walk to the Baker Street Tube and catch the Circle Line.

The raiders hadn't gone home yet and, as he was approaching Marylebone Road, he became conscious of engine noise followed by an odd whistling sound. Moments later an apartment block on the other side of the road exploded. Merlin was blown off his feet and enveloped by a dark cloud of smoke. For a second or two he lost consciousness then, lying flat on his back and staring up at the gleaming disc of the moon and the black shadows passing across it, he confirmed to his own satisfaction that he was still alive. He was rising carefully to his feet, his body bruised but intact, when a shot rang out. The sound of running feet followed, then Merlin found himself on his back again, bowled over this time by a man hurtling into him from somewhere to his left. He stood up again with an effort and looked down the small side street from which the man must have come. He made his way stiffly along the street and came to the ruin of a building, which was still smouldering in parts and was probably a casualty of the day before. Merlin couldn't quite decide whether it had been a residential building or an office. He walked carefully around a crater in the pavement, which the moon had helpfully illuminated and stepped gingerly through what he assumed had once been the front door. Suddenly he was aware of a murmur of voices and somewhere at the back of the building a cigarette glowed.

He took another tentative step forward and then another. The noises became clearer and he was able to make out a few words – "Bastard – get him – boxes" and some others clearly not English but too indistinct for him to identify the language. On his next step forward his foot got caught in something and there was the sound of shifting rubble.

"Who's there? Come on, my friends, let's get out of here."

By the time Merlin had got his foot unstuck, there were no more voices and the men, whoever they were, had evidently disappeared. He thought for a moment about having a good look around, but decided that it was too dangerous in the dark and made his way back to Marylebone Road. Strangely, the pain in his shoulder had gone away completely.

CHAPTER 8

Monday, September 9

The all clear sounded again just after six. Voronov had slept soundly through the night in his own bed and was irritated to be disturbed by the siren at such an early hour. He looked over at his wife. She was wisely wearing black eyepads and earplugs. She didn't share Voronov's blind faith in his indestructibility, but had not wanted to upset him by not sharing his bed, so she had drunk half a bottle of vodka and several large glasses of a rather fine Bordeaux before retiring. Her mouth was half-open and she was breathing regularly. From experience, Voronov estimated that she'd be out of it till lunchtime. He tugged at a rope that hung on the wall on his side of the bed. Shortly afterwards a bleary-eyed Maksim appeared at the door.

"Ah. You're still alive I see. Did you sleep well in the cellar?" Maksim shook his head.

"Hmm. Well, I slept particularly well until that infernal noise went off." Voronov stroked his beard slowly.

"Very well. Tea, if you please. And quickly. I have a terrible thirst."

Maksim disappeared and Voronov lumbered out of the bed. He walked over to the French windows in front of him, pulled back the curtains and stepped out onto the balcony. Everything seemed as it had been before. In the rapidly improving light, Voronov saw a milkman doing his rounds.

Only in England, he thought. The Germans had showered hundreds of tons of explosives on London over two nights and half the city had been blown to smithereens, yet the milkman was still calmly out on his rounds at six in the morning. "An amazing country!" he shouted, chuckling to himself. The milkman looked up and waved.

Voronov turned back in and went to the bathroom. He stared at himself in the mirror above the sink. His eyes were bloodshot, but then they were always bloodshot. His nose was thick, round and heavily veined. A typical Russian drinker's nose, as his wife pointed out whenever he dared to criticise her own alcoholic consumption. His thick, woolly hair was greyer than a year ago, which, aesthetically speaking, was for the best, as it now made a better match with his thick, grey beard. Sifting through the latter, Voronov picked out small remnants of last night's meal – a breadcrumb or two, the odd caviar egg, a scrap of beef. He ran the cold tap, bent down and splashed his face several times. He removed a small, black-lacquered box from the cabinet to his right, took out two pills and drank several glasses of cold water, with the last of which he took the pills. He had a bit of a headache, but no worse than usual. He shook his head. He needed to be in good form as it was going to be a busy day, as well, he hoped, as an enjoyable one.

★ ★ ★

Jack Stewart led his weary team through the door of the Chelsea Fire Station. He walked down the corridor, turned into the canteen and sat heavily on one of the chairs at the main table. His team did likewise, with the exception of Francis Evans, who wandered off towards the bunk room.

"Gawd! You lot look like death warmed up. Better get the tea on." Elsie and the other helper, Jean, were short, plump, middle-aged cockney ladies who might have been sisters but weren't. Elsie busily set to with a vast kettle and a teapot almost as big, while Jean began making sandwiches. Every man's face was streaked with soot and as they sat in the unventilated warm room, trails of blackened perspiration dropped down onto the table, their clothes and the floor.

Evans reappeared carrying a book, which he dropped in front of Stewart. "There you are. *The Art of J M W Turner*. I brought it from home yesterday, but didn't have a chance to give it to you."

Stewart reached over for a towel hanging over a nearby chair and wiped his face and hands.

"Oh, don't worry about getting it dirty. I've got another copy as it happens."

It was a big glossy book with more pictures than words. Stewart's eyes felt as if someone had poured vinegar into them and rubbing them with his blackened hands only made them worse. He eventually managed to focus on the pages in front of him. He flicked idly through until he came to Turner's picture of the Houses of Parliament going up in flames. That was a gap in his history then – he had never realised that Parliament had burned down in the first half of the nineteenth century. He stared intently at the brilliant glowing image Turner had painted. The viewpoint of the painting was the south side of Westminster Bridge and buildings, river, bridge and people all merged into a roaring outburst of colour and violence.

"Glorious, isn't it? I think that's one of his best. You know, it's taken as read by the artistic establishment that France has been the fount of artistic innovation over the past fifty years. They say that the French invented impressionism, for example – but what can be more impressionistic than this painting, created long before all those French chaps – Monet, Seurat, Renoir and so on. Wonderful!"

Stewart felt himself being drawn into Turner's brilliant creation. He could feel the flames swirling in his face just as, a few hours before, he had gazed helplessly as he watched the catastrophic effect that a string of incendiary bombs falling in quick succession had had on a rubber tyre factory. He closed the book and nodded at Evans. "Thanks. I'll look at it more closely when I've had a bit of a rest. Let's just hope what's happening in the painting doesn't repeat itself!"

★ ★ ★

Merlin stepped carefully around the large pool of smouldering sludge. Madame Tussauds had taken a direct hit the previous night and he presumed that he was looking at the last remains of some of the famous waxworks' stock-in-trade. Eerily, some parts of the sludge retained human form. Here and there it disgorged an arm, a leg or a tortured face.

Merlin stepped over something that looked like Jean Harlow's head and then over the head of either George Formby or Stanley Baldwin, he wasn't sure. Like Merlin, Madame Tussauds had had an eventful Sunday night.

His shoulder pain having cleared up and despite his bruises and the aircraft noise, he had a surprisingly good and deep sleep when he'd got home. In bright early morning light, Merlin was walking along Marylebone Road, trying to find the ruined building of the night before. A little beyond Madame Tussauds on the other side of the road, he found it. To his left was the still burning shell of the bombed flats whose explosion had blown him off his feet and opposite was the side street from which the running man had emerged. As he turned into it, he saw a cat racing along the cobbles in pursuit of something. No doubt the rats were everywhere. He stepped across the road and around the bomb crater and stood at the door through which he had passed only a few hours before. The building was no longer smouldering. The frame of the front door remained intact, as did a small portion of the front wall to the right of the door. A brass nameplate remained undamaged. On it were the words "Grand Duchy and Oriental Trading Company Limited". Merlin took a small notebook out of his jacket top pocket and jotted down the name. He walked through the doorway and picked his way over the splintered floorboards towards the back of the house where he thought he'd seen the men.

"Oi, mate. Better get out of there. This thing could come down at any minute."

Merlin looked back to see the outline of an ARP warden framed by the front door against the bright sunlight. The image reminded him of a scene in a Western he'd been to see with Alice. "It's alright. I'm a policeman."

"Well, being a policeman is not going to stop the roof of this place coming down on you. I suggest you make your way back over here and carefully."

"I'll just be a few minutes."

"Suit yourself. It's your funeral." The warden disappeared. Merlin moved forward carefully. Some sunlight was filtering through holes in the walls and the roof, but this had the effect of making the areas of the house not lit by sun even gloomier and harder for his eyes to penetrate. He thought he could see something shining in the corner, but was it just a trick of the light? He took another couple of wary steps.

★ ★ ★

The restaurant was tucked away in a narrow street off Trafalgar Square. It had been here for years. Its Georgian owner had arrived on a boat from Batumi the week before Queen Victoria died. He had rapidly married an English girl and fathered three sons, all of whom, with much noisy argument, maintained their father's establishment today, while he, supposedly retired, brooded over their efforts in a back room. Voronov was a regular. There was not really enough call in London for an exclusively Russian restaurant, let alone a Georgian one, so the chef, the youngest son, Josef, offered a wide range of British and European cuisine on the menu. If you wanted steak and chips or steak and kidney pie, you could get it, provided they had the meat. If you wanted something more continental, you could get that too. For a hard core of regulars, there was, however, a comprehensive Russian menu, with Georgian dishes a speciality.

Voronov was early and was drinking his second lemon vodka of the day while happily browsing the Russian menu. It was a little unadventurous, but he really felt like some traditional soup to start. The Muzhuzhi cold soup made from pork legs, ears and tails was always excellent. He had it on Misha's rather dubious authority that pork tails were good for the sex drive. Not that he had noticed any particular failings in that area recently. His wife had no grounds for complaint and he still had plenty spare for Alexandra, that perfect specimen of young Russian womanhood he had discovered in Harrods at the beginning of the summer, and indeed for other challenges. That's what today's lunch was all about.

★ ★ ★

Merlin sat at his desk, removed what he had found in Marylebone from his pocket and placed it in front of him. The object sparkled in the bright sunlight coming through the window. It was a small ingot measuring four inches by two and appeared to be pure gold. Turning it over in his hand he saw that there were different designs engraved on the two larger sides. He reached into a desk drawer and took out his new reading glasses. They didn't seem to work as well as they did on print and he found the designs a little fuzzy. One engraving appeared to be of a horse and the other, which was a little larger and clearer to him, depicted an eagle wearing a crown.

Sergeant Bridges came into the room.

"Here, Sam, have a look at this."

Bridges whistled when he picked up the bar. "Gold, isn't it? Very nice. Worth a bit, I should think." He took it to the window. "Eagle on one side and unicorn on the other. Wonder what that means?"

"I thought it was just a horse."

"No, there's a small horn at the front. Where did you get it?"

Merlin recounted to Bridges his experience of the previous night and his visit of the morning.

"Obviously something fishy going on. What did you say the name on the building was?"

"Grand Duchy and Oriental Trading Company."

"Want me to check it out?"

75

"Please, Sergeant. Can you also get in touch with Inspector Goodman downstairs. There's very little he doesn't know about coins and bullion. See whether he or his contacts can identify this little item."

Bridges turned to leave.

"Oh, and Sam, we have a missing person to investigate. I'll tell you about it when you get back."

★ ★ ★

Mikhail hurried out of the kitchen with the two plates for table three. It was surprisingly busy for a Monday. He hadn't managed to get a bite to eat for himself yet today and the spicy fumes rising from the two plates of piping hot lamb stew he was carrying were getting to him. He deposited the plates carefully in front of the regular customers, Russian embassy officials, one civilian and one military, and smiled obsequiously. The man in the uniform, Grishin he thought his name was, nodded stiffly while the civilian ignored him. Mikhail looked up to see Voronov waving at him. Another vodka he supposed as Voronov was still waiting for his guest. As he made his way to the gloomy corner table at the back, which Voronov always favoured, he saw the restaurant door opening and a woman enter. No ordinary woman either. He paused to whistle under his breath. She had very short, very black hair, large pools of eyes and the most kissable lips. She was simply but elegantly dressed. She looked over at him. "Mr Voronov. I'm looking for Mr Voronov's table."

The lucky bastard. What did a beauty like this see in that ugly, old bear? *Well*, he thought to himself as he extended his arm to indicate where Voronov was sitting, *that's obvious isn't it; it's what makes the world go round – money, property, gold, jewels* – Voronov had plenty of all of those. Mikhail sighed. He and the woman arrived at Voronov's table simultaneously. Voronov rose stiffly to his feet and kissed his guest's hand.

"Ah, Mikhail, another menu please and another vodka. Would you care for something to drink, my dear? No. Well, perhaps some wine with the meal. Bring me the wine list, will you? And some water. Please sit down, Countess, I am delighted that you have found the time to join me. Delighted. And we have so much to talk about, you and I."

As Mikhail handed a second menu to the Countess, he noticed that she was very pale and that her smile seemed forced. Ah well, perhaps Voronov would have to put in some extra work for this one.

★ ★ ★

Merlin was still puzzling about the gold he had found when he realised it was lunchtime. He decided to find out how his friend Jack Stewart was bearing up. As he walked down the stairs, he toyed with the idea of getting a car from the pool, but just as he got outside he could see a bus moving slowly along the Embankment. He broke into a run and managed to get onto it just as the traffic lights in front of Big Ben were turning green. Twenty minutes later he jumped off on the King's Road, turned down Flood Street and found the Chelsea AFS station around the corner from one of his and Stewart's favourite haunts, The Surprise pub.

As soon as he pushed through the swing doors, he found Stewart, or rather heard him, tearing a strip off a couple of firemen.

"Why on earth haven't you got that pump fixed? You've had six hours since we got back. I said everyone could have a little rest, but by little rest I didn't mean six hours. It's a small job anyway and shouldn't take more than half an hour."

Merlin heard a stuttered apologetic response.

"That's no bloody excuse. Well, get on with it now anyway. We're probably only a short time away from the next raid. Go on, off you go." Stewart emerged from behind a bright red door, shaking his head. Stewart's frame never did have much meat on it, but Merlin thought his friend was thinner than the last time he'd seen him.

A broad grin split the fireman's face. "Well, this is a nice surprise. Frank Merlin, welcome to my humble abode. 'Mid pleasures and palaces though we may roam. Be it ever so humble, there's no place like home!'"

Like Merlin, Stewart was a great lover of poetry and through their many years of friendship they had enjoyed proclaiming favourite lines to each other. "Have you got any time to be taken out of your humble abode, Jack? Time for a quick one round the corner?"

Stewart consulted his watch. "I shouldn't, but alright. A very quick one."

Minutes later, both men were nursing modest half-pints of mild while trying to get to grips with two rather stale pork pies.

"So, how are you finding it, Jack?"

"Finding it. How am I finding it? Well, I don't know if I have the words to be honest, Frank. Hellish. Stomach-churning. Knackering. Those are some not very good words. Strangely, also exhilarating, awe-inspiring, invigorating. Those are some good words. And Byron had some better. How does it go now?

'For the Angel of Death spread his wings on the blast,

And breathed in the face of the foe as he passed,

And the eyes of the sleepers waxed deadly and chill,

And their hearts but once heaved, and forever grew still!'"

"Muy bueno! Beautiful. Anyway, I thought you'd like to know that I've been thinking of you. To tell the truth, I'm still upset the A.C. blocked me from joining up. I can't help feeling that I should be doing something more worthwhile in this war."

"Oh, don't feel like that. You're doing just as important a job. Didn't you just get that creepy little woman-murderer his just desserts? You know I've been twiddling my thumbs for months waiting for some action. It's just the case that now the fire service's moment in the spotlight has finally arrived. It's probably going to be a long moment, but…" Stewart shrugged.

"How are your men holding up?"

"Very well, all things considered. They've been brilliant. I have to bawl them out sometimes, but the sense of camaraderie is wonderful – some young lads, some older men showing guts and resilience in hair-raising circumstances they could never have imagined before this war. Helps to give me belief and confidence that we're going to lick those Nazi bastards. Anyway, enough of me and mine, what are you up to? And how's the luscious Sonia?"

"She's fine. Refusing my advice that she get out of London into the country, of course. Her brother's on the scene. A pilot in one of the Polish squadrons. Seems a nice chap."

"Well, I'll bet he's a busy boy at the moment. Working on anything interesting?"

"A couple of things. I'm just about to start looking for one of Sonia's compatriots. A pilot in her brother's squadron who's gone missing. And Gatehouse has also involved me in sorting out a response to looting."

"Looting?"

"Apparently there have been significant outbreaks of looting since the bombing started in August. Quite surprising levels of activity in the suburbs and now in the last few days in central London. Have you come across anything?"

"Not really. We've been too busy concentrating on the fires themselves rather than the aftermath. I hadn't really thought about it, to be honest. I suppose it's just human nature, the worst of it, but human nature all the same. I can't think that any of my men would be capable even if the opportunity arose. I'll keep more of an eye out from now, if I can. So how has the A.C. involved you?"

"Typical Whitehall. The levels of looting are frightening them. There's no civil defence contingency plan. The A.C. was put on the spot in some meeting and did as he usually does in such circumstances, turned to me, after, of course, bawling me out quite unjustifiably for not anticipating and planning for such a problem myself."

"So what's being done?"

"There's to be a committee. I've got my Inspector Johnson to sit on it. They are meeting on Wednesday. Apparently there's going to be someone from your lot in it. Have you heard of a man called Sir Archibald Steele?"

Stewart laughed. "Sure I have. I know him well. Some people in the service call me his protégé! In any event he was very instrumental in getting me my promotion."

"Good man?"

"One of the best."

"Well, that's nice to know. I'll tell Johnson."

A siren sounded. Stewart drained his glass. "I'd better be off."

"Good luck, my friend."

Stewart touched the peak of his cap in mock salute and disappeared through the door. Merlin ordered a cheese sandwich to take away the taste of the mouldy pork pie. It was equally unpalatable.

★ ★ ★

Voronov cradled the glass of red Georgian wine and looked intently at Countess Tarkowski. She had chosen the cold meat salad despite his fervent entreaties to attempt one of the Georgian delicacies on offer. "My dear, they have meat here you can't find in many other places. They have a line into the Russian embassy's kitchen. The lamb is out of this world – try the Chanahi or perhaps the Buglama stew. You'll love it."

But no, cold cuts would be fine, thank you, for the lady. And she'd only eaten half a slice of ham as far as he could see. Every time he had looked at her, her dark eyes had been concentrated on her plate or the table. She drank only water and he could discern a faint tremble in the hand that raised her glass.

Well, she might stint her food, but he wouldn't. He demolished the chilled soup in quick order and then, having been unable to choose between two dishes, he had them both

– the Chanahi lamb stew and the Khachapuri savoury pie. Delicious! And he had talked, of course. Talk was one of his great specialities. He had talked about some of his Russian adventures, bowdlerised in deference to his gracious companion, about his friends, about the powerful men he knew all over Europe. He had talked about everything under the sun except what he had arranged the lunch for. She had said little, toying desultorily with her lettuce and occasionally allowing the hint of a smile to move her lips.

Why was she so dull today? At the party she had been an impressively lively hostess, laughing and chatting gaily with everyone. Ah, yes, but then – she was no fool. He had presumed on an old brief acquaintance with the Count and Countess in pre-war Warsaw to gatecrash the soirée his sources had told him about and had taken the opportunity to pass her a message. When he had caught sight of her reading the note he had given her when leaving the party, he had seen the shadow quickly fall over her face. She loved her family. That was why she was here – but she had no illusions.

Mikhail came to remove the plates.

"A dessert, Countess. You should try the butter cake. It is sublime!"

The Countess shook her head.

"Ah. Two coffees then. And I'll have some of that Georgian brandy that your family keeps for best. A cigarette for you perhaps, my dear. Yes? No. Very well. I'll have a cigar. My usual."

After Mikhail disappeared the Countess finished her glass of water and looked directly at Voronov for the first time. "Your stories are all very interesting, Mr Voronov, but perhaps you could get to the point of our meeting. You said in your note that you knew of Karol's situation and, what were the exact words again, that one favour might be returned with another. What exactly did you mean by that?"

Voronov swirled the remaining dregs of his wine in the glass before draining it. At the outset, he had insisted on deferring any discussion about his note till after they had eaten. Now it was time for business. "My dear, I apologise for not coming to the point a little earlier. I thought it would be nice if we could get to know each other a little better."

"Very well. Now we know each other a little better, what do you have to say about Karol?"

Voronov stroked his beard and shook his head slowly. "Such a story. Such a story. A brave man, your Karol, but perhaps not such a sensible man, if I may say so."

The Countess pursed her lips. "I would call him a brave man of principle myself. If it is not sensible to be a man of principle and to stand up for those principles, then, yes, perhaps he is as you say."

"Ah, principle! Such a nice word. But principle is an expensive thing to have in such times, especially in a little country like Poland, at the mercy of two monsters, as it is."

"Can we please dispense with the sophistry and get to the point? My brother Karol is in prison in Moscow. He made the mistake of placing Polish patriotism ahead of his personal well-being and refused to become a puppet administrator in the half of my country swallowed by your Mr Stalin. This was an annoying and unexpected affront, hence Karol's removal in short order to the Lubianka. I assume he remains there, although for all I know he may already have been removed to Siberia or indeed may be dead."

"He is alive, my dear." Voronov saw the Countess' beautiful, dark eyes water. She took a deep breath.

"Are you sure?"

"I am sure. You may trust me. I have very reliable sources."

"And is he still in Moscow?"

"He is, although there is some talk of moving him back to Poland."

Hope brought colour to her face for the first time that day. "You mean he is to be freed?"

"That rather depends."

"Depends. Depends on what?"

"On you, my dear."

The Countess shivered. Her paleness returned. "This, I presume, is the favour of which you spoke?"

Mikhail appeared with Voronov's brandy and cigar. Voronov clipped the end off the cigar, lit it and drew on it in a leisurely fashion. He picked up the brandy glass and put his large, red nose in it, savouring the smell at length before tasting. Finally, he looked back at the Countess. "A favour, Countess. Yes, a favour. You can do me a favour." He suddenly reached out a hairy hand and placed it over the Countess's. She tried to withdraw, but Voronov's grip was too firm. "Perhaps you can even do me more than one favour." His wet lips pulled back from his teeth in an approximation of a grin and he winked. "And for one or perhaps more favours, I can help Karol."

"How?"

"Well, my dear. I am sure you know how well connected I am with the authorities back there. I can call even the Big Man a friend, although Comrade Stalin's view of friendship is perhaps a little unorthodox. I need information, Countess. You may be in a position to provide this information to me. If you can do what I want, then I can pull strings. Depending on the quality of your information and, let us say, how accommodating you are in your work, I may be able to improve his condition and get him out or even get him to England."

"And if I can provide this information, whatever it is, how on earth will I know whether you are pulling the strings for Karol?"

"You will have to take my word for it, Countess."

"And if I do not trust your word?"

"If you do not, your brother has no hope. And how will you feel if you had the chance to help him and refused? You must trust me, my dear. I am Karol's only hope. Give me what I want and you could be dining with him in this restaurant by Christmas."

The Countess looked away before reaching out for Voronov's brandy glass. She drained it, slammed the empty glass back on the table and stared at Voronov. "You had better tell me what it is you want to know."

★ ★ ★

Some of the mechanics were playing football on the grass behind the huts. Jan watched them through the window of his room.

"Like a game?" Miro Kubicki flourished his pack of cards in Jan's face. Printed on special Polish paper at the beginning of the century, the cards had been designed by some relative of his who fancied himself as a Polish version of Toulouse-Lautrec. Kubicki insisted that all games be played with his cards. Since he had a very good record of winning, Jan was seriously beginning to suspect that the cards were marked.

"No thanks, Miro. There's no one else to play anyway."

Kubicki sat down heavily on the rickety chair in Jan's quarters. "Where's Jerzy then?"

Jan had just finished cleaning his shoes and his hands were covered in flecks of black polish. He reached under his bed and found a handkerchief with which to clean himself. "Gone up to town, I think. Got special dispensation at short notice from Kellett."

"Lucky we haven't had any action today."

Jan nodded, then shrugged his shoulders. "I don't know what he had to do in town. He was a bit cagey about it. Rather like Ziggy was the night he disappeared."

"Oh, well. A man of many secrets, eh? What about a game of bezique? That's a two-handed card game."

Jan sighed. "Don't we need another pack for that?"

"Eh, voilà!" Kubicki provided a second pack from his trouser pocket. "Not as nice as my cousin's pack, but it will do."

★ ★ ★

The A.C. stood stiffly at his window, hands behind his back, looking down at the river. Merlin noticed a new photograph of the A.C.'s wife and sons on his desk. While Mrs Gatehouse's charms were now fading, Merlin knew that she had been quite a looker in her day. Unfortunately, it seemed as if the boys were taking after their father.

"Operation Cromwell, Frank, that's what they call it."

"Sir?"

"On Saturday, Operation Cromwell was activated."

Merlin rubbed his right thigh, where he had a large bruise from his fall of the night before. "And what is Operation Cromwell, sir?"

"I mentioned it in a memo I sent you the other day. You really must keep up with your paperwork, Frank. The launch of Operation Cromwell means that the government believes invasion is imminent or, to put it another way, the Eastern and Southern Commands have been put in a state of readiness for invasion."

"Does that mean that German boats have been sighted crossing the Channel or that German paratroopers have been seen landing?"

Gatehouse turned from the window, his thin lips twitching in an approximation of a smile. "I believe that there was a bit of panic in the Home Guard as that was what they thought 'Cromwell' meant, but no. I think it's just a reasonable precaution in light of what's happening up above. The Chiefs of Staff have taken the view that all this heavy bombing of the city is a softening up procedure and a precursor to invasion."

"Seems a reasonable assumption, I suppose. By the way, any idea why our guns have been so quiet? Everyone I hear keeps asking – where are the bloody guns? Those bombers just seem to keep on coming at will."

The A.C. sat down, picked up a pencil and rolled it rather irritatingly back and forth along the top of his desk. "Well, I think, if the truth be told, the Luftwaffe caught the ack-ack people a little on the hop. I believe that over the past few weeks most of the guns have been deployed to where the attacks were initially taking place – to factories and airfields in the country. This has left London a little short."

"I presume someone is hurrying to get them back?"

"I think General Pile is on the case. He's in charge of the Anti-Aircraft Command."

"And what about the air force? They've been brilliant of course, but in the last few days I heard several people moaning that they didn't seem to be knocking so many of the bombers out of the sky."

"Ah, yes. Well, I think the problem there is the visibility. The fighters aren't so effective at night anyway, but with this incredible barrage of munitions…" The A.C. shook his head. "The towering columns of smoke and flame are making things very difficult for our pilots."

"Everything alright with you at home, sir?"

"Yes, Frank. Our little square in Kensington has been spared so far. I tried to get Mrs Gatehouse to go to our cottage near Guildford, but no hope. Luckily, the boys are in their school in Northamptonshire, so they're well out of it. And you?"

Merlin shrugged. "Yes, so far. Amazingly, nothing has come near my block. I just feel I should be doing something to help."

"You are doing something vitally important, Frank. The fight against crime must go on. Speaking of which, what are your thoughts on the looting issue we discussed last week?"

"I've put Johnson on to it. He's a good man. I think he has a meeting on Wednesday. I haven't seen him yet today, so I hope he's…" Merlin looked out of the window.

"Yes, yes, Frank. I'm sure he's… alright. Well, I won't detain you anymore."

Merlin stood up and walked to the door. As he was halfway out of the office, he turned. "Got a disappearance to investigate. A Polish airman. He vanished into thin air. Thought I might look into it myself."

The A.C. seemed to be finding the file he had just opened very interesting. He spoke without looking up. "Fine, Frank. Whatever you think. My God, I've just got the figures for reported looting incidents over the weekend. They are dramatically worse than I would have expected. Find Johnson as quickly as you can. I'd like to give him the benefit of my views before he starts his work. And Frank…"

"Yes, sir."

"Keep a close eye on Johnson's work yourself. I'm holding you responsible."

CHAPTER 9

Tuesday, September 10

Tarkowski emerged from his taxi in one of the numerous ancient alleyways of the City of London. The Bank of England, still intact despite the best efforts of Goering's bombers, was just a hundred yards away. No longer intact was the building covering one side of the lane. Tarkowski tried to remember the name of the building. He had been a frequent visitor to this little corner of the City since his arrival in London, but for the life of him he could not remember what it was called. Something "Equitable", wasn't it? "Yorkshire Equitable House" or "Lancashire Equitable House". Something like that. Anyway, whatever it was called, it was now a smouldering hole in the ground. Rather amazingly, considering the narrowness of the lane and the proximity of the buildings, the property housing the bank which he was about to visit had as yet suffered no visible damage at the hands of the bombers, although it had suffered some at the hands of a graffiti artist who had daubed an unimaginative but to the point personal message in white paint to the Fuhrer – "Fuck off Adolf "– on the wall to the right of the entrance.

Tarkowski grasped his old leather briefcase tightly to his chest as he nodded at the uniformed doorman and passed through the heavy oak doors into the building's reception area. On the left was an ancient lift manned by an equally ancient lift operator. "Third floor, please."

Tarkowski turned to his right out of the lift and strode purposefully down a dark corridor. At the end was a large, black door on which he knocked sharply. The small bronze nameplate to the right of the door proclaimed this to be the London office of the Polish Commonwealth Trading Bank.

A small, wizened man with a few tufts of grey hair sprouting out at random from an otherwise hairless head greeted the Count warmly. "Your Excellency, your Excellency, welcome again. How good of you to grace us with your honourable presence. May I take your hat?"

The man bounced with excitement as he took the honourable gentleman's trilby and hung it on a stand in the corner. "Mr de Souza is expecting you. Yes, he's expecting you. Indeed he is. May I show you through? Perhaps some tea? Yes. Yes. I shall bring it straightaway. Come, your Excellency, please."

The little clerk knocked quickly at the door behind his desk and with a grand gesture bade the Count enter.

"Ah. Count Tarkowski. A pleasure to see you." A rotund, heavy-featured, middle-aged man rose from behind a mahogany partners desk. He wore a tail coat, striped trousers and sported a cream silk cravat at his neck. A luxuriant pile of bouffant black hair crowned his large head. As he vigorously shook the Count's hand, sprinkles of dandruff fell onto the shoulders of his coat. "Come, Count. Please. Take a seat."

Mr Eugene de Souza indicated two plush leather sofas to the left of his desk. On the wall behind them was a large seventeenth-century map of the Great Polish Commonwealth. The print showed Poland at the peak of its territorial imperium, encompassing not only the ancient traditional Polish lands but also the Grand Duchy of Lithuania and much of the Ukraine. Tarkowski paused a moment to admire this brightly coloured reminder of Poland at its greatest, before taking his seat.

De Souza sat down opposite him. "And so, Count Tarkowski. May I ask to what I owe this pleasure? Is this a private visit or are you here in an official capacity?"

"A little of both, de Souza. On the personal side, you may have heard—"

The office door opened and the clerk Wertheim entered, pushing a small trolley. He glided up to them and set down a tray with two cups and saucers and a teapot on the low table that separated the Count and de Souza. "Will you be needing anything else, sirs?"

De Souza shook his head. "Can you go and drop that package at the Bank of England now Wertheim? It's urgently required." Wertheim nodded his assent and oozed out.

Tarkowski was amused, as usual, by Wertheim's Dickensian manner and appearance. He would have commented on it to his companion were it not for de Souza's equally Dickensian air.

"You were saying, Count." De Souza leaned forward to pour the tea.

"I don't know if you heard about the offices?"

De Souza looked back blankly.

"It only happened on Saturday. The offices took a direct hit on Saturday night or early Sunday morning, I'm not sure which. "

"My commiserations. Were there any casualties?"

"None that I'm aware of."

"And, er…" The banker lowered his voice. "Did the goods suffer any damage?"

"Most fortunately, I had just had most of them removed to my house. There may be one or two items lost and most of the records and papers, of course. Naturally, I got my people to make a thorough search of the ruins. I stopped off on my way today and they gave me the valuables that survived. I have them here."

The Count paused and opened his briefcase. He withdrew a cloth bag and opened it to reveal a glint of gold. "Worryingly, my men encountered a little difficulty. They believe one or two of these may have been stolen from them."

"Goodness me. And do you know who—"

"It was dark and my men did not get a clear look at him, but I have an idea. In any event I was just wondering if you would be so kind as to take these into your care for the time being."

"Why, of course. I'll escort you myself to the safety deposit room downstairs." A brief smile of appreciation crossed the Count's face. De Souza frowned. "Do you not think it would be wise to bring the rest of the consignment from your house? I should think our vaults are considerably more secure and bomb-proof."

Tarkowski pondered for a moment. "I have been giving it some thought, de Souza. That may be the best option."

The bank manager nodded. "May I ask, sir, whether you received the information I gave your wife on the telephone the other day?"

"The information regarding an inquisitive gentleman, you mean? Yes, thank you, de Souza. I did. It is good to know we have such a reliable friend in you." The Count reached into his briefcase again and took out some papers. "Now perhaps we can move on to the official business."

★ ★ ★

As Merlin got out of the car at the entrance to the Northolt aerodrome, an aircraft roared overhead. WPC Robinson spoke, but he couldn't hear a word. He walked over to the guard box and showed his CID card to the young soldier manning the entrance. The soldier went back into the box and after a brief conversation on the phone, returned and opened the gates. "The Squadron Leader's in that hut over there, sir, the third on the right."

Merlin got back in beside Robinson and she drove the car into the base. "What did you say just then, Constable?"

"I was saying that that was a Wellington above us."

"Well up on your aeroplanes, are you?"

"My brother has an obsessive interest in them. I suppose some of it might have rubbed off."

Merlin pointed at the hut to which they had been directed. "Park it just over there."

"Do you want me to come in, sir?"

"Of course, Constable. You are 'in loco' Bridges this morning, as he is otherwise engaged sorting something out for the A.C. I don't intend you to be just a driver."

As they got out of the car, a couple of young officers passed by. One wolf-whistled while the other made a great show of removing his hat and bowing. The wolf-whistler exclaimed, "My, oh my" in a Canadian accent, while the other muttered something in a language that Merlin knew to be Polish. Robinson blushed and kept her head down as she followed her boss through the door.

"Chief Inspector Merlin, I take it. Pleased to meet you." Squadron Leader Kellett put down his pipe and rose in greeting. Standing next to his desk was Jan Sieczko, who nodded at Merlin and Robinson and extended a hand.

"Rather amazingly, Inspector, you find us twiddling our thumbs. No action yet today, so we are at your disposal, for the moment at least. Can I offer you anything?"

"No, thank you, sir. I am conscious that you may be called away at any minute so I think it's best to get on with it."

Kellett nodded and pointed to the canvas chairs in front of his desk.

"So, Squadron Leader, you have a missing Polish flyer. Jan here doesn't believe that this chap Kilinski is the deserting kind and tells me that you agree that we should look into it."

"Yes, that's right. He's a good pilot. A slightly difficult man, but then after all these fellows have been through," he gestured towards Sieczko, "what's a little awkwardness. Can't say I've really spent much time with the chap, but I'd put money on his being a good fellow. I know he fought bravely over Poland and would be very surprised if he is a deserter."

He looked down at a folder he had in front of him. "This is a copy of our file on him. There's a picture here too."

Kellett pushed the folder across the desk. Merlin picked up the photograph and found himself looking at Ziggy Kilinski. The face looked older than that of a twenty-year-old man. Dark, hollow eyes, slightly flared nostrils and a strangely twisted mouth on which the ghost of a smile played. A cowlick of black hair escaped from under the flying gear on his head.

"Strange-looking chap, isn't he?" The telephone on Kellett's desk suddenly rang loudly. "Yes. Yes. Very well. I'll be right over." He put the phone down. "I'm terribly sorry, but I have to go to a meeting with some other senior officers. It's only just been called. Will it be alright if I leave you in Sieczko's hands?"

"Yes, of course. I'd like to see Kilinski's billet, if I may."

Sieczko jumped to his feet. "Come. I'll show you to Ziggy's hut. It's only a short walk." Outside there was more activity than there had been when they'd arrived. A group of men in oily overalls were standing behind the hut being given some instructions by two officers speaking alternately in English and Polish. Another group, this one made up of pilots, was setting up deckchairs outside the next-door hut. Further away, a number of fighter aircraft, Hurricanes and Spitfires, were being refuelled.

"It's just along here." They arrived at a hut some two hundred yards from Kellett's. Two pilots were playing cards on a small table outside the door. One of them looked up and exchanged a few words in Polish with Sieczko, after which he rose and introduced himself to Merlin. "Miro Kubicki, sir. At your command, Inspector." He gave a small bow and shook hands. "And at yours, mademoiselle." He reached for Robinson's hand and kissed it.

The constable reddened. "Oh, pleased to meet you, I'm sure."

Kubicki pointed at his companion. "That ugly specimen over there with the beautiful black eye, which he won't tell us how he got, is Jerzy Kowalski."

Kowalski glared at Kubicki, then put out his cigarette, rose and bowed. "So you are here to help us find our comrade Kilinski?"

"Yes, Mr Kowalski, we were hoping to have a look inside if that's alright with you."

"Alright, sir? Why, of course it's alright. Please. Make

yourself at home. Come." Kowalski opened the door, which bore a design that looked like some variation on the American flag with stars surrounding a red grid and what looked like a hat and two scythes. At the bottom were the figures 303.

"Our squadron insignia, sir, 303 squadron – the Kosciuszko squadron. Mr Kosciuszko was a Polish hero in the American War of Independence. One of the few occasions in history where you and we were on opposite sides, I believe. He was an engineer of brilliance who helped Mr Washington with his defences against the British. After that he was a hero at home fighting against the Russia of Catherine the Great. Unfortunately, despite his great efforts, he and we lost and Poland was wiped from the map by the Russians and, of course, the Prussians. That was over 140 years ago and here we are again. Except this time Mr Kosciuszko will be avenged and Poland will rise again, independent and free."

"He's a great one for history is our Jerzy." Kubicki shook his head. "Come on. Let the poor people in. It's Kilinski they're concerned with not Kosciuszko." Kubicki pushed through the door and beckoned Merlin down a narrow corridor. He turned into a room on the right. A double bunk bed took up most of the space in the room. An upturned wooden crate by the window served as a table. Some laundry hung from a rope hung across the room. "This is Kilinksi's room. Up until three weeks ago he shared it with another man, Petr Marowitz. However, sadly, Marowitz died in a stupid accident. We hadn't been allowed into battle at that point so poor old Marowitz didn't last to see any real action. Anyway, Kilinski has had the luxury of having this place to himself for a while. I don't know if Kellett's got round to deciding who should have the spare bunk."

"What was the accident?"

"Somehow Marowitz ended up walking into an active propeller. Took his head clean off."

Robinson blanched.

"How unfortunate. May I, Mr Kowalski?" The pilot stepped

94

aside to let Merlin go past him into the room. He saw something lodged under the lower of the bunk beds and bent down to find an old, blue trunk with a rusty padlock. There was no name or initial to indicate its owner. "Kilinski's or Marowitz's?"

"They took Marowitz's stuff away, after the accident."

"Well, I think it would be helpful if we had a look inside, if you gentlemen don't object."

Sieczko, Kubicki and Kowalski murmured their agreement. Merlin and Robinson had a quick look around to see if they could find a key, but were unsuccessful. Robinson did, however, find two old photographs on the windowsill behind a curtain.

"Can one of you find me something to deal with this padlock?" Merlin heaved the trunk onto the lower of the bunk beds. Kubicki grunted and disappeared down the corridor.

"Look at these, sir. I wonder which one is Ziggy." Robinson showed him a picture of two young boys, one around eight or nine and the other maybe four or five. They were both dark-haired and smiling broadly at the camera. Merlin looked carefully at the photograph and thought he recognised Ziggy's mouth in the younger boy. The second photograph portrayed a grey-haired woman looking self-consciously into the camera.

"His mother, I suppose, and a brother. He had a brother, did he, Jan?"

"Yes, but he wouldn't talk about him. Wouldn't even say what he was called."

"Dead, do you think?"

"Perhaps, but as I say, Ziggy kept, how do you say, mummy on the subject."

The two officers smiled, but did not correct Jan's idiosyncratic slang. Kubicki returned with a small steel rod and quickly broke the padlock. Merlin paused before opening the trunk. "Perhaps you gentlemen wouldn't mind…?"

The three Polish officers nodded and started for the door. "No, Jan. It would be helpful if one of you could stay."

The two other pilots shrugged and saluted jauntily. "À bientôt, mam'selle." Kowalski winked his bruised eye. The door closed behind them.

Merlin bent down and lifted the trunk lid. There were a few layers of clothing, neatly folded and packed, at the top. He carefully removed them and put them on a small table by the room's only window. At the bottom of the trunk, two books, a box camera and a chess set. One of the books was an art book of some sort with a Polish commentary. Merlin handed it to Jan, who translated the title as *Great Polish Art of the Classical Period*.

"Ziggy liked to talk about art and history. He was always talking to me about Polish artists and architects." Merlin handed the other book, which was thick and worn, to Jan. "That's the Torah. Our bible."

Merlin looked thoughtfully at Jan. As Sonia had told him that she was half-Jewish, he didn't have to be Sherlock Holmes to deduce that Jan was also. "So Ziggy was Jewish, was he?"

"Yes. To be honest, I don't think Ziggy Kilinski was his real name."

"Do you know what that was?"

"No, he never told me."

"I see. Was it commonly known that he was Jewish?"

"Possibly; I've never discussed it with anyone."

"Do people know that you are?"

"Maybe. Maybe not. I haven't had any problems about it, though Jews are not exactly popular in Poland."

"Hmm." Merlin looked down again into the trunk and noticed a small pocket on the side. He reached in and pulled out a business card embossed ornately with the name of Count Adam Tarkowski and a London phone number and address. "Moving in high circles, wasn't he? Did Ziggy go up to London much, Jan?"

"A few times. As I think you know, we were only brought out of reserve very recently and so had quite a bit of time on our hands in August. Ziggy perhaps went into town more than most. I thought he might have a girlfriend but he denied it."

Dipping into the pocket again Merlin found what looked like a cutting from a newspaper. There were no words on it, just a photograph. "What do you think, Constable? Looks like some sort of bracelet or necklace."

"Perhaps South American, sir?"

"You think? Well, we'll need to check this out." Merlin continued to rummage in the trunk, but found nothing else of interest. The loudspeaker just outside the hut suddenly crackled to life with an urgent voice instructing the pilots to get to their planes. A klaxon started up close by. Jan looked at them, shrugged his shoulders apologetically then ran out of the door.

Back in the car, Merlin had another look at the cutting, admiring the intricacy of the portrayed object's design. Even without his new glasses he could see that it was a beautiful work of art. Although the photograph was in black and white and he couldn't tell for certain, he would bet that this beautiful thing was made of gold.

He sat back and tapped a finger on the window as Robinson started the engine. "A few things to work with, Constable. This cutting, Count what's his name—"

"Tarkowski, sir."

"Yes, Tarkowski's card."

"And we know Ziggy was a Jew, sir, and went up to London several times."

"Yes. We'll have to find who he was seeing. And we'd better get the portrait from his file circulated."

Robinson nodded and Merlin waved to acknowledge the guard as they drove through the gates.

★ ★ ★

Francis Evans trudged wearily up the three flights of stairs that led to his poky flat just off Kensington Church Street. He struggled, as always, with the front door lock. He really should get a new lock installed, but at the moment every penny counted. It was the landlord's responsibility really but he'd never get that old miser to do anything. Meanwhile, he now felt it had been rather stupid to lend Stewart his Turner book, if lend was what he had done. He'd left the terms of the transaction rather ambiguous, saying that he had another copy at home. One of his two great weaknesses was the delusion of or at least the pretension to grandeur. On consideration, pretension was probably worse – if one was deluded, at least one couldn't help it. Anyway – he should have sold that book – sold all his books, in fact. He was, as usual, struggling to pay the month's rent and he could get a modestly tidy sum from Sullivan, the bookseller round the corner. He still had some nice stuff. Remnants of his once soaring career in the halls of academe.

He made his way to the tiny bathroom of his bedsit and took a pillbox out of the cabinet above the sink. There were a couple of aspirin left and he threw them into his mouth and sucked thirstily on the cold tap. Glancing in the mirror at the few wisps of hair clinging valiantly to his scalp, he returned to the main room and rummaged around on his desk for the letter he'd received from his old Cambridge colleague the day before. They'd had a bit of a fling at Cambridge. Well, more than a fling really. A full-blown passionate affair. They'd been friends, lovers and colleagues together. Two young fellows setting ablaze the relatively undeveloped discipline of the history of art. They shared the same interests and outlook and had shared everything else for a while. All had been going swimmingly until that fateful trip to London in 1938. He was researching Poussin and an expert from the Sorbonne was visiting University College briefly to give a few lectures on that subject. He'd booked himself in to the Strand Palace and had an evening to kill before his appointment with the Frenchman the following morning. After a steak dinner, he'd had a few drinks in a pub off Leicester Square and then headed home. Caught short, he'd popped into the nearest public convenience. A young man had approached him at the urinal. A moment's glance. A nod, then an instant of madness. His second great weakness. While they were in the cubicle they heard a loud banging on the door. The constable who confronted them was fat and red-faced. "Come on, you disgusting little perverts. You're nicked." And so ended his academic career. He got six months in Wormwood Scrubs and not a word from his lover. His hair fell out. Afterwards he had a series of menial jobs in the bookshops of Charing Cross. He didn't suffer fools gladly, of course, so holding on to the jobs was not easy. Then the war had come along and thankfully brought some relief, with the challenge of the AFS. He liked most of the crew and Stewart in particular, who was no fool, despite his impoverished background and lack of formal education.

He found the letter written in an elegant hand. Elegance was a word that could always be applied to the writer, as once it would have been to Francis Evans.

He took the letter and flopped on the bed. Better get a good sleep because his next shift was only six hours away. He sniffed the envelope, which still had a faint whiff of their favoured eau de toilette. Too expensive for him now, of course. His reading spectacles had fallen from the bedside table to the floor and he stretched to retrieve them. "Now then," he said aloud to himself. "Let's have another look at what Mr Anthony Blunt has to say for himself."

CHAPTER 10

Wednesday, September 11

It was seven in the morning, but the pub had already been open for a few hours and the atmosphere was thick enough to bottle. The Old Red Cow had stood in its corner of Smithfield since the Middle Ages or even before – no one quite knew how long. All the pubs around the market opened early in the morning to serve the butchers, wholesalers, buyers, sellers, delivery men, porters and other odd job men whose lives revolved around London's ancient meat market. Jake Dobson knew Smithfield and the area surrounding it like the back of his hand as his family had had a wholesale stall there since the turn of the century. As the twenty-four-year-old black sheep of the Dobson family, he had nothing to do with the business, but still spent most of his spare time in and around the market. He kept his meagre belongings in a dosshouse just off St John Street and laid his head down there most days after an early morning session at the Cow. His nights he mostly spent on his new lucrative job with Billy. This job had prospects and he had high hopes of moving up in the world. Perhaps he could say goodbye to the world of smelly, damp, insect-ridden dosshouses forever. His older comrade Billy had a little more stability in his life – a small two-up two-down in Bethnal Green housed him, a crabby wife and two wild teenage boys, the older and nastier of whom Billy wanted to add to their little team.

"Did you speak to that smooth bugger with the ginger bonce then?"

"Yeah, Jakie boy. I got the geezer on the blower. He's going to come over to the lock-up today."

"When?"

"We've got to be there at four. You'll have plenty of time for a nap."

Jake blew his nose into the cuff of his jacket and spat on the floor. "Is he coming on his own?"

"Maybe with another geezer. 'Someone to give an educated appraisal', were the words he used."

"So after that we get our bees and honey?"

Billy downed his pint of best and lit a cigarette. "That's the general idea – they value it, then they pay for it."

"Think we can trust him?"

"Came good with the dosh last time, didn't he?"

"Yeah, I know, but this stuff's better quality and there's more of it. I don't want to be short-changed on it."

Billy laughed. "Get you! The man of business. For your whole life you haven't had enough coppers to buy a pot to piss in. Now you're worried about being short-changed. Don't you worry. We're not going to get stiffed on this. If they don't come up with the goods, we can find someone else. There are plenty of other greedy buggers out there. Now finish your pint and go and have a rest. After we've seen these blokes, I think we're in for another busy evening."

They pushed through the pub doors into a drizzly morning. Across the road, one of the market towers teetered precariously. Some scaffolding had been put up on Monday after the market had taken a bit of a pounding from the bombers, but it didn't look to Jake as if it would hold for much longer. "Best keep away from that, Billy. Someone's going to get clobbered by it if they don't pull it down."

"Don't you fear, Jakie boy. I'm off up here."

Billy strode away up Snow Hill and waved while Jake went in the opposite direction, cutting through a few back lanes to avoid the market itself. "Jakie boy." How he hated Billy speaking to him like he was a kid. He yawned then smiled, thinking of what he was going to do with the money he was about to get.

The looting committee meeting had begun promptly at 8.30 and had finished two and a half hours later. Not a minute too soon in Peter Johnson's view. Not much had been achieved apart from his meeting his co-members on the committee. The committee had been kept mercifully small – a couple of middle-ranking civil servants, a senior fellow from the ARP, a retired major from the Home Guard and the rather charming Scottish man from the AFS. In the hallway outside the meeting room this tall and languid man, Sir Archibald Steele, came over to Johnson. "May I walk you back to your office, Inspector? I think the rain has stopped now and I need a bit of air to blow the cobwebs away."

As they walked towards Parliament Square, Steele gave Johnson the benefit of his views on their fellow committee members. "Craig's alright, I suppose. He's quite on the ball for a young office civil servant, which isn't saying a lot, and as for Matthewson, he's just a time-serving nonentity. The ARP fellow's a jumped-up little prat – I've had a few run-ins with him in the last couple of months. The major's not a bad old stick, but I wouldn't expect much of a contribution from him, which leaves us pretty much holding the ball."

Johnson swerved to avoid an oncoming taxi, as he struggled to keep pace with his colleague as they crossed the road.

"Sorry, Inspector. I forget how fast I walk sometimes. Too much tramping over the moors of my homeland. My wife is always ticking me off for it."

"Not to worry, Mr, er… Sir… er."

"Archie, if you please. No point in pomp and ceremony with me. And may I…?"

"Of course. Peter. Please."

"Well, Peter, I think you know one of my protégés."

They reached the turning on to the Embankment.

"I do?"

"Yes, Jack Stewart. He's a friend of your boss, I believe?"

"Oh, yes. Jack Stewart. An interesting man. He and DCI Merlin are great pals. Like to spout poetry at each other over a pint or two."

"Indeed. Indeed. A remarkable brain Jack has, all the more so considering the poverty of his childhood and education."

"Yes. I know he's also been a great support to the Chief Inspector during his, erm…"

"Yes, yes. I know. Poor fellow lost his wife and I understand Jack played a blinder helping him through it."

They came to a halt at the entrance to Scotland Yard. "I have no idea how we are going to make this committee effective, have you, Inspector? Our manpower in the fire service is already stretched to capacity and things are likely to get a lot worse. I believe you chaps are in the same position?"

"We're all doing pretty much double-time. I think a coordinated response to the looting problem is going to be very difficult. I was talking to Inspector Merlin about it yesterday. Obviously much of the looting, if it occurs as anticipated, will be one-off and opportunistic."

Steele nodded his agreement.

"With such ad hoc looting, Archie, all we can hope to do is catch as many as possible and give them heavy sentences. However, where there is evidence of coordinated looting, we can perhaps aim to be more effective and influential."

"How do you mean?"

Johnson set down his briefcase and folded his arms. "It's possible that we may find looters operating in gangs with some sort of organised approach. They may target certain areas."

"The richer ones obviously."

"Yes, Archie. Mayfair, Chelsea, Kensington and so on. I would be surprised if we don't find gangs working in partnership with professional fences and thieves."

Steele extracted a handkerchief from his jacket and blew his nose discreetly. "Excuse me. And how do we approach that problem?"

"Well, I don't think the committee is really going to achieve anything. You and I know it's not an effective vehicle. However, if you and I and our people pool our resources to some extent then we can find a way to target those professional looters and bring them to justice."

Steele smiled. "I like your thinking, laddie. You and I'll make up our own little sub-committee of action. I'll get my boys to keep their ears to the ground, yours will do likewise, and we'll work out a plan." A couple of officers passing by on their way into the Yard raised their eyebrows as Steele's voice increased in volume. "Then we'll get these bastards! I'll be in touch shortly, Peter. You can count on it." Steele strode off down the Embankment at double-pace, turning briefly to wave.

★ ★ ★

Back at the Yard, Bridges had some unpleasant news. "Inspector Goodman died in the raid last night."

"Dios mio! And his family?"

"The whole lot of them. Wife and three children and grandma. A direct hit on his house in Hackney. Not surprisingly, his department is in turmoil. Jimmy Edgar, his number two, also happens to be in hospital with appendicitis, which doesn't help."

"Dear God. Poor man, poor man." Merlin shook his head and closed his eyes for a moment.

"What do you want me to do with the gold, sir?"

"It's not just the gold. Look at this, Sergeant. I was going to refer this to Goodman as well." Constable Robinson, who was sitting opposite Merlin, passed an envelope across the desk to Bridges.

Bridges opened it and removed the cutting. "Some sort of lady's necklace?"

"Perhaps, Sergeant. Found in Ziggy Kilinski's trunk."

Robinson cleared her throat quietly. "May I say something, sir?"

"Fire away, Constable."

"My brother Edward is an expert on South America. He used to teach Spanish history at Cambridge before the war. Perhaps I could show him the picture?"

"Where is he?"

"He scraped home from Dunkirk and is now based at Chelsea barracks."

"Alright, Constable, why not? Get round there now and see if he can help."

"What about the gold bar, sir?"

"There must be a specialist in this sort of thing in London. Have another word with someone in poor Goodman's department. At least one of the juniors there should be able to tell you where to look. Otherwise just trawl through the phone book for bullion or coin specialists."

"Very well, sir."

"And there's another lead, Sergeant. Chap called Tarkowski. Let me explain."

★ ★ ★

Bridges had rung the London number on the business card Merlin had found in Northolt, which proved to be that of the Polish government in exile. Count Tarkowski, who, according to his loyal secretary, was a very highly regarded senior adviser to that government, was not planning to be in the office that day. His secretary was unaware of his exact plans, but agreed to try and contact him at home to arrange an appointment. She was successful and so Merlin and his sergeant drew up outside Tarkowski's large, vine-covered property a half a mile or so off the Finchley Road at eleven o'clock precisely.

Minutes later they sat together on a leather sofa in a warm, sunlit study before their well-groomed host who was perched on a high-seated chair behind a large partners desk.

"My back, gentlemen. I am a martyr to my back. This is the only type of chair on which I can do my work. I was in the cavalry in the first war and had a number of unfortunate falls. Hence this, er…"

"Sorry to hear that, sir. Now, as we said on the phone, we wondered whether you could tell us anything about this compatriot of yours, a pilot in the Kosciuszko Squadron?"

"Ah, the Kosciuszko! You do not know what a pride wells in the heart of any Polish patriot when he hears that name. Perhaps you do not know the history of this—"

"We know it, sir. Anyway, the pilot in question, known as Ziggy Kilinski, has gone missing. We are responding to a request from his squadron to find him. We searched his belongings in his room in Northolt and found your business card. Can you tell us what dealings you had with Mr Kilinski? This is a photograph of him by the way."

Tarkowski glanced briefly at the proffered photograph then cleared his throat. "Well, gentlemen—"

At that moment the study door opened and a woman entered the room.

"Ah, my dear. Gentlemen, may I introduce my wife, Maria."

The policemen rose and nodded their heads in acknowledgement. Merlin was struck by the Countess' understated, simple beauty. He was assuredly acquiring a keener awareness of the charms of Polish women this year.

The Countess smiled a greeting. "Is there anything wrong, dear?"

"No, no, my love. The policemen are simply making some routine enquiries about a fellow Pole. Nothing for you to worry about."

"Ah. Good. I am just going into town to have my hair done. I'll see you at tea-time?"

"Yes, I'm here all day." The Count crossed the room, took up his wife's hand and kissed it. As she withdrew her delicate hand, Merlin thought he detected a slight tremor in the fingers and the Countess' still-present smile seemed to take on a rather nervous quality. She turned on her heels and departed with a little wave.

"You have a charming wife, Count."

The Count perched himself back on his chair. "How kind you are, Chief Inspector. Yes, she is très charmante. Like all of us she has been through much, but she tries to keep her spirits up – as do we all, Chief Inspector."

Merlin coughed politely and tapped the photograph, which now lay on Tarkowski's desk.

"Of course, gentlemen. Back to business. Yes, I remember meeting a Mr Kilinski in this very study. He requested a meeting. One of my particular areas of responsibility with the Polish government in exile – how I detest the need for those last two words – is finance. Mr or rather Pilot Officer Kilinski was interested in knowing about our finances."

"By 'our' finances, I take it you mean that of the Polish government in exile?"

"Just so, Chief Inspector. He wanted to know about our sources. I was unable to satisfy his curiosity."

"And who are your sources?"

"I can't really discuss that with you as it is obviously a matter of government confidentiality. That is the very response I gave to Kilinski."

Merlin scratched his cheek thoughtfully. Outside they could hear the sound of birdsong and the hum of distant traffic. "I wonder why he wanted to know about your government finances?"

The Count twisted in his chair and winced with pain. "I've no idea. Sorry. My back. Forgive me for a moment." The Count reached into one of his desk drawers and took out a couple of pills, which he took with the remaining dregs of a teacup on the desk. "I wish I could enlighten you. I did reassure him, as I would any Polish citizen, that what we had would be sufficient to keep up the fight until the glorious day when independence would be restored, but I could not go into specifics."

"We found a photograph of what looks like an ancient necklace. We are having it checked out now. One of my colleagues thinks it might have South American origin. Did Mr Kilinski show you anything like that?"

The Count grimaced again and he stood up and walked to the window, flexing his arms above his head. He looked out of the window. "No. No necklaces. Nothing like that. Now, gentlemen, if that's all, as you can see, I'm not having one of my best mornings." The Count turned and shook his head wearily. "My doctor here tells me there is some kind of operation I could have, but I'd then be laid out on my back for six months, which is something I cannot afford."

"When was your meeting with Kilinski, Count?"

"Perhaps two weeks or so ago. I can't remember exactly which day. No doubt my secretary would have the details."

"And was there anything else you remember about Mr Kilinski?"

"No. I'm afraid not, Chief Inspector. Seemed a nice enough boy. A little anxious, but then that is what you'd expect in one about to face aerial combat, I think. No, I gave him my answer and he departed."

The Count raised an arm, shuddered, then closed his eyes. Without opening them, he rang a bell on his desk. "An agonising back spasm, gentlemen. Forgive me, but I really cannot continue." A man appeared. "Andrei, I need to lie down. Help me upstairs." Merlin cast a wary eye at Bridges and reluctantly rose to his feet.

★ ★ ★

Francis Evans reported in at the Chelsea AFS station at midday. He was perspiring for some reason although, despite the sun having come out, it felt like a brisk autumnal day. "Anyone seen Stewart?"

"He's just popped out for a packet of fags. Back in a minute." Bill Cooper was lounging with his feet over the arm of a rackety old armchair in the corner. He had a copy of the day's edition of the *Daily Mirror* in his hands. Evans saw the headline "Cloud Dodgers in the Blitz". He thought "cloud dodgers" seemed a rather poetic description and wondered to what the story referred, but knew that if he asked the notoriously verbose Cooper he would be stuck there forever. He went into the washroom and splashed his face with water.

When he emerged, Stewart was back. "Hello, Chief. Can I have a word?"

Stewart opened his cigarette packet and offered Evans one. The two men lit up and sat down at the large table that took up most of the space in the back end of the station. "I need to get away for a couple of hours later today. Will that be possible?"

"Better ask Goering not me."

"Yes, of course, if there's a raid then I'll be here, but if nothing's doing around 3 or 3.30 do you mind if I pop out for a short time? I've not far to go."

Stewart thought for a moment. Evans had proven himself a brave and diligent firefighter and had never asked for anything before. He'd also been generous with that fascinating Turner book. He decided to cut him some slack. "Got to see a girl? Is that it?"

Evans blushed. "No. No. Just a little bit of business someone's asked me to help out with. Is it alright?"

Stewart drew on his cigarette, then slowly exhaled. The smoke spiralled away above them. "Very well, Mr Evans. If nothing's doing here you can get off at – is it 3 or 3.30 you want?"

"I think 3.15 might be best."

"Very well, 3.15 and back at?"

"If I see the bombers coming in, I'll head straight back, but otherwise say 5.30?"

"Fine. Meanwhile there's a little bit of paperwork I could do with some help on."

"Of course. Of course."

Stewart withdrew to the other end of the station room and returned with some forms that required review and completion. Evans made short work of these, then walked over to the tea-urn and brewed himself a strong cup. He found himself a quiet corner to sit and pulled Blunt's letter out of his jacket for one more read through.

"My dear Francis,
A thousand heartfelt apologies for being such a poor friend. You will, I hope, understand that when your unfortunate accident occurred I found it difficult to calculate the appropriate response. No doubt you will be able to advise me that it was not the one I took, but there appeared to be a number of difficulties, which I do not wish to spell out, but which I believe you will be able to divine. Leaving that matter aside, I happened to run into a common acquaintance of ours the other day who advised me of your current circumstances. I am sorry that you are finding it difficult to gain employment suited to your great intellectual ability or indeed as I understand to gain and retain gainful employment of any sort. I was told that financially things are very tight, although this has not held you back from offering your services to the country at this dire time – bravo for joining the AFS and, platitudinous as it is, I cannot refrain from asking you to look after yourself in your dangerous work. In any event, returning to financial matters, I may be in a position to help you earn some more money. A foreign friend of mine requires some artistic advice. I shall not spell this out here, but I have asked him to contact you at your address. If, of course, you do not care to undertake the work, I quite understand, but it would certainly be remunerative. The gentleman or one of his associates will visit you on Tuesday at 5pm. If your other duties call you away at the time, he will leave a note as to where he can be contacted. Good luck. Yours, Anthony."

Evans had indeed been contacted by a Russian gentleman named Trubetskoi, a stocky fellow of middle height with a shock of dyed red hair. He had explained that he had some paintings and other antique treasures in storage and would appreciate Evans' opinion on them. Evans had explained that pictures rather than antiques were his speciality, but Trubetskoi had waved his hand imperiously and given him a card with an address in Shepherd's Bush and a meeting time on it. This was the meeting he had to go to.

He set down the letter. His heart was pounding. Whilst he was excited at the prospect of making some money for easy work, apparently on a regular basis, he felt uncomfortable. There was something worrying about Trubetskoi that he couldn't put his finger on – and how was he a friend of Blunt? Blunt had often discussed his communist leanings with Evans. Was there some kind of connection there?

Cooper wandered up and threw his newspaper in front of Evans. "Fancy a read? Some interesting stuff. Did you know…?" Evans tuned out as Cooper gave him a summary of all the stories he had read in the paper. Was there a word that meant the opposite of précis? If there was, it was applicable.

★ ★ ★

Merlin was sharing with Bridges his suspicions about Tarkowski, when Robinson came in, a little flustered but smiling. Merlin waved her to a seat as Bridges gave him his opinion. "He gave us the bum's rush, sir. No doubt about it. Shifty is what I'd call him."

"Indeed, Sergeant. I think it's fair to say he wasn't completely open with us and he certainly overplayed the backache. I wonder why?" He ran a hand through his hair. "Well, Constable, you seem pleased. What have you to tell us?"

"I found my brother at the barracks. He confirmed our initial thoughts, sir. He's pretty sure the picture is of an Aztec amulet from the time of Montezuma. He remembers reading a study of artefacts from that period and believes he saw a picture of something similar if not the same piece."

"Montezuma? How fascinating. I was only reading about him the other night. And is it gold?"

"Almost certainly, with gemstones for the eyes."

"Well, well. Something from one of the most interesting periods in history or certainly Spanish history."

"Would that Montezuma be the same one as in Montezuma's Revenge?"

"Very funny, Sergeant."

"What is Montezuma's Revenge, sir?"

"You don't know, Constable? I am surprised. What a sheltered life you must have lived. How would you delicately define it, Sergeant?"

"Begging the constable's pardon, sir, it's where you've got the runs after eating something too spicy."

Robinson smiled. "We called it something different at my school, sir."

"You know, I don't think we'll go any further down that road. So then, I wonder what Kilinski has got to do with Montezuma?"

"One other thing, sir. Edward is also a very keen numismatist."

Bridges looked puzzled. "What's that when it's at home?"

"Coin expert, Sergeant. And so, Constable?"

"I mentioned the ingot to him and he said there was a coin shop in Soho whose owner knew more about that sort of thing than anyone."

"That's excellent, Constable. I'll go with you to see this fellow, but you should still have a word with Goodman's team, Sergeant, to see if they can help. And don't forget that Grand Duchy company. Let's get to the bottom of that."

★ ★ ★

It wasn't really sunbathing weather at Northolt, but Jan Sieczko and his friends nevertheless awaited their next scramble in three rickety deckchairs, their eyes closed and their faces turned up towards an intermittently sunny sky. As Jan looked up he saw the trail of a small plane, probably a reconnaissance flight, cross in and out of the small patches of blue sky above them. To his right, Kubicki puffed lazily on an ancient Meerschaum pipe he had inherited from someone on his adventurous journey from Poland through Romania and the Middle East and ultimately to London. On close examination it looked as if it was going to fall to pieces at any moment, but somehow it survived. To his left, Kowalski petted a small mongrel puppy in his lap that he and Kubicki had found, apparently homeless, near the base. They had named it Sasha after some friend back in Poland.

Jan stood up suddenly and did some bends and physical jerks. "Come on, you lazy sods. Do some exercise. You might have to run out to the planes at any second. You'll be as slow as shit, sitting there like that!"

Kubicki continued happily puffing away on his pipe, waving a hand dismissively. Kowalski's dog, which had been dozing, woke up and snapped squeakily at Jan.

"There now. Look what you've done. Disturbed poor Sasha's sleep. Sit down, Jan, and don't be an idiot." Kowalski pulled his hat down over his eyes and made an obscene gesture with his right hand. Jan laughed and settled back in his chair. "I wonder how the policeman is getting on with finding Ziggy."

Kubicki removed his pipe from his mouth for the first time in an hour. "He's gone, Jan. Don't get your hopes up. Something bad has happened to him."

"Don't say that, Miro. It's… I'm sure Merlin will get to the bottom of it. Eh, Jerzy?"

Kowalski grunted then began to whistle the tune to an old Polish ballad.

Kubicki shook his pipe and tapped it on the side of the chair. "Certainly an unlucky room that one – first, Marowitz, then Kilinski. If they reallocate rooms, I'd avoid that one, my friends, if I were you."

Jan sank back into his chair. "Poor old Marowitz. I still don't understand how he managed to walk into the propellor like that. It was dark I know, but still."

"And what a mess to clean up." Kubicki reached to the ground for his tobacco pouch and refilled his pipebowl.

Jan shuddered. "You knew Marowitz at university, didn't you, Jerzy?" Another grunt from Kowalski before he threw Kubicki a lighter. His hat remained in position. The dog had gone back to sleep.

"Leave him, Jan. You know he prefers to be a miserable sod before action." Kubicki's face was again enveloped in smoke. "I must say, I didn't particularly know Marowitz, but he seemed alright. Very inquisitive though. Always asking questions about things. Nosy little bugger, really."

Jan closed his eyes again. *Yes, that was true*, he thought, Marowitz was always asking him questions about his family. Perhaps that's why Jerzy seemed rather cool with him, despite the fact that they'd known each other for years. Studied law in the same year, if Jan remembered correctly. Then again Miro was one to talk. He also couldn't stop asking personal questions. Oh, well. Marowitz was dead and gone and God rest his soul, but God now had more important things to do. He had to preserve the souls of Jan and his friends. Reconnaissance and radar told them a huge bomber formation was on its way. They'd be in the air for sure in a couple of hours.

★ ★ ★

Merlin and Robinson found Williams' Coin Emporium in a small side street off Shaftesbury Avenue. The doorbell rattled noisily as they entered and a neat little man hurried up to them, followed by an enormously fat cat. "Get back, Boris, there's nothing for you to fuss yourself about." The man spoke with a delicate foreign accent. "Good afternoon, sir, madam. How can I help you?"

Merlin removed his hat and made the introductions.

The little man smiled politely and waved them towards a desk located in the back of the shop. "It is not often we get police in the shop, is it, Boris, and never, I think, a pretty, young policewoman?" Mr Williams, as Merlin assumed him to be, guided them to a battered, old, red divan before taking up his seat behind the desk. "And so, Chief Inspector, how can I help you?"

Merlin nodded at Robinson.

"My brother, Edward Robinson, suggested we come to you."

"Ah, yes. Young Edward. A very clever boy. And you are his beautiful sister. I hope he is well. I heard he got back safely from the beaches?"

"Yes, he's fine. He suggested, Mr Williams—"

The shop owner chuckled. He was dressed very dapperly with a green handkerchief poking out of his top pocket, which matched the green of his tie and the mottled tweed of his suit. "Williams is the name on the shop, but the real name is Wyczinski, Josef Wyczinski. Joe Williams is a lot easier for your countrymen."

"Well, Mr Wyczinski."

"Very well pronounced, young lady. I sense latent linguistic skills."

Merlin brushed some cat hairs from his coat. "That would be a Polish name, would it not, sir?"

"Indeed it would, Chief Inspector."

Robinson continued. "We have an item that may be relevant to an investigation we are conducting. We were hoping you might be able to identify it for us."

"I shall do my best."

Merlin had put the ingot in a small cloth bag, which he now produced and opened. He laid the gold bar on Wyczinski's desk.

Wyczinski put on a pair of white gloves, took a magnifying glass from the side of the desk and carefully picked up the gold. "Mmm. A fine piece of work indeed." He switched on a small desk lamp to his right and held the ingot in the light. "Yes. Please bear with me a moment. I just need to confirm something." He disappeared up a rackety spiral staircase behind the desk and returned some minutes later with a very large, leather-bound book, which he set down in front of him. Clouds of dust dispersed in all directions as he opened the pages.

"I am sorry, but I haven't had cause to look at this book for some time." After a few minutes' browsing, Wyczinski turned the book around. "Eh voilà! There is your piece of gold." There indeed was a large black and white photograph of Merlin's ingot. Wyczinski rose to join them on the other side of his desk. "This, officers, the unicorn surrounded by these two six-pointed stars in the right-hand corners and clusters of six swords in the left, is the family badge of the Stanislawicki family, a famous and noble Polish family. In its time, if I recall correctly, the Roman figure six in the badge related to the six brothers who laid the foundations of the family's success in the fifteenth century. Here, if I turn a page, you'll see the notes. Yes, there, 'the six Stanislawicki brothers were great warriors who helped destroy the power of the Teutonic Knights. All but one of them died at the great Battle of Grunewald in 1410 leaving Stanislaw Stanislawicki as the sole survivor. He was ennobled, given extensive lands in southern Poland by King Wladislaw Jagiello and his family remained one of the pre-eminent Polish dynasties for centuries. A specific reason for the use of the symbol of the unicorn is not known, save that of the general context of purity attaching to that figure in medieval thought.' There you have it!" Wyczinski picked the book up and returned to his seat. He closed the book with a flourish, generating more dust clouds and picked up the small bar.

"The eagle on the other side is a representation of the White Eagle of Poland. Legend has it that Poland's founder, Lech, established the first capital of the country on the spot where he discovered a white eagle's nest. Ingots like these would have been used as a form of currency in the regions controlled by the Stanislawicki family, but not as currency in general circulation. These would have been high-value tender used by noblemen, wealthy businessmen, the Church and, most importantly, by the family itself. Above all, I believe it would have served as a staple form of repository for the family's wealth, kept under lock and key in the treasuries of their castles." He held the ingot under his desk lamp again. "This example is in remarkably good condition. It looks as if it could have been minted yesterday. But of course it must date back many centuries. Remarkable! Remarkable!" He chuckled and reached out to stroke his cat, which, belying its corpulence, had jumped up nimbly to settle in an alcove next to the desk. "Remarkable, eh, Boris? I wonder how such an interesting artefact ended up in the hands of the London Constabulary?"

"I found it in a bombed-out building in Marylebone."

"Indeed, Chief Inspector. However did it get there?"

"That's what we'd like to find out. Do you have much knowledge of the Polish community in London?"

The cat made an unpleasant screeching sound as Wyczinski withdrew his hand from its back. "No, I'm afraid not. I am – what is the word – an integrated Pole. I have been here for over thirty years. In that time I think I have met only four or five other Poles. My wife is English, Chief Inspector, and in the way of things we mostly socialise with her friends. Of course, now that there has been such a wave of Poles coming here, perhaps I shall meet more – especially if they have items such as this."

"Do you know anything of what happened to the Stanislawicki family? Are they still around?"

Wyczinski leaned back in his chair and smoothed his tie. "I believe that the line has continued. On infrequent occasions I read Polish newspapers and I do recall reading about people of that name in the years before the war. I think there was a Count Stanislawicki I read about in the business pages, but in what context I cannot recall. I presume he is part of that same noble family. Of course, with the German invasion, who knows what has happened to the man and the rest of his family."

Merlin rose to his feet. "Well, you have been most wonderfully helpful, sir. Is it possible for us to borrow that book for a short while?"

"Of course. Would you like me to wrap it up for you?"

"Please." Wyczinski bound the book in some cloth and passed it to Merlin who turned for the door.

"Don't forget this." Wyczinski handed Merlin the gold bar.

"Of course, thank you. One last question. What is something like this worth?"

"I'd probably buy it from you for £200★ or so and there would probably be a collector who'd give me £250 or perhaps £300. Give or take, its gold content is probably worth that."

★ ★ ★

Evans' feelings of discomfort had grown more acute. He was standing outside a rather grubby lock-up in Shepherd's Bush. He had been the first to arrive, but then had been joined by two rough and ready fellows who'd grunted a greeting to him. Now one of them was unlocking the double-padlock on the door, while the other was blowing a particularly foul-smelling tobacco smoke in his face. "Where's your mate then?"

"Mate?"

"You know. The ginger geezer. Funny accent. Smooth bugger."

"Oh, Mr Trubetskoi. Well, I'm sure he'll be here any minute."

Jake swore. "This bloody padlock needs a good oiling. I can't…"

"Let me do it. Here. See, easy as clockwork."

"Thanks, Billy."

As they were beckoning Evans through the doors, a car pulled up and Trubetskoi emerged from the rear. "Alright, Maksim, you wait around the corner on the main street. I'll be

---

★Value of £1 in 1940 is roughly estimated at about £40 today.

half an hour, maybe longer. If anyone noses around, just drive off for a while. Mr Evans? You made it. Very good. Ah, I see the other gentlemen are here also. Is everything unpacked and on display? Very well, shall we proceed to business?"

Billy switched a light on to reveal a small treasure trove of paintings, antique furniture and other valuables.

"So, Mr Evans. You see here the goods that my partners and I have in storage. Some beautiful stuff, is it not?"

Evans nodded. "Is this really the best place in which to keep these items? Surely you could warehouse them more appropriately in town."

Trubetskoi raised a bushy red eyebrow – *surely he doesn't dye those*, Evans thought. "In town, you say, Mr Evans. With Goering's bombardment going on, you think one of those nice, big warehouses by the river would be appropriate?"

"Why, of course not, but surely you could get somewhere just out of London that's better than this?"

"Well, Mr Evans. Once you have assisted us in our valuation of these items, all of which have been purchased in the past eighteen months…" Billy and Jake sniggered. "As I say, once we have valued them properly, we may remove them to safer ground."

Evans scratched his head. "But, surely, if you purchased these items in auction or however, you must have a reasonable idea as to their value?" A ripple of irritation moved over Trubetskoi's face. He had a black cane with a silver top in his right hand and he raised it in the air and pointed it at Evans.

"Your friend in Cambridge recommended you to us as an expert in art, Mr Evans, not as an expert in asking questions. For whatever reasons, which are frankly none of your business, we wish to have your views on these items. For this advice, you will be paid well. I understand that money is of some importance to you as you have none. Now, may we proceed?"

Evans could feel himself blushing. Trubetskoi's two associates continued to snigger. *Well*, he thought, *I need the money and beggars can't be choosers*. He'd just have to swallow his pride and banish the discomfort he was feeling and get on with it. "Very well. I'll go through the pictures. As to the furniture, I can also give you a view, but it will be less reliable than as regards the paintings."

Trubetskoi tapped one of his shiny black shoes with his cane and smiled. "Please, go ahead." Jake walked to the back of the lock-up and removed the tarpaulin covering the crates. Evans followed him, pulling out a notebook from his trouser pocket. From the first crate he removed a delicate nineteenth-century watercolour and started to write.

CHAPTER 11

Cartagena, Spain 1937

Rain drifted in from the west in intermittent squalls. The wind ruffled the papers of the manifest and occasionally dislodged one from the Colonel's clipboard, requiring one or other of his guards to hurry and retrieve it. He sat under a dripping awning on the quayside watching the sodden sailors working away at their task. Grishin cleaned his spectacles for what seemed like the hundredth time. It was gone midnight and he was desperate for his bed, but he had to see the job through. He thought with irritation of Orlov, his superior, who had dumped this job on him. Orlov would get all the credit for it, of course. No doubt he was enjoying the comforts of his beautiful Spanish mistress' bed at this moment. Grishin stroked his greying moustache then waved at one of the naval officers supervising the loading. "How much longer do you think?"

"Another four hours I should think, senõr. We are on the last ship now. Another twenty lorry loads or thereabouts?"

"Thank you, Captain. Carry on." Grishin took out a hipflask from inside his greatcoat and took a swig. This Spanish brandy wasn't so bad when you got used to it. "Hey, Sasha. Want a drop?"

Grishin's second-in-command emerged from the gloom to his left. "No, thank you, Colonel. My stomach is playing me up tonight."

"Must be that paella you had for dinner. I warned you to keep to the ham."

"Yes, Colonel. You were no doubt right, as always." Sasha settled back into his canvas chair and pulled his hat down over his forehead.

At 5.30am, the captain reported that loading was complete. Three hours later, as the first glimmer of light illuminated the cloudbanks to the east, a black government vehicle pulled up to Grishin's station. Two men got out of the back and walked over to the Russian group.

"I thought you were aiming to be here at six, Senõr Mendez Aspe? Sasha and my boys have been sitting in this god-awful place since yesterday lunchtime. I would have thought you might have the decency to keep to your appointments!"

Mendez Aspe, a tall, skeletal man from the Spanish Treasury turned to his companion, a similar physical specimen but even taller than he, and shrugged. "My apologies, Colonel. The road was not in the best condition because of the weather. It's a good job we had got the gold down here already. If we had been transporting it by road from Madrid this week I think it would never have got here."

Grishin grunted, drank again from the brandy flask and rose to his feet. "Very well, gentlemen. Let's get to business. My assistant, Sasha here, whom you both know, has had a couple of our accountants making a physical audit of the material now loaded onto our vessels. At the same time, your treasury officials have been doing the same. I have here the manifest of your people responsible for the material in the caves where it was stored. This shows a total of 7,800 boxes in the consignment. Sasha, go and get your men and Senõr Mendez Aspe's people and let's see if everything tallies. Then I can go and have a long soak in a bath, a good breakfast and twelve hours' sleep! Off you go."

Sasha headed off in the direction of the nearest lorries while Grishin accepted the invitation of the Spanish officials to join them in the drier and warmer comfort of the Hispano-Suiza limousine they had travelled in. Feeling a little more benign, Grishin offered his flask around.

Mendez Aspe and his colleague shook their heads and declined. "So, Colonel. You will not be travelling with the consignment yourself?"

"No. Sasha and several others from my NKVD team will be going on board."

"In the circumstances, do you not think it wise to accompany the goods yourself? This is, after all, the largest part of our transfer to you. Soon, in Moscow and in your banks in France, you will hold safe for us our entire gold resources – the fourth largest gold reserves in the world."

"Just so, senõr, but I am quite happy that Sasha and his men, together with our comrades of the merchant marine and security party aboard, will be able to get the gold safely to its destination."

Mendez Aspe's colleague angrily spat something out in Spanish, which Grishin failed to follow. Mendez Aspe patted his colleague's shoulder soothingly. "My colleague is not happy about this transfer, Colonel. Nor are many other of our colleagues in government circles. But then, as I have told him many times, what choice do we have? Your great Generalissimo Stalin is the only one who is prepared to arm us in our struggle with the vile Generalissimo we ourselves have spawned and who threatens our democracy and lifeblood with his fascistic plans. Naturally, your Senõr Stalin wants payment for this help and if the Spanish gold reserves represent our only viable security for credit, it is only natural that such security be provided. Is that not so?"

Grishin licked the sticky remnants of brandy from his moustache. "High finance is not my thing, Senõr. All I know is that your government authorised the transfer and my superiors asked me to handle the shipment. Anything else is above me."

"Come now, Colonel. You are one of the two top NKVD men in Spain. I think you are being far too modest. In any event, the decision has been made and it is pointless for us now to second-guess the decisions of our superiors. Let us hope that our Republican cause is soon victorious and these treasures of Spain can be returned swiftly to their home, after deduction, of course, of the relevant consideration payable to your government." Mendez Aspe leaned back in his seat and closed his eyes for a moment. "Wonderful treasures there are too. You, I believe, have seen nothing but the boxes, but I had the chance to view some of these magnificent items before they were shipped out of Madrid. There are not just boring nuggets of gold and silver, but marvellous treasures of Spain's truly golden age. Not just coins, but artefacts of surpassing beauty. Aztec and Inca jewellery and ornaments whose artistry defies belief." He opened his eyes and his cheeks flushed. "The permanent removal of such pieces would be a crime beyond… beyond…" His words trailed away as someone knocked at the car door window.

Grishin wiped the condensation from the glass. "Here's Sasha. We'd better get out."

Sasha introduced the two Russian auditors and their three Spanish counterparts. For several minutes these men compared their paperwork, while Grishin and the two civil servants stood aside and made small talk. It had at last stopped raining and there was a patch of bright blue sky above them. Grishin noticed that the auditors' voices were becoming louder though he couldn't hear what they were saying. Eventually, Sasha rejoined them. "There's a small discrepancy, sir."

Grishin raised an eyebrow.

"Our people say that we have loaded 7,900 cases, but the Spaniards say that it's 7,800 cases."

"That's the figure that tallies with my manifest, is it not?"

"Yes, sir." Sasha handed Grishin the manifest so that he could check for himself.

"So, senõrs. My manifest and your auditors say that we are shipping 7,800 cases, while my people say the actual figure is 7,900. What shall we do? We have no time for a recount if we are to make the tide and my instructions are to do that."

"One moment, Colonel." Mendez Aspe walked away a few yards with his colleague and exchanged words. When they returned, Mendez Aspe raised his arms and shrugged. "Colonel. Our storage manifest and our auditors here say it's 7,800 cases. Perhaps we Spaniards are a little more advanced at arithmetic than you Russians. We are happy to sign off on 7,800 cases."

Grishin ignored the slur and smiled politely. "You will allow me a moment, senõrs?"

"Of course."

He beckoned to Sasha and the two men walked off towards the sea. "I don't know how to explain it, Colonel. These two are very good, thorough men."

"I'm sure, Sasha. And I'd put money on their being right. In any event, there is only one path for us. If we insist that we are right and in fact we are not, we shall have to explain the absence of 100 cases to Comrade Stalin. What's that at current values, do you think?"

124

"I'd guess around $6 to $7 million."

Grishin sucked his breath in sharply. "I do not care to think of the pleasures that would await us in the Lubianka in such circumstances. So as I say, our path is clear, is it not? If by following it, Moscow ends up with a surplus of 100 cases, so be it. They won't give us any medals, but at least we'll be alive."

They returned to the Spaniards. Grishin bowed his head to Mendez Aspe. "We shall defer to the advanced Spanish intellect. The number of cases counted is 7,800 and that will be the figure on the ship manifest. Are we in accord?" The Spaniards nodded and all shook hands.

"The cargo will reach Odessa when, Colonel?"

"It's a voyage of seven days, senõr. Not too long. Now if you will forgive me, my bed awaits. Come on, Sasha, let's get back into town. You have a couple of hours until the tide. You can at least wash the cold out in a nice hot bath before leaving."

Sasha lay back in the water. He couldn't stop thinking about it. Gold worth over $6 million. He knew in his bones that his people had got the count right. Perhaps more than $7million. That gold no longer existed, on paper. Would its loss be noticed? The Spanish wouldn't miss it and his government wouldn't know. Physically it was two normal lorry loads, fifty cases each. When they unloaded in Odessa, 160 lorries would be required to move the cargo from the ships to the Odessa railway cargo area for onward transfer to Moscow. Who was to be in overall charge of the transhipment? He, Sasha, was. A detachment of 173 NKVD Rifle Regiment would be meeting the ships, but again they would be under his command. Four ships, 160 lorries, or should that be 162 to include the non-existent gold? And was it definitely to be transhipped by rail? These details had not yet been confirmed. He had been told to await final orders when en route. Despite the warmth of the bath, he shivered. $6 or $7million? 160 or 162 lorries? Rail or road? He had a lot of thinking to do.

★ ★ ★

Colonel Valery Grishin looked gloomily across his desk at the picture of Stalin, the "Vozhd"*, on the opposite wall. He stood up and strolled around his large, comfortable office at the back of the Russian embassy. He could swear as always that the Chief's eyes were following him around the room. That might be an illusion, but the fact that Stalin's eyes penetrated everywhere and everyone was indisputable.

He looked out of the window at the Kensington Palace Gardens behind the embassy and then over at the palace itself on his right. He understood that the building had been cleared of the minor royalty and retainers who normally lived there. No doubt they had all decamped to safe luxury in the country.

In many ways this was not a bad posting. After the difficult years in Spain he had gone back to Moscow for a while. The Chief had been going through a particularly paranoid period – but then when was he not going through a paranoid period? Grishin had been lucky to survive that. Scores of his colleagues in the military and many other friends and associates had fallen victim to one or other of Stalin's purges, but he had come out yet again with his career, family and life intact. Yes, he was a lucky sod, just like that bastard Voronov, who he kept on seeing out and about in London. Given Voronov's past history with the Chief he was very surprised that he had not received instructions to liquidate him. Amazingly, it seemed as if Stalin had a soft spot for him! To think of Stalin having a soft spot for anyone was, of course, absurd. He was spluttering with laughter at this mad thought as his secretary, Ania, entered the room with the cup of Turkish coffee he had asked for minutes before.

"Thank you, my dear. Is the ambassador back yet?"

"No, Valery Stepanovich, not yet."

The ambassador, Ivan Maisky, had an impossible job. Just

---

*Vozhd – Russian for the Leader or Chief particularly associated with Stalin.

before the outbreak of war, Stalin had agreed to the signing of the Molotov–Ribbentrop Pact. Dressed up as a mutual "non-aggression" treaty, it allowed for the division of the spoils of Eastern Europe between the two countries, which rapidly succeeded Hitler's invasion of Poland in September 1939. Britain went to war to save Poland. Russia took advantage of the German invasion of Poland to share in carving it up. Didn't that mean that Britain and Russia were at war? Not according to the niceties of diplomacy and Maisky was doing his very best to maintain the niceties. Grishin sat down at his desk and knocked the coffee back.

"Thank you, my dear, that will be all." Grishin watched Ania's pert bottom, tightly encased in a green dress, as it moved with a life of its own to the door and out of the room. He might have to pay his respects to that bottom again soon. It had been too long.

Grishin's office title was Deputy Military Attaché, but he was in effect the embassy's Chief Spy. The Deputy Commercial Secretary had until three months ago performed that role, but some unpleasantness back home had led to his recall and, so far as Grishin could tell, although it had not been officially confirmed, his liquidation. He had had to pick up the pieces and there were a lot of pieces to pick up. The Soviet spy network in Britain was extensive and ranged high and low. Aristocrats, politicians, professors, scientists, MI5 and MI6 officers, journalists, trade unionists, secretaries, coal miners – he had the lot. Keeping them under control and keeping his masters in Moscow happy was a big, big job. That's why he had no time for distractions. Voronov was a distraction. He picked up a report on Kyril Ivanovitch Voronov, prepared by one of his men a while ago. It was attached to a thick file on the man who had a network of expatriates in London, which often intersected with his own. He was a liability and he knew the best way to remove a liability. However, what about the "soft spot"? If he took matters into his own hands, what repercussions might there be with the Chief?

127

He stood up and went to look out at the park again and thought of Spain. That stupid idiot Sasha. Did he really think that such a thing would not be noticed? Grishin thought he had managed to cover his tracks on this one, but what if someone shone a light on the affair again?

He shouted for Ania, who hurried in, fluttering her pale eyelashes alluringly. "I am going for a walk in the park, Ania. What are you doing tonight?"

★ ★ ★

Jack Stewart's group had been on duty all night around St Paul's where the Germans had had considerable success, though the cathedral remained untouched.

"Goodness, Chief. This is a tragedy." Evans took off his hat and wiped his face. Soot covered nearly every inch of his face and almost hairless head. The whites of his eyes stood out like searchlights in the black-out.

"Of course, it's a tragedy. This whole war's a tragedy, Evans."

Evans joined Stewart on one of the steps leading up to the cathedral. "No, I mean this is a particular tragedy. This whole area next to the cathedral, Paternoster Row. It's been the heartland of literary London for centuries – the booksellers, the printers, the binders and so on. As the City has been to business, Paternoster Row has been to books. Now look at it."

Stewart looked up though he knew well enough what he'd see. The shells and skeletons of buildings and here and there a surviving building blackened and faltering on its foundations. Most of the easily found bodies had been ferried off in ambulances by now, but there were still bodies to be discovered amid the wreckage of bricks, timber and slate, and he could see figures moving carefully in the dark on that errand. His group had just been relieved by an AFS station from Paddington and they were taking a breather before returning to Chelsea. Their session of duty had not been without personal loss.

"Who'll tell Cooper's wife?"

"Oh, someone at headquarters. I'd do it myself, but when I discussed it in principle with Archie Steele a few weeks ago, he said I should leave it to the ordinary channels. Some bureaucrat will go and see her. I'm going to send a message though. Tell her she can come to the station and see me if she likes."

The two men fell silent. Bill Cooper had been training the hose at one of the crumbling old printing houses that Evans had been lamenting when a piece of falling masonry had landed on him and killed him outright. When they'd managed to get him out from under the stone and bricks, they found his face had been smashed almost beyond recognition.

Evans swallowed hard as this grisly vision played again in his mind. "A good chap. A little long-winded, but a good chap."

Stewart patted him on the shoulder. "Did you get that little bit of business successfully concluded?"

The image of Cooper's pulped face receded to be replaced by the smug leer of the red-headed Russian. "Yes. Thanks for giving me the time."

Evans had gone through the paintings meticulously. There had been several choice items – an early Turner, a Van Ruisdael, a Blake drawing, a portrait that looked very much like a Rembrandt but which he had categorised after a little thought as "school of". He had had to race through everything and the furniture had only been given a cursory look. He'd totalled everything up at a provisional value of at least two thousand pounds. Trubetskoi had been very pleased and gave him five guineas. "Guineas is what you pay in the arts world, is it not, Mr Evans? So guineas it shall be." Five guineas would go a long way for Evans. It was more than he had expected and more work of the same nature was promised. The hot work of the night had taken his mind off the subject, but now that Stewart had reminded him of it, the nagging doubt reasserted itself. It was good money and he desperately needed it, but what on earth was he getting himself into?

"Come on then, Mr Evans, let's get going. Can you round everyone up?"

As they turned, there were warning shouts to their right and they remained motionless as one of the surviving buildings crumbled noisily to the ground.

★ ★ ★

Voronov had a good view of the street from his study and he saw Trubetskoi strolling jauntily down it from a long way off. He was twirling that stupid stick of his and looking very pleased with himself. Voronov didn't know why he was looking so self-satisfied, but no doubt he would soon find out. Misha Trubetskoi and he went back a long time and they had been through many things together. They had saved each other's lives on more than one occasion. In the Polish campaign of 1921, Trubetskoi had thrown a grenade at a couple of Polish officers who were about to put a bullet through Voronov's forehead. Years later, when Stalin's Poisonous Dwarf, Yezhov, had taken a liking to Trubetskoi's then wife and wanted her husband out of the way, Voronov had interceded with Stalin and saved his partner. And there had been other times. They were like brothers now. That being said, there was no avoiding it, brave and adventurous as Trubetskoi might be, he was not the sharpest pin in the box. He thought he was, but there was a great gulf between illusion and reality.

"Ah, Misha, there you are. Did you have a good evening?"

Trubetskoi threw his coat and stick onto the chaise-longue by the door and sat down heavily on one of the two leather armchairs in the room. Above him a large portrait of a younger-looking Kyril jovially surveyed the room. "Excellent, my dear Kyril. Excellent. Despite the firework display laid on by our German friends, I found two brave young ladies of the night who were prepared to return chéz Misha. One was a blonde – natural mind – and the other a rather striking brunette. A most agreeable evening."

Voronov tugged at his beard. "Good. I'm sure you could do with a strong coffee. Maksim!" The servant had anticipated his master and appeared promptly with two Turkish coffees.

"Some toast perhaps, Misha, an egg maybe?"

Trubetskoi shook his head and Maksim departed at the flick of a Voronov finger. "And so, my friend. How did your meeting go yesterday afternoon?"

Trubetskoi raised his legs onto a footstool and, removing a silver toothpick from somewhere in his jacket, dug violently at his teeth. "I had some beef last night. This lousy English meat always gets stuck in my teeth. Ah. That's better." He spat a small remnant of meat into the fire on his left. "Yes. The meeting. It went well, I think." He smiled complacently across at his partner.

"And?"

"Well. This chap who Blunt recommended. Didn't really take to him. Asking questions. Superior sort of fellow. However, he certainly knew his stuff. Valued everything at around a thousand pounds★."

Voronov laughed. "So, Misha. Knowing you, the real figure was what, say three thousand? Come on. Don't try your luck with me. I always find out, don't I?"

Trubetskoi stiffened and assumed a hurt expression. "Kyril, please. How can you think that I would—"

"Shall I call Mr Evans then? Maksim!"

The servant appeared instantly.

Trubetskoi's features relaxed. "No. No. Kyril. Just my little joke. Just testing your observational skills are all there. Clear off, Maksim."

With a nod from his master, Maksim disappeared.

"It was around two thousand. I swear on my mother's grave. Not a bad sum."

Voronov pulled a cigar from a box on a shelf behind him before offering one to Trubetskoi. "So, Misha, if two grand is

★Value of £1 in 1940 is roughly estimated at about £40 today.

the real figure, I assume you didn't give that number to our two cockney friends?"

Trubetskoi drew vigorously on the cigar to get it going. Satisfied that this task had been accomplished, he sat back in his chair, blowing smoke rings at the ceiling. "Kyril, my friend. Please. What do you take me for? When this Evans creature had finished, I drew him aside. They did not hear the figure from him. Once I had the details, I got rid of him and gave the men a figure of five hundred."

"Five hundred! You idiot! Why didn't you tell them two or one hundred even?"

Trubetskoi sat up. Indigestion coloured his already rosy cheeks. "These men are not morons, as you take me for. Five hundred was a credible figure."

"Huh!"

Trubetskoi leaned back into the chair.

"So what terms did you agree?"

"I said we'd split the balance of the proceeds down the middle, after the deduction of a hundred for selling expenses. When we've got our disposal arrangements in hand I said I'd give them a hundred up front. They quarrelled about this and I'd taken some cash with me, so I've already given them fifty in 'readies' as they say."

A large piece of ash fell onto Voronov's waistcoat and he brushed it away. "Did they suspect anything?"

"My dear Kyril, this is your old Misha. Of course they suspected nothing. I am as smooth as silk."

"And who do you have in mind for the disposal?"

"I'm not sure. There are a couple of candidates. I'll check them out and let you know which I think best."

Voronov grunted. Another chunk of ash grazed his beard before falling to the floor. He bent to open a drawer in the desk and removed a bottle of vodka and two glasses. "So. Here's to good business."

The two men stood and clinked glasses. In the distance a siren began to wail.

"How are you getting on with the lady, Kyril?"

Voronov tugged at his beard. "She will succumb to my charms, gradually, Misha. I'll get what we need soon, don't you worry."

★ ★ ★

Merlin was looking for Bridges and wandered down the corridor. Passing the small cubby hole on the right where the tea and biscuits were, he found Robinson and Cole in what appeared to be a deep conversation, hands touching across the small table at which they were seated.

"Anyone seen the sergeant?"

They jumped at his voice and Robinson's face flushed.

"I'm here, sir." Bridges appeared from the other end of the corridor and Merlin followed him back to the office.

"Something going on there, Sam?"

"I believe there is, sir."

"Not very keen on office romances."

"Me neither, sir."

"God knows what the A.C. will say."

Merlin seated himself at the desk.

"Cole asked me if he could be allowed to help Johnson in his looting investigation, sir."

Merlin pushed a pile of papers to the side of his desk. "Did he now? Well, yes, let him. Might take his mind off the beauteous Claire. Get him to come and see me."

"Your brother's been trying to get hold of you."

"Has he? Thank you, Sergeant." He pressed a button on his telephone and got a line. Merlin's younger brother Charlie had been lucky and unlucky. Caught in the worst fighting at Dunkirk, he had been fortunate enough to escape from France with his life. Unluckily, he had left a leg behind. A happy and well-balanced young man before the war, when he had worked at a bank, his injury had left him bitter and resentful. Charlie had spent nearly two months recuperating in hospital, but

133

since the end of July he had been sitting in his wheelchair at home in Fulham, passing on his depression and misery to his family. Beatrice and Paul, his wife and young son, were doing their best to support him, but they were having a bad time of it and Merlin didn't know what he could do to help.

"Hola, big brother. Como estás?"

"I'm alright, Charlie, how about you?"

"What do you think? Fine I suppose for a one-legged cripple with no future."

"Come on now. Beatrice was telling me the other day that Martins Bank sent you a nice letter wishing you well in your recovery. She thought they were hinting they'd take you back."

The line crackled with pent-up frustration. "What does she know. They didn't spell it out, did they?"

"What can I do for you, Charlie? I'm pretty busy at the moment."

"It's alright for you. El Grande Jefe de Scotland Yard. You've got a life!"

"Look, Charlie, what do you want?"

The breathing at the other end of the line became less intense. "It's the boy. He hasn't seen you for a while. Wants to kick a ball with his uncle. Can't do it with his dad, can he? Can you come around some time? Maybe Saturday?"

"I'll be there, Charlie. Around lunchtime." As Merlin replaced the receiver with a sigh, Cole came excitedly into the room.

★ ★ ★

Wyczinski's book, opened at the relevant page, took up half of Merlin's desk. Robinson, seated opposite him, was just recovering from a bout of sneezing brought on by the dust accumulated in the book's ancient pages.

"Teutonic Knights on one hand and Aztec treasure on the other. I am beginning to think we are in a Rider Haggard novel."

"Yes, sir."

"Any more on the necklace?"

"Sorry, sir. Edward hasn't got back to me yet."

"Strange coincidence that this gold ingot turns out to be Polish, isn't it?"

Robinson crossed her legs and looked thoughtful. Merlin walked to the window and looked down at the sandbagging lined along the Embankment. It was bright, sunny and warm again. He felt a sudden urge for a Fisherman's Friend, which he staved off by biting a fingernail. "Most things come down to the basic motives – love, hate, greed, revenge. Assuming Kilinski has been the victim of a crime, I wonder which it is here?"

Robinson uncrossed her legs. *Yes, very shapely*, Merlin thought. Good job Sonia hadn't seen Robinson. He had discovered her jealous streak when he had remarked on an attractive girl on the beach the other day. "Too soon to tell yet, sir."

"You're right, of course. The fellow might just have fallen down a hole. Find the sergeant and see what else we can discover about Tarkowski. There may be some diplomatic niceties to deal with because of his status, but something about him smells and I'm going to find out what and why. Now I've just got to go upstairs and find out what your uncle – sorry, the A.C. – is jumping up and down about."

★ ★ ★

The A.C. twitched in his chair. "Look, Frank, I said I didn't mind you looking into this Polish flyer fellow's case, but I hope it's not going to take up too much of your time." The A.C. looked as if he was sucking a particularly sour boiled sweet.

"An investigation is an investigation, sir. I can't go at it half-cock. If something untoward has happened to Kilinski, I need to pursue all possibilities."

"Ah, but that's the thing, Frank, isn't it? We don't know that this chap hasn't just gone on some almighty bender somewhere, do we? Or run off with some floozy."

"From what his colleagues tell me, I don't think that's what happened, but, of course, I can't rule it out."

"Hmm." The A.C. licked his razor thin lips and shifted in his chair. They could hear shouting outside and the A.C. raised an eyebrow at Merlin, who stood and wandered over to the window.

A detachment of British soldiers had stopped on the Embankment just below. A small crowd watched from the pavement as two bedraggled men in the soldiers' care knelt on the road and drank greedily from water containers. Some young men in the crowd jeered, but the others watched in silence. When they had finished drinking, one of the soldiers helped them to their feet and marched them off towards Charing Cross.

"What is it, Frank?"

"German prisoners being taken somewhere. The Tower maybe."

"I think not. Unless they've got Goering down there. They're going to the station and then off to one of the camps in the country, I should think. Now come back here and tell me what else is going on."

★ ★ ★

Air Warden Webster finally had a moment to sit down and eat the tomato and cheese sandwich that his wife had stuffed in his pocket when he'd gone on duty the night before. By rights of what he'd seen in the past fifteen hours or so, he shouldn't really have much appetite, but nevertheless he was starving. He sat down on a smooth block of stone resting on a mountain of rubble and tucked in. The sandwich was washed down with a bottle of milk he'd found amazingly intact at the doorstep of a door to a house that no longer existed. He'd been pulling people and bodies out of the ruins all night, but his stomach was in good shape. *Getting used to it*, he supposed.

He'd had several nights like this now. The sun found its way through the smoke and dust and struck his forehead. The stone was big enough for him to stretch out on and he leaned back and enjoyed the warmth of the sun. His mate Terry had called it a day and headed off to the nearest ARP canteen and everyone else seemed to have cleared off from this particular spot just off the Euston Road as well. The eerie silence was broken only by the ticking of an old grandfather clock resting precariously against the exposed wall of a shattered shell of a house to his right. He closed his eyes, exhaustion and the soothing rhythm of the clock bringing him close to sleep. A sudden rustling noise jolted him awake. All of a sudden he felt little feet running over his face. The sandwich rose in his mouth and as he stood up he saw several large rats burrowing beneath some rubble to his right. With an effort he kept his sandwich down. *Time to go home*, he thought, brushing himself down before bending to pick up his hat and mask. This time he could see what the rats were up to and he vomited. After he had thrown up, he took a deep breath and charged the rats, flailing his arms and shouting at the top of his voice. They scampered away. Grunting, he pulled back a large piece of masonry to reveal quite clearly their handiwork. The man's nose had been chewed off, as had most of the fleshy parts of his face – or, he wondered, was some of that decomposition? Perhaps the body had been there for a few days? He cleared away some more rubble. The dead man was wearing a flyer's uniform. There were wings on his lapel with something written in needlework, which he couldn't make out under all the filth and dust. He heard some footsteps.

"Oi. Mate. Another body here. Can you give me a hand?" As he turned back to clear away some more of the rocks, he noticed something glinting in the rubble.

★ ★ ★

Voronov had suggested meeting at the Savoy or the Ritz, but

the Countess had said that would be far too dangerous as there were all sorts of acquaintances they might bump into. And so he found himself in this rather nondescript hotel near Russell Square. As she'd pointed out, it was quite big, so their presence there wouldn't necessarily stick out – and the rooms were perfectly comfortable, though bland and soulless – and he was a man of soul! Still, the prize was his and even if the surroundings were not to his liking, he was not going to be put off his enjoyment of that prize.

There was a light tap at the door. He jumped up, ran a hand through his oiled hair, straightened his tie and ruffled his beard to ensure the absence of unsightly detritus. The door opened to reveal the Countess, looking attractively demure.

"Come in. Come in, my dear. So glad you could make it." He hurried her into the room, grasped her shaking hand and pulled her towards the window. "A fine view of the back of the Liverpool Insurance Company. I'm sure you agree, my little Maria, it is one we can do without." He snapped the window blind down abruptly, leaving the room lit only by a small ugly bedside lamp. "A drink? I took the liberty of bringing a fine '36 Dom Perignon. The chilling facilities here are, I'm afraid, rather inadequate, but the bottle was cold when I got here and I have left it in the basin in cold water. Shall we?"

The Countess nodded with resignation as she lowered herself onto the large metal postered bed. Voronov removed the champagne flutes from his briefcase, made a big show of popping the cork and poured out two glasses.

An hour later he sat up in the bed, puffing happily on a large Corona cigar. It had been a pleasurable experience. Not, as was usually the case, completely up to expectations, but certainly worthwhile. A B or maybe even a B plus. Of course, she was not a willing participant, but that could cut both ways in the lovemaking experience. With a willing party there was pleasure but no challenge – with a partner such as the Countess there was the challenge of provoking a real response. For all his ugliness and violence, he knew he was a skilled lover who was quite capable of making a woman, even the most beautiful woman, forget his absence of physical charms and be taken to the heights of ecstasy. He had, as they said in this benighted country, pulled out all the stops and the Countess had not avoided receiving pleasure from him, hard though she had tried to. She was certainly relaxed enough to have dozed off by his side. Her nose twitched rather charmingly as she adjusted her position in her sleep. The bed sheet slipped to reveal what he considered the perfect breast – not too long, not too small, a handful for a big-handed man like himself. He pulled the sheet further back and admired her. Considering all she'd been through, she was in remarkably good shape. He felt the signs of reviving capability below. Their arrangement, as far as he was concerned, did not preclude repeat performances. Replacing his cigar in the ashtray, he reached out for that perfect handful. They could discuss the other matter later.

★ ★ ★

"It is surprising how easily one could get used to the screams in this place," mumbled Andrei as he sat in his own faeces, finishing the bowl of thin gruel which would be his only meal of the day. Something had happened to Andrei in the past four weeks, something had snapped. Not so difficult to understand really. He had been in the Lubianka for nine months, although if asked he would not be able to say how long. In the desperate, cold gloom of Moscow's notorious prison, minutes, hours, days, weeks, months, years all melted indistinguishably into each other. There were events, of course, to punctuate the time – mealtimes, although the paltry tasteless rations provided rarely made these red letter moments. Far more memorable were the beatings, the interrogations, the threats and the carrying out of threats, the screams and, of course, the blood. However, the thing that had snapped in

Andrei made him almost impervious to all of these events. He was ill, emaciated, swimming in his own waste, freezing or boiling depending on the season and he was going to die soon. He had accepted this and now lived in a state of irrational, gibbering cheerfulness.

Karol had given up trying to talk to Andrei. Whatever happened, he was determined to keep his mind to the end. Rising stiffly to his feet, he summoned up all his reserves of strength and began banging loudly on the door. "For Christ's sake, someone come and clear up in here. Andrei's shit himself again. Please, someone." The effort of banging and shouting completely drained him and he fell back down on the thin straw mattress in his corner of the cell. After a while he could hear heavy steps, then the door clanked open. The guard was short and built like a small tank. He had crossed eyes, but Karol couldn't see them in the dark of the cell. The guard leaned over and punched Karol on the back of his neck.

"What the fuck is your problem, you Polish pig? Smells like roses in here, doesn't it, Andrei?"

Andrei nodded enthusiastically.

"See, your friend's happy. No more complaints, you Polish scum."

As the guard aimed another blow at Karol's head, the sound of footsteps reverberated down the corridor. A small man with very thick lens glasses pushed his way past the guard and into the room. He was followed by a taller, wiry man carrying a briefcase. The guard dissolved into spasms of obsequiousness and was despatched by the shorter man's waved hand. Both of Karol's new visitors wore nondescript dark suits and brilliant white shirts, but no ties. Both men wrinkled their noses in disgust at the stink in the cell.

"Come, my Polish friend. We are going to give you a little break from this sewer."

Karol was prodded out of the door, along several corridors, down some stairs and eventually into a room he by now knew quite well. For once he was offered a cigarette, which he sucked on gratefully. Then the questions began. The same old questions to which he gave the same old answers. Hour after hour after hour.

★ ★ ★

A thin drizzle was pattering against the window panes as Merlin sat thinking at his desk. He had just read a newspaper report of Churchill's latest broadcast the day before. Churchill had said that if Hitler was going to invade, it had to happen soon as the weather would deteriorate and the large invasion fleet, which had evidently been mustered by the Nazis in the ports of Germany, Holland, Belgium and France, could not be left waiting forever at anchor as British aircraft and warships in the Channel pounded them. Drawing on his profound love and knowledge of British history, he had compared the moment with the time when Drake was finishing his game of bowls as the Spanish Armada broke or when Nelson stood between Britain and Napoleon's Grand Army. Merlin, with deference to Churchill, thought it felt a lot worse. Drake and Nelson had triumphed and with the long view of history it seemed inevitable that they would do so. He felt no inevitability about the victory of British power now. It suddenly occurred to him that tomorrow was Friday the 13th – for whom would it be unlucky?

The phone rang. Merlin picked up the receiver as Bridges came through the door. "Yes? I see. When exactly? We'll be there as soon as we can."

Bridges looked at him enquiringly.

"They've found a body off Euston Road. Wearing a flyer's uniform. Let's go."

CHAPTER 12

Mexico 1519

The large burning orb of the midday sun beat down relentlessly on the agitated crowd milling around the square in front of the great temple. The inhabitants of the great Aztec capital of Tenochtitlan were excited by the news coming from the coast. An army had disembarked from a flotilla of great canoes, which had arrived from the east over the Great Sea. This force was now travelling steadily through the subject lands of their mighty ruler, Montezuma, with all indications that its intended destination was their holy city of the lake. All sorts of rumours were circulating about the nature of these men. The priests were saying that they were not men at all but gods, whose arrival had been foretold by the startling natural phenomena of recent times – the column of fire stretching from earth to sky, which had appeared every midnight for a year; the two temples destroyed by fire and lightning; the comet seen by day; the bird whose head had a mirror in it in which the approaching army had first revealed itself to the great Emperor. These men or gods were strange white creatures riding on four-legged monsters like deer. Their bodies were covered with thick dark material and their faces sported bushy red or black beards. In their caravan were new strange weapons of warfare capable of rivalling in noise and power the loudest thunderstorm. As the air hummed with this gossip, at the foot of the temple stairs, close by the rack holding the countless skulls of victims sacrificed to the great gods, a fight broke out between the supporters of rival interpretations of events; swords were drawn and blood was spilt.

High above the crowds, the great Emperor noticed this commotion and sighed. He fingered the ornate imperial amulet, which hung glittering around his neck, then stared up briefly at the burning sun. What should he do? Should he treat with these gods to protect his great kingdom from their wrath or should he listen to those of his advisers who insisted that these creatures would bleed if cut and should be attacked without delay? But then to attack was not so easy – the newcomers were travelling through lands subservient to his power, but not loyal to it. The Totonacs, for one, were rumoured to be keen to use the foreigners to assist their independence. The Tlaxcalans likewise.

Then again, what did these creatures want? He had heard they had a great hunger for gold and he and his people certainly had an abundance of that. He glanced to his right at the open door of the temple treasury. The sun's rays were flooding through the doorway and a blinding glare of reflection bounced back from the multitude of golden statues, vases, ornaments and other artefacts kept there in honour of Huitzilopochtli, the Sun God of War, Quetzalcoatl and the other great gods of the cosmos.

Montezuma sighed again. He looked across the wide platform that lay just beneath the high apex of the temple. His priests were busy preparing the sacrifice to his left and he heard the whimpering of the victims. One of them looked up and dared to stare at her Emperor. She was a pretty young thing with long, flowing black hair, deep, dark eyes and a perfect figure. She was naked, as were the other three maidens who were to die to propitiate the gods and, Montezuma prayed, to secure guidance as to how best to resolve his current passing problem. Now the victims were brought forward by the guards to the great stone table in the middle of the platform. Their whimpering halted as they faced the truth of their fate. The pretty, dark girl kept her gaze on the Emperor and he fancied that he saw there a defiant glare. Montezuma looked down at his beautifully crafted, golden amulet, which took the form of two snakes entwined, their eyes flawless emeralds glittering in the burning sun. A thought occurred to him. He stood and raised a hand to the Chief Priest, who halted proceedings. Montezuma strode towards the girl and removed the amulet from his neck. He would place it around her shivering neck and after the knife had done its work and her heart had been plucked from her slender frame, the cremation of her body would blend her ashes with the molten metal to provide a majestic offering of sacrificed beauty to the gods – surely then he would be given the *guidance he required? He held the amulet out. The girl stared beneath her briefly at the masterpiece of intricate workmanship and a tear dropped onto the flawless metal. As he lifted the amulet up to place it around her neck the silence was suddenly broken by a loud cawing noise and a large, black bird swooped down and plucked the amulet from Montezuma's fingers. The bird rose high in the air before swooping down again and dropping the amulet in front of the treasury door. The Emperor looked hard at the girl before turning and walking back to his seat. A servant hurriedly retrieved the amulet and at a nod from the Emperor replaced it around the royal neck. His idea was clearly not pleasing to the gods. The girl could die without decoration. He shaded his eyes from the sun with his hand then nodded at the Chief Priest, who resumed chanting before proceeding with his grisly work.*

★ ★ ★

Friday, September 13, 1940

Tarkowski blearily removed the bedcover from his face and slowly opened his eyes. His head throbbed. Another endless meeting followed by several rounds of Polish plum brandy with the general and his cronies had played havoc with his brain cells. He rolled onto his side and grimaced as his back creaked in sympathy with his head. The high ceiling above him shimmered in the distance as his ears began to register an unusual sound. His wife was not by his side, but, as he levered himself up on his elbows, he could see the back of her dressing gown in the bathroom facing him. Her shoulders were trembling, he could see, and the unusual sound was that of her crying. Maria had never been one for tears. Even during the worst moments of their flight from Poland, when it looked as if they would lose everything including their lives, she had never shed a tear. Not even when one brother's death had been reported and then Karol's capture had become known had she wept – not in front of him anyway.

He rose stiffly from the bed and walked to the bathroom. He placed his hands on her shoulders. "What is it, my darling? This is not like you."

Maria's shoulders fell for a moment, then she turned and melted into his arms. "Oh. Adam. Adam. I am so unhappy!"

"Please, darling. Tell me. Who or what is causing this?"

"It's Karol. Voronov thinks he can help, but for a price. He knows or thinks he knows about—"

"What does that fat, jumped-up, Russian thing know? How dare he!"

"He says he has contacts who can help, if we…"

"Calm down, Maria. I doubt very much he can do anything for Karol and we must not succumb to blackmail."

The Countess started to sob again. How could she begin to explain to her husband that for love she had already paid part of Voronov's price?

★ ★ ★

Merlin drummed his fingers on the desk in irritation. He had had a frustrating night. Due to an unexploded bomb scare on the Embankment, he and Bridges had been confined to the Yard for three hours. When they had eventually arrived at the makeshift mortuary near Euston it was late, dark and raining. No one knew anything about a dead flyer. On their way home a raid had started up. The raiding party didn't seem as vast as on some previous nights, but their targets seemed to include Euston Road and the Strand. Bridges had driven skilfully to avoid a couple of bomb craters, smoking and flickering with flames, and when they got back to the Yard they had decided to hole up there for the night.

There was a shelter at the bottom of the building, but they had some bedding to lay out in Merlin's office and they had both dossed down there. Sleep had largely evaded Merlin, however. Bridges' regular snoring didn't help, but the ack-ack barrage was the main culprit. London's defence forces had finally got their act together now and the guns rhythmically boomed out for hours. Eventually Merlin had nodded off for an hour or two.

"Sergeant. Get on to the ARP people and the Medical Corps people and try and track down someone sensible who can lead us to this body. The doctor who called me yesterday was a Lieutenant Ross." Merlin's fingers drummed some more. A firm knock on the door preceded the entrance of Constable Robinson.

Bridges had not yet tidied up the loose bedding and Robinson stepped gingerly between the blankets and sheets.

"Yes, Robinson. What have you for me this morning?"

"I had dinner with my brother last night. I went out to his house in Chiswick. He had a night's leave. Anyway, as promised, he had done a little more research regarding the amulet. Here's his report."

Robinson put a brown envelope on the desk.

"Please summarise, Constable."

"He's done a bit more reading and thinks he's actually identified the piece. There's a reference in one of the books to an amulet with this design of intertwined snakes being worn by Montezuma himself."

"Montezuma himself? How interesting."

"He has provided a lot of other esoteric information, which I don't think is particularly relevant, but I did ask him who might own such an item now. He said obviously it might have belonged to a museum in the Americas or Europe. There are also, of course, private collectors. Perhaps the biggest owner of items such as this before the war was the Spanish government."

"That's not a surprise to me, Constable. The Spanish conquest of the Aztecs and Incas, Cortes, the Spanish treasure fleet and so on. Easy to forget after the insanity of the Civil War how great and rich a nation Spain once was. But what has all this got to do with a Polish airman?" Merlin stared up at his Goya print. "Any idea how much it's worth?"

"He couldn't estimate a value, but thinks it must be worth a bomb."

As Merlin scratched his nose in thought, Bridges returned. "I've tracked down Lieutenant Ross. He was very apologetic. Said he and his subordinates were dragged away to help with some casualties in St John's Wood. He's at the mortuary now and can show us the body."

"Will the warden who discovered it be there?"

"I'll ring and ask, sir."

"It would help if he is, Sergeant."

★ ★ ★

Trubetskoi had asked Evans to be available around lunchtime that day, which proved to be no problem as Stewart's brigade had been given a day's much-needed leave.

The routine was the same. The dingy lock-up in Shepherd's Bush, the cocky cockney duo and some items of surprisingly good quality. Evans gave his view again to Trubetskoi out of earshot of Jake and Billy and got his money again, but remained troubled. On this occasion, he followed the Russian to the end of the street where his driver was waiting as before. After they drove off, Evans hailed a passing taxi and asked him to follow Trubetskoi's car. As they passed down Kensington High Street, traffic was held up by a fire engine that had somehow toppled onto its side in the middle of the street. Eventually they arrived at Eaton Square and Evans shuddered as they passed the nice place where Blunt and he had stayed on occasional trips up to London. The Russian car turned off the Square and parked by an imposing-looking detached house facing on to Upper Belgrave Street.

It was drizzling as Evans got out of the taxi and he pulled up the collar of his threadbare raincoat. A siren had gone off as they had approached Chelsea and now Evans could see a small group of aircraft above. As he loitered on the pavement opposite the house Trubetskoi had entered, he heard distant explosions from the direction of Whitehall. He ought really to find a shelter, but his experiences of the Blitz so far were hardening him to danger. He decided to wait it out to see whether the house might reveal any secrets.

He was rewarded half an hour later when the door opened and Trubetskoi stepped out onto the pavement with a large, bearded man. Trubetskoi's driver, who followed them out, looked nervously up at the sky. The bearded man slapped the driver on the back and roared with laughter as he pushed him into the driver's seat. Then he and Trubetskoi got into the back seat and the car drove away. Evans ran after a passing taxi, but it didn't stop and he watched the car disappear from view. At least now, he thought, he had some better idea of the people paying him – and ritzy as their location was, Evans was far from reassured about the probity of his new employers.

★ ★ ★

A thin beam of sunlight struggled through the recently opened hole in the roof to illuminate the nave of the church.

Merlin stood by the open cardboard coffin, regretting his decision to bring Robinson along with Bridges. As Air Warden Webster had explained, the corpse had been got at by a band of rats and the result was not a pretty sight. Merlin could not recognise in the mush of the ravaged facial features the young man in Kilinski's file photo. The corpse was wearing a filthy RAF uniform on which the badge of rank and name seemed to have been unpicked. The man's pockets were empty according to the medic in charge, Lieutenant Ross, a stocky, red-faced man with a limp. Webster said that he had not had time to do a proper search around the area as the bombs had started dropping again, but he had noticed something unusual near the body and he had given it to the lieutenant.

"Here it is, Chief Inspector. Very decent of Webster to hand it in – I'm sure many men would have pocketed it for themselves." Webster blushed and shuffled his feet. Ross reached into his jacket and produced a small gold bar.

Merlin felt a strange sensation of excitement as he took the bar from Ross and turned it in his hand. "Madre de Dios! I suppose we should now call this a 'Stanislawicki ingot'." He held it up for the sergeant and constable to see. "So, Mr Webster, can you tell me exactly where you found this body?"

Webster struggled to restrain a yawn. "Sorry, sir, a long night. I found this chap in the rubble of a building just off the Marylebone Road."

"That's interesting. And where was the gold ingot?"

"Just below the body, sir. Perhaps a yard or less away."

"Could it have fallen from his hand or pocket or somehow otherwise been dislodged from his clothing?"

"Quite possibly, sir."

"I'd appreciate it if you could show us where you found him when we are finished here."

Webster nodded wearily.

"Bridges, your eyes are better than mine. Have a look at the badge on the collar. It's a bit grubby and torn, but tell me what you can see."

Bridges bent down and brushed some dirt from the badge. "I can make out three letters – 'L', 'N' and I think that's an 'I'."

"Kilinski then?"

Merlin's two colleagues nodded.

"Looks to me like an attempt might have been made to obliterate the name deliberately, sir. Though, then again, it could just have been the rats."

"Thank you, Sergeant. What's the set up, Lieutenant? I know this is only a temporary location. Where do the bodies go from here?"

"We send them up to the St Pancras mortuary. If they are not claimed in a few days, they are buried."

Merlin moved back as a couple of wardens pushed past with a loaded stretcher. The stink of putrefaction mingled with the smoke drifting down from the smouldering rafters. He could feel his stomach churning and his eyes beginning to water.

"Please pass instructions to St Pancras not to dispose of this body. Any views on cause of death?"

Ross smiled ruefully. "How about falling under the proverbial ton of bricks?"

"But you haven't examined the corpse."

"Inspector, look around you. Do you think I have the time to examine the dead ones? I have been up to my ears for the last forty-eight hours concentrating on the survivors. Somehow my superiors expect me to keep an eye on this place while also performing my duties with the injured arriving at St Barts. No, I haven't examined the corpse."

Merlin reached out to touch Ross' shoulder. "Sorry, Lieutenant, I didn't mean to suggest any negligence on your part. It's just that I'll need to arrange a post-mortem for this chap. Perhaps you could mention that to the authorities at St Pancras. Is Bentley Purchase still the coroner?"

Ross wiped some grime from his cheek. "He is. Sir Bernard Spilsbury also does much of his work there."

Bridges eyes widened a little. "Isn't he the pathologist chap who nailed Crippen, sir?"

"That's him. When I was a young sergeant, I met him while working on the Brighton trunk murders. A very clever chap."

Merlin shook hands with Ross. "Well, Lieutenant. I'll rely on you to ask Spilsbury or whoever else is in charge to look after this body carefully. We'll get in touch with them about the post-mortem."

A loud creaking noise was followed by the sound of timber falling to the ground nearby, just missing a passing warden. "Come on, you two, before we join Kilinski in a box as well. Let's see where Mr Webster found the poor chap."

★ ★ ★

Jake Dobson tossed and turned on the flimsy bed in his dingy rented room. Last night had been very dodgy. Very dodgy indeed. Billy and he had found some good stuff in the wreck of an old residential house in Covent Garden and they had received prompt cash payment from the Russian that afternoon. He was worried though. The dangers were increasing – both the physical danger and the danger of apprehension. As they had been leaving the ruins with a nice load of artwork and gold and silver, Billy had tripped on something that he realised with horror was an unexploded bomb. Nothing had happened, but still... Then as they'd got out into the street a warden had accosted them. Before entering the building, they had tried, as usual, to gauge its distance from what seemed to be the bombers' main target areas for the night and thus get a lead as to the likely absence of wardens, firemen and soldiers. That night the bombers' focus seemed to be the City, and Covent Garden had seemed safe but... Anyway, he had smashed the warden's head with a heavy silver lamp stand he had in his bag and they had got away safely this time.

And then he knew for certain that the Russians were shafting them. Regardless of the value of the items – and, of course, they had to have their profit – he thought that danger money should be factored in. Billy thought he was the clever one while Jake's pathetically unsuccessful life to date did not indicate great talent or brainpower – but Jake knew when he was being diddled even if Billy did not. He had noticed that Trubetskoi made a point of lurking in a corner with the poncy valuer to discuss the goods. He knew that Trubetskoi was up to no good, but Billy seemed to be perfectly happy with the wodge of cash they got up front and the promise of a cut in the understated proceeds of sale. He'd like to get Evans in a dark alley and squeeze the truth out of him. Maybe after their next meeting he'd get a chance. He wouldn't tell Billy about it as he'd probably be old womanish and warn him off. It wouldn't take much to get the information out of Evans but then again, perhaps he was a straight shooter and wouldn't have a problem giving him the proper valuation.

He reached out a hand and grabbed the half bottle of brandy from the floor. Pleased that he had come up with a course of action that should resolve his concerns, he took a long swig, then lay his head back on the thin and grubby pillow. Within minutes he was asleep.

★ ★ ★

Inspector Johnson had arranged to meet Jack Stewart at his station to discuss the looting problem. The place seemed to be empty when Johnson arrived, but he could hear a faint sound of snoring somewhere in the back.

In a small alcove behind the tea station, Jack Stewart was catching forty winks, perched a little precariously on two chairs. As Johnson approached, one eye snapped open. "Hello, Peter, how are you?"

"Fine, Jack. Couldn't you find somewhere more comfortable to take a nap?"

Stewart swung his legs to the floor. "Wasn't really intending to take a nap. Just nodded off waiting for you."

Johnson smiled. "Where is everyone?"

"Day's leave. Been at it pretty much non-stop since this all began. As the raiding intensity has softened just a little for the last few days, the powers that be said we could have a break. Battersea station is covering for us. We'll be back at it tomorrow. I think it's only the calm before another storm. What can I do for you, Peter?"

Johnson rubbed his upper lip, still missing his late lamented Ronald Colman moustache. "DCI Merlin has mentioned the looting problems to you?"

"Och, yes. That he has. As has my boss, Sir Archibald. He mentioned that the two of you were getting your heads together on this."

"Have you come across any looters?"

Stewart stifled a yawn. "I've seen people around the action who didn't appear to have any reason or right to be around…

but as for people actually in the act of looting, no, I haven't, as I told Frank. That's not to say I don't believe it's going on."

"Hmm." Johnson finished his tea and looked up at the rain spattering a nearby window. "Sir Archibald and I were chatting and we had an idea I'd like to run by you."

"Fire away."

"What if we attached a police officer to your team so he could keep an eye out?"

Stewart rubbed his eyes. "You realise what we are doing is not a walk in the park?"

"Of course, I know it will be extremely dangerous."

"Who are you thinking of?"

"Myself actually, perhaps with one other officer."

Stewart chuckled. "Well, I always knew you Geordies were mad buggers and now you've confirmed it. I have no objection, provided you don't get in the way of the team. Who's the lucky fella who's going to be your partner?"

"I was thinking of DC Cole, you know him, I think?"

"Aye, nice lad. The champion runner. Should come in handy bringing the bastards down, eh?"

The two men stood and shook hands. "If you are back on duty tomorrow, how about tomorrow night?"

"Tomorrow night it is, Peter. We'll look forward to your company. Keep in touch with Sir Archibald. He'll be able to tell you where we are being deployed."

★ ★ ★

Merlin chewed on a soggy corned beef sandwich at his desk, puzzling as to why Bridges had not been able to find anything at all on the Grand Duchy and Oriental Trading company. It wasn't registered as a British company and there was no record of it as a branch of an overseas one. Perhaps it was just a front for something else. The sergeant, who was sitting opposite him, had just telephoned the St Pancras mortuary. Neither Bentley Purchase nor Sir Bernard Spilsbury were around, but Bridges had managed to speak to one of the deputy coroners and passed on the message about the need for a post-mortem.

Webster had shown them where he had found Kilinski's body. It turned out to be just a hundred yards or so from the Grand Duchy building on the other side of the Euston Road.

The office door swung open and A.C. Gatehouse strode into the room. Merlin lowered his feet from the desk and brushed the sandwich crumbs from his lapels. The A.C. smiled affably at the two men. "How's your wife coming along, Bridges? Is the infant due soon?"

"December, sir."

"Ah yes. I was a December child, you know. Born Christmas Day in fact. Well, best of luck to you both."

"Thank you, sir."

"Mind if I have a private word with DCI Merlin, Bridges? Won't be long."

Bridges hurried out and the A.C. seated himself at the desk opposite Merlin. "Frank, I was just wondering whether you could, er… let me know how my niece, I mean, Detective Constable Robinson is coming along? I'm seeing my sister at Claridges for dinner tonight and she's sure to want a report."

Merlin had met the A.C.'s sister once. She was a female carbon copy of the A.C. – tall, gaunt and not exactly beautiful. He hadn't been able to work out how this spectral apparition had given birth to the beautiful Claire. Presumably the father was very handsome, in spite of which he had ended up with her mother.

"She's doing exceptionally well, sir. A very bright girl. Willing to learn and very quick on the uptake. She is proving a valuable addition to the team."

A.C. Gatehouse's thin lips stretched to their maximum extent as he beamed at Merlin's summary. Then his features stiffened and darkened. "Constable Cole. I understand that she may, mmm, be spooning with him?"

Merlin struggled to keep a straight face. "Spooning, sir?"

"You know what I mean, Frank. And you can wipe that silly smirk off your face, if you please."

Merlin attempted to compose his unreliable facial muscles. "I understand they are good friends, sir. As you know, I am rather too busy to have time to register much about the private lives of my officers."

The A.C. harrumphed. "Yes, well. I have never condoned the development of relationships among my officers, Chief Inspector – and apart from that he's entirely unsuitable, of course."

"Seems a very nice lad to me."

"Why hasn't he been called up?"

"As you well know, sir, short-staffed as we are, the services have been told to keep off our people."

"Why hasn't he made a noise about it, eh? You made a noise about wanting to join up again. So did Bridges, despite his unfortunate condition." Sergeant Bridges had been turned down for service at the beginning of the year, to Merlin's relief, due to the misfortune of his having six toes on one foot. "He's not yellow, is he?"

Whatever remained of any smirk on Merlin's face now mutated into a glower of anger. "As a matter of fact, he has been to see me about the subject. Said he was keen to do his bit and I gave him a version of the same speech you gave me. No doubt you remember it, sir. Something along the lines of the country and more specifically you, sir, needing our best officers here. How did you put it again? 'If we didn't keep our best officers here then chaos would ensue and chaos is worth a hundred divisions to Mr Hitler.' I think those were the words."

A.C. Gatehouse shifted in his chair then gave Merlin a wry smile. "Yes, well put indeed, wasn't it? Well, I'm happy to hear that about Constable Cole. Very happy, but he's still the wrong sort of chap for Claire. You must discourage them. I shall certainly be having a word with Claire if you don't."

Despite his own reservations about the relationship, Merlin was about to speak further in defence of Cole by citing his volunteering to join Johnson in the looting investigation when Johnson himself came in to the room.

"Oh, sorry, sir. Sirs. Didn't realise you were, er…"

The A.C. jumped to his feet. "Not to worry, Inspector. We are almost finished. Getting anywhere with that Polish goose chase, Frank? As I said, I don't want you wasting—"

"We found his body. Trying to arrange a post-mortem now."

"Oh? Come and tell me about it later. I have to go to another one of those interminable meetings in Whitehall."

★ ★ ★

They were sitting in the mess at Northolt after lunch, staring into their cups.

"Give me yours, sir. Let me have a look."

Jan Sieczko slid his cup over to Corporal Tom Reilley, one of the squadron mechanics.

"I'm not sure I want you to do this, Corporal."

"Just a bit of a lark, sir. My old gypsy nan taught me how to read tea leaves."

"Go on, Jan, let him have a go. He'll probably tell you something you don't know such as you will be in danger and watch out for a man with an unfortunate haircut and a toothbrush moustache." Jerzy was the third person at the table. Jan shook his head and pulled back the cup. "Oh, well, Reilley. If Jan is going to be such a faintheart, why don't you read mine?"

"Your English is coming on very well Mr Kowalski, sir, if I may say so. 'Faintheart', that's a very good word for a Polish chap to be knowing. Now, let's have a look."

Reilley picked up Kowalski's cup, poured any remaining liquid into an ashtray, shook the cup then carefully examined the patterns made at the bottom of the cup by the tea leaves.

"Very interesting. Mmm. Yes." Reilley turned the cup this way and that for a while, before depositing it back on the table with a satisfied grunt.

156

"Well. What did you see?"

"Very interesting, in fact fascinating, Mr Kowalski, sir." Reilley produced a toothpick from one of his jacket pockets and applied it to his protruding front teeth.

"Well, come on then. Let's have it."

"Very nice meat pie at lunch that was."

Jan chuckled as he watched Jerzy squirming impatiently in his seat. "Oh come on, Reilley, put him out of his misery. It's all rubbish anyway. Get on with it before he explodes."

Reilley put his toothpick back in his pocket and folded his arms.

"I saw a dark and beautiful lady. An unhappy lady."

"Must be that nice WAAF girl you were leading up the garden path the other night in the pub."

"This lady has a secret. A secret she has shared with you, sir."

Kowalski laughed rather nervously as he lit a cigarette. "All the ladies have secrets, do they not?"

Jan picked up his friend's cup and examined the tea leaves carefully. "So which tea leaf says 'lady' and which says 'secret'?"

"Oh, this is rubbish, Jan. Come on. Let's get some fresh air." Kowalski got to his feet.

"It's a very ancient art, gentlemen. No need to be so rude. Even has a fancy name. Now what was it?" As Reilley pondered, Jan saw Squadron Leader Kellett come into the room, look round briefly, then head in their direction.

"Tasseography!"

"What?"

"That's the name for it, Pilot Officer Sieczko. Tasseography. A good word for you to get your Polish tongue around. Now, let me have a look at your cup? It's—" Reilley was cut short by Kellett's arrival at their table. The three men stood to attention.

"Sit down, gentlemen. Not you, Reilley. I need to speak to these officers in private, if you don't mind."

"That's alright, sir. I need to get back to the kites anyway."

Reilley offered a rather slapdash salute and wandered off to the main door. Kellett sat down. "I'm afraid I have some rather bad news for you. I just got a call from DCI Merlin. Apparently Kilinski has been found dead."

Jan closed his eyes for a moment and raised a hand to his mouth.

"Where, sir?" Kowalski reached out a hand to pat Jan's shoulder.

"In the rubble of a bombed building in the centre of London."

Jan lowered his hand and absentmindedly lifted his empty tea cup to his lips. "So he got killed in a raid?"

"Sounds like it. Merlin didn't say any more, other than to ask that you, Sieczko, might help identify the body. It's pretty banged up apparently."

"How do they know for certain that it's him?"

"He didn't say. Presumably he's in his uniform and we are not missing any other Polish pilots."

"Where do they want me to go?"

"St Pancras mortuary."

"But how can I go, sir? There might be—"

"I've checked with Bomber Command and there seems to be nothing brewing at the moment. I'll organise a car for you straightaway and you could be there and back in a couple of hours. A straight run on the A40. Come on."

★ ★ ★

Augustus Wertheim sat thinking in the small reception area he called his own just outside de Souza's office. He had been named for the great Roman Emperor. His father had been a successful grain merchant in a small town that had at various times in its history been Polish, Lithuanian and Ukrainian. Ignatius Wertheim had a great passion for all things Roman and had passed this passion on to his son. Of course, none of his father's extensive collection of Roman artefacts and coins had made their way with his son to London, but Augustus Wertheim remembered that collection very well. His father had asked him to catalogue it for him and if he concentrated just a little he could reproduce that catalogue almost photographically in his mind.

Wertheim had made his way to London just before the First World War. His father and the rest of his family had perished in one of the pogroms which every so often flared up in that part of the world. Young Augustus had been returning from market at a neighbouring town where, from a distance, he could see the flames. The Wertheim house was clearly visible on the edge of town and there was no mistaking what was happening. He approached to what he thought was a safe distance and watched from behind a cart. Though small and wiry, he had stood up for himself many times at school and proved himself no coward, but he knew that bravery in this situation was futile. There was nothing he could do. He could still hear the cries of his parents and sisters as the flames licked higher and higher over the house. When it was dark he walked up to the charred skeleton of his home. He retched as he saw what appeared to be the remains of his family. Under the charcoaled floorboards at the back of the house in what had been the main dining room, he found what he was looking for. A box with some money. A very tidy sum. Enough to get him far away – to Berlin maybe or to Paris. Perhaps even as far as London. And, yes, he had got to London and he had made a life. The tidy sum, however, was long gone and now he had to rely on a not overly generous clerk's salary. The fact was he needed more money and was always looking for ways to make it.

He pushed the button and the coins dropped into the machine of the telephone box behind the Bank of England. A gruff voice growled a greeting down the line.

"He came in on Tuesday."

"Why haven't you told me before?"

"I haven't had a chance."

The voice at the other end chuckled rather unpleasantly. Wertheim obviously wasn't going to explain that he'd been having second thoughts about this arrangement. The money in prospect was attractive, but the danger was not. "And so, what did he want?"

"I don't know everything, but I know that he made a deposit."

"Of what?"

"I can't say. De Souza sent me out on an errand. One of the other clerks saw Tarkowski with a cloth bag. He thought it looked quite heavy. De Souza himself took the Count to the safety deposit room and put whatever it was away in one of the deposit boxes for which only he and Tarkowski have the keys."

"Hmm. This is not much you are telling me, my friend. I shall need more, much more than this if you wish to profit by our association."

Wertheim heard the pips and put some more pennies in. "But you asked me to tell you of Tarkowski's dealings with the bank and I am doing so."

Wertheim could hear voices in the background at the other end of the line.

"I shall put a small amount down on your account, my friend. I would put some more down if somehow you were able to get a key and tell me exactly what de Souza deposited. That would be worth something, I think."

"But I can't… I mean… I haven't got a key."

"A clever man will find a way, I am sure, my friend. A clever and inventive man like you, eh?"

The phone line clicked to show that the connection had been ended. Wertheim slipped out of the kiosk into Threadneedle Street and began walking back to the Polish Commonwealth Bank. He was thinking hard and didn't see the small crater ahead of him. As he fell, he cracked his right elbow hard on the pavement.

"Ah, there you are, Wertheim. Are you alright?" De Souza bent and helped his employee to his feet.

Wertheim grimaced with pain. "Thank you, sir."

"You've got to be careful, Wertheim. There are so many pitfalls to watch out for in this unfortunate city!"

★ ★ ★

Merlin looked out of the car window at another collapsed building and remembered that the date matched his bleak mood. "Do you realise it's Friday the 13th today, Sergeant?"

Merlin and Bridges were driving back from St Pancras Mortuary, where Jan Sieczko had been able to confirm Kilinski's identity despite the mess the rats had made of his face. Height, hair, the uniform and the gold had all been indicative, but the clincher was Kilinski's right hand. Kilinski had lost part of his little finger in a crash-landing when defending his homeland from the Nazi invasion. Jan recognised the stump on Kilinski's hand. Jan had assumed that Kilinski had been killed in the raid and his assumption had been allowed to stand. Merlin looked forward to hearing the results of the post-mortem.

Bridges eased their car past some heavy masonry that had tumbled into Charing Cross Road from a damaged office building. "Unlucky day for quite a few people, I'd say, sir."

"Certainly for Kilinski."

"Wouldn't that have been the day he bought it?"

"I suppose so if you want to be pedantic, Sergeant."

They passed St Martin in the Fields, which had so far escaped damage and was in fact being used as an air raid shelter. They were still having lunchtime classical concerts there and a sign advertised a performance of Handel's Water Music for the coming Sunday. Perhaps he would take Sonia if he had time.

★ ★ ★

The Count summoned the waiter and ordered a bottle of Krug.

161

He had brought his wife to Claridges for dinner to see if he could cheer her up and take her mind off things. He had also made some attempt during the day to see whether some further enquiries could be made about Karol. Voronov had told Maria that Karol was still alive in the Lubianka. The use of the word "alive" for an inhabitant of the Lubianka was, Tarkowski guessed, something of an exaggeration. In any event, one of Sikorski's adjutants, Tomaczewski, a Pole of noble ancestry like himself, was a family friend of Sir Stafford Cripps, who in May had taken up the thankless position of British Ambassador to Soviet Russia. Thanks to the Ribbentrop–Molotov Treaty, under which Russia and Germany had agreed a non-aggression pact, Russia had joined Germany in carving up Poland and various other countries in Eastern Europe. Cripps had been given the herculean task of extracting Russia from this agreement and bringing Stalin into the fold. This seemed to the Count to be a very long shot and he doubted Cripps had any influence to wield in Moscow at all. However, Tomaczewski had promised to get word to Cripps to enquire about Karol's current status. Any real news would be good news to Maria, he hoped. He told her of his efforts over the second glass of champagne, but she seemed little impressed.

"I know he is in prison and is alive. How can this Cripps person get him out? I don't think Stalin and his cronies will give a fig for Mr Cripps."

"Sir Stafford, my love. Sir Stafford Cripps."

"You think Stalin will be impressed with this knighthood, Adam? Pfft." She clicked her fingers in disgust. "We must deal with Voronov. It is a crook like him that Stalin will respect."

Tarkowski finished off his champagne glass. "Are we not at risk of overstating Karol's importance here? Perhaps the great leader is unaware of Karol's existence. It is a case of dealing with lesser creatures."

Maria laughed disdainfully. "I am sure Stalin knows of Karol. I should think that Stalin's favourite bedside reading is a list of all his prisoners at the Lubianka and a record of their daily tortures."

"Hmm." Tarkowski was aware of several pairs of eyes looking over at the sound of Maria's raised voice. "Perhaps we should order, dear."

As he called for the menu, a tall, forbidding man in evening wear passed by his table in the company of an equally tall and forbidding female. The man caught the Count's eye. "Ah, Count. Good evening to you. My sister Maud. This is Count Tarkowski, dear. A leading member of the Polish government in exile."

The Count rose to his feet. "Good evening, Commissioner. We prefer to leave the 'in exile' bit out, of course."

"Indeed, indeed, my apologies, Count, Countess. I hope all is well with you, insofar as it can be of course. Yes, well. Do enjoy your dinner. Come along, my dear." Maud cast a glacial smile back at the couple as she followed in her brother's wake.

As they watched the A.C. and his sister clumsily edge their way through the tables, the Countess giggled. "What a strange pair! Who is he?"

"The Metropolitan Police Assistant Commissioner, my dear. Quite a powerful man." Pleased that his wife had relaxed enough to laugh, the Count decided to focus on the menu. The Dover sole was always good here. Little sign of shortage or restraint yet in Claridges. Thank God!

CHAPTER 13

Saturday, September 14

It was just after midnight and Johnson and Cole were standing in a corner of Buckingham Palace courtyard.

"Not quite where you imagined we'd spend the night, eh, Cole?"

"No, sir. My mum will never believe it."

It had been raining on and off all evening and a gusty wind had just got up and was swirling down the Mall.

The Germans had not come in their greatest numbers that evening, but there had still been a steady flow of bombers. It seemed to Johnson that a plane was passing over them every ten or fifteen minutes. For the first time, bombs had landed in front of the palace, doing some damage to the Victoria Memorial, and also at the other side of the courtyard from where they stood and where Jack Stewart and his team were now dealing with a number of burning vehicles. The palace itself had not yet been hit as far as Johnson could see. A roving searchlight caught the bright colours of the Royal Standard fluttering high above the two policemen. As Johnson understood it, if the Standard was flying, the King was in residence. He wondered whether there was some special luxurious air raid shelter beneath the palace where the royal family were now huddling away from the bombs.

"The King and his family must be somewhere down below, don't you think, Cole?"

Cole was about to answer when a look of astonishment came over his face. "No, I don't think so, sir."

Johnson followed Cole's gaze and turned to see a slight man in evening suit approaching them. His face, illuminated by the glare of the fires around them, was instantly recognisable.

"G… good evening o… o… officers. Are you sure you are s… safe over here?"

Johnson seldom found himself tongue-tied, but he was now. It was Cole who found his voice first.

"We are fine, sir. Thank you."

A voice sounded in the dark behind the King. "Bertie, where are you?"

"Here I am, d… darling. I am with these brave p… p… policemen."

The slight figure of the Queen emerged from the murk to the right. She was wearing a fur coat despite the blasts of heat blowing across the courtyard. "Good evening, gentlemen. Is it sensible of you to be here? The firemen seem to have everything in hand."

Johnson finally found his voice. "We are attached to the Auxiliary Fire Service, your… er… Majesty. On a special mission."

The King withdrew a cigarette case from his pocket and lit up. His wife put her arm through his. "Oh, that sounds exciting, doesn't it, Bertie? Might one enquire as to what that might be?"

"Well, your, er, well, we are trying to get to grips with the looting problem."

"Oh, yes. Absolutely dreadful. Mr Churchill was telling us about the p… p… problem the other night. However, Mr… er…"

"Johnson, sir. Inspector Johnson and this is Detective Constable Cole."

"G… good to make your acquaintance, gentlemen. I was just going to s… say that you might be in the wrong p… place for that… I… I think that these s… swine would have to be pretty stupid to try that game here, eh, my dear?"

The unlikely group was suddenly lit up by the glare of a bomb exploding behind them in St James's Park. The air was quickly filled by the angry complaints of the park's avian inhabitants. Then another explosion sounded, this time more distant, in the direction of Westminster.

"Bertie, my dear, perhaps we had better go back in. There's courage and then there's foolhardiness. It's not going to help the country much if the next bomb lands on your head."

The King flicked cigarette ash in irritation on the ground, then gave the policemen an apologetic smile. "Always d… do what your wife tells you, g… gentlemen. Isn't that always b… best? Very well, my dear, l… lead on. Pleasure to meet you both. T… take care. Your country needs you."

The royal couple disappeared into the dark and Johnson and Cole stood in stunned silence for a while. From the point of view of their mission, of course, Johnson knew that the King was quite right. Because the bombing had brought Stewart's team to the royal home, they would learn nothing about looters tonight. They had, however, had an experience they would never forget. Suddenly they broke into laughter.

Jack Stewart came up to them, looking bedraggled, exhausted and confused. "What's so funny then?"

"You wouldn't believe it, Jack."

"Why don't you try me?"

★ ★ ★

Sir Bernard Spilsbury had passed a disturbed night in his St John's Wood house. However, it was not the bombing this time that had ruined his sleep, as it had for most of the previous week. Rather, he thought, the improperly prepared haddock he had consumed at dinner at his club. Also, no doubt, his digestion had not been helped by the encounter after dinner with Sir Norman Birkett, the renowned advocate, who had given him such a hard time over his evidence in the "Brighton trunk" case a few years ago. During the inter-war period, Spilsbury, accepted by all as the founder of the science of forensic pathology, had been regarded almost as a god-like figure. *Time* magazine had described him as "the living successor to the mythical Sherlock Holmes". He had been unchallenged as the leading medical expert witness in murder cases ever since his crucial evidence in the infamous case of Dr Crippen. However, in recent years there had been a slight weakening of his pre-eminence, which had all started with this blasted Birkett fellow. He brooded on this as his chauffeur-driven car drew up to the St Pancras Coroner's Court. As his driver opened the door, he looked down to check that his habitual spats were as pristine as usual, or rather as pristine as usual at the start of his day – frequently by the end of it they were flecked with blood. He picked up his battered Gladstone bag from the seat beside him and extricated his long, thin body from the car.

As he entered the hallway of the building he spotted the chief coroner emerging from a door to his right. "Ah, Bentley, my dear man. How goes it?"

An elegant middle-aged man with a spray of silvery hair above his ears walked briskly over to him. "Busy, busy, Bernard, as always. There's a body waiting for you downstairs, if you are free. Post-mortem requested by the Yard, chap by the name of Merlin requested haste. The deceased is a Polish pilot who seems to have suffered the natural consequences of being in the wrong place at the wrong time during a German raid, but the police think there might more to it. Can you do it?"

"Of course, my dear fellow. Who better?"

★ ★ ★

Miro Kubicki sat in the cockpit of his Hurricane, his dark head throbbing in time with the engine. He had drunk a little too much vodka with his friends last night to mourn Kilinski. Jan had clearly been very upset and Jerzy very gloomy. As far as he was concerned, the pushy little Jewish prick had got what was coming to him. Kilinski had pretended not to be a Jew, but Miro could always tell. His father had educated him well about how to treat Jews. When out hunting once with his father and grandfather in their estate near Krakow, they had come across a small caravan containing a family of proverbial wandering Jews – a father, mother and two teenage boys. Such sport they had had – his father had told the males they had a ten-minute start; they ran off into the woods and then they were mercilessly run down and hacked to death. Returning to the caravan, his grandfather had insisted on Miro having the wailing mother, a woman who would have been quite attractive were it not for the tears rolling down her cheeks and the shrieking of her distorted mouth. After he had done his business, for what was only the second time in his young life, his father had pulled out his revolver and shot her neatly in the middle of her forehead. The caravan had been torched and the hunting party had happily made its way home. The estate and his family's wealth had disappeared several years ago now, of course. All thanks to Jewish bankers and his father's profligacy. God, he hated Jews.

He knew, of course, that Jan had some Jewish blood in him. Perhaps that's why he was so upset about Kilinski – these people always bonded together, didn't they? He had a soft spot for Jan though – he didn't look Jewish and he had such charm. His sister was a bit of a looker too, as he had noticed on her recent trip to the base. Jerzy had said something about the policeman walking out with her. That was a pity, but things might change. Many things changed overnight in this war.

One of the ground crew waved at him. The blocks were away. He saw Jan manoeuvring his plane in front of him and then accelerating into the sky. They were heading southeast towards Dover and the Channel. The concentration required for flying his Hurricane soon drove away his headache. How many kills could he add to his tally today?

★ ★ ★

Merlin had arranged to meet Sonia at 11am by the main kiosk in St James's Park. They bought some currant-buns and cups of tea and sat by the lake, watching a group of ducks dive-bombing the water.

"So, it is sad about Jan's friend, Frank. Do you know how he died?"

"No. He was in the rubble of a bombed building so the obvious cause is being crushed by debris. I just feel that's not the answer. It appears that he was on some sort of personal mission and I can't believe that he was just a mundane bombing casualty. There should be a post-mortem going on now."

Sonia idly tore off a piece of bun and threw it towards the ducks. "Any idea at all about this 'mission' he was on?"

"Not really. There are just a few scattered clues. We found some gold on him. It has the stamp of some ancient Polish family on it."

"Which family?"

"Stanislawicki. Did I pronounce that right?"

Sonia threw the rest of her bun towards the ducks. "Very good, Frank. I have heard the name. I think they have been around a long time, yes?"

"Apparently so. We also found a picture of an ancient Aztec necklace or amulet or whatever it's called. Kilinski also paid a visit to a leading member of the Polish delegation here in London, a Count Tarkowski."

"Again, I recognise the name. Why was he visiting this man? What had Ziggy to do with the Polish delegation?"

"I don't know. Tarkowski was not very forthcoming. He said Ziggy had asked a question about the finances of the Polish government in exile."

Some of the ducks were now wandering up to Sonia in hope of further food. "I only met Ziggy once or twice. A gloomy fellow. Jan said he was good fun, but I couldn't see it myself."

"There was a family picture in his room. He had a brother who Jan said he wouldn't talk about."

"Yes, I remember him mentioning that. Some sort of craftsman, he said."

"Looks like he told you more than Jan. Must be that pretty face that loosened his mouth."

Merlin reached up to stroke Sonia's cheek and smiled. Sonia pulled her head away sharply. "Don't, Frank. The poor man's dead."

"Sorry, my dear."

Sonia turned back to him and put her arms around his shoulders. "No, I am sorry, my darling. I don't know why I reacted like that. It just seems that death is everywhere around us. I try to keep your English stiff upper lip, but sometimes…"

Merlin hugged her tight then planted his lips on hers. They held their embrace until a park warden approached them, making loud tutting noises.

Merlin stood up and pulled her to her feet. "I have to go and see my miserable brother now, Sonia. You are welcome to come, but it's not going to help cheer you up."

Sonia withdrew a handkerchief from her handbag and wiped her nose. "No, darling. Thank you, but I said I'd do the afternoon shift at the shop today. Will I see you tonight?"

"I am not sure. I am going to pop into the Yard after I've seen Charlie – I'll call you from there. Oh, by the way, there's a classical concert on at St Martin's Lane tomorrow. Handel, I think. Shall we?"

Sonia nodded enthusiastically before kissing him on the cheek and hurrying away towards the park gate.

★ ★ ★

"Como te va, Carlos?" Charlie Merlin, or Carlos Merino as he had been christened, glanced at his brother from the wheelchair in a corner of the room by the fireplace. The brothers shook hands and Frank took the chair on the other side of the fireplace and attempted a hearty cheerfulness he did not feel.

"Where are Beatrice and the boy?"

"They just nipped out to the local shop to get something. Biscuits for you, I should think."

"Ah. Do you need anything while we are waiting?"

"A spare leg would come in handy."

Merlin sighed. He hoped that his sister-in-law and nephew's trip was a brief one.

"Sorry, Frank. I just can't help myself." A small tear tracked its way down his left cheek.

"Oh, Charlie." A squall of rain thumped suddenly against the back window and they both held their breath for a moment, then smiled.

"I guess if the weather's bad our German friends might find the Channel a bit of a handful. Any insights at the Yard as to Hitler's plans?"

"Nothing that you don't know or guess, I should think. He and Goering hope to pummel us into submission in the air, then sweep in and take over. There are reports everywhere of troops and ships massing off France. As far as I can see, the RAF are doing a great job, but how long can they keep it up?"

"Just so. Not much longer, I'd say, but then my outlook on everything is pessimistic now. Let's change the subject." Charlie raised his good leg in front of him and moved it from side to side.

"You know the annoying thing is that sometimes when I wake up in the morning, I can feel the leg that's missing. I begin to think for a moment that by some miracle its grown back." He lowered his leg and helped himself to a cigarette from a packet on a small table by his side.

"Still off the weed, are you Frank?"

"Yes."

Charlie lit up and blew a cigarette circle in the air. "Any interesting jobs on?"

"I'm on one concerning a missing Polish pilot at the moment." Merlin proceeded to summarise the case to his brother, ending with the enquiries made of Tarkowski about Polish government finances.

"I had some dealings regarding Poland when I was working at the bank before the war."

"Oh, yes."

"Martins Bank was the correspondent bank of a Polish bank, what was its name now?" Charlie shook ash into an ashtray as he tried to remember.

"Yes, I have it. There was a bank called the Polish Commonwealth Trading Bank. I had to oversee the paperwork on some large financial transfers from Poland in 1939. There were a few accounts set up, the names meaning nothing to me, but I understood from the manager of that bank that they were government transfers. He didn't spell it out, but he hinted that it was some cautious forward thinking by the authorities, in case things turned out as in fact they did."

"A lot of money?"

"Oh, yes, millions in sterling terms. There was some bullion too, as I recall."

"You don't by any chance recall the name of the manager you dealt with?" Charlie stubbed his cigarette out and fumbled for another.

"De something, I think. De Souza, that's it. Eugene de Souza."

They heard the front door slamming and Charlie's young son, Paul, ran into the room and jumped on his uncle. His wife, Beatrice, followed, carrying a large shopping bag. As she put it down, she sighed with relief before walking over to pat Merlin's hand. "There you are, Frank. You'll stop for lunch, of course. I managed to get hold of some nice lamb chops."

★ ★ ★

At the sound of the voice on the other end of the telephone, Grishin's blood ran cold. Down the line he could somehow sense Beria's pitiless eyes inspecting his soul through those sinister spectacles of his, while from across the room the relentless eyes in Stalin's portrait did the same. It was only a few months since Beria had prompted Stalin into ordering the massacre at Katyn. Around 20,000 of Poland's finest men had perished including nearly all of the Polish military officers taken prisoner by the invading Soviet forces in 1939. A few officers had survived to undergo interrogation in the Lubianka and Beria's call had been about one of them. Apparently this officer had, as Beria put it, inevitably seen fit to accommodate his interrogators with the answers to their questions, after a little discomfort. Grishin knew well what agonies "a little discomfort" might encompass.

"There has been a development that might interest you, Grishin." Beria's wheedling voice always went through Grishin like a fingernail on a blackboard.

"Yes, Comrade Beria."

"You may recall from your time in Spain that various shipments of bullion were made to us in consideration of the substantial assistance we were giving the ultimately useless Republican forces."

Grishin shuddered. "Yes, Comrade."

"By chance a while back, it was discovered that there had been a discrepancy in one of the shipments."

"Was there, Comrade?"

"You know very well, Grishin. Don't pretend otherwise. One of your subordinates – a Pole, you can never trust a Pole, of course – stole millions of roubles worth of gold from the Soviet State. Unfortunately, the man died before we tracked him down. You know all this, of course."

Grishin cleared his throat. "I do not."

"There, there, Grishin. No need to say anything. The Vozhd is all-seeing and all-knowing and so are his loyal chief lieutenants, such as I." Grishin could imagine him preening and puffing himself up like a peacock as he sat at his desk in the Lubianka. "Overall you acquitted yourself well in Spain and haven't put a foot wrong since then. While not forgotten or forgiven, the great leader has chosen, how shall we say, to put your failing concerning the gold in abeyance."

"But I had nothing to do with any theft! I—"

"That is enough, Grishin. Just be grateful. In any event, as

I said, there has been a development. We have been unable to find the missing gold. There was a view that it had ended up with some of your assistant's friends in Krakow, who had transported it to America. Another line of enquiry pointed to its having ended up in France. Our German friends have been accommodating in affording assistance to our agents in Paris, but to no avail. Now, however, we have other testimony from this Polish officer."

"Which is, Comrade?"

"That the gold was melted down and transferred via Brussels to London."

"To where in London?"

"Unfortunately, the witness in question has not yet revealed that, but we shall get it out of him, I am sure."

"And the gold? What form does it now take?"

"I'll send you a copy of the witness' testimony when we've finished with him. Then I shall expect you to act!"

★ ★ ★

The squadron was scrambled just after half past two and they were in the thick of it an hour later. The German bombers were back in force and there were hundreds of aircraft in the sky above London. The Spitfires were targeting the Messerschmitt fighter escorts while the Hurricanes' focus was the bombers themselves. Jan and Jerzy found themselves chasing two Heinkel bombers, which had somehow become detached from their escorts somewhere over east London. As they closed in on their prey, a spray of bullets suddenly ripped across Jan's windscreen and a trickle of blood blinded his left eye. He also felt a dull pain in his left shoulder. The Hurricane's handling seemed to be unaffected, but visibility was seriously impaired. Looking to his right he could see Jerzy's plane banking above him and he saw a line of tracers aimed at a target he couldn't see. He decided to pull away to the left. There was no hope of him tracking down the bombers now and the best he could do was to get safely home. As he couldn't see the plane that attacked him, he didn't rate his chances very highly.

As he flew the plane onto a westerly course, he was able to see the great River Thames meandering between the dockland below. It had been cloudy for most of the day, but now the sun found its way through briefly and the water sparkled in the momentary rays.

A loud explosion sounded close above him and he twisted the aeroplane onto a northerly course. Out of the corner of his eye he could see a trail of black smoke and then, as he steadied, he was able to look down and see an aircraft plummeting towards the glittering mass of water. He couldn't tell if it was Jerzy's Hurricane or the assailant's Messerschmitt. Gripping the control firmly, he mumbled an old Jewish prayer he remembered from his childhood. As the last word escaped his mouth, a plane appeared high above him and waggled its wings before diving down, turning beneath him and pulling up on his right side. Jerzy was sticking his thumb in the air and Jan nodded back. They would both live to fight another day.

★ ★ ★

Merlin sat at his desk, oblivious to the sound of the anti-aircraft guns on the other side of the river and the steady drone of bombers above. *It's amazing what you can get used to*, he thought. There was some paperwork on his desk, which he couldn't get his head around. He had managed to absorb a couple of notes; one message from Johnson to say that he and Cole had survived the night, but, for reasons he would explain in person, had made no progress with their task. The second note was from Bridges mentioning that he had remembered he had a friend whose wife was Polish and did some work for the Polish government in exile.

Removing his new glasses, he attempted to read a new

175

security leaflet someone, no doubt Bridges, had left on his desk. He held it at a distance and then close up, but it was no good either way and he put the spectacles back on. Merlin had been a good sportsman in his time, nearly playing football at a professional level. That was how he had met Jack Stewart. He remained very fit and could handle himself well in a fight as had already been proven several times in the past year. If he needed glasses, so be it. Perhaps he would have to wear glasses all the time soon. Most other parts of the Merlin machine were functioning well. The undercarriage area appeared to be in particularly good nick, after a few years under wraps. He blushed at the thought of Sonia's perfect naked body and her bewitching face. They had not shared a bed now for a few nights. Perhaps tonight…?

The phone rang. A clipped voice at the other line introduced the caller. "Spilsbury here. Gather you are the chap interested in one of my corpses. The pilot."

"Ah, yes. Sir Bernard. Thank you very much for calling. Should I come out to St Pancras?"

"I can tell you my findings over the phone or you can meet me at my club, the Junior Carlton Club of Pall Mall. Do you know it? It's number thirty."

Merlin knew he would regret foregoing a second encounter with the founder of modern forensic medicine. "I shall be happy to learn what you have to say in person, Sir Bernard. What time?"

"In forty-five minutes at 5pm. It is my habit to have a glass of sherry at that hour. Perhaps you can join me for a glass."

"Indeed, a pleasure, sir."

The connection was broken and Merlin sat back for a moment in contemplation of his forthcoming meeting. Then he leaned forward and, reaching past the Eiffel Tower paperweight, he grabbed his favourite pen and a piece of notepaper. Once he knew the cause of death, he wanted to interview Tarkowski again. It would be worth interviewing the Count's wife too. Then there was this chap Charlie had mentioned, de Souza. It might be useful to see him – in fact, he would arrange to see him before seeing the Tarkowskis. Perhaps he should also try and see someone else at the Polish legation, again depending on what he might learn from de Souza. Then again he was sure he could get more from the pilots and the base. He scribbled notes down and then picked up the telephone and dialled Sonia's number. There was no answer and Merlin then remembered she was working the afternoon. She wouldn't be home until six or seven, he thought. He could surprise her. They could go to that cosy Italian place around the corner from her place. By rights he shouldn't have much of an appetite after the hearty lunch that Beatrice had given him, but he felt that by 7pm he would be voracious again. He wondered whether it might have something to do with love.

★ ★ ★

Voronov pulled back the landscape portrait of one of the endless Russian steppes and dialled the combination 21121879. The figures derived from a seminal birth date in Russian history. Of course, the Georgian sheepshagger didn't really like the idea that he had done anything as humdrum as to be born – in his mind he had been hewn out of granite or, perhaps more appropriate to his current assumed name, forged in a steel mill. Stalin, Man of Steel – well, it rolled a lot more easily off the tongue than Dzhugashvili, that had to be said. Josef Dzhugashvili and he went back a long way – both young revolutionaries, both criminals, both ruthless and violent. Voronov kept his violent side well hidden these days, cloaked in a general air of bonhomie and laughter. But it was still there and he could feel it bubbling close to the surface tonight. There was no particular reason for it, but this side of him needed an airing every so often so that it did not explode out of him unbidden.

He reached into the safe and pulled out a bundle of notes,

held together by a rubber band. Whistling tunelessly, he made his way back to his desk and fell into his chair. "Maksim, where are you?"

His servant appeared at the door.

"You are looking guilty, Maksim. What have you been up to?"

"Nothing, Kyril Ivanovitch. I was just having a cup of tea."

"Laced with some of my best vodka, no doubt."

"No, no. I'd never do that."

"Do you take me for a complete idiot, Maksim? Anyway, I'm not going to get in to that now. I can't find my Tokarev revolver in the desk. Where is it?"

Maksim shuffled to his feet and stared miserably at his master. "I took it out to give it a good clean."

Voronov leaned back in his chair and belched loudly. He stared hard at Maksim. "You did, did you? And is the gun now cleaned and ready for use?"

The servant nervously picked at his nose. "And who might you want to use it on, Kyril Ivanovitch?"

Voronov banged his fist on the desk. "That's none of your fucking business! And if you don't bring it to me here tout de suite, it'll be you I'll be using as target practice."

Maksim scurried away.

Voronov ran his hand through his beard under which the skin had started to itch as it usually did when he got irritated. To be truthful, he didn't know what he was going to do with the revolver. He might take some pot shots out of the window at whatever domestic animals were foolish enough to come within range. He might just go for a walk in the park and shoot some birds. He needed to do something to relieve the violent tension he felt building in him. Was it Trubetskoi and his stupidity that had provoked this? Or the lack of progress on the gold? Perhaps he just needed another session with the Countess? She had seemed to enjoy the rough stuff or was he deluding himself? He rose from his chair. "Maksim, where the hell is that gun?"

Merlin arrived at the Junior Carlton Club just after five. He was shown by a porter to a large library cum bar at the far corner of which he recognised the eminent pathologist already sipping a small sherry. Sir Bernard Spilsbury rose briefly from his seat and extended a hand. Merlin shook it and took the only other seat at the table, which faced on to a busy Pall Mall.

"Chief Inspector Merlin? Have we met before?"

"Once, Sir Bernard. When I was a sergeant, I worked on the Brighton trunk murders."

Sir Bernard's hawk-like features, naturally bleak, became a little bleaker. "Ah, yes, the worm Mancini. Not one of my favourite cases as you may imagine, Chief Inspector." The pathologist's heavy-lidded eyes momentarily closed as he sipped his drink. "A travesty of justice. The man was guilty."

"Yes, sir. I believe he was, but Norman Birkett—"

"Was on top form, I have to concede, and Mancini gave a wonderfully theatrical performance in the dock. However, he murdered the girl, without doubt. One day my evidence will be verified, mark my words."

Merlin became aware of a strange smell, but then remembered that Sir Bernard famously carried everywhere with him a permanent scent of the formaldehyde and other chemicals associated with the investigation of dead bodies. He wondered what Lady Spilsbury thought about it.

Now he had a chance to look at Sir Bernard more closely, he realised that the scientist had aged considerably in the six or so years since he had last seen him. He had heard something about a stroke. The man's voice and demeanour though were as firm and self-confident as always.

"So, Merlin, to this latest case. Pilot Officer Kilinski, Zygmunt, I think?"

"That's the name we have, sir, although I think it might prove to be an alias."

"Indeed. Well, that's nothing to me, is it? I am here to give you the facts about the unfortunate man's death."

"Yes, sir."

Spilsbury leaned back slightly in his chair and signalled a waiter. "Please forgive my manners. I haven't offered you a drink. Will you have a sherry? I am having a fine dry sherry from one of the best names in Jerez. Will that do?"

Merlin nodded. "Thank you."

The waiter hurried away.

"Now. The officer, as I guess you rightly surmised, did not die from injuries caused by being in a collapsed building. The man was already dead. Where was the building by the way?"

"Marylebone."

"Ah, yes. Well, the cause of death was poison. Rat poison to be precise. Or to be even more precise, probably Battle's Vermin Killer, the best-selling rodent exterminator, which, without getting too technical, is a paste laced with white phosphorous. This is, as you may imagine, highly toxic to rats and no less so to human beings."

"I see, Sir Bernard. How—"

"Let me finish, Inspector. Death by this poison is a highly unpleasant and painful experience. In chemical terms, acid in the digestive system reacts with the phosphide to generate the toxic gas, phosphine. The process of death involves, at various stages, nausea and vomiting, delirium, cramps and various other unpleasant symptoms, and culminates in complete collapse of the central nervous system, jaundice, coma, failure of kidneys, liver and heart, and, ultimately, unsurprisingly, death."

Merlin's sherry arrived, but he ignored it.

"I hope I haven't put you off your drink, Inspector."

Spilsbury finished his and asked for another.

"Time of death, Sir Bernard?"

"The body was in a dreadful state, of course. The best I can say is some time in the three or four days before it was found."

"I see. So any time from last Sunday or Monday. Is it possible that Kilinski consumed the poison accidentally?"

"It is possible, Inspector. This poison is frequently spread on scraps of food to attract the vermin. If Kilinski consumed such a scrap of food, even a small dose can be quite lethal. But why would he?"

"Could he have drunk it?"

"Of course. Now, Kilinski appears to have been a fit, young man, as one would expect from a serving RAF officer. Unfortunately, because of the damage done to the body caused by falling timber and masonry, it is difficult to discern whether there was any other physical violence done to him, such as might occur, for example, in the forced administration of poison. His hands and wrists were badly mangled in the collapse of the building. I thought I saw some sign of constriction on the wrists, but, really, the evidence is inconclusive."

Merlin finally began his sherry. As part-Spaniard, he ought to like one of that country's most famous products, but he had never really got the taste. It gave him a headache too, as did port and madeira or any other fortified wine.

"By constriction you mean as in marks caused by a rope?"

"Yes, but I cannot opine authoritatively. It is just a possibility."

"Hmm. Well, thank you very much, Sir Bernard. Is there anything else you would like to add?"

"No, Inspector. A horrible death. Foul play is my guess. Best of luck finding the culprits. Any ideas?"

Merlin rose from the table. "A few lines of enquiry, Sir Bernard, but nothing concrete enough to share for the moment."

Sir Bernard rose stiffly to his feet. "Quite right, Inspector. Keep your lip buttoned until you have analysed everything thoroughly. That's what I do, you know. But when I've completed my analysis, I come to a view that is always correct, whatever the jury in the Brighton trunk case might think!"

★ ★ ★

"How is Jan, doctor?" Kowalski stood outside the RAF Northolt base hospital, anxiously biting a fingernail.

The RAF doctor was a young man who looked like he should still be in school. "Don't worry, Mr Kowalski, he'll live. He's got a graze to his forehead and a bullet in his shoulder. He won't be flying for a little bit, but he's alright."

Kowalski relaxed a little. "Can he have visitors?"

"No, I've just given him some morphine and I'd rather let him rest for now. Ah, here's another friend."

Kowalski turned to see Miro Kubicki running towards the hospital.

"What happened?"

"Well, while you were swanning around over the estuary, I saved Jan's life."

"What do you mean swanning around? I downed a Heinkel, thank you very much. How is he?"

Kowalski explained Jan's wounds. The two men stared together at the ground. "Come on, let's get a drink."

The pub had only just opened and for once they were the only two RAF personnel in there. Both men ordered vodka rather than beer and they sat exhausted staring at their double measures, preferring for the moment the anticipation to the act.

"Did you know anything much about Kilinski's background, Jerzy?"

"No, why should I?"

Kowalski decided he'd had enough anticipation and knocked his glass back with a grimace. Kubicki followed suit, greedily wrapping his thick lips around the glass. "Takes it out of you, doesn't it, my friend?"

"You always were the master of understatement, Miro."

Kubicki grunted. "Of course, Kilinski was a Jewboy, wasn't he? Marowitz knew a little. Said he had some bee in his bonnet about something that happened back in Poland."

Kowalski smiled. "The man owed you money, I believe, Miro. Bit of a turn-up for the book. Usually it's the other way round, isn't it, with Jews I mean?"

"Yes, he owed me card debts. Didn't seem to be fussed about paying them either. I—" Kowalski rose abruptly and headed to the bar, returning shortly with another round of vodkas.

"I wonder how it is back there at home?"

"It is hell, as you well know, Miro. Your family is there as is mine. God knows what is happening, but it will not be pleasant."

"Are your parents still in Warsaw?"

"As far as I know."

"My lot are in Krakow. An apartment just off the Rynek Glowny."

"Yes, I know, a small flat off the main square. You've told me before, frequently."

Kubicki finished his second vodka. "Sorry. I am getting repetitious in my old age. There is some old saying that a week of war ages a soldier by a year. On that basis I'm about fifty-two years older, aren't I? You too."

Kowalski stifled a laugh. "You are speaking some real rubbish tonight."

"You must forgive an old man. Of course, I have some cousins in Warsaw. I used to stay up there on holidays every so often. Big, old house in the centre. Where does your family live?"

"In Warsaw town. My parents and my sister Agneta."

"Isn't that your mother's name as well?"

"Yes, it's a tradition in the family that the first-born daughter is called Agneta, the second Maria and the third Karolina."

"And is there a tradition for the boys' names?"

"No, just for the girls. My father, the first-born as am I, is called Aleksander." Kowalski stubbed out his cigarette, ran a hand over the small scar on his cheek, then lit another. The bar was starting to fill up and the men nodded to a group of ground staff leaning against the bar.

"I was looking at the dog the other day and wondering

about my cousin Sasha. Any news on your Sasha?"

"Let's not talk about such things." Kowalski was silent for a while. Then he looked up at the ceiling, rubbing his hands fiercely. "My friend, Miro, there are some English words that I need here for you. What are they again?" He closed his eyes.

"What do you mean, Jerzy?"

Kowalski's opened his eyes and smiled. "That's it. Nosy parker! You, Miro Kubicki, are being a nosy parker. In fact you are often a nosy parker! Now, keep your questions to yourself and go and get us another drink. I feel like getting, er, what's that other good English word?"

"Drunk, Jerzy?"

"Yes, but there's a jollier English word for it. Oh, yes! Blotto, Jerzy. Let's get blotto!"

★ ★ ★

Sonia came to the door in the striped pinafore she always wore when she was cooking. "Oh, I thought we might go to Carlo's round the corner, for a treat."

"Well, no, Frank, I am cooking as you can see."

He leaned down to kiss her. "Is there enough for two?"

She pushed him away laughing. "Of course, you idiot Mr Policeman."

"I called, but, of course, you were working. I had to pop out for a meeting and then I thought I'd try pot luck."

"Well, your luck is in the pot, if that's how you say it."

He laughingly attempted to grab her and she pulled away. "I must see to the food. If you want a drink, there is a bottle of beer in the kitchen."

Merlin followed her into the tiny kitchen, found the bottle of Bass and opened it. "Can I help?"

"Yes, by getting out."

"What are we having?"

"My special Polish goulash. Don't ask what's in it. I won't

claim to have the perfect ingredients, but given the way things are, I don't think I have done too badly."

"When did you manage to shop?"

"Between our going to the park and starting back at Swan and Edgar. They have some good food shops in Soho, you know."

"I'll take your word for it, darling." Merlin sat himself down on a sofa and enjoyed the beer. It managed to remove the taste of the sherry, which had lingered unpleasantly in his mouth on his long walk from Pall Mall.

The goulash was wonderful. He hadn't been able to work out exactly what he was eating, but he didn't care. For once his belt was straining to contain his belly. He sat down on the sofa and put the radio on.

Having decided that they would try and go to the Handel concert on Sunday, they were snuggling up together listening to the radio on which the Bert Ambrose Band were just starting to play a medley of dance tunes when the telephone rang. Merlin had pulled a few strings at the GPO to get Sonia a telephone ahead of the long queue. He felt a little guilty about using his position to get favours, but it had certainly made his life much easier. Sonia jumped up to answer the call, still excited with her new toy, but her excitement was soon dampened by the person on the other end of the line.

"Can I see him? No. But surely… Very well. What number do I call? Wait, let me get a pen and paper." Merlin rummaged in his discarded jacket and handed her his notebook and pencil. She wrote down the number. "And you are sure he will be alright? Yes. Thank you, doctor. Goodbye."

Sonia sat down by Merlin and started to cry. Merlin put his arms around her and hugged her tight. Between sobs she told him about Jan's injuries. "I really should go and see him now. There don't seem to be any bombers around tonight. Can we go and get your car and—"

"The doctor said he was sedated and that there was no need to worry, didn't he?"

185

Sonia nodded meekly.

"Well, let's wait until tomorrow and then you can ring them. If he's asleep and under medication, there's nothing to be achieved tonight."

Sonia's sobbing gradually subsided. "You are right, Frank. Of course. I think we can forget the concert though. Come on, let's go to bed. The washing up can wait until tomorrow."

As Frank lay with Sonia in his arms, her now calm and serene face lit up by the shaft of moonlight that shone through the half-closed curtains of the bedroom, he couldn't help thinking about Ziggy Kilinski and his cruel death. Someone in the Polish squadron must know something that would help in the investigation. He must have confided in someone about his past. If he drove Sonia up to the base tomorrow, he could do some poking around. Maybe Kellett had some more papers on the man. He had been given a very basic personnel sheet, but maybe there was more information in the files.

Sonia stirred, an eye opened and her hand played around Merlin's bare stomach. He forgot about Kilinski.

CHAPTER 14

Sunday, September 15

The car rumbled to a halt in the driveway outside 11 Group Headquarters at RAF Uxbridge. Hillingdon House, which had become RAF Uxbridge, was a rambling, old mansion dating back in parts to the eighteenth century. It was here that Air Vice Marshall Keith Park, a tall, craggy New Zealander, was overseeing the Royal Air Force's struggle in the Battle of Britain.

"It always amuses me, my dear, to recall that this estate was built by a German soldier. The Duke of Schamberg, for it was he, served under William of Orange. He got a knighthood in the Battle of the Boyne, if I recall correctly, and—"

"Yes, Winston, you told me all this the last night. Now, do you not think we should get out of the car?"

"Yes, dear." The Prime Minister banged on the window and his young male secretary, who had already exited the front seat, opened the door. Struggling with his cane and his cigar, the PM finally made it safely onto the gravel in front of the main door. Keith Park was already waiting, with a small group of officers, and brisk greetings and introductions were exchanged.

"Right, gentlemen and Mrs Churchill, I think you may recall the way, but best follow me." Park led the party through the grounds, eventually arriving amongst some bushes at a small door, which appeared to be an entrance to nowhere. One of Park's officers opened the door and led the way down a long and steep flight of stairs. They went down two levels then along a corridor with several doors. Park assembled the party outside one of them. "Alright, Mrs Churchill? And you, sir?"

"Yes, Park. I'm fine. Fit as a fiddle, you know." A puff of cigar smoke followed his exclamation.

"May I remind you, Prime Minister, that our air conditioning can't cope with cigarette or cigar smoke."

Winston Churchill pouted back at Park for a moment before handing his cigar to his secretary. "Put it out and keep it safe, please, Henry."

Henry extinguished the cigar unhappily and placed the soggy item in his coat pocket.

"Thank you, sir." Park opened the door and they entered the control room or, as it was more commonly called now by the officers, the Battle of Britain Ops Room. A large room, two floors high, revealed itself to them. In the middle of the room was what at first looked to be a large, brown table, but which on second viewing emerged as a map of southern England, the Channel and the northern coast of Europe. Several WAAFs stood around the map or plotting table holding wooden poles with a block at the end, with which they could manoeuvre small models representing squadrons of aircraft around the table. There were seats positioned above the table and stairs to individual control rooms behind curved and tinted-glass windows.

The room was a hub of relentless activity.

"I guess that we are going to have a rather busy day, Prime Minister, Mrs Churchill. Our intelligence sources suggest that Herr Hitler may be at the end of his tether. If the Germans are to launch their invasion, which we know they are fully prepared for, they would be unwise to wait much longer before the autumnal weather really sets in. The cloud and rain of the last few days seem to have cleared for the moment and I thought when I awoke and saw the sun shining that today might be a big one. Now, perhaps I can explain what everyone is doing."

Park took his guests around the room, introducing them to people and asking them to describe their duties to the Prime Minister and his wife. Churchill asked an attractive, young

WAAF at the plotting table what the model she had just placed on the map represented. "That's the Kosciuszko Squadron, sir. Flying out of RAF Northolt."

"Ah, yes, the brave Poles. I understand that they are magnificent pilots, Park?"

The Air Vice Marshall, whose subordinates had had some difficulties with the headstrong Poles, nodded. "As long as they are obeying orders, Prime Minister, yes, indeed, they are fine airmen." Another young WAAF hurried up to and handed Park a message. He read it and grunted. "As I thought, Prime Minister. I believe we are about to have some heavy action. May I…?"

"Of course, Air Vice Marshall. You must get on with your job. What news?"

"We've just had a radar report of a build up of enemy aircraft near Dieppe and there's another formation approaching Dover. I doubt that these will be the first and last."

"The ghastly Hun is trying to deliver a knock-out blow, eh, Park?"

"Indeed, Prime Minister. Would you like to take a seat and observe?"

"Yes, yes. Give me my cigar, Henry. I may not be able to smoke it, but I shall gain some comfort and reward from having it between my lips, as we observe what transpires. Go to it, Park, and God speed!"

Park went up the stairs and disappeared into one of the glassed-in control rooms. After watching him go, Churchill winked at the WAAF he had spoken to and, with his wife and secretary, eased himself into one of the rows of seats above the plotting table, from which vantage point they watched the proceedings with intense interest.

★ ★ ★

Merlin arrived mid-morning at the Northolt base. Sonia was

189

angry with him because he had allowed her to sleep in. She would have wanted to arrive at the crack of dawn to see Jan and Merlin guessed this, but she had looked so angelic in the bed and so peaceful after the stress of the previous night that he had not woken her. Then they had had to go to the Yard to get the car, which added another half an hour. A few sharp words had been exchanged, but she had calmed eventually as they sped down the A40, placing her hand on his as it rested on the gear stick.

The guard at the gate glanced briefly at Merlin's warrant card and frowned. "All hell is breaking loose today, sir. In you go."

As they drove up to the main administration building, Merlin could see what he meant. People were running in what seemed to be every direction, but more generally in the direction of the planes and the runways. As they got out of the car, Merlin saw Jan's two friends, Kowalski and Kubicki, racing past, pulling on their jackets. Jerzy saw Merlin and Sonia and waved before disappearing around a corner. Merlin ushered Sonia into the building and they walked up to a prim-looking WAAF sitting at a desk upon which Merlin placed his warrant card. "I know it's probably a stupid question, but what's happening?"

The WAAF picked up the card and sniffed. "It is rather a stupid question, Chief Inspector. We're having a scramble, obviously. There's rather a lot of incoming and everyone is going up."

"I see. Well, this is Miss Sieczko, Jan Sieczko's sister. We understand he was injured yesterday and she'd like to see him."

The girl, for now that they were close up Merlin could see she was not much more than that, sniffed again. "This isn't the best time, but as you've come all the way out here you'd better go ahead. The medical block is fifty yards to the left as you step out of the door here. You can't miss it. There's a red cross on the front door."

In the hospital it didn't take them long to find Jan, who was sitting up in his bed, accepting a drink of water from a nurse. He had bandages on his face, around the top of his head and on his left shoulder. Sonia burst into tears then pulled herself together and leaned forward to kiss Jan's face gingerly, taking care to avoid the injuries. Jan said what sounded like some soothing words in Polish before acknowledging Merlin. "It's only some grazes, you know, Frank." Merlin nodded and extended a hand to Jan.

Sonia spoke some more Polish before reverting to English for Frank's benefit. "He says it's just grazes, but a bullet went clean through his shoulder. That is not a graze!"

Jan gave his sister a feeble smile. "Look, my darling sister. It was a clean injury. They say my shoulder will recover fine. The disaster of it is I am missing out today! It could be the biggest day of the war and I'm stuck in this stupid bed." He banged his free right hand on the bedside table and fumed for a while before shouting to the nurse to get his sister and her friend a cup of tea.

Sonia began to talk in Polish again, gripping Jan's hand tightly. Merlin looked around. There was only one other patient in the ward, in a bed at the far end. He was groaning pitifully, his body almost completely swathed in bandages. An officer unknown to Merlin approached the bed.

"Badly burnt, I'm afraid. They are doing the best they can. I'm Kellett's number two, Chief Inspector. Vincent is the name. Flight Lieutenant Vincent. Front desk told me you were here, so I thought I'd pop over."

Vincent's right arm was in a sling. He moved towards Jan's bed. "We two crocks are missing out today, eh, Sieczko?"

"Yes, sir."

"I collected a windowfull of glass in my arm, Chief Inspector. Thought yesterday I'd still be able to manage, but woke up with no feeling in my fingers and the medicos tell me I can't go up."

"What's the situation, Flight Lieutenant?"

"Latest reports from Uxbridge are that there's a force of over 200 bombers, with a host of escort aircrafts, over Calais and they are heading our way. Pretty much everyone is being scrambled. Here our 303 and 229 Hurricanes are now getting airborne. The Spitfire squadrons at Biggin Hill, Hornchurch and Warmwell are doing likewise, I believe. Then no doubt the Hurricane squadrons at Kenley, Debden and Hendon will be—" Vincent was interrupted by the sound of breaking glass as Jan knocked a jug of water off his bedside table, waving his arm in frustration.

"Now, now, Sieczko. Get a grip, man. Nothing we can do about missing out today. Just concentrate on getting fit as soon as possible."

Jan sighed and Sonia put her arm around his good shoulder and gave him a hug.

Merlin thought for a moment. "As you are here, sir, do you mind if we have a word about Kilinski?"

Vincent looked a little surprised. "The Yard never sleeps, is that it, Chief Inspector? Well, I can give you a few minutes. I'll need to get over to the ops room shortly. Come along, let's go to the Squadron Leader's office."

"Back in a moment, darling."

Sonia nodded and grasped her brother's hand tightly.

Kellett's office was in the main administration building. "I was just wondering, Flight Lieutenant, if I could have a look at Ziggy's personnel file?"

"I understood that your girl took a carbon copy away with her last time."

"I know and I saw it, but I was just hoping to see the file itself just in case…"

"That's alright. It's here in this filing cabinet. Just give me a moment." Vincent opened a drawer with his good left hand. "Here it is. Do you also want another look at his belongings? I've got them stored in a cupboard just outside. I can get someone to bring them in here, if you like."

"Yes, why not. I'd be grateful."

Vincent went out to organise Kilinski's belongings, leaving Merlin with the file. This was his first proper look at it. Robinson had told him the file wasn't particularly helpful, so he had only given it a quick glance. She was a clever girl, but she was young and inexperienced. She could have missed something.

★ ★ ★

Cole and Robinson had agreed to meet up in a pub in Richmond for a lunchtime drink and a sandwich. They had both had a bit of a trek to get to the White Cross. Both lived with their parents; she in Hampton and he in north London. She had come by bus, he by underground.

They sat by the window looking at the Thames, which was twinkling in some welcome sunshine, and chewing their ham sandwiches. They had not been able to meet up for a few days and Cole had enjoyed with great relish telling of his encounter with royalty. Claire Robinson had made an attempt to be impressed, but Cole could see she wasn't quite herself. "What's up, Claire?"

Robinson sipped at her gin fizz and gave him a weak smile. "You are up, you idiot."

"What?"

"Why on earth did you agree to go on these foolhardy errands with Inspector Johnson? Surely they could have found someone else?"

Cole stretched his long legs out under the table and looked bemused. He would never understand women. "Thought you'd be proud of me getting out there into the thick of it, chasing down looters."

"More like getting yourself blown up."

Cole reached over and grasped Robinson's hand. "Sorry, Claire, but it's my… my duty, isn't it?"

Robinson shook her head, smiled weakly then pecked him on the cheek. "Yes, I suppose it is. Well, at least the Germans did you a favour last night by staying away."

"That's not going to last long though, is it? Anyway, I worry about you. The way things are, anyone could cop it in a raid."

"Yes, but you are exposing yourself to particular danger, chasing around all the hotspots with the AFS."

Cole sipped his beer and decided there was nothing more to be said on this subject and hoped Claire would decide the same. Just then, a thickset man burst through the door and loudly demanded a pint. As he waited, he was muttering something under his breath. Cole could just make out the word "hell". The barman returned with his drink and noticed his agitation. "Anything the matter, mate?"

The man downed half his pint before answering. "Just drove my van up from Sussex. Hundreds, maybe thousands of them, I don't know."

"Thousands of what?"

"Planes, German planes. Hordes, yes, that's the word, hordes of Nazi bombers. How much is a horde?"

The barman shrugged his shoulders.

"Well, however many that is, that's how many there were. Biggest bunch I've seen yet. I heard there was a huge wave of bombers earlier as well. London's going to take a pounding today, I bet."

Cole and Robinson exchanged worried glances, then he put his arm around her. "I'd better go back into town and see if I can find Johnson."

★ ★ ★

Merlin could hear the sound of returning aircraft. He looked at his watch. He was surprised to see that it was just after two o'clock. His investigation had been productive. Robinson had been right about the file. It was a simple, skimpy outline of Kilinski – a birthday in 1920, a birthplace in Warsaw, no other family details and a brief outline of his flying service in Poland.

He had spent an hour or two trying to read into it anything informative to the case, but had failed. Kilinski's belongings, however, had yielded something after very careful scrutiny – one item that Merlin found in the back pocket of a pair of trousers, a receipt for a bill in a restaurant off Trafalgar Square called Odessa. Then, from another trouser pocket, the business card of Eugene de Souza, General Manager of the Polish Commonwealth Trading Bank. His prospective interview with Mr de Souza was instantly moved up to the head of his list for the following morning.

As he shut the lid of Kilinski's trunk, Squadron Leader Kellett appeared at the door, grinning broadly, his face covered in grime. "We've fought the bastards off for now."

"Where are they?"

"Most are already limping back to France. Our pilots and guns did brilliantly. The Germans dropped a lot of bombs, of course, but not many on central London, which was their main target. As for our men, squadron 303 performed magnificently. No losses and a number of claimed hits." Kellett banged a table with his fist. "My God, Goering will be smarting!"

"Is that it for today, do you think?"

"I think there might be another wave on the way. I've told the boys we must be ready for anything. Vincent looked after you, I understand?"

Merlin nodded. He decided that he would very much like to have a further chat with members of the squadron about Kilinski, but now was not the time. Indeed the way things were going in the air, it might not be the time for the foreseeable future. He would have to see what interviews with de Souza, the Tarkowskis and perhaps other Poles in the legation would reveal. He shook hands with Kellett, thanked him, wished him all the best and headed back to collect Sonia.

Jan was asleep when he reached the hospital bed.

"They've sedated him because his shoulder was giving him real pain."

Merlin might have asked Jan about the restaurant or if Kilinski had ever mentioned de Souza, but clearly it was time to go. Sonia protested, but she was by now completely exhausted by all the emotion and in the end came quietly.

★ ★ ★

Sam Bridges and his wife were taking a walk in Battersea Park when they heard it. The heavy drone of a large aeroplane grew louder and louder, but there was something wrong about the sound. Increasingly it was accompanied by a clattering, juddering noise.

Bridges took Iris under the cover of a park hut and they turned to watch the stricken aircraft appear from over the top of Prince of Wales Mansions trailing a stream of black smoke. They could see sparks of flame flaring on one of the wings. Higher above, Bridges thought he could see a couple of Spitfires shadowing what presumably had been their target. As the bomber passed above them, the engines made a screeching sound as the pilot struggled to find some thrust.

After it had passed over them, Bridges ran in the direction of the Thames and moments later heard a loud explosion. Reaching the roadway nearest the river he could see a tall column of smoke and flames rising from the direction of Victoria.

Back at the hut he found Iris sitting on a bench, crying. "What's the matter, love?"

"A fine gentleman, you are! Deserting your pregnant wife like that."

Bridges sat down beside her and put an arm around her shoulders. "Sorry, Iris. Got caught up in the moment."

Iris dabbed her nose with a handkerchief. "What happened then?"

"Well, it crashed. Somewhere in Victoria."

"Theirs or ours?"

"One of their bombers, a Dornier I think, but some civilians will have got hurt when it came down, I shouldn't wonder."

Iris shuddered. "Put your hand here, Sam. She's giving me a right old kicking."

"What do you mean she? It's young Winston, isn't it?" He put his hand on her stomach and indeed felt a tremor against his fingers. "He's a right old one, isn't he? Going to play for Chelsea, I think!"

"What do you mean Chelsea, Sam Bridges? He's going to be a Gunner just like his old uncle Alf, God rest his soul!"

"Alright, alright, Iris. Whatever you say. Let's get back home now and have a nice cup of tea."

★ ★ ★

Billy and he weren't going out this Sunday night and with a thick packet of crisp notes in his pocket, Jake Dobson had decided he would relax and enjoy a change of scene. He hadn't been up west for a drink for a while – he'd been there for work, of course, but that was different. No, today he fancied a good walk. As a night-worker his day started late of course. He had slept like a baby through the morning bombing and it was after three when he got dressed and walked out of his dosshouse. He bought himself a fry-up in a café in Hatton Garden, then made his way through Holborn and up Oxford Street until he came to Hyde Park. He stood for a while at Speakers' Corner, listening to some maniac ranting on about how we could win the war if we all became vegetarians. Someone in Smithfield market had told him the other day that Hitler was a vegetarian. He thought about contributing this snippet of information to the debate, but let it go. From his perspective anyway, he didn't want the war to end. He was making too much money out of it. Then again, he thought, as he sauntered down Bayswater Road, he wasn't making as much as he should be. His stomach began to churn again as he thought about the way he was being cheated. A drink would take his mind off this, but the pubs weren't open yet.

He turned to the park and headed towards the Serpentine. Despite the buzz of planes high above and the threat they posed, there were plenty of people out taking a Sunday walk. When he reached the lake he decided to rest his feet for a moment and sat at the end of a bench. The ducks and other waterfowl waddling and fluttering all around him didn't seem to be suffering too much from the war yet. A big, brown duck in front of him would do very nicely for Sunday tea, he thought idly. There was no possibility of him pulling that off though, not with all these crowds around. He couldn't remember the last time he'd eaten duck. Of course, with the money burning a hole in his pocket he could afford to go to the finest restaurant and order one. He looked down at his shabby trousers. Not in these duds though. He must get himself some new clothes and then he'd be able to enjoy himself a little more.

A pretty, blonde girl wandered past with some sort of mongrel dog on a lead. Jake whistled at her but received two fingers in response as the girl hurried away giggling.

"Fuck you," Jake shouted. The man at the other end of the bench tut-tutted. The two men stared at each other for a moment before they recognised each other.

"My God, it's you, ain't it? Mister lardy-da Evans."

"Oh!" Evans became a little flustered and the sheets of the newspaper he had been trying to read began to fall apart. He bent down to retrieve two of them, which had dropped underneath the bench.

When he straightened up, Jake had edged along the bench and was only an inch or two away. "Quite a coincidence meeting up like this, Mr Evans, ain't it?"

"Yes, quite, er, Mr…"

"You can call me Jake. No need to stand on ceremony seein' as we are so closely linked in business, eh, Mr Evans? What's your first name then?"

"Francis."

"Hmm. What a nice name."

Jake looked up at the sky. "Don't know what's really happening up there, do you? Can't see or hear any more bombs dropping now, but I reckon something'll be happening again soon."

"Yes, no doubt you are right. In any event, I must get going. Have a good day." He attempted to rise, but Jake clasped his coat with a powerful hand and pulled him back to the seat.

"No need to rush, Frankie boy. Such a lovely day and it's nice for me to have a bit of company. Don't see much of anyone apart from Billy and, I have to tell you, he's a boring old fart. No, stay, let's chat." Jake relinquished his grip on Evans' coat and started to pick his nose. Evans registered his disgust. "Oh, pardon me. I must mind my manners, mustn't I?" Jake withdrew his finger and wiped it on his trousers.

"My old dad, God rest his soul, used to play this trick when I was a nipper. He put his finger up one nostril like this and hummed 'Any Old Iron' then pulled it out and stopped humming. Like he had a gramophone up there or something. Heh! He was a card, my old man."

As Jake gazed mistily into the distance, recalling the comic skills of his late parent, Evans made another move to rise, but Jake's hand shot out again to restrain him. "Alright, alright. I know you don't want to be stuck here on this bench with lowly old me, eh, Francis? But let's have a little word. A business discussion, you might call it."

"What business?" Evans nervously folded his newspaper.

Jake leaned forward close to Evans' face. "I know you know."

"Know what, Jake? Please stop speaking in riddles."

"Riddles, eh? I'll riddle you, mate."

Evans jerked back his head, recoiling at Jake's foul breath. "Look, I've got to go. Say plainly what you have to say."

Jake leaned back and smiled. "I know that Billy and I are being given the bum's rush on your valuations of the loot. I am right, aren't I?"

"How would I know? I give my ideas on value to Mr Trubetskoi, who then discusses them with you. If he gives you different figures from mine, what can I do about it?"

"You can tell us direct next time, can't you?"

"Well, if Mr Trubetskoi is amenable, I—"

"We'll make sure he's a… bloody… menable! And you'd better watch out, mate, because I'm bloody close to the end of my tether on this." Jake raised his fist in a menacing manner and bared his teeth. "Billy and I are busting a gut in bloody awful conditions. Most people would shit themselves if they went through what Billy and I go through. All I want is a fair whack! But I'm not afraid of causing physical pain to people who shaft me. Have I made myself clear, Mr lardy-da Francis Evans?"

Evans stood up, the newspaper rustling in his shaking hands. "Very clear. Now, if you don't mind?"

"Nah. Off you go. Just think of me when the bombs are coming down tomorrow night. Making you rich!"

"As a matter of fact, I shall be…" Evans bit his tongue. What need was there for this thug to know of his fire service.

"What's that?"

"Never mind. Good day to you."

Jake watched Evans hurry off towards Kensington. *The pubs must be open soon*, he thought, and he headed off in the opposite direction, thinking of that nice little place in Belgravia where they served a lovely pint of Fullers.

Evans too went in search of a drink. It was now absolutely clear to him what he had become involved with and he was sick with fear.

CHAPTER 15

Warsaw 1938

David couldn't help himself. He could quite easily have avoided this particular street on his journey across the city. Several other cross-streets could have served his purpose as he made his way out of Nalewki, the ancient Jewish quarter of Warsaw. Yet it was to Dzielna Street that his legs automatically led him. And there it was, the grim building that had been his home for just over twelve months. Wisps of smoke rose slowly from a chimney just behind the grimy walls, which stretched out far along the street ahead of him. The ache in his right arm, which had been with him ever since his stay there, sharpened as if to warn him of the folly of approaching so close. The two guards at the gate stared dully at him as he halted briefly and rubbed the painful arm vigorously with his left hand. One of the guards muttered something to his colleague and then shouted out. "Hey, Jewboy. What are you up to? I'd move along if I were you. Unless you're looking for cheap accommodation. If you are, we might be able to help you."

The guard launched a gobbet of spit at David, who stumbled before running to the other side of the street, narrowly avoiding being hit by a coal haulier's horse and carriage. He could hear the guards laughing and felt his forehead prickle with perspiration. He cursed himself for taking this route and for his cowardice in running away from the guards. He breathed deeply and glanced across the road at the jeering guards before fixing his eyes firmly on the pavement ahead of him and walking away as calmly as he could manage. He would not pay his compliments to the Pawiak Prison again – not on a voluntary basis at least. Shuddering at this thought, he turned across Zamenhofa, which was clogged with morning traffic, turned right and then left by the Mostowski Palace. After pausing briefly to take in the clean, neo-classical lines of that elegant building, he carried on down towards the Krasinski Gardens. As he turned his head to the right, his eye was caught by a flash of sunlight glinting on the high dome of the Great Synagogue of Warsaw. He bowed his head and offered a brief prayer seeking God's favour. It was not the first prayer he had offered up for divine support in his new assignment. If things went wrong, he could end up behind those forbidding, grey prison walls again. Hannah said he was mad to take on the job, but then he needed to put food on the table for her and the twins. How else was he going to do that without making use of his God-given skills? And what choice had he anyway, given who was asking him?

David crossed the wide boulevard and passed through the gateway into the gardens. The raucous traffic noise receded and some of his tension eased as he breathed in the more fragrant air. He stopped and took a breather on a bench overlooking the small garden lake. An old man wearing a skull-cap under a stovepipe hat sat at the other end of the bench, fingering his thick, grey beard. In front of him, a small boy out for a walk with his nanny was feeding bread to the ducks. It was April and spring had well and truly arrived in Warsaw. As David left home that morning, there had been a brief sharp shower, but now a surprisingly strong sun was making its presence felt. Only a few of the early morning clouds remained. As the ducks squabbled over the bread, David smiled, closed his eyes and raised his face to the sun. It's good to be alive, he thought. When you've survived the horrors of somewhere like Pawiak, the simplest of life's pleasures can be profound.

The louder quacking of the ducks as the little boy ran out of bread roused him from his brief reverie. He opened his eyes and sat forward with a jolt then turned to the old man, who smiled and raised his hat.

David returned the compliment, then pulled the gold watch his grandfather had given him out of his waistcoat pocket. "Damn, I'm going to be late. Good day, sir. I must be on my way."

The ducks gathered hungrily around another bread-bearing small child, a girl this time, as he strode off round the lake and towards the baroque opulence of the Krasinski Palace. He lovingly fingered the watch in his pocket with his free hand. It had only been retrieved from the pawnshop a week ago. He'd thought he'd lost it forever and couldn't believe that the broker hadn't sold it. Goldschmidt had been a school friend of David's Uncle Samuel and maybe that had softened his heart a little, although compassion was not a common trait in that profession.

The Krasinski Palace had been built in the late seventeenth century for a mayor of Warsaw. David had learned all about its design and construction in his studies. The ornamental reliefs above the façade of the palace had been sculpted by Andreas Schluter, who had gone on to do more great work in his native Germany. There was no time, however, to dawdle gazing at the meticulously crafted heroic dress of the Roman figures, as David had done many times before. He hurried on out of the gardens and turned into Miodowa Street. More baroque and neo-classical architectural splendours presented themselves there, but David kept his head down and moved as quickly as he could down the street towards his rendezvous in the Old Town. After passing behind the Branicki Palace, he turned left and raised his eyes. The bronze statue of King Zygmunt III glinted in the sun on top of its tall, granite column in the Castle Square. As David entered the square, he bumped into a blind man who was trying to sell his last few copies of one of the daily newspapers. He apologised and the man wandered off shouting out something about the Polish team's recent qualification for the football World Cup and then about anti-Jewish riots in Dabrowa.

A small crowd was milling in front of the Royal Castle, another baroque masterpiece whose walls displayed different shades of colour as the sun dipped in and out of the light cloud cover – one moment orange, another salmon pink, another rose. He suddenly saw the crowd's subject of interest – a tall bear wearing a Turkish fez and a brown waistcoat. The animal was under the control of a grizzled, old hunchback, who danced about clumsily and was mimicked in even more laboured fashion by the bear, which growled plaintively at the onlookers. David hurried on and entered Piwna Street, one of the streets leading from Castle Square to the Rynek Starego Miasta, the heart of Warsaw, the Old Town Market Square. It was there that his destination lay.

It was a very busy market day and people crowded into the narrow passages between the stalls that covered all but the very centre of the square. There, a group of colourfully dressed jugglers and acrobats were entertaining those of the crowd not intent on buying any of the wide range of food, clothing, old books, cutlery or pictures on offer. The sounds of violins and tambourines mingled with the indignant squawks of chicken and other fowl, the disgruntled squeaking of pigs, the barking of dogs and the shouts of merchants selling their wares.

Slowly David pushed his way through the throng towards the far corner of the square diagonally opposite from where he had entered it. As he shrugged off a juggler pestering him unsuccessfully for a contribution, he noticed a stall selling playing cards, dice and a ragbag of other sources of amusement. He waved a hand at the youthful proprietor, who smiled broadly back at him, revealing a large gap where his two front teeth should have been. "Yes, sir, what can I do for you?"

David bowed, in the process knocking a ragdoll from its resting place on the stall to the ground. Beads of sweat poured down his forehead as he bent down to pick up the doll. The square was stifling and he was wearing a thick, coarse suit and had walked a good distance. He would be glad to get into the shade of the house. But before he did that, he would do a little something for his younger brother. After all, he now had some money and soon, if all went well, he would have more. "I see you have some chess pieces. Do you have a full set with a board?"

The stall owner reached down under the stall table and with a flourish produced a board, a little faded in colour, but serviceable. From a corner of the stall table he picked up a wooden box and slid back the cover. "A full set, sir. Check if you like, but they're all there. A fine set, sir. No doubt about it."

David smiled apologetically as he meticulously removed the slightly faded chess pieces from their box and counted them out, despite the young man's assurances, black first then white. "Yes, very good. I think these will do. How much?"

"Three zloty."

"You are joking my friend. One zloty."

The stallholder sucked in his breath and shook his head. "Two zloty."

The two men haggled for a few minutes and settled on one zloty and fifty groszy. David handed over the money.

"Shall I wrap it, sir?" The stallholder pulled some old newspaper out from a box at his feet.

"Yes, please, but can you keep it for me? I have an appointment nearby. I will be back in an hour. Will that be alright?"

The toothless grin again. "Of course, sir. I'll be here for the rest of the day. Don't worry."

"Good. See you later then."

The stallholder bowed low and doffed his cap again.

Worrying that it was probably unwise to place such trust in a market vendor, David slipped through the narrow gap between a stall selling homemade jams and honey and another selling kettles and pots and pans and found himself in front of an impressive doorway. Up two steps and set a few feet back from the pavement was a high, broad, oak door, to reach which he had to step through a magnificent stone portal. Some of the masonry above the door was covered in gilt and in the centre stood a unicorn with a bright, golden horn. With one hoof raised and its head turned, it stared imperiously into the square.

David stepped up from the pavement and reached for the heavy, black door knocker. He struck the door twice and could hear the sound of the vibrating oak echoing in the room beyond.

A white-haired man in an old-fashioned, green servant's uniform appeared at the door. He had a long, bushy, white moustache, the ends of which hung down well below his chin.

"I am—"

The man put his finger to his lips. He looked coldly at David. "Yes, I know. You are expected. Please, come in."

David went in and stepped onto a highly polished, marble floor. Above him, dark oak beams traversed the ceiling and around the walls were scattered heavily framed and forbidding portraits of members of the Polish nobility through the ages.

205

"I will let the master know you are here." The servant inclined his head towards a high-backed, wooden chair in the far corner of the room, which was otherwise devoid of furniture. Then he disappeared through another thick, oak door and David sat down carefully on what proved to be a singularly uncomfortable chair.

He glanced up and noticed that the ceiling in between the strong old beams was covered in faded, decorative artwork. The unicorn featured heavily as did various other mythical or non-mythical animals. David presumed that there was some symbolic, heraldic meaning in the design. He looked down to appreciate the beauty and symmetry of the star-patterned marble floor and then stood up and stretched his arms in the air. The pain in his right arm was pounding again and he rubbed it vigorously. He sat back down and began to relax, only then to be assailed by fresh uncertainties. Perhaps Hannah was right and this job could only lead to trouble? But what choice did he have? His talent was what created the opportunity, but then again, without his talent he would still be languishing in the Pawiak Prison. What other choice did he have? Survival was at stake.

He heard steps in the adjoining room. The door flew open and David stood up. His right arm shuddered in a brief spasm.

"Ah, there you are. Come, come, my clever friend. Come through here, if you please."

★ ★ ★

Monday, September 16, 1940

Merlin propped his newspaper against the large saltcellar on the café table and read the headlines of the *Daily Herald*.

The main headline blared "175 NAZI PLANES DOWN". Others read "RAF Triumphs in Biggest Air Battles of War", "Raiders Chased Back to the Channel" and "RAF Puts Goering in Shade". A second huge wave of bombers had crossed the Channel on Sunday afternoon and had been as effectively repulsed by Britain's Hurricanes and Spitfires as they had been in the morning's raid. Merlin wondered whether the figures for German losses had been overstated as usual, but, having been at Northolt himself the previous day, he knew that the thrust of the stories was correct. Something like 400 enemy planes had set out during the day to destroy London and they had palpably failed to do so. A small number of bombers had got through to the heart of the capital, but relatively little damage had been done. There was a sense in the newspapers that some turning point might have been reached, which was reflected in the cheerful atmosphere in Tony's Café. He finished his tea, nodded to Tony and left some coppers on the table. Within minutes he was in his office at the Yard.

Bridges was tidying up Merlin's desk and WPC Robinson was hovering at the door.

"Everyone alright then? Survived the weekend in good shape, did we?" Merlin sat down at his desk and they exchanged words about the RAF's apparent great success on Sunday.

"Did you hear about Inspector Johnson and Tommy Cole's entertaining night?"

"No, what happened?"

Robinson smiled. "The AFS group they are attached to was at Buckingham Palace."

"I heard it got bombed. Are they alright?"

"Very much so, sir – but they had an encounter with their majesties."

"Their majesties, Robinson? You mean they met the King and Queen?"

"Apparently so, sir. They were—"

At this moment, Cole appeared at the door.

"So, here is the man himself! Am I to congratulate you on a knighthood, Cole?"

Cole reddened with embarrassment then haltingly told his story.

"Well, well, Cole. Perhaps I ought to join you on your next outing. Who knows who we'll meet, though it will be hard to top that. Any other developments on the looting?"

"No, sir. We thought we might go out last night but couldn't hook up with Mr Stewart."

Merlin nodded and pulled his chair closer to his desk. "Alright, let's get back to work. Sergeant, I've got two jobs for you. First, I'd like you to go and see that Polish wife of your friend and see if she can help us as regards Tarkowski. Then I want you to check out the restaurant in Trafalgar Square that Kilinski went to and see if they remember him. Robinson, you and I are going to see a bank manager. Cole, you'd better go and find Inspector Johnson and discover what's on the menu for today. Tell him I may join you tonight if something's organised."

★ ★ ★

Bridges drove to Pimlico where his friend Raymond Hargreaves, a railway engineer, and his wife, Lenke, lived in a small cottage. Bridges had met Ray a couple of times at the football before the war. He was an old schoolfriend of PC Harry Jones, who'd caught a bullet in the face when interrupting a burglary in Jermyn Street the day before the Germans invaded Poland and whom both Bridges and Hargreaves mourned deeply. Lenke was a tall, dark-haired woman, who smiled welcomingly at him. She led the way into her cosy living room. "Raymond is out at work at the moment. Is there anything wrong? He's not in trouble, is he?"

"No, no. Not at all."

Bridges declined the customary offer of refreshment and followed Lenke into her brightly furnished sitting room. "It's to do with your interpreting work, Mrs Hargreaves. We are seeking information on someone who works with the Polish government in exile."

"Oh, yes. I do some work for them from time to time."

"Have you ever come across a gentleman called Tarkowski, Count Tarkowski?"

"Indeed, I have. He is a very senior adviser to the government. I have done some translating work for him. A charming gentleman of the old school – why do you want to know about him?"

"Do you know anything about his history?"

Mrs Hargreaves leaned forward on her seat. "Do you think it's alright for me to talk? They are all so secretive. I wouldn't like to be breaking any confidentiality. I'd hate to lose my work there. The money comes in very handy for Ray and me."

"I have no desire to compromise you. Just a bit of general background, Mrs Hargreaves. A Polish flyer has gone missing and the Count may have had some contact with him. It's really routine. Can you tell me what the Count does?"

"Well, as I said, he's an adviser of some sort. Doesn't seem to have a formal title. Obviously he's, how do you say, very well connected, being a Count and all. He seems to have some diplomatic responsibilities and some financial ones. I believe he has some responsibility for raising and managing funds for the Polish government."

"Is he a wealthy man himself?"

"I suppose so, Sergeant. Who knows? Some people managed to get out of Poland with their money, others didn't. I myself had no money to get out with." A strained smile spread across her thin lips.

"Did you ever see any Polish air force personnel at the Count's offices?"

"Sergeant, I am only a part-time worker. I do not sit in the offices taking note of the many people coming in and out."

"No, indeed, Mrs Hargreaves. I was just wondering on the off chance."

"I have seen people in uniforms, of course, and no doubt some of them were air force uniforms, but I paid no attention really."

"I see. Generally, what is your impression of Count Tarkowski?"

"As I said, a well-mannered gentleman. It is clear that he has been through tough times, as we Poles all have, but a gentleman, certainly."

"Was there any gossip in the office about the Count and his wife?"

"Gossip, Sergeant? I do not involve myself in gossip. Certainly, no."

"Do you know anything about his family?"

"Only that he has a beautiful wife. Saw her in his office one day. She's an aristocrat as well. Someone did tell me her family name. What was it now? I should remember as it's quite a well-known family in Poland. Stan… Stanislawicki, that's it. Stanislawicki."

★ ★ ★

The little clerk could not hide his surprise as Merlin presented the warrant card to him. "Goodness, Chief Inspector Merlin. What can you possibly want with Mr de Souza? He is a very busy man, you know. Very busy. I shall be happy to make an appointment for you later in the week. Would Thursday be convenient for you?"

"With all due respect, Mr…"

"Wertheim, Chief Inspector, Augustus Wertheim at your service."

"Well, with respect, Mr Wertheim, Thursday would not be convenient, no. Today and now, however, will suit and I would be grateful if you could inform Mr de Souza that we are here."

Wertheim fiddled with his spectacles and scratched his nose. "Well, this is most irregular, most irregular." He got up from his desk, turned and went through a door behind him. Moments later he reappeared and beckoned Merlin and Robinson through. The solid figure who stood to welcome them seemed to Merlin to be the epitome of an old-fashioned City banker, save for the slight air of foreign exoticism.

"Officers. Please, come, sit down, please. Wertheim, some tea if—"

"That won't be necessary, Mr de Souza. Thank you."

Wertheim disappeared back into his office and picked up the telephone on his desk.

★ ★ ★

The Odessa restaurant was not yet open for business when Bridges arrived and he had to bang several times on the door before he got any attention.

"We serve lunch from twelve noon, can't you…?" Mikhail became silent as he regarded the burly form of Sam Bridges waving his warrant card in front of him.

"May I come in?"

Mikhail's heart skipped a beat as he thought about the two illegal aliens currently peeling vegetables in the kitchen.

"We run a good restaurant here, sir. No problems. No hanky panky. No trouble with the police."

"Alright, alright, keep your hair on Mr…?"

"Mikhail. Just call me Mikhail. I am head waiter." Mikhail led Bridges through an ornate vestibule, decorated in deepest red, and into the main restaurant where he indicated a table and pulled out two chairs. Apron-clad waiters bustled around them, setting tables and frequently shouting at each other in a language Bridges took to be Russian.

"I am here to ask you about a customer. Do you recall a Mr Kilinski dining here ever? Mr or rather Pilot Officer Kilinski, he was a Polish RAF officer."

"Was?"

"Unfortunately, he is now dead."

Mikhail blanched. Against the pallor of the waiter's skin, Bridges noticed that Mikhail's eyes were a little bloodshot. "Dead. You mean from food poisoning?"

"No, no. Nothing like that. I just want to know if you recall him dining here and, if so, who he dined with."

"No, no. I don't remember such a person. No."

Bridges watched Mikhail's eyes shifting back and forth to the kitchen. "You're quite sure about that? You can say that without looking at your reservation book?"

"No Polish flyers in here. Never. I am sure."

"You must get plenty of servicemen customers in here. Are you so familiar with all the uniforms that you can rule Mr Kilinski out?"

Mikhail's eyes moved towards a location near the main door where Bridges assumed the reservation book was kept. "I have look if you want, but…"

"I tell you what, Mikhail, why don't you bring it over here? We can then have a look at it together."

Mikhail shrugged, got up and, barging his way past a couple of the waiters, retrieved the book. He smirked as Bridges opened the thick volume to find all the entries written in Cyrillic script.

"Ah." Bridges thought for a moment before slapping the covers of the book back together. "Perhaps the best thing is for me to take this with me. The Yard is bound to have access to someone who can read it. And you can come with me to look at a photograph we have of Kilinski back at the Yard."

Mikhail's smile disappeared. "You cannot do this. We need book!"

Bridges set the book down on the table and sighed. "Look, Mikhail. Why don't you just help me out here? You are clearly holding out on me. I can make life very difficult for you and the people who own this place. You are foreigners, Russians. We are at war. Your people are on the same side as our enemies. I could probably get you closed down in a moment. So why not make your life easier and assist us?"

"Not Russian. We are Georgians!"

"Excuse me, but isn't Stalin a Georgian?"

Mikhail squirmed in his seat, ran a hand through his hair and decided to break the habit of a lifetime and tell the truth. "The book won't help you, but I remember a Polish flyer coming just a week or two ago and I remember his name being mentioned by the person he met here. I have very good memory for names. For head waiter is very important to

212

remember names. Good memory for names often means good tips."

"That's good, Mikhail. And who did he have lunch with?"

"Very dangerous man. If he finds out I tell you, he could do much damage. That's why I no like to answer you."

"Don't worry, we won't mention you, Mikhail."

Mikhail looked towards the kitchen. His boss was away for the week. The decision was his to make. "A man called Voronov. Kyril Voronov."

"And who is he?"

A bead of perspiration made its way down Mikhail's forehead. "A rich Russian. Lives here in London. Kilinski had lunch with him and another man. They had quite a heated discussion, but then Voronov and his friend left in a hurry, leaving Kilinski to pay the bill. That's one reason I remember it well, as Voronov is very free with his money. He usually pays for everything and leaves big tips. That time Kilinski got stuck with the bill and he could only just scrape the money together."

"And when would this lunch have taken place?"

"Last week of August, I think. Voronov has us hold a permanent table here at lunchtime, so it won't be in the book, but I'm sure it was last week August. A Wednesday or Thursday, perhaps. Voronov, yes, a dangerous man. You watch out!"

★ ★ ★

"So, Mr de Souza, the late Pilot Officer Kilinski arranged an appointment with you in order to set up an account at the bank?"

"Yes, Chief Inspector. He had heard that a large number of Polish people held accounts here and wished to avail himself of that service."

"And when would that have been exactly?"

De Souza consulted the fat red diary on his desk. "That

would have been the afternoon of Wednesday, August 28th."

"Did he have much money to deposit?"

De Souza shook his head and a few flakes of dandruff fell onto his shoulder. "We didn't really get that far."

"Hmm." Merlin glanced at Robinson. "Can you show Mr de Souza our little cutting, Constable?"

Robinson produced the photograph of the Aztec amulet and laid it on de Souza's desk.

De Souza picked it up and studied it. "A beautiful piece."

"Have you seen this amulet, sir?"

"No, why no. I haven't seen this photograph. No."

"Mr Kilinski didn't show it to you?"

"No."

"Do you know what it is?"

De Souza took a magnifying glass out of one of his desk drawers and looked again at the photograph. "It is clearly an item of value and antiquity. South American, perhaps?" Laying the glass down, he leaned his elbows on the desk, steepled his hands in front of him and smiled.

"On a more general note, sir, do you have any dealings with the Polish government in exile? Do they have an account here?"

"I am not really at liberty to discuss our account holders, Chief Inspector. Perhaps—"

"I am conducting a murder enquiry, sir. Mr Kilinski was the victim of a murder and I need to pursue every avenue. If you choose not to be forthcoming, I could return here later with a warrant to go over your books. If—"

De Souza shook his head rapidly, dislodging another small flurry of dandruff, and waved a hand in the air. "There'll be no need of that, gentlemen. No need. Yes, the Polish government is a client here."

"And would they have substantial deposits here?"

"Indeed, they do. Fortunately, they prudently transferred substantial funds in advance of the German invasion."

"Did that include gold bullion and the like?"

"Er… yes. It did."

Merlin felt a twinge in his shoulder and decided to get up from the uncomfortable chair and stretch his legs. He moved over to the window, which overlooked what looked like a newly created bombsite. A couple of mangy-looking dogs were being chased off the rubble by a warden, while in the road below he could see a captured German pilot being marched in the direction of the Bank of England.

When he turned round, de Souza was sitting up expectantly at his desk like an over-eager dog. "And do many members of the Polish government or legation, or whatever you call it, maintain accounts here?"

"Yes, some do."

"Does Count Tarkowski keep an account here?"

The banker blinked in momentary surprise. "The Count does have business with the bank, yes."

Merlin felt the pain easing as he sat back down in the chair. "He has deposits here?"

De Souza squirmed awkwardly in his seat. "He does."

"Might I enquire what he has with you?"

"Really, Chief Inspector. There must be a limit. I shall be happy to discuss the Count's deposits here in his presence. I think that is only fair."

"Does he have bullion here?"

De Souza rose and moved over to a sideboard where he poured himself a glass of water. "Please, Chief Inspector. Can we not call the Count and—"

"Kilinski didn't just have the photograph of that gold necklace in his possession. He also had some gold – of Polish origin apparently." He rummaged in his jacket pockets then produced the ingot. "Just like this in fact. Have you seen one of these before?"

"I… I…"

"Did Kilinski show you this, sir? He had a bee in his bonnet, you see. I don't know exactly what his mission was, but there are various links beginning to come clear to me. He had a photograph of this magnificent amulet, he had an example of this ancient Polish currency, he went to see the Count, a prominent Pole in this country, he came to see you, a prominent banker to the Poles in this country, and then he died violently. Someone didn't want him to chase down whatever he was seeking and someone stopped him. That's how it looks to me. Was it you, Mr de Souza?" Merlin stood up again and leaned over the desk, staring fiercely at the now cowering banker.

"Of course not, Chief Inspector, why would I do something like that?"

Merlin's face resumed its normal equable look and he eased himself back into his chair. "Mr de Souza, I need help. Your wholehearted assistance, not the guarded response I feel I am getting from you. If you have nothing to hide, please help me. I know you have client responsibilities as a banker, but these, I am afraid, have to go by the board when we are investigating murder."

"Of course, Chief Inspector. Please excuse me a moment." De Souza rose slowly to his feet and walked over to the sideboard where he poured himself a large, neat whisky. He indicated two other empty glasses, but Merlin shook his head. Seated again at his desk, he took a large mouthful of the drink and leaned back in his chair. "I don't know the exact family background, but somehow the Count appears to be a very rich man. I am not a Pole myself, gentlemen – my own background is Hungarian."

The bank manager finished his Scotch and poured another glass from the decanter which he had brought to his desk. Having decided to open up, he now relaxed into his task. "No doubt the Count had large estates, but as such wealth is obviously not portable, I assume the Count had substantial other assets. In any event, on his arrival here from Poland in January, I think it was, of this year, he made a large deposit of gold bullion."

"How much did he deposit?"

"Well, it was around five hundred thousand pounds worth, or two million dollars."

"And in what form?"

"In the form of these ingots. I have not been given information as to the antiquity or artistic worth of the ingots, but our valuation is simply based on the actual gold content at current prices."

"And where is this gold?"

"In our vaults below."

Robinson tapped a pencil on her notebook. "And is that all of the gold the Count has?"

De Souza scratched his chin. "Well, no, there is apparently more, young lady."

"And where does the Count keep that?"

"I have advised him most strongly against this, but he has most of it in his home. He did have storage in some business premises, but the building was bombed out last week. I understand he has moved most of what was there to his house."

"And you think that might have substantial worth as well?"

"Certainly, millions of pounds' worth, I believe. The Count did not wish to have all his eggs in one basket, so to speak."

"These bombed business premises. Would they, by any chance, operate under the name Grand Duchy and Oriental Trading?"

"Yes, they do, or anyway did."

Merlin relieved the returning pain in his shoulder by standing up and walking to the window again. "And does the gold you hold earn him any interest?"

De Souza reached down into a drawer beneath him and produced a document. "It does not, Chief Inspector. It appreciates or not, as the case may be." He fingered the document. "I hope I am not going to get into trouble for telling you, but this document is a loan agreement."

"Between who?"

"Between the Count and the Polish government in exile. It enables the government to use the gold as collateral for funds that my bank makes available from time to time."

"Didn't you say that the government had its own funds?"

"Some, Chief Inspector, but I believe the task of running a government in exile and supporting resistance activities in Poland is an expensive one."

Merlin resumed his seat. "So the Count is a true patriot?"

"It would appear so, yes." De Souza opened a small packet. "Turkish cigarettes. One of my vices. Can I interest you?"

Merlin and Robinson declined. De Souza lit up, filling the room with a pungent aroma and smoke which made Robinson's eyes water.

"Turning to Kilinski."

"Ah, yes, the flyer. Well, as I said, he came to see me, wishing to open a deposit. We discussed the formalities. Then he produced the necklace or amulet or whatever you call it. Said he'd like to deposit it with us. Asked me if I thought it was valuable."

"He had the actual amulet?"

"Yes, indeed, a very beautiful item."

"Why on earth didn't you tell us in the first place?"

De Souza shrugged. "A banker's first reaction is to respect customer confidentiality."

"Hmm. Well, what did you say?"

"Well, of course, I could see it was a beautiful item. Said I'd check out the gold content and get it appraised for him if he wanted. He declined forcefully, saying he could get someone else to do it."

"Did he say where he got it?"

"Called it a family heirloom. I can't pretend I wasn't a little surprised. He seemed to be a very ordinary boy. Jewish, I should have thought. We can always tell our own, you know. A fellow from some poor ghetto in Warsaw or Krakow or Stettin or somewhere like that, I would guess, who had somehow elevated himself into the Polish Air Force. Where would a boy like that get such a beautiful thing? Perhaps he stole it or looted it in the invasion of Poland or maybe even here, in this blisskrieg of the Nazis." The second whisky appeared to have gone to de Souza's head and his words were becoming a little slurred.

"And the ingot? Did he show you the ingot?"

The banker picked up the gold bar, which Merlin had left on the desk, and held it up so that it caught the light from the window. "He did. Asked me whether I had seen any others like it." De Souza set the ingot back down on the desk.

"And did you tell him?"

"I did not. That would have been a definite breach of client confidentiality."

"And what did Kilinski say?"

"He was rather rude. Said he didn't believe me. Mentioned Tarkowski and said that he must have plenty of them. Asked if Tarkowski had an account with us. I remained silent."

"And then?"

"He stood up. Picked up his ingot and his amulet, said that he wasn't sure about the account and that he'd think about it and then said good day."

"And that was that?"

"Yes, that was that. Except…"

"Yes?"

"Except he returned to see me again the following week. The Friday before last it was, I think."

"That would have been what date, sir?"

De Souza consulted his desk diary. "The 6th, Chief Inspector. September the 6th."

"And?"

"He was here for minutes only just to tell me he had changed his mind about me valuing the amulet."

Merlin raised his eyebrows at Robinson. "You mean you have it, sir?"

The banker rose and walked a little unsteadily over to a portrait of a smug-looking, Victorian gentleman on the wall to his right. The painting swung back to reveal a small safe. With surprisingly deft fingers he applied the combination, opened the safe door and removed something.

Back at the desk, he carefully laid the object, wrapped in a white cloth, in front of Merlin. "Et voilà." With a sigh, de Souza pulled back the cloth to reveal the entwined snakes of Montezuma, which glinted in the light from the office window.

Merlin caught his breath. Robinson let out a gasp of admiration.

"Yes, a beautiful item, isn't it? My contact in Hatton Garden valued it at ten thousand pounds, but to the right collector it might be worth much more."

"If you don't mind, sir, I'd better take this into my custody."

De Souza looked wistfully at the sparkling necklace. "Very well, Chief Inspector. Although Mr Kilinski is no more, I had better have a receipt for form's sake."

Merlin removed a page of paper from his own notebook and scribbled on it.

"Thank you."

Merlin rewrapped the amulet in its cloth and put it in his pocket. "When Kilinski left after his first visit, did you contact Tarkowski?"

De Souza removed a handkerchief from his top pocket and mopped his forehead. "Excuse me, Chief Inspector, I am not used to alcohol at this time of day."

"Did you contact the Count?"

"I felt duty bound to let him know, as a major customer of the bank, that someone was going round asking questions about him and furthermore flourishing a gold ingot like those we had in our vaults . I sent him a message via his wife."

"Did you mention the amulet?"

"No. I saw no need."

Merlin felt a twinge of cramp and stretched a leg underneath de Souza's desk. "What was the Count's response?"

"When I last saw him he expressed his thanks for keeping him informed. That was all."

A siren began wailing in the distance and Merlin looked over at Robinson. "Any questions, Constable?"

"Yes, sir. Just one thing, Mr de Souza. Or rather two. On the second occasion you saw him, did Mr Kilinski look in good shape? I mean did he look like he was sleeping rough?"

"He was perfectly presentable."

"And was he in uniform or civvies?"

"He was wearing a dark suit, shirt and tie, on his second visit."

"But you know he was a pilot?"

"Of course. He was wearing his uniform on his first."

"Thank you, sir. That's all I had to ask."

The two officers rose and headed for the door from behind which the faint sound of scurrying footsteps could be heard.

★ ★ ★

Back at the Yard, Merlin listened intently as Bridges explained what he had learned from Lenke and then from Mikhail at the restaurant. When he had finished, he swung a leg onto the desk and looked thoughtfully out of the window.

"Shall I rustle up a drink, sir? Still got the taste of that awful cigarette smoke in my mouth." Robinson coughed to emphasise her point.

As Robinson disappeared through the door, Merlin rummaged in the bottom drawer of his desk and found the two Fisherman's Friends lozenges from the packet he'd discovered earlier underneath some old files in his filing cabinet. He didn't bother offering one to Bridges, who, he knew, detested them and popped them both into his mouth. After sucking hard for a moment, he recounted the details of the de Souza interview to the sergeant.

"Well, at last we have found out about the Grand Duchy company. An unregistered foreign company, I suppose. Why on earth do you think de Souza was so cagey about the amulet, sir?"

"Greed, Sergeant. He had the amulet, unknown to us, when I told him Kilinski was dead. He probably thought he might be able to get away with pocketing it for himself. Then, when I pursued further, he got cold feet." Merlin could feel the adrenalin beginning to flow as it always did when things began to move and come together in a case. Robinson returned, he tidied the papers on his desk and cleared his throat.

"I think we can summarise the facts regarding Kilinski as follows –

One – He was in possession of an ancient Aztec gold amulet and a gold ingot stamped with the arms or design of the Stanislawicki family of Poland.

Two – The gold bar is part of, yes, let's give it the word, a treasure owned or controlled by Count Tarkowski, a member of the Stanislawicki family, some of which is deposited at the Polish Commonwealth Bank and some of which is apparently stashed in his house, having previously been kept in the now ruined offices of his Grand Duchy and Oriental Trading company.

Three – Kilinski, an apparently loyal and well-regarded RAF pilot, having made several visits to London to make enquiries, was provoked to desert the service, for desert he certainly did, in pursuit of a mission to track down the treasure or the owner or owners of that treasure, or someone connected with such owners.

Four – Tarkowski has been unforthcoming to us about his contact with Kilinski and appears to have something to hide.

Five – A wealthy Russian émigré called Voronov somehow features in the mix as Kilinski met up with him recently. The importance of this apparently heated meeting is not clear.

Six – Kilinski's body was found not far from Tarkowski's business premises. Whatever Kilinski was seeking may have led someone to murder him at some time in the early part of last week. Perhaps Kilinski wanted some or all of the treasure for himself. Perhaps he had information with which he hoped to blackmail the owner of the gold. Then again perhaps someone known to us or unknown had a grudge against him unrelated to the gold. Perhaps… well, there are several perhapses.

"Did I miss anything?"

"Seven, sir, that, as Robinson pointed out, Kilinski was staying somewhere other than on the streets and that he had a change of clothes."

"Quite so, Sergeant. Kilinski was missing, pursuing his vendetta or whatever it was for a week or so. He either stayed at a hotel or rented room or with a friend. We should check that out. But the first task for us, as I originally calculated, is to have another word with the Count. He might be able to open everything up for us, if we can get him to talk."

"What about Voronov, sir?"

"Have a word with Five, Sergeant."

"Five, sir?"

"That's MI5, Constable. They might have something on a rich Russian émigré like him."

"Should I—?"

"If you can dig anything up on your own, Constable, go ahead. Sergeant, make the call to Five and then let's track down Tarkowski."

★ ★ ★

Voronov put down the telephone. Wertheim was proving to be a useful addition to his payroll. More useful anyway than that hot-headed young Pole. If the police were closing in on Tarkowski, he had better move quickly if he was going to get his hands on any of the gold. The Countess had told him that all of the gold was at the Commonwealth Bank. He had suspected this was a lie and now, thanks to Wertheim, he knew it. What a fool Tarkowski was to keep what could well be a large portion of it in his house. However solid the cellar or attic or wherever it was that he had stored it, it would not keep Voronov out. He would have to move quickly. Maksim would have to track down Trubetskoi. Perhaps his looting gang could be put to a new use. Tonight might be too soon to organise everything, but he could aim at tomorrow.

"Maksim, where the hell are you?"

★ ★ ★

Bridges pulled the car to a halt outside the Polish embassy in Portland Place. The policemen understood that Tarkowski normally worked out of the embassy building on Mondays. It was raining heavily and they hurried through the front door. They presented their credentials, a phone call was made and they were ushered by an elderly porter through the austere entrance hall, along a long corridor and into an office at the back of the building. Merlin caught a glimpse of the BBC head office out of one of the windows. A pretty, red-headed girl sat at a desk to the left of a large door beyond which, Merlin assumed, was Tarkowski's inner sanctum. "Good morning, gentlemen. You are the policemen?"

The two men nodded and introduced themselves.

"I'm afraid the Count hasn't arrived yet. I don't know what's happened. He's normally here by now."

"We'll just wait here, if you don't mind, miss." The secretary gave Bridges a twinkling smile. "Please, go ahead. It is nice to have some handsome, male company." Bridges blushed as the two men sat down on a scuffed leather sofa by the window. They declined the offer of tea and the secretary went back to her work and began clattering away on the typewriter.

"Excuse me, Miss…"

"Wajda. Cristina Wajda, Chief Inspector."

"I was just wondering. We are investigating the murder of a fellow countryman of yours."

"Oh dear."

"A Polish pilot called Kilinski. He met the Count at his home, we understand. It just occurred to me that he might have tried to see the Count here and that you might have met him?"

The secretary considered, her finger touching her pouting lips in a rather attractive pose, or so Merlin thought. She looked up and nodded. "I did meet him. He came when the Count was out once. You say he is dead, poor man. A skinny fellow, a strange face but in a funny way not bad-looking. Very intense eyes. I remember he had a girl with him."

"A girl?"

"I couldn't get rid of him. He said he was going to wait until the Count came and sat where you are sitting for twenty minutes or so. Then a girl – well, I say a girl, but I know her – she came and said she wasn't going to wait for him any longer. He got in a bit of a temper, she stomped away down the corridor and he followed her. That's the last I saw of him."

"You say you know this girl?"

Cristina examined her varnished fingernails carefully for a moment then looked back at Merlin. "She's a waitress at a Polish restaurant in Kensington."

"You know her name?"

"Sophie Radzinski. She's from Gdansk like me. Poor Sophie. I presume she was sweet on this flyer. Does she know he's dead?"

"Probably not. I don't know about you, Sergeant, but I'm getting a bit peckish. We might end up waiting for Tarkowski all day. I'm quite partial to Polish food these days. And you can wipe that knowing smirk off your face right now. Let's go and get a spot of lunch at this place. Where exactly is it, Miss Wajda?"

★ ★ ★

A small terrier was greedily eating some pork scratchings the pub landlady had tipped into a bowl by the door as the two men made their entrance. A few workmen stood by the bar, but otherwise the place was empty.

"We shouldn't really be doing this, should we, Mr Stewart?"

"A spot of spirits in the blood won't go amiss, my friend."

Jack Stewart had dragged Evans out of the AFS station for a quick drink in The Surprise. "Go on, get that down your neck."

Evans had asked for a rum and black and continued to sip it carefully as Stewart knocked back his pint of beer and scotch chaser. Stewart had bought a plate of cheese and onion sandwiches as well and Evans, not having eaten anything since his unfortunate encounter in the park the day before, tucked in heartily.

"Let other poets raise a fracas
Bout vines, an' wines, an' drucken Bacchus,
An' crabbit names an' stories wrack us,
An' grate our lug:
I sing the juice Scotch bear can mak us,
In glass or jug."

Evans smiled at Stewart in confusion.

"Burns on scotch, Mr Evans. A very fine poet and a very fine drink. As paintings are to you, so poetry, albeit in a more modest sense, is to me. My policeman friend Frank Merlin and I like to have a gentlemanly poetry competition over a drink from time to time. We aim to produce a poetry quotation the other can't identify. I'm afraid to say that he wins more often than I do."

"An admirable pastime, if I may say so." Evans dithered over the last sandwich.

"Go on, man. Help yourself. This Blitz business makes a man hungry and thirsty. I think I'll get another plate."

"Fine, sir. When you get back, I just wanted to ask about something that's worrying me."

Stewart disappeared to the bar, returning with another

226

round of drinks. "Sandwiches will be a couple of minutes. Fire away then. I hope you're not going to quiz me about my knowledge of JMW Turner. I'm afraid I haven't had the time to look at your book yet."

"No, nothing like that. It's just some valuation work I've been asked to do. There appears to be something fishy…"

Just then, an attractive young woman in a Wren's uniform entered the pub with a couple of girlfriends in civvies. She immediately spotted Stewart, strode over and banged her handbag on the table. "There you are, Jackie boy, trying to avoid me, are you?" She stamped her feet rather theatrically, dislodging a few locks of frizzy blonde hair from beneath her hat.

Stewart sat back and grinned. "Hell, no, Brenda. Why would I want to avoid you? Don't you know there's a war on? I've been putting out fires all over London for days. Come and sit down here. Let me remove that pout from your pretty little face." He pulled Brenda towards him and kissed her on the lips. She pushed him away, but with a broad grin. "Oh, you sweet-talker."

"What'll it be then, Bren? Gin and It? My friend Mr Evans and I can't stay long, but we'll have the one with you, as long as you behave."

Evans stood up as the second round of sandwiches arrived. The landlord's terrier sidled up to him, scratchings finished, assessing his potential as a source of food. "Let me, Mr Stewart. It's my shout." Thanks to Trubetskoi's money, at least he could buy his round these days.

Stewart reached over and pulled Evans back into his seat. "No, no. My girl, my shout. I'll do it. But what was it you wanted to ask?"

"Oh, forget it. Another time perhaps. I think I'll be getting back to the station. Wouldn't want to be a gooseberry."

"Don't be silly. I'm not going to be long myself. Just need to put the girl in a holding pattern." Stewart chuckled and slapped Evans on the back.

227

"No, no, sir. I'll get back to the station. See you there." As he pushed through the door, he could hear the Wren giggling. "Come on, Jackie boy. Get on with it. A girl could die of thirst here."

★ ★ ★

The Polka restaurant was in a side street close to South Kensington Tube. It was not a big place and the walls were covered with a collection of garish abstract paintings, which made the place seem even smaller than it was. As they waited for attention, Merlin counted eight tables of which all but one were occupied. A young man with oily hair burst out of what was obviously the kitchen door, shouting loudly at someone behind him. He strode towards the policemen and brusquely waved an arm in the direction of the one empty table. As they sat down, he slammed two menus and a bowl of bread in front of them, then disappeared back into the kitchen. Strong garlicky meat smells wafted through the air. The other customers all appeared to be paying rapt attention to their food and only one or two looked up to check out the new arrivals.

The kitchen door banged open again to reveal a short, thin, dark-haired girl, who brought the policemen two glasses of water and enquired in a strong Polish accent whether they would like anything else to drink.

"No, thank you, miss. Are you Sophie Radzinski?"

The waitress flushed and squeezed her hands together anxiously. "Yes, that is my name."

"Do you mind if—?"

The oily-haired man appeared from nowhere and shouted something in Polish at the girl.

"I am sorry, sir. We are very busy. I do not have time to chat."

Bridges stood up and tapped the young man's shoulder and displayed his warrant card. "We need to ask a few questions of this young lady, sir."

"But we are busy, as you see. Cannot this—?"

"Why don't you do some serving yourself? We are going to ask Miss Radzinski here to sit down for a moment. Just hold your horses and we'll be as quick as we can."

The young man reddened and muttered something as he went back into the kitchen from where they heard the sound of clanging pots and pans.

"Thank you, Sergeant. Miss Radzinski, do you know a Polish pilot called Kilinski?"

A shadow passed over Sophie's face. Her very bright, red lipstick contrasted strikingly with the paleness of her face. Despite the make-up, she looked little more than a girl. "Something's happened to him, hasn't it?"

"I'm afraid it has."

"He is dead, yes? Shot down by those Nazi killers?"

"Dead, yes, but not in the air."

Sophie shook her head and looked off into the distance. Merlin expected tears and was conscious of how insensitively he had broached the news. "I am sorry if—"

The girl's eyes bored into him. They had no tears. "Save your apologies, policeman. Death is death. I have lived with death for some time. Another death of someone I loved. There have been so many."

"Had you known Mr Kilinski long?" Bridges grabbed a bread roll and nibbled at it awkwardly.

"A few months. He was a nice boy."

"Did you see much of him in the last week or so?"

Sophie sighed and looked out of the restaurant window. A fire engine drove noisily past. "Yes, he stayed with me for a week or so. He had some clothes there from earlier in the summer. Said he had leave because of some injury. He seemed alright to me. If I asked what the injury was, he said it was a, how do you say, psychological injury and laughed."

"Where do you live?" Merlin had copied Bridges and was picking at a roll.

"I have a small bedsit in Bermondsey. It is cramped but

cosy." Now, at last, a small tear appeared on the girl's cheek. "How did he die?"

"I'm sorry, but he was murdered."

With a sharp gulp of breath, Sophie closed her eyes. Then she slowly breathed out and looked at Merlin. "Glupi chlopak! That stupid boy. I told him to take care."

"Do you know what he was up to, Miss Radzinski?"

The oily-haired maitre d', or whatever he was, came up and glared at Merlin before delivering a dish to another table.

"I hope you are not going to lose me my job, Inspector?" Sophie brushed away a lock of hair.

"Don't worry, we'll have a word with your boss after."

"Better make it a scary word. He's a bastard. So, you want to know what I know about Simon?"

"You know his real name?"

"Yes, Simon Nozyk. He tells me after we know each other a little. Said he had to have another name for the air force. I didn't understand really. Simon told me a story about his brother. I don't know the whole story, but he had a clever brother. This brother fell in with some family of rich Poles for whom he did some kind of work. They didn't pay him much, but he was a Jew who had been in jail, so he was glad to get something with which to support his young family. That's what Simon said anyway. Simon was the younger brother and he appeared to have idol…" She struggled momentarily for the right English word "Idolised, yes, that is it – he idolised David. Then some time in 1938, I think it was, David didn't come home from work. Simon and his family never saw him again. They reported him missing to the authorities, but received little attention. He was a poor Jew, after all."

Merlin thought for a second of Sonia and her background. There was and had been anti-Semitism in England, but nothing like that in Poland and other Eastern European countries. "How can this have led to Simon's mission here in London?"

"David had never told Simon the name of the people he was working for, but Simon thought he might have found the house where they lived, as he had played truant one day and followed him into town. It was a big house in the main square of the Old City in Warsaw. After David's disappearance, he investigated some more and found out who the family were."

"Did he tell you who the family were?"

"No."

Merlin grabbed another bread roll. "Am I to think that Simon connected David's disappearance to these employers in some way?"

"His mission was to find the connection. He had some clues. David had given him a small, locked, black box. He told Simon he was doing some dangerous work. In case anything happened to him, he wanted Simon to have the box. He gave him the key, knowing how honest Simon was and how much he loved him. After David's disappearance, Simon, of course, opened the box. In it he found some gold pieces and a necklace of gold. Very beautiful. He showed me."

"And he was trying to connect these gold items to whatever happened to David?"

"He needed to know what happened to his brother, of course. He had those few clues and he felt he could find the answer here in London."

★ ★ ★

It was gone one by the time Count Tarkowski reached his office. "My meeting with Sikorski went on forever, Miss Wajda. Anything for me?"

"There were two policemen here to see you, sir, Chief Inspector Merlin and Sergeant Bridges."

"I see."

"They couldn't wait any longer, sir, and went for some lunch. Didn't say if they'd be back."

"Anything else?"

Miss Wajda toyed with the idea of mentioning Kilinski and his girlfriend, but decided that it would be best to keep well out of all that business. The Count was a good boss, but who knew what he was really up to. "Mr de Souza from the bank tried to get hold of you."

"Get him on the telephone, would you?"

"The last time he called he said he was going out and would be out for the rest of the day. Something about having a tooth out. To be honest, sir, he sounded as if he was already under the laughing gas."

"How do you mean?"

"He sounded a little drunk."

"That's not like him."

"Said he'd call back tomorrow morning."

The Count went into his office, sat at his desk and thought. He wasn't going to hang around for those policemen to return. Life seemed to be getting even more complicated. What should he do?

Pain shot up his spine as he stood up a little too abruptly. "I am going to get something to eat myself, Miss Wajda. I may or may not return today. Have you finished writing up that report I gave you, the one about the Gestapo's latest activities in Warsaw?"

Miss Wajda's face whitened. "I have just begun, sir. The material is, um…"

"Yes, I am sorry. It does not make very pleasant reading, does it? If you like, I can ask someone, perhaps Andrei upstairs, to do it?"

"No, no, sir. It is my job and I'll get it done by tonight. Is it true though? What they are doing?"

Tarkowski nodded sadly. "And worse, my dear. Much worse."

★ ★ ★

When they got back to the Yard, Merlin tried to get hold of Sir Bernard Spilsbury. He wanted to see whether the detailed autopsy report on Kilinski was ready yet. There was no reply on the numbers Merlin had. As he replaced the receiver, the A.C. came in. "I couldn't help hearing the name Spilsbury as I stood at the door, Frank. Why are you trying to get him?"

"He did the post-mortem on our Polish flyer, sir. There's no answer."

"I doubt you'll get one for a day or two. His son was killed in the bombing on Sunday night."

"Very sorry to hear that, sir. The poor man. Only son?"

"Yes, talented medic apparently." The A.C. turned away to look disapprovingly at one of the prints Merlin had hung, contrary to regulation, on his wall. "I think there may be a brother. Who is that ghastly chap up there?" This was not the first time the A.C. had asked this question.

"Dr Gachet, sir, by Van Gogh."

"Fellow chopped his ear off, didn't he? A madman. If you do have to break the rules by hanging pictures in this office, Frank, couldn't you put up something British – a nice Gainsborough perhaps?"

"I'll give it some thought, sir. Was there anything else? I've got rather a lot of—"

"Yes, yes. I'm sure you have." The A.C. rose stiffly to his feet. "I saw a Polish acquaintance of mine at the restaurant the other night. Fellow called Tarkowski. Wondered whether he might be able to assist you with your dead flyer case."

Merlin chuckled. "Oh yes, he can help us alright."

The A.C. looked bemused. "Should I have a word with him then?"

"No, sir. You can leave that to me."

★ ★ ★

A line of schoolboys in neat blue uniforms filed noisily beneath Voronov's study window. He turned to his desk and picked up the telephone. "Have you spoken to them yet?"

"No. They are meant to ring me some time this afternoon."

"Will they be on the job tonight?"

"That's what they were planning, Kyril."

"Hmm." Voronov leaned back in his chair and looked out of the window again. "If they call, we might be able to cancel their job and organise something for tonight. If they don't, we'll have to do it tomorrow, but no later. Is there no way you can contact them yourself, Misha?"

"No. The arrangement is that they call me. They are reliable about it."

A figure in a gabardine mac walked along the pavement opposite, not for the first time that day.

"Very well. Let me know when they do." Voronov slammed the phone down and poured himself a brandy from the crystal decanter he had liberated from a bombed house around the corner. He had been followed or watched many times in his life and he had developed a fine intuition for the techniques employed. The moment he had seen the fellow down below, the hairs on his neck had tingled and he knew. The second sighting of the man only confirmed an already established fact. Who was it this time? He should have told Misha to keep an eye out. One of the advantages of his house was that it had a cellar door, which opened onto a small alleyway to the rear of the house, which in turn led on to a mews and then to Eaton Square. He would have Misha investigate whether that exit was known to whoever had decided to keep tabs on what Kyril Voronov was doing.

★ ★ ★

Their reflections smiled back at them from the long mirror behind the bar of the Ritz.

"You are looking very beautiful tonight."

Sonia blushed and giggled. "Don't be silly, Frank. I am just in my work clothes."

"And very lovely work clothes they are." Merlin raised his beer glass and clinked it against Sonia's glass of champagne.

"I have never had champagne before, Frank. Are we celebrating something?"

"Being alive, my darling. Being alive." Before leaving the Yard, Merlin had found out from Johnson that Stewart's AFS team were covering Piccadilly that night and had arranged to meet him at the end of Savile Row at ten. Perhaps unwisely, he had wandered over to Swan and Edgar and found Sonia just as they were shutting up shop. The Ritz was only a short walk down Piccadilly and Sonia deserved a treat.

"The bubbles are going up my nose." Sonia giggled again.

"Don't worry, dear, you'll get used to it. All women do."

"Used to what, Frank?"

"Luxury. Champagne. Flowers. Breakfast in bed."

"Now you are talking. I'll have scrambled eggs on toast tomorrow morning, if you please."

Merlin finished his beer and ordered a glass of champagne for himself. "Haven't had one of these in a long time."

They clinked glasses again. Silent for a moment, they observed the other customers of the Ritz bar. A group of naval officers in one corner seemed to be laughing non-stop. From the insignia he could see on their jackets, Merlin thought they might be submariners. He shuddered. That was one thing he wouldn't be able to do – live in a metal tube at the bottom of the ocean for days at a time; bad enough in itself without the worry of being bombed or mined by the opposition. In another corner, two elderly ladies in fur stoles and an abundance of jewellery seemed to be enjoying the stiff Martinis on offer in the establishment.

"Did she like champagne, Frank?"

"Who?"

"Did Alice like champagne?"

Merlin had never really discussed his late wife with Sonia. He had never felt comfortable talking about Alice to anyone. Yet now, all of a sudden, he didn't mind, not with Sonia, at any rate. "She did indeed. Pol Roger was her favourite. Someone told me that's Mr Churchill's favourite tipple too."

"Was she from a, how do you say it, a good background?"

"Her parents were very comfortable. Lived, or rather, live,

as her mother is still alive, in a big pile near Guildford. Her father was a very well-known lawyer. A judge, in fact. Yes, quite an eminent family."

Sonia's face clouded. "Not like me then. A poor Polish nobody."

Merlin placed his hand on hers. "Don't be silly. I don't care about your background. I didn't care about hers and neither did she. She was very down to earth. Had to be, didn't she, to marry a lowly, clodhopping copper like myself?"

"What does clodhopping mean, Frank?"

"Hmm… never mind."

Sonia laughed and kissed his cheek. In the distance they could hear the roar of engines. The siren had blown a while ago, but they had been determined not to let Hitler ruin their brief hour or so of pleasure.

"Another one for you, my darling Sonia? Before the place goes up in smoke?"

"Alright then, what is the phrase you use, Frank? If you twist my arm."

★ ★ ★

After bundling a complaining Sonia into a taxi, Merlin crossed the road and went up Bond Street, heading for his rendezvous with Johnson and Stewart. He turned right into Burlington Gardens and eventually found Stewart and Cole halfway down Savile Row. Cole was pointing his torch into one of the posh tailor shops that lined the street. The tailors' dummies seemed strangely sinister to Merlin and he shivered. "Where's Jack Stewart, Inspector?"

Johnson nodded down the street where Merlin could see firemen, illuminated by the towering flames, training their hoses on a burning building. "Stewart's down there with his men. The place took a hit about an hour ago."

Merlin could just make out Stewart standing beside one of the hoses supervising the operation. Even at his seventy or so yards' distance, Merlin could feel the heat generated by the fire.

"Cole and I were just doing some exploring." A crackle of gunfire sounded in the distance.

"Very good, Peter. Let's carry on up here. This should be prime looting territory. All these fancy shops, galleries and so on and the Royal Arcade just round the corner." The policemen wandered up towards the top end of the street. The blackout was well observed in this hub of British tailoring and they came across nothing unusual. There had been no aircraft noise for a while, but, when they reached the corner, they could again hear the whirr and buzz of the Luftwaffe coming in for second helpings.

Johnson looked up. "Here they come again."

Merlin stopped by the entrance to the Albany. "As the Inspector knows, Constable, the flats here in the Albany, or sets as they are called, are amongst the most exclusive in London. Waiting list as long as your arm. Aristocrats, politicians, writers – plenty of famous ones here. Byron, Gladstone, Macaulay, amongst others."

"Any film stars, sir?"

"Yes, Cole. Someone told me that Leslie Howard had one of…" Merlin paused and looked up. "Hear that?"

An eerie whistling sound directly above heralded the imminent arrival of a bomb. Merlin turned and pushed Johnson and the young constable in the direction of Bond Street. "Run! For Christ's sake, run!"

★ ★ ★

Tarkowski could hear explosions in the distance and there was a misty glow in the sky at the end of his street. The telephone rang and he turned away from the study window and returned to his desk. The room was lit only by the small lamp on a table behind him. He hurriedly swallowed a couple of painkillers with a glass of water, then picked up the receiver.

"I am so glad you phoned. Are you alright? Good. Look, I need your help. I want to move the rest of the gold. It's best all round, I think, to get it into the safety of the bank." A flash of light outside briefly illuminated the room. "Do you think you can get away tomorrow? With luck, yes? Let's hope then. I need to speak to the bank, but I am trying to get transport organised for the afternoon. There are a few good men at the legation who I trust. If you could bring another reliable body that would be good. Trouble? It's possible. Anyway, call me in the morning to confirm."

Tarkowski put the phone down and closed his eyes. There was a noise at the door and his wife entered. She was wearing an old dressing gown and her face was plastered with beauty cream, but she was still the most beautiful woman alive to him.

"You are moving it tomorrow then?"

Tarkowski nodded.

"And he's coming to help."

Tarkowski nodded again.

"May God be with us."

★ ★ ★

The bomb landed at the north end of Burlington Arcade. Stewart, Evans and three other firemen were swiftly on the scene, having left the rest of the team dowsing the burning embers of the bombed building on Savile Row. The explosion had set off several of the alarms in the Arcade. Jack Stewart arrived with a couple of his men. Stewart wiped some grime from his face. "Not as bad as I first thought, Evans." Gentle flames were licking away at the roof of a building next to the Arcade and fallen masonry almost blocked its entrance. Stewart climbed over the rubble and tentatively edged into the Arcade. Glass was everywhere. In one shop to their right, the antique watches on display were splattered with debris. There was some movement behind him. "Hey. Who's that? Frank, is that you? Are you alright?"

Merlin rose awkwardly to his feet, coughing dust. He was

covered in plaster and glass, as were his two colleagues. "Just about, Jack. Are you alive, you two?"

Johnson and Cole grunted in the affirmative.

Stewart shone his torch into the Arcade. "Looks like nearly all the shops have had their windows blown out. There's a lot of valuable stuff here. I think…" Another bomb exploded not so far away and the men were rocked on their feet. "Christ, that was close. The noble Lord Tennyson comes to mind, eh, Frank? 'Into the Valley of Death…'"

"Yes, Jack, but we are not quite six hundred."

"Fair point, my friend. I reckon we should stay put here for a moment. Now where's Evans gone?"

Merlin pointed. "Someone's just gone down to the other end of the Arcade. Is that him?"

Stewart shouted Evans' name with no response save the echo of his own voice from the Arcade walls. A moment later, the Arcade walls echoed again, this time with the sound of running footsteps and an out of breath Evans appeared.

"What the hell, Evans? Looks like you've seen a ghost." Stewart reached out and helped Evans over the large concrete slab that had partially blocked the Arcade entrance.

As Evans had reached the far end of the Arcade, he had seen a couple of men clearing out one of the jewellery shops. What Stewart had taken to be terror in Evans' face was in fact a mixture of fear and indecision. In the light of their torches, Evans had recognised his new associates, Jake and Billy. Should he… tell? He decided that he had no option. "Looters. A couple of them down there. In one of the jewellery shops."

Merlin patted Johnson's shoulder. "Come on." Merlin led the way, Johnson and Cole behind, carefully edging down the gallery behind the light of his torch. He presumed that the thieves ahead had heard Evans' running footfall and would be prepared for something. When they were about twenty yards from the Piccadilly end of the Arcade, his torch caught a glint of eyes. Cole hurried past him and the looters shouted something to each other. A shot rang out.

The gunfire glare blinded Merlin for a moment. He heard Johnson shout. "Tommy, are you alright?" As his vision cleared, Merlin saw that Cole had crumpled to the ground against a shop window. He was breathing heavily and as Merlin and Johnson turned their torches on him they saw a pool of blood seeping onto the floor to his left.

Merlin caught his breath. "The bastards." Another shot rang out and the bullet hurtled just between Merlin and Johnson into the already cracked window of the shop. Then they heard the sound of racing feet. Johnson was torn for a moment between concern for the condition of his colleague and the need to chase the looters, but Merlin flew off at once. "Come on, Peter!" The men had at least twenty yards on them. As Merlin ran through the gallery exit into Piccadilly, he felt the heat of another bullet whizzing past his head. He withdrew into the cover of the Arcade and by the time he looked out again, the thieves had disappeared into the safety of the blackout. He felt for Johnson's arm. "Bugger it!"

From off towards Picadilly Circus, they could hear the whistle of another bomb descending and they turned and hurried back down the Arcade to Cole. Johnson flashed his torch and sighed with relief when he saw that he was conscious. "I think he's going to be alright, sir." Cole gasped for air. "It's my shoulder. Hurts like buggery, but I'm not a goner yet."

Merlin felt his own shoulder ache for a second or two in sympathy. "What on earth were you thinking, charging off like that, eh? You don't need to prove your courage to me, you know, Tommy. Anyway, can you walk? We need to get you out of here." Cole got awkwardly to his feet with his colleagues' help. As they struggled slowly back down the gallery, a thunderous roar indicated another bomb strike somewhere nearby and when the three men finally clambered over the rubble at the top end of the Arcade, yet another explosion sounded from somewhere in the direction of Regent Street.

"Christ, it's coming down everywhere." Johnson's torch lit

upon Evans' face. He and Stewart were talking to an ARP warden a few yards from the entrance.

"Any medics to hand? I have an injured officer here."

"What happened down there?" Stewart hurried over with Evans and the warden and helped Cole to sit down on a collapsed wall opposite the Arcade.

Merlin wiped his forehead. "The chaps you spotted, Mr Evans, had a shooter. Cole took a bullet in the shoulder. I think he'll be fine, but he needs urgent attention. The looters unfortunately got away."

"I saw an ambulance just now turning into Savile Row." The warden had an Irish accent. "I've got a first aid box with me though. Perhaps…?"

Evans shook his head. "I'll go and get the ambulance. You see what you can do." He ran off towards Gieves & Hawkes' shop at the end of Savile Row his face now displaying a grim determination. As he turned into the road, a nearby building took a direct hit, but he kept running through the smoke and falling debris. Behind him, Cole told Merlin and Johnson he felt good enough to walk to the ambulance himself with some assistance and they followed, while Stewart ran off to find the rest of his men. As the policemen and the warden turned into Savile Row, they saw the ambulance approaching them through the flames and smoke. Johnson flagged it down.

"Can we have a bit of help here?" Cole was helped into the back of the van, which also housed what appeared to be an injured lady of the night. "Alright, ducks? Cuddle up close, why don't you?"

Johnson tried to follow Cole in, but the orderly pushed him back. "No room here, mate. We'll be taking your friend here to the Westminster. Come and find him there."

Merlin flashed his warrant card and glared at the ambulance man.

"Alright, pal. If you insist."

"See you later, Peter. I'll look after Cole, don't worry. And see what happened to Evans."

The Lubianka had finally broken him. It wasn't one thing that had done it, but the accumulation of things. The beating, the lack of sleep, the cold, the endlessly repeated questions, the simulated executions, the stink of the cell and of his disgusting cell-mate. Finally, something had broken in Karol and the words had come gushing out – all that he knew about the leaders of the Polish government in exile, about his erstwhile military comrades, about the Polish Secret Service such as it now was and about the money and the gold. He did not know what time it was when he had given up the ghost. He did not know what time it was now. Hours later, a day?

He glanced over at Andrei, who was muttering unintelligibly while waving his hand at the wall. For once, it suddenly dawned on Karol, Andrei's actions appeared to have an element of purpose. He seemed to be pointing at something. Karol rose from the stinking floor.

"What is it, Andrei? What are you trying to tell me?" Andrei's gibbering rose in intensity. Karol bent down to examine the brickwork which Andrei seemed to be focusing on. Then he saw it. A faint glimmer in the gloom of the cell. There was a slight gap between two of the bricks and he reached into it and withdrew the sliver of broken knife, which Andrei must have secreted there. He patted his cellmate's hand. "Thank you, my friend."

Andrei withdrew to the other side of the cell, a trace of a smile appearing on his slack mouth. Bracing himself, Karol stood up, said a brief prayer, turned up the palm of his right hand and opened the veins of his wrist.

CHAPTER 16

Tuesday, September 17

One of the mechanics had given them a lift to South Ruislip and Northolt Junction and now their train clattered merrily along the rails through the suburban metroland of west London.

Kubicki extracted a cigarette from the packet Kowalski waved in front of him. "Thanks. What exactly is it we are going to do in London, Jerzy?"

"After a very nice lunch in the West End, we are going to help some friends move some boxes."

"Can't they get some labourers to help? I don't see why—"

"Look, I don't think we'll need to actually use our hands, Miro. It's just that my friend wants a little security, in case anything goes wrong."

Miro lit his cigarette. "I don't understand why you are being so secretive. What the hell is in these boxes? Must be something of value obviously. Why won't you tell me?"

Kowalski looked out into the tiny gardens of the two-up two-downs running along the railside. He might as well tell him, he thought. When they were at his cousin's place, it would probably become clear enough anyway. "You are an inquisitive soul, Miro, aren't you? Always pestering me with questions. Very well, it is gold bullion. From the home country. It was stored in a building that was bombed and moved to a private house. Now it's thought safer that it goes to the bank. Is that clear enough for you? We are going to my friend's house to keep an eye out, just in case anything goes wrong."

Miro blew a smoke circle towards the ceiling of the compartment, of which they were the sole occupants. "Gold, eh?" He licked his thick lips.

★ ★ ★

The rain was pattering rhythmically on the window panes of Merlin's office as Johnson entered. Merlin was trying as ever to sort out the newly accumulated clutter on his desk. After a moment, he stopped, seemingly satisfied, though to Johnson's eye it still looked a mess.

"How's Cole doing, sir?"

"He'll be alright. It's only a flesh wound. Then again the doctors said mine was a flesh wound, but it's still giving me gyp."

"Sorry to hear that, sir." Johnson took a seat. "I've got some interesting information." He paused to rub his eyes, which were still red and stinging from the previous night's fire and smoke. "That chap Evans."

"Oh, yes? I meant to ask. What happened to him?"

"When he ran to get the ambulance for Cole he got hit by some falling masonry. After you went off with Cole, Stewart found him."

"Is he dead?"

"No, he was lucky. Just a concussion and a broken bone or two. He's in the hospital now. The point is that when Stewart found him and he had come round, he was a bit fevered and was going on about relieving his conscience. Said he knew who the looters were. Names of Jake and Billy."

"How on earth…?"

"Apparently, Evans had been asked to value some paintings and other valuables. He's some kind of art expert by training. A Russian friend of a friend had recruited him. He now realises that these items must have been looted by these fellows Jake and Billy who were in the Russian's employ."

"And you got all of this from Jack?"

"Yes, sir."

"Did he have a name for the Russian?"

"Trubetskoi. What is more, when Evans became suspicious,

he followed him home one time to a property near Eaton Square. He managed to give Stewart the address."

Bridges appeared at the door. "Ah, Sergeant, just the man. Anything back from Five yet on that Russian?"

"No, sir. They've been their usual unhelpful selves. Said they'd get back to us, but haven't. It may not matter anyway."

"How so?"

"Robinson managed to dig up Voronov's address through someone she knows at the Home Office. He's a registered alien. Has a big house off Eaton Square. I have the address."

"Where is Robinson?"

"I let her go and see Cole at the hospital on condition she gets back within the hour."

"Alright. Well, the Inspector has another address off Eaton Square. I wonder if they match?"

★ ★ ★

"Honest, guv. You're going to have to pay up a large amount of dosh, if you want help with this. Everything is getting far too close to the knuckle, ain't it, Billy? Look, see how his hands are shaking – not one for nerves normally, are you, Billy?"

Billy wiped some of the smudged smoke burns from his face with his sleeve. "We were far too close to the action yesterday, Jakie boy. I said we should lay off the main target areas as usual, but you wouldn't listen." Billy sighed. "Anyway, Jakie's right, Mr Trubetskoi. We almost copped it last night. And remember, it's a capital offence now. If we're caught, we are for the drop. Pay up, as Jakie says. The odds are shortening against us and you're not going to get us for pennies."

"What is this pay up you are talking about, gentlemen?" The three men were in the Shepherd's Bush lock-up where the two looters had hurried, empty-handed, scared and furious, from Piccadilly. A few hours' uncomfortable sleep had been grabbed on beds fashioned from torn cardboard boxes and rags. Both men were in a foul mood and Trubetskoi realised that he did not have much bargaining power. "A hundred quid for the job. Is that good enough?"

Jake laughed sarcastically. "Hundred quid each, mate. And fifty quid each bonus for successful completion."

Trubetskoi pursed his lips. "Very well."

"And what's in these boxes we are after anyway? If we manage to nick them and they are so valuable, we should have a taste of whatever it is, eh, Billy?"

Trubetskoi had already realised that if he and Voronov were successful in obtaining Tarkowski's gold, they would certainly have no further need for this looting sideline and no further use for Billy and Jake. Whatever he agreed to, a bullet each in the head would be their ultimate reward.

"Whatever you say, gentlemen. You may have a good taste, as you say. Now, may I outline the programme for you?"

★ ★ ★

Eugene de Souza's head was throbbing. He had vowed to himself several times since waking that he was never going to drink again. Madame de Souza had given him a terrible going over at breakfast and thoughts of murder had jostled with those of remorse all morning. That little necklace would have given him a nice big bonus too. With the proceeds he'd have found the financial demands of Pearl at the Windmill a little easier to accommodate. Although he had sat at his desk as usual from nine until one shuffling papers, no meaningful work had been done. It was now lunchtime and he thought a little fresh air might help. He shuffled to his office door, which was slightly ajar, and reached up to the coat stand for his British Warm. Although it was mild outside, the hangover was giving him the shivers.

As he slowly put the coat on, he could hear Wertheim's voice whispering on the phone outside. Now at last prepared for the elements, de Souza stood still as he felt a surge of bile suddenly rise to his throat. He remained still for a short while to ensure that he did not have an unfortunate accident. As he waited, the sense of the words Wertheim was speaking penetrated his brain.

"Yes, they are moving the goods here sometime today, Mr Voronov. What? Sorry, sir. I won't mention your name again, but there's nothing to worry about. He's locked in his office with a massive hangover, oblivious to everything. We've been told to be ready to receive the goods some time between five and seven tonight and I've agreed to stay in to facilitate the deposit. If you are going to act, you had better get on with it. Yes, sorry, but I have made myself clear, no? And you remember our arrangement, funds to be... Yes? Very well. Good luck, sir." The phone was replaced on its receiver.

Despite the great loss of brain cells he had suffered over the past twenty-four hours, de Souza understood fully what he had just heard. He had had his suspicions for a while about Wertheim and these had finally proved justified. Placing his homburg on his head, he walked through the door. He would deal with the clerk tomorrow, but first things first. "Off to lunch, Wertheim. Back in an hour."

The clerk bowed obsequiously. In the street, de Souza turned right and walked towards the public phone box on Lombard Street. He pulled out his small pocket notebook and found the Count's number.

★ ★ ★

The man in the gabardine mac was nowhere to be seen as Voronov paced in front of the windows of his study. The telephone rang. "Thank God. Where have you been? Never mind. Have you got the men organised? Good. Wertheim tells me they are shifting the gold to the bank this evening. We have to be there this afternoon. I suggest you get over to the house now with the men and get the lie of the land. Keep out of sight." He glanced over at the old Russian clock on the sideboard. "It's 2.30 now. You should be there in an hour at the latest. I am going to join you. You have a map, of course. There is a road leading away from Tarkowski's to the right as you look from his house. It's called Snowdon Drive. I'll meet you there. Well out of sight of the house, of course. Don't do anything until I get there!"

He looked out of the window one more time. No one. Perhaps he had been imagining things yesterday. Like most Russians, he lived in a natural state of paranoia, but maybe this time he was wrong.

Voronov put the telephone down and reached into the bottom drawer of his desk. He had two handguns – a Smith and Wesson .357 Magnum, which the man he had bought it from had told him was the most powerful handgun in the world; and the trusty Tokarev TT, which Maksim had cleaned for him the other day and which might not be the most powerful handgun in the world but had done him good service over many years. In the drawer there was also a canvas bag into which he put the guns and plenty of ammunition. The study door was open and he shouted through it. "Maksim. Get your skinny arse up here. We are going out."

Maksim appeared out of breath. "Where are we going?"

"Take this bag and get the car. Pull it around to the back entrance. I should put a coat on, if I were you. A thick one. I am going to put a little excitement into your dreary life!"

★ ★ ★

Count Tarkowski was sitting at his desk thinking about what de Souza had just told him. It was no surprise, of course. Thank God he had called Jerzy. The front door bell rang and he hurried out of his study to answer it.

"Come on in Jerzy. And who is this you have got with you?" Jerzy made the introduction. "Ah, Miro Kubicki? We met once in Warsaw before the war, I think. Welcome, welcome to my house."

The Count and his guests exchanged pleasantries in the hallway of his house as several workmen manouevred around them moving what appeared to be very heavy wooden crates. Tarkowski was clearly very nervous and sweat was trickling down his forehead and cheeks into his wing-collar.

"What is the plan, exactly, Adam? How much is to be moved and how?"

The Count inclined his head towards a door on their right and the two pilots followed Tarkowski into his study. When they were seated, Tarkowski opened the bottle of vodka that was on his desk with some glasses. He poured out three full measures and pushed two glasses towards the men now sitting opposite him, raising his own glass in a toast. "To Poland, gentlemen!" They tossed back the drinks and Tarkowski poured refills.

"Adam, before you get us drunk, which I doubt is the wisest thing to do, can you tell us what is happening? I have told Miro what the cargo is, and I have told him of its vital importance to Poland, so you can speak freely."

The Count shot a concerned look at Kowalski for a moment as if questioning his indiscretion then relaxed. "A very large truck will arrive here at between 3.30 and 4.30. Originally, I had arranged the transfer to take place under cover of darkness, but I have information suggesting that it might be more prudent to accelerate the process. The men you see are extremely reliable men employed by the Polish embassy. Patriots all who know the value of the cargo to their country. When the lorry arrives, all the sixty or so boxes will be assembled in the hallway and front reception room. The boxes will be moved onto the truck and down to the Polish Commonwealth Bank branch in the City where my banker has arranged for them to be deposited in the safety of the bank's vault where the remainder of the gold is already held. It is all quite straightforward, but, as I told you, Jerzy, I felt it might be useful for you and a friend to be here, just in case."

Kubicki had tired of looking at his second vodka and drank it, replacing the glass on the desk with a bang. "Forgive me, Count, but what do you mean by 'just in case'? And what exactly is 'information suggesting that it might be more prudent to accelerate the process'?"

The Count looked down at his feet for a moment, then winced as he felt a spasm of back pain. "Well, bluntly, it means that there are people who are interested in taking the gold off our hands."

Kubicki used a finger to remove some of the tough beef they had had for lunch from between his teeth, then waggled it at the Count. "What sort of people?"

"Russians, Miro. Ruthless people."

"Shit, Jerzy, what the hell have you got me into?"

★ ★ ★

"Christ! Of all the times to call a review meeting." Merlin had just emerged from a two-hour meeting of senior officers convened at short notice by the A.C., the main purpose of which had been for the A.C. to let off steam about the harassment he had been receiving from the Metropolitan Commissioner and the Home Secretary about a variety of subjects. Gatehouse had taken it out on everyone, but had had a particular go at Merlin about the looting.

"Robinson's back, sir."

"Get her, Sergeant."

Robinson appeared, a little paler in the face than usual.

"How is he then?"

"He seems to be doing alright, sir."

"Good. Did the sergeant tell you about the address we got from Johnson, the one this fellow Evans gave us for the Russian Trubetskoi?"

"Yes, sir. And it matches the one I got for Voronov."

Merlin looked up and stared hard at his print of Dr Gachet. "What are we to make of this? This Voronov fellow is popping up everywhere. Lunch with Kilinski. In cahoots with looters. What do you think, Sergeant?"

"I wonder if he has any links with Tarkowski?"

"I wouldn't be surprised. I think before we see Voronov, we should ask Tarkowski about him. And we have other things to ask the Count. Let's get going. We'll try him at home again."

★ ★ ★

It was by pure chance that Grishin had decided to pay a visit to Platonov on this particular afternoon. His driver had the day off so he drove himself. He enjoyed driving in London. At least there was the challenge of some traffic to negotiate unlike in Moscow, where government vehicles had the central streets largely to themselves. He pulled up a block away from the target house and stiffly extracted himself from the car. He lit up a small cigar and sauntered down the pavement, past a crowd of workmen clearing the debris of a bombed terrace house, keeping an eye out for his man. After looking around unsuccessfully for ten minutes and mentally commending Platonov for his professional invisibility, he heard the word "Comrade" and Platonov emerged wearing his gabardine mac from behind a large refuse bin in the mews across the road from the back of Voronov's house.

"Ah, dobryj dyen, Sergei. There you are. Well done! I doubt they'd spot you there. Anything doing?"

"Yes, sir. His servant just went to get a car from a garage around the corner. He's parked over there behind that van. At the end of that alleyway opposite is a back entrance to Voronov's house. He's been using it a bit."

Grishin chewed on the end of his cigar. "Does that mean he spotted you?"

"I don't think so, sir. A man like him – I should think he has plenty of enemies to avoid at the front door. Anyway, it's not as if this back door is some sort of a secret passage – if he thinks it can't be found, he's deluded."

"Huh! Deluded I suppose is one of many choice words we

could use about Kyril Ivanovitch Voronov."

Sergei Platonov was a cadaverously thin man, with a disproportionately large head that looked as if it might topple off his neck at any time. As his shoulders heaved with laughter at Grishin's words, this possibility seemed ever more likely.

"I suppose it might be interesting to see where Voronov is going. I have my car down the street. Shall we—"

"If you follow me back down here sir, we can double back round to your car without Voronov's driver seeing us."

"Very well, Sergei. Let's be quick. Here he comes. You are armed?"

Platonov opened his coat a little to display a revolver jammed in his trouser waist. "And I have a spare strapped to my back."

★ ★ ★

The Count and the pilots had moved back into the hallway, which, together with all the ground floor rooms, was now completely filled with large crates.

"Have you got any weapons, Count?"

"Nothing apart from my old service weapon."

Kubicki cast a concerned look at Kowalski. One of the workmen came over to Tarkowski and told him that everything had now been brought up from the cellar and that the transport should be arriving any minute.

Kubicki's concern had changed to irritation. "But excuse me, Count. You say these Russians are ruthless people. Do you not think they will arm themselves? It would have been better, Jerzy, if you had thought this through and we could have brought something with us."

Kowalski shrugged. "I wasn't aware that these Russians posed such an immediate threat, Miro. Anyway, the transport will be here in a minute. It is broad daylight and we are almost in the centre of London. You are worrying unnecessarily." At that moment, they heard the sound of an engine and creaking brakes. The Count opened the front door and looked out anxiously. "The lorry is here. Come on, let's get everything aboard."

★ ★ ★

"Kyril, over here!" Trubetskoi waved Voronov's car down by a postbox in the middle of Snowdon Drive.

Voronov wound down his window and beamed at his partner. "I have come. All is well! And I assume these two fine gentlemen are the colleagues of whom I have heard so much."

Billy and Jake stepped out from the cover of some bushes and touched their hats in acknowledgement.

"There really was no need for you to come, Kyril. We can handle it."

Voronov opened the car door and hauled himself out onto the pavement. "No, Misha. It is a case of 'all hands to the deck', as the English say. And Maksim here was yearning for some adventure."

Maksim, who remained in the driver's seat, turned and offered a weak smile.

"What is happening?"

"A couple of handy-looking RAF pilots arrived at the house a while ago. Poles I should think. Seems like Tarkowski must have taken pains to have some extra security. He must know something is up. This is not going to be, as they say here, a piece of cake, Kyril. There are also plenty of men loading boxes onto the truck, which arrived a moment ago."

"The gold?"

"What else?"

"And you all have your guns?"

"Of course, Kyril, what do you take me for?"

Trubetskoi guided Voronov to a gap in the bushes at the end of the road from where they could get a good view of the loading operation in process. "Ah, there, I see that Polish bastard." Voronov sighed. "And is that the lovely Countess I

253

can see? Yes, such a fragrant beauty. Will I taste of it again? Probably not after today."

"What was that, Kyril?"

"Nothing, Misha. Nothing. And where are these RAF men you mentioned? Ah, there they are. Fine strapping men, no doubt, but no match for us, I think." Voronov slapped the shoulders of their two cockney accomplices. "Now, let us all get in my car. There is room for all. We shall go over the plan one more time. Where is the vehicle you stole earlier and came in? Ah, yes, over there, good."

★ ★ ★

The Countess appeared and walked towards her husband and the two pilots who were talking on the pavement in front of their house. She embraced Kowalski and kissed him on the cheek, shook Kubicki's hand then turned to her husband. "My darling, why don't you take this? It might come in useful."

The Countess produced a small Colt revolver from her handbag. The Count made a sign to indicate that her offer was unnecessary, but Kubicki grasped his arm. "Take it, Count. I'll have it and Jerzy can have your service pistol. I know you said it was old, but we might as well. I dare say we have had more practice with firearms than you recently. Any more ammunition?"

The Count smiled wanly at his wife. "My darling. Could you get the bullets from my drawer in the bureau?"

Twenty minutes later, the loading of the gold was complete. The afternoon light softened as the sun moved behind some clouds. The Count looked up and down the apparently empty street. "I can't see anything untoward, can you, gentlemen?"

Nothing disturbed the peace of the Hampstead afternoon save for the gentle chugging of the lorry engine, which the driver had just restarted. The three Poles got into the cab alongside the driver, a heavyset man with a sour face. It was a tight fit. The gears were engaged and the vehicle moved off and turned down Snowdon Drive, heading for the Finchley Road.

In his car, Voronov sat up. "Here comes the lorry, Maksim. Trubetskoi and the two Englishmen will be following it in their Austin and you follow them. There, they are turning right."

Voronov was stating the obvious, but Maksim did as he was told. As he turned the Packard saloon into another leafy suburban street, there was a heavy revving engine sound and then fifty yards ahead they saw the Austin driven by Jake accelerate past Tarkowski's truck and pull in front of it. With a screech of brakes, the lorry came to a halt, its cargo shifting noisily on its flat-bed but remaining in position. A mixture of Russian and English curses filled the air as Misha Trubetskoi and Billy jumped out of the Austin and ran up to level their guns at the driver's cabin.

Voronov put a hand on his servant's arm. "Stop here, Maksim. Let's keep our distance."

The abrupt halt had thrown the lorry driver, the Count and the two Polish officers hard against the windscreen. The Count was at the open passenger side window, looking dazed and Trubetskoi hurried to place his revolver against the Count's forehead.

"You know why we are here, my Polish friend. I have many men with me. Slowly does it. Get out with your hands up and you..." He addressed himself to Kowalski, who was sitting next to the Count. "No funny business or the Count will be joining his ancestors." As Billy covered the driver and Kubicki on the other side of the cab, Trubetskoi grasped the door handle and pulled.

★ ★ ★

The Countess sat in her bedroom, trembling. She did not have a good feeling about things. On the dressing table was a picture of her beautiful boy Karol, sharing a beer with some friends on their old country estate outside Warsaw. She remembered the day the photograph had been taken. There had been a game of tennis in which Karol had excelled, as always. Tennis, riding, shooting, swimming – Karol had been wonderfully good at all these things. A handsome, well-built, young man. Now what sort of shape was he in, assuming he was in any shape at all?

Reaching into one of the dressing table drawers she pulled out one of the ingots. She had kept one back as a memento. It was probably not wise, but… The artistry that had produced the ingots was wonderful. To have such a talent must be a joy. But then, to die with such a talent not properly fulfilled – that was truly tragic. Her beloved Karol had so many talents to fulfil, not just sporting ones but more important ones. In the right world Karol would be a prime minister, a general, a… The Countess's train of thought was interrupted by a strange noise. She hadn't heard it for a while, but recalled the familiar sound from the time when they were escaping from Poland. It was the sound of small arms gunfire.

★ ★ ★

The Count stepped carefully down from the cab, still covered by the revolver in Trubetskoi's hand. Before following him, Kowalski touched Kubicki's arm and whispered in Polish, "Let's be careful, Miro. We don't know how many men we are dealing with."

When the four men were all out of the cab and gathered in front of the lorry, the Count still with a gun at his head, Trubetskoi made a dismissive gesture with his free hand and shouted "clear off" to the driver, who was cowering in terror beside Kubicki. The man needed no second bidding and ran as fast as his fat legs would carry him until he was around the corner and out of sight. Jake got out from behind the wheel of the Austin and joined Trubetskoi and Billy.

Tarkowski looked with disdain at Trubetskoi as he used

his free hand to pat the Count down for weapons. Then the Russian pointed at Kowalski and Kubicki. "Your weapons. Hand them over. Now!" Kowalski hesitated then handed over his gun without resistance. But as Trubetskoi took the pistol, a thin smile of triumph playing on his lips, Kubicki suddenly pulled his revolver from his waistband and raised the muzzle to Trubetskoi's forehead. "You are not having my gun, you fucker." As he watched the confidence drain from Trubetskoi's face, he smiled and pulled the trigger. Trubetskoi stood for a moment, mouth agape and the black hole in the middle of his forehead opening like a third eye, before he slumped to the ground. As he fell, a spasm in his hand caused his finger to pull the trigger of the gun he was holding to the Count's head and the Count gave a strangulated cry as he too fell to the ground. The two lifeless bodies came to rest only inches from each other, their leaking heads combining to produce a single viscous and expanding pool of red blood.

It all happened very fast. Kowalski, Kubicki and the two cockneys stood transfixed by the scene for a moment, unaware of the sudden arrival of Voronov, who darted forward with impressive speed for a man of his bulk and clubbed Kubicki over the head with his Tokarev pistol. Kubicki groaned and fell to his knees before sliding slowly down the grille of the lorry. Kowalski was still too dazed even to be aware of the danger he was in. He knelt down to close the Count's eyes, oblivious to the gun in Voronov's hand that was trained on him. Voronov also knelt down, maintaining his gaze on Kowalski, and touched Trubetskoi's hand. He muttered a few inaudible words in Russian to his dead compatriot then stood up to face Kowalski. His face was distorted with fury and he kicked Kubicki's inert but breathing body savagely. His voice as he spoke to Kowalski in fluent Polish, however, was measured and even.

"You had better come with us. Your foolish friend has caused the completely unnecessary deaths of the Count and my good friend. I should kill you both for that, but…" He waved his free hand in the air and shouted over his shoulder in Russian. "Maksim. Bring the magnum and load this gentleman into the car." Maksim appeared, gun in hand, and grabbed Kowalski by the arm as Voronov instructed Jake and Billy to drag the unconscious Miro and follow Maksim. Voronov told them that he would remain by the lorry covering them.

Maksim was just about to open one of the car doors for Kowalski when a young woman in a nanny's uniform appeared at the gate of a house a few yards further down from where the lorry had pulled over. As she turned to close the gate behind her she saw the scene for the first time – the dead men, Miro's unconscious body, the blood, the guns. She screamed in terror. Maksim, Jake and Billy looked back in confusion at Voronov, who was walking over to the woman and in that instant Kowalski took his chance and bolted. He ran as fast as he could along the edge of the pavement, which was bordered in the most part by thick hedges, hoping desperately they would provide some protection from his pursuers. There was the crack of a gun report and he heard the bullet whistle inches above his head. He ran another twenty yards then stopped and hid behind a tree. Hearing the sound of squealing tyres he poked his head out and looked back to see Voronov's saloon accelerating away with the lorry following behind.

★ ★ ★

Merlin and his team arrived a little later than intended because they had had to divert around a bomb-crater just outside the Lord's cricket ground. As they pulled up, they saw the Countess standing rigidly outside her front door, staring hard into the distance, as if looking for something. A number of men who looked like workmen stood around her, seeming equally confused. Then Merlin heard a cracking noise, and another. "Was that what I think it was, Sergeant?"

"Sounded like gunshots, sir."

One of the workmen pointed at the next road junction and shouted something about a lorry. The Countess turned slowly to look at him, her hands clenched tightly together in front of her, and shouted her husband's name. "Adam!"

Merlin got back in the car and Bridges took off, taking the first turning down Snowdon Drive in search of the source of the shots. At the end of the road, Bridges paused briefly until Merlin directed him to the right. "There. Be careful." The stolen Austin remained where it had stopped, pulled in at right angles to the kerb. There were no other vehicles in sight. "Approach carefully, Sam."

Merlin could see three motionless figures, two in the road near the car and one on the pavement a few yards away. "You'd better stay in the car, Constable."

"Certainly not, sir."

Merlin decided to ignore Robinson's insubordination. "Very well, but stay close to me."

Bridges walked over and knelt down to look at the first of the bodies in the road. "The Count, sir. Looks like he's had it." A thin stream of red liquid trickled from the corner of Tarkowski's mouth as he lay, his head face up, in the blood-soaked gutter.

"This one's alive." Robinson knelt by the man on the pavement who was wearing a Polish Air Force uniform. While the back of his head sported a very ugly-looking bloody wound, his eyelids were fluttering. Merlin knelt down beside her. "Why it's Jan's friend Kubicki. What the hell is he doing here?"

Bridges turned to the final body. "This one's dead too, sir. Both men killed with a bullet in the skull." Bridges stood up and told Robinson to find a police box to call for an ambulance. "I saw one around the corner." Merlin looked down at the second corpse. "Who's this then?" Strands of red hair hung over Trubetskoi's sightless eyes, which seemed to stare up at him in amused surprise. The face looked Slavic to him.

"Look at those tyre marks, sir."

"Yes, Sergeant. A large vehicle brought to a halt by this car. The lorry the man was shouting about presumably. A hijacking?" They inspected the car, which revealed nothing of immediate note. Robinson returned and said that an ambulance and more officers were on their way.

"Look, Constable, you'd better stay here with our injured man and those other poor fellows. Which way do you think they might have taken the lorry, Sergeant?"

"If we keep going in this direction, we'll get to the Finchley Road. That's our best bet, I should think."

As the two men got back into their car they heard more gunfire. "Hurry, Sam!"

★ ★ ★

Kowalski hid behind a tree and paused for breath as the police car rushed past him. He muttered a string of violent Polish curses. That idiot, Miro! If only he could have been a little more patient. He replayed in his mind what had just happened. God, what an idiot!

His first thought when he stopped running was to find the Countess and tell her the terrible news, but the arrival of the police car suggested to him that this might not be wise. If he went back to her, he would have to answer all sorts of awkward questions from the police. And what about Miro? He had seen that the hijackers had left him on the pavement. He should have gone back for him, of course, but the police would no doubt sort his friend out. He was alive and he had a thick skull. As for the hijackers, they were probably well away by now. At least two of them were Russians. Government men probably. Well, they had the gold and there was nothing to be done. He had done his best to help Tarkowski, but he'd better get back to Northolt. His plane should be fixed by now and there would be Germans to kill tomorrow. He was breathing more easily now and his nerves were no longer jangling. He walked calmly away from the tree. It wouldn't take him too long to get to Marylebone Station.

★ ★ ★

The lorry had not made it to the Finchley Road. As they approached the junction, Merlin and Bridges came across it halted in the road, its path blocked by a long, foreign-looking limousine with diplomatic number plates. Another smart saloon car sat beside it. A stocky, grey-haired and moustachioed man in a grey overcoat and a skinny fellow in a gabardine mackintosh were pointing guns at a large, bearded man and two scruffy heavies. The bearded man was handing over a gun to the man in the overcoat. Merlin got out of his car and shouted, "Please, everyone lower your guns."

The grey-haired man shouted back, "I am a Russian Embassy Official. Grishin is the name. These men are thieves in possession of Russian government property, which I am requisitioning."

"That is as may be, but you must lower your gun, sir."

"Only when you have these crooks under control."

Merlin told Bridges to stand back and began walking slowly towards the men. A shot rang out and he flattened himself on the road. He was unharmed, but heard one of the Russian officials, the skinny one, cry out before falling to the ground.

Voronov laughed. "Well done, Maksim!" As Grishin anxiously searched for the source of the shot, Voronov escaped around the side of the lorry and into someone's front garden, while Jake and Billy ran hell for leather into a small lane between the houses behind them and disappeared. When Grishin and Platonov had stopped Voronov's car and the lorry minutes before with their own roadblock, they hadn't noticed Maksim, who still had Voronov's Smith and Wesson, slipping out of the Packard and behind some dustbins near the car. Voronov now moved from the garden, under cover of some bushes, to join

Maksim and took possesion of the gun. Grishin meanwhile ran behind his car and was joined there moments later by Platonov, who had only been grazed by Maksim's shot.

Merlin hurried back and knelt down behind the police Austin with Bridges. Moments later there was a shout as Maksim broke his cover. Somehow he avoided the hail of bullets from Grishin and Platonov and made it to the entrance of the lane down which Jake and Billy had escaped. He cast a brief glance back at his boss before vanishing from sight.

"Maksim, you bastard! Come back…"

"Come out, Kyril Ivanovitch. This is idiotic. You have no hope." Merlin could see that Grishin was reloading as he shouted in Russian to the bearded man.

"Ha, Valery Grishin. I spit on you. You know I have a hundred lives. I have thwarted our great leader Comrade Stalin many times. Why not once again?"

More bullets pinged against the metal of the bins and the Packard before Voronov burst from his cover, maintaining his fire as he ran towards the lane down which the others had made their escape. Grishin needed to reload, but Platonov got off another couple of shots, one of which was successful. Voronov came to a halt, staggered a few steps, then slowly crumpled to the ground. All was silence, save for the hissing sound of the steam escaping from the Packard's bullet-damaged radiator. After a cautious minute's wait, Grishin slowly emerged from behind his car and walked the few yards towards the fallen body. He turned Voronov over with his foot and saw that he was still breathing. Voronov opened his eyes, coughed up some blood, and smiled up at him. Grunting with pain and effort, he reached up to grasp Grishin's wrist. "I have enjoyed my lives, my friend." He attempted a chuckle. "So I guess this really was my hundredth." A stream of blood stained his beard. "Such a messy end, eh? Please give my regards to Josef Vissarionovich. I wish him pleasure of his gold." His grasp relaxed and the great luck of which Voronov was so proud finally ran out.

★ ★ ★

After some to'ing and fro'ing with the A.C., who had had to consult several lofty civil servants, Merlin had arranged for the lorry's contents to be deposited that evening in the vaults of the Bank of England. Grishin had ranted and raved at him in Hampstead and followed him to Scotland Yard, insisting that the gold was Russian property and should be entrusted to his care. The Russians had made representations to the Foreign Office, the Treasury and the Prime Minister's Office, all to no avail.

Miro Kubicki was recovering from his concussion at the Hampstead General Hospital and hadn't yet been questioned. The Countess was still distraught and in no fit state for interrogation. The second dead man at the original hijacking scene had been identified by papers on his body as Misha Trubetskoi, Voronov's business partner and partner in crime.

Robinson had been kind enough to make Merlin a hot chocolate, which he was now enjoying in his office as his cuckoo clock sounded to tell him it was midnight. He hoped the exact story of what had happened in Hampstead that afternoon would become clearer tomorrow. He was doodling with a pencil on the blotting pad on his desk and found himself writing down the name of Kilinski. A lot had happened, but would any of it lead them any closer to Kilinski's killer? The night's bombing seemed to have subsided. He shut his eyes. *Best to give my brain a rest until the morning,* he thought.

CHAPTER 17

Wednesday, September 18

The moon had appeared from behind the clouds and lit up their faces. After escaping, they had run like madmen down Finchley Road, pushing their way past pedestrians and attracting much attention. By the time they reached Swiss Cottage, they felt sure they were not being chased, but who was to say that there had not been a police alert. They slowed down to a walk, but their hearts were still beating double time. As they passed St John's Wood Tube Station, a policeman turned the corner of the road and almost bumped into them. When he had showed no other interest than to warn them to watch where they were going, they relaxed a little more. After resting on a seat in Regent's Park, they had found a pub, congratulated themselves on their survival, drunk a skinful and then set off to walk home. A bombing raid had delayed their journey and they had found shelter in a derelict office block.

"I think the bombers have gone now, Billy."

"Haven't heard the all clear, have you?"

"Nah, but it's all quiet, listen."

"Alright. Let's get going." They rose from the linoleum floor of what had been the reception area for an accounting firm called Thomsons, as a large sign hanging upside down above the main doorway informed them. They made their way towards Marylebone High Street and then on to Euston Road. As they turned right and headed towards the City and East End, they suddenly became aware of aircraft engine noise. They looked up and saw a light in the distance somewhere over Oxford Street. "Looks like someone's come a cropper." Billy turned and kicked a large stone in front of him.

Jake had stopped and was looking back. "I don't think it's a fighter. It's too big."

The men resumed their journey, aware of increasing noise. They began to run. The roar became intense. Panic suffused the men's faces. Moments later, the stricken flaming Heinkel bomber crashed onto Euston Road, down which it ploughed for a hundred yards or so, taking a few parked cars, a stray dog, and Jake and Billy with it.

★ ★ ★

The team, including the newly returned Constable Cole with his arm in a sling, had gathered in Merlin's office. "Thank you, everyone. You alright, Cole? Good. Well, we had a rather exciting day yesterday. Sorry you and Cole missed all the fun, Peter. I feel I can now say I know what it was like to live in the Wild West. First shot at in the Arcade on Monday night, then yesterday again in Hampstead. All a bit like the Gunfight at the OK Corral."

Merlin was feeling very good this morning. What was it the Prime Minister had said in his youthful memoirs? "There is nothing more exhilarating than to be shot at without result." In the Arcade, he had avoided a bullet clearly intended for him and although in the Russian shootout no bullets had been aimed at him, several had passed within inches of his head.

"The question is, of course, what the hell was that all about? Well, Colonel Grishin has told me a story. As some of you know, the Colonel has been moving heaven and earth to get the gold from the lorry on behalf of the Russian government. The story, of course, justifies the Russian entitlement to this gold, and we should bear that in mind in judging its veracity. Anyway, according to Grishin, some time ago, in the Spanish Civil War, the Republican side – that's the bunch that eventually lost, by the way – agreed to send Mr Stalin a large shipment of gold as some sort of security for all the financial and material help the Russians were giving them.

Spain had a lot of gold from its years of empire in the Americas and was at the time one of the five leading bullion owners in the world. In any event, when the shipment was sent, a small part – still worth a fortune – was siphoned off somehow on arrival in Odessa. In due course, the Russians became aware of this and worked hard to identify potential culprits. After a while they focused on a Pole, an officer who had served the Russians in Spain, as the main culprit. Somehow he had managed to get the gold through the apparently porous local national borders to accomplices in Poland." Merlin paused to check he had everyone's attention. "Now, these accomplices were members of his family, which was, according to Grishin, Count Tarkowski's family, or more specifically, the Countess' family. The Polish officer's name was Alexander or Sasha Stanislawicki."

"The Stanisawicki ingots."

"The ingots indeed, Constable Robinson. Stanislawicki is Countess Tarkowski's maiden name and Sasha was her brother. The gold, when it arrived in Poland, probably Warsaw according to Grishin, was in many forms. Much of it was ancient Aztec or Inca gold jewellery or body decoration. Grishin thinks, and this seems to be a sensible assumption, that the Stanislawickis felt it unsafe to keep the gold in the form in which it arrived. They had the gold melted down and then turned into ingots with the Stanislawicki crest on them. If anyone came looking, they could simply claim that the gold was family gold and had been in the family for generations. The family was well known to be powerful and wealthy, though Grishin says there were hints that their finances might have become strained. Somehow or other, Tarkowski and the family managed to get the gold to London. Grishin only became aware of this latter fact in the past few days. Voronov was a Russian émigré in London whom Grishin knew to be up to no good and had placed under observation. The man was apparently a notorious crook and fraudster, who had lived something of a charmed life. Grishin said he was quite close to

Stalin. It's my understanding that proximity to Stalin often proves deadly, but Voronov somehow managed to keep on good terms. Grishin by chance happened to be following Voronov yesterday, witnessed the hijacking and put two and two together regarding the gold. He has been good enough to give me the embassy's full background report on Voronov, which is being translated for us now. That, for what it's worth, is his story."

Johnson raised a hand. "So, if Voronov and his partner were sponsoring looting expeditions, that would appear to be in character?"

"Yes, it would, Peter. And I have been thinking that the men who scarpered from the scene in Hampstead yesterday might be the looters who shot poor Cole here."

"Not poor, sir."

"Sorry, Cole, bad choice of words – brave Cole here, I mean."

"Where does all this leave us with Kilinski, sir?"

"Good question, Sergeant. Obviously we have to speak to the Countess. There is, however, a slight problem. The A.C. has been on to me. The Polish Legation have insisted that the Countess be left in peace to come to terms with her loss. I told the A.C. that I would try and be understanding, but that I would need to see her as soon as possible. The A.C. asked me to put any interview off for a day, but I said I didn't think I could do that." Merlin paused. "That was not very popular."

"When can we see her then, sir?"

"I'll leave it until this afternoon. There's one other person we should speak to and that's Kubicki. Do we know if he's still in the hospital, Sergeant?"

"He checked out this morning. Went back to base."

"Very well. Another trip out to Northolt, I think. You come with me, Robinson. Sergeant, you'd better stay here, fend Grishin off and tidy up any loose ends from yesterday. Peter, you and Cole generated an excellent looting lead, but it looks like the big fish in this particular case have copped it."

"Not to worry, sir. The small fry may reappear and there are plenty of others out there. We'll get back on the job with Stewart as soon as Cole is able—"

"I am able now, sir."

"That's the spirit, Cole, but I think you'd better wait until that sling is off, eh?"

"Yes, sir."

★ ★ ★

Miro Kubicki was seething and his head was throbbing. The staff at the hospital had not been keen for him to leave, but he had insisted.

When he arrived at the base, he went straight to Kowalski's hut. Jerzy was by his bed, putting his final bit of kit on as the squadron was due in the air imminently.

Kubicki's first action was to throw a punch, but he was weak and Kowalski easily deflected it. "What the hell, Miro, what are you doing? What's wrong with you?"

Miro fell onto the bed and put his head in his hands. "Ty draniu, Kowalski, you bastard. You took me off on what was very nearly a suicide mission yesterday. I was almost killed and then you left me for dead with those bastards and ran off. Then you ask what is wrong."

"Look. I'm sorry. It would have been better if you had kept calm, but—"

"You are a bastard, Jerzy. I fought like a man at least. What have you really been up to with those people, the Count and everyone?"

Kowalski shrugged, smiled enigmatically and disappeared through the door.

An hour later when the policeman arrived to see him with the pretty girl, Kubicki was lying on his bed with a wet towel on his forehead. Physically he was feeling a little better, but his anger had not subsided. He told them everything about what had happened the day before. They were, of course, previously unaware of Kowalski's participation in events. He had no compunction about telling them.

"He seemed very close to these people, the Count and Countess. You should speak to the Countess about him. Where was all this gold from? He wouldn't tell me. He drags me along to help without telling me that there were some mad Russians prepared to go to war for this gold. What was he thinking?"

"Where is he now?"

"In the air, Inspector. Up above, free as a bird."

★ ★ ★

The two Messerschmitts came out of the sun on his right. Kowalski could see them clearly, but he thought the two other squadron planes on his left might be blinded. He waggled his wings and dived, hoping that they would get the message to follow him. His radio was on the blink for some reason. As he bottomed out of his dive, he saw that his friends had been slow off the mark and the German planes were almost on them. Squeezing the maximum out of the Hurricane, he rose steeply and flipped back over and behind the Messerschmitts. His mistake was not to notice another German fighter coming out of the sun. The two RAF planes beneath him were now under fire. Flames began to flicker from one of them. Jerzy squeezed the trigger and sent a line of tracers beneath him, catching the tail of one of the Germans. Moments later there was an explosion and he could see that half of his left wing had gone. The third Messerschmitt closed in for the kill. Splinters of glass sprayed his cheeks as the bullets grazed the windscreen. As the plane began to spiral down, he managed to cross himself. He thought of the good things he had done and prayed forgiveness for the bad. He thought of Maria and Adam and the Stanislawickis. He thought of Jan and Miro. And he thought of Kilinski.

★ ★ ★

Merlin had asked the station commander at Northolt to call him when Kowalski returned from his mission. Back at the Yard, he picked at a currant bun that Bridges had brought in from Tony's Café and pondered what to do. There was a brief knock on the door and the A.C. entered. "Ah, Frank. There you are."

Merlin rose, but the A.C. nodded him back into his chair as his mottled teeth revealed themselves in a wintry smile. "Just a quick word. I thought you should know, I've had quite a bit of flak about your battle in Hampstead yesterday. No. No. You needn't get worked up. I told everybody that it was an incident that would have happened whether you were there or not and the fortuitous fact of your presence prevented things getting much worse. In any event, the Home Secretary was most anxious that this matter get resolved as soon as possible. He was very shocked, of course – he used similar words to yours, though instead of talking about a cowboy gunfight, he said something about Chicago gangsters. The long and short of it is that you are to ignore the complaints of the Poles and if getting to the bottom of things requires a vigorous interrogation of this unfortunate Polish lady, you are to get on with it."

"Thank you, sir."

★ ★ ★

"I am afraid the Countess is still not fit to receive visitors."

Merlin squeezed the telephone receiver tight in irritation. "Look, Doctor Molik. There have been two gunfights on the suburban streets of Hampstead. I have three bodies. All something to do with a pile of gold in the Count and Countess' possession. The Countess is the only person who can cast full light on these events. Regardless of what you—"

"But, Chief Inspector, it is not only I insisting that the Countess be left in peace. General Sikorski, the leader of the Polish government in exile is adamant that—"

Merlin rose from his seat. "Look, Doctor, I don't care whether it's you, Sikorski, the Prime Minister or the King of

England insisting. I am on my way to see the lady." He slammed down the phone and grabbed his coat.

They arrived at the Tarkowski residence just after two. At the door they were met by the doctor who was a short, balding man with a wispy, grey beard. He remonstrated with Merlin again, but his complaints were halted by an imperious voice from above. "Stop it, Doctor. I will see them. They are only doing their jobs." The Countess, dressed in black, descended the staircase slowly and elegantly, before leading Merlin and his colleagues into her drawing room. A large, life-size portrait of a dashing young man in military uniform, brandishing a sword in the air, dominated the room.

"My father, Count Stanislawicki." The Countess waved a hand at the chairs in front of the fireplace above which the portrait was placed and everyone sat down. "It was painted when he was commanding his regiment at the turn of the century. Of course, Poland only existed as a province of Russia then. For all of the nineteenth century, Polish independence was a distant aspiration. It was only in 1918, after the Great War, that Russia gave Poland back her independence and even then, it took only a few years for the Russian army to be back at the gates of Warsaw. My father fought with Pilsudski then and for once the Poles triumphed. Stalin fought on the Russian side then, did you know that? Being the coward that he was, of course, he skulked in the rearguard. Yes, my father was a brave man. I say was, although he is still alive, or so the last letter from the Mother Superior advised me. He is now only a husk of a man. His mind has gone. There was no way he could make the journey here, so we entrusted him to the care of the nuns at a convent deep in the country."

The Countess stared up at her father's portrait and a tear ran down her cheek. She collected herself, brushed the tear away with her hand and faced Merlin. "Now, Chief Inspector. Ask your questions."

Robinson took out her notebook and sat forward, pen poised.

The Countess drew in her breath. "My, Inspector. You have come well supplied with clerks. The Nazis are very good at clerking by all accounts." She paused to look out of the window. "Ah, but forgive me, my dear, the comparison is ill-judged. Please forgive a bitter woman." Robinson bobbed her head to acknowledge the apology.

Merlin cleared his throat. "I am very sorry about your husband, Countess. As you know, he was murdered by Voronov's gang. Voronov, as you may not know, is also now dead. We know that the Count was transporting a large quantity of gold to a bank in the City. This bank already holds gold bullion on your husband's account. We also have an allegation from the Russian embassy that this gold was stolen a few years before the war from a consignment of gold being shipped from Spain to Russia. Perhaps you could elaborate on all this for us?"

The Countess looked hard at Merlin then transferred her gaze to Robinson. "You are a very pretty girl to be in the police, young lady." Robinson blushed. "Would you be so good as to go to the bureau in the corner over there and pour me a small glass of plum brandy? It's in the decanter on the right." Robinson looked across at Merlin to seek approval, then went to get the drink.

"Forgive my manners in not offering you anything, gentlemen, but I am sure being on duty precludes such refreshment." The Countess took the glass from Robinson and took a sip. "First of all, Chief Inspector, I will tell you all I know with one exception. I do not propose to discuss these ludicrous claims concerning the provenance of the gold with you. Or, let me put it another way – I state unequivocally that the gold belongs to my family, as it has belonged for countless generations, and that the Russian claims are without foundation. This gold is serving or is intended to serve a noble purpose, that is, the support of our Polish government here in London. There is much work to be done back in the homeland. The Count was devoted to his country." The Countess paused to drink again. "So, Kyril Voronov is dead, is he?"

"He was shot at the second shootout."

The Countess' lips parted in a sour smile. "Voronov was a vile man. A murderer and a blackmailer. I have a brother in prison in Moscow. Voronov promised to help him if I… if I did certain things. He also knew somehow about our gold and wanted me to help him steal it."

"And did you?"

The Countess shaded her eyes with her right hand. "I did something I regret, but did not lead him to the gold. He used his contacts and found his own way. My husband had this gold in storage in a commercial building, which was bombed. He moved it here, but obviously that was not suitable and hence he made arrangements to move the gold to the bank yesterday. Voronov learned about these arrangements from a clerk at the bank and came with his cronies to rob us of the gold. He killed my husband, but… well, there it is."

Merlin leaned forward in his chair. "What were Miro Kubicki and Jerzy Kowalski doing here?"

"They came to provide moral and physical support. My husband was worried about the danger of transporting the gold, justifiably, as we now know. He asked Jerzy to come and Jerzy brought Mr Kubicki. I understand he got a blow on the head. Is he alright?"

"He's recovering. Do you know what happened to Jerzy?"

"Yes, he rang me last night to offer me his sympathies and to say that he got safely back to his base."

"And what is Jerzy Kowalski to you, Countess?"

"He is my nephew, my sister's son."

"Are you close?"

The Countess reached again for her drink and finished the glass. "Of course. He is a charming, loveable boy. A hero too."

"Ziggy Kilinski?"

"What about him?"

"We have a theory that Kilinski was on some sort of mission to do with his brother. He also had one or more of your gold

273

ingots and an ancient Aztec amulet. We also had the distinct feeling that the Count was not truthful with us about his meetings with Kilinski. Can you tell us more?"

The Countess stared into the distance for a moment and seemed to be wrestling with her thoughts. She reached some sort of resolution. "His real name was Simon Nozyk. He had a brother called David who was a skilled craftsman who worked for my family. He turned his hand to many things. We had a fine collection of art, jewels and so on. One day David disappeared. His brother was trying to find out what happened to him. Unfortunately he had got it into his head that we had had something to do with it."

"And this was why Kilinski contacted you? He had connected you to David?"

"Yes."

Merlin rubbed his forehead and sighed. "Do you have any idea about what happened to David?"

"None I'm afraid, but Kilinski would not believe us. He also knew about our gold and indeed had got hold of a sample of it, although I know nothing of the amulet you mention. He told my husband he had met Voronov who had clearly filled his head with these false rumours about the provenance of the gold. He began to make threats about using this knowledge to embarrass us and make us reveal to him what he thought might be the truth about David. He became more than just a pest. He felt he could blackmail us."

"And did Kowalski know what Kilinski was about?"

"I told him."

"And what did he do?"

"I believe Mr Kilinski disappeared before Jerzy could speak to him."

"Did—" Merlin was interrupted by a commotion at the front door. Moments later, Grishin burst into the room followed by two burly men in military uniform. "And so, Countess Tarkowski, have you been telling Mr Merlin about your stolen gold?"

The Countess stood, her face beetroot red with anger. "The gold is ours!" Grishin produced a document from the briefcase he was carrying.

"Not according to this, dear lady. Do you recognise the signature? Go on, look."

The Countess put on her spectacles and grasped the last page of the document that Grishin was holding in front of her. She looked and read, then, with a piercing cry of recognition, buckled to the floor. Constable Robinson hurried forward to try and catch her but was too late. Merlin and Bridges bent down and helped the Countess carefully to her feet and back into her chair.

Grishin continued contemptuously. "Yes, your dear brother Karol describes here in detail how your other beloved dead brother Sasha stole the gold from our shipment from Spain, taking advantage of a bureaucratic error. How he, Karol and your cousin Kowalski brought the gold overland through the mountain forests to Poland. How the gold jewellery and Spanish bars were melted down and recast with your family crest. And, finally, how you managed to get the gold to London before the Nazis could get their filthy hands on it."

The Countess sat rigid in her chair. "And Karol?"

"Is dead, Countess. By his own hand apparently, though you may choose to believe otherwise."

Silent tears rolled down Maria Tarkowski's alabaster cheeks. Robinson placed a consoling hand on her shoulder.

Merlin gave Grishin a hard look. "Could this not have been handled a little more delicately, Colonel?"

Grishin stroked his moustache and laughed. "Delicately! You are sitting on millions of pounds' worth of our gold, Chief Inspector. Gold stolen by this woman's family. No doubt she has been sitting here telling you a pack of lies. Perhaps now you will get the truth from her."

"With respect, Colonel, I would suggest the gold belongs to Spain before anyone. You stole it from the legitimate government of Spain at the time, did you not?"

"Stole? No, my friend, a legitimate commercial transaction.

They wanted arms and had to pay for them or provide security for payment. The Spaniards can whistle for the gold, Chief Inspector."

Doctor Molik appeared at the door and sprang to the Countess's side. "Come, my dear. Come upstairs. The Countess needs rest, gentlemen. I told you she was not yet fit to be talked to."

★ ★ ★

Back in the office, Merlin picked up the telephone and listened. "Yes, sir. I see. I am sorry. Thanks for letting me know."

Merlin pushed back his chair and sighed. "That was Northolt. Kowalski did not return from his mission. He's been posted missing, but two of his fellow pilots think they might have seen him shot out of the air."

"That poor woman."

"Poor woman indeed, Robinson. But I am certain that poor woman is a liar." Merlin rubbed his forehead. "So, according to her, Kilinski's brother disappeared. She claims she has no idea why or how. Kilinski didn't believe her. What did he think? Whatever, clearly he was being an infernal pest to the Tarkowskis. Is that why he in turn disappeared and died? Or was that for some completely different reason?"

"Perhaps Kilinski was operating as some sort of agent for Voronov?"

Merlin twirled a pencil in his fingers. "Perhaps, Constable. Still a lot of imponderables. The fact remains that of the living, the Countess is the one who knows the most. We must have another crack at her when we can. I am going for a little walk to clear my head."

When Merlin returned an hour later from his stroll along the Embankment he found the phone ringing again. He was just replacing the receiver when Bridges came in. " That was the Countess's doctor, Sergeant. He sounded very strained. Let's go. Where's Robinson?"

"Getting a translation of Grishin's document, sir. Someone at the Foreign Office is sorting it for her. What was the message?"

"Just to get there pronto. Come on."

★ ★ ★

The doctor opened the door to them. He looked exhausted and said nothing, but pointed to the stairs. When they reached the landing on the top of the stairs, the doctor called out, "It's the bedroom on the right at the front of the house."

The policemen entered a large double bedroom. The curtains were half drawn and the room was quite dark. A single bedside lamp illuminated the body on the bed. Propped up against the pillows and clad still in the dress of their earlier meeting, the Countess seemed to be gazing out of the window, her eyes wide open, her face strangely unmarked by the agonies of violent death.

Doctor Molik came into the room. "I found her there an hour and a half or so after you left. Method of death? There is a brandy glass on the carpet on the other side of the bed and an empty bottle of sleeping pills."

Merlin moved carefully around the bed. "Did she do anything in particular or speak to anyone in that hour and a half?"

The doctor sat down wearily in a small chair by the window. "The phone rang once downstairs. There is an extension on the bedside table, as you can see. I assumed that she picked it up."

"And when you found her, was she in the throes of death or...?"

"No, she was dead." The doctor raised a hand and pointed at something on the bed. "That letter is addressed to you." Merlin walked around and saw his name spelled out clearly on an envelope. He picked it up and opened it carefully.

"My dear Chief Inspector Merlin, I have just received a call from the RAF at Northolt to tell me that Jerzy is missing, presumed dead. It appears that God is determined to punish me greatly for my misdeeds. In the space of a few hours I have lost my husband, my nephew and my beloved son. In light of the anger my Maker obviously feels about what I have done, it seems prudent that I unburden myself fully before I meet him and hopefully join my loved ones.

You will, no doubt, be surprised to see the words 'my beloved son'. Apparently, this is one secret the Russian torturers failed to extract from Karol. It is a secret that I have kept for his lifetime, save from my closest and dearest. Yes, Karol was indeed not my brother but my son, the result of a youthful indiscretion long before I met the Count. In that society of ours, the truth could not be admitted. However, my father was remarkably understanding. My mother was dead and he presented Karol to the world as his adopted son and a new brother for his children. It goes without saying that I would have done anything for my son. Anything! Whatever I did do to try and save him, I cannot regret, even though I failed.

Karol's confession about the gold, secured under torture, might normally be regarded as worthless. However, given the unhappiness that the gold has brought to my family and the evil that has been done because of it, it is probably best now to admit that the story is as Grishin tells it. I am sorry if this admission deprives my government of useful resources in these dire times, but it is going to take more than a few crates of gold bullion to save Poland now. Our fate is in British and, with luck, American hands and may God bless all your efforts. I cannot resist pointing out that this theft by Poles from Russians is a mere drop in the ocean compared with the thefts by Russians from Poles over the centuries.

My younger brother, Sasha, was a bit of an adventurer. Well, perhaps that is an understatement. He somehow ended up as a communist secret policeman for our greatest enemy, but then saw an opportunity to deprive that enemy of some gold and took it successfully. The gold needed to be melted down and disguised. David Nozyk had the skills to help us to do this and we hired him. As you have seen, he did an excellent job. Then he disappeared. I lied to you about not knowing anything about this. Too many lies. The truth about David's disappearance is as follows. David was a very clever man. After a while he felt his contribution was not being properly appreciated. In other words he became greedy. At some point there was an argument about money. We also discovered that he had been taking some gold items for himself. The amulet in his brother's possession was clearly one such item. Karol confronted him about this in our house in Warsaw, there was an argument and fists were raised. My son never knew his own strength. He hit Nozyk and as he fell he knocked his head on the edge of a marble table. He was killed instantly. Karol arranged for his body to be buried. Nozyk had worked for us on a strict basis of secrecy and we believed and hoped that no one, including his family, knew about his relationship with us. My son was extremely remorseful about what had happened and anonymously, through a private charity, made provision for Nozyk's family. In particular an eye was kept out for David's younger brother, Simon, and steps were taken to enable him to fulfil his ambition and join the Polish Air Force. We heard later that he was, for whatever reason, going under the name of Kilinski.

A few weeks ago, Kilinski appeared on the scene. He came to see my husband a few times. He said that his brother had left him some gold items – ingots, an amulet. While still in Poland, he said he had been able to identify the design on the coin as that of the Stanislawicki coat of arms. His brother had disappeared and his family had presumed him dead. He also knew that David had visited our house in Warsaw. He wanted to know what connection David had had with us. My husband fobbed him off. We then became aware that he was spying on us. He lurked outside the house and outside my husband's office. Someone tried to interfere with the transfer of gold from my husband's commercial premises here and we assumed that was him. He harassed our bank manager. Somehow he managed to piece together most of the story and threatened to expose us. He consorted, as you know, with the madman Voronov. Eventually we had had enough, or rather I had. My husband was too kind and gentle a man. When he was out of London for the day at the beginning of last week, I saw Kilinski lurking outside late in the morning. Jerzy happened to ring me and I told him that Kilinski's pestering was becoming unbearable. I asked him if he could plead family problems to obtain an afternoon's leave. He promised to borrow someone's car and come to me. Jerzy adored me. I knew he would do anything I asked. Kilinski was still loitering at lunchtime and I invited him in for a sandwich and a drink. I offered him a brandy, then another. I don't think he was much of a drinker. He became a little inebriated and morose and was telling me about his brother. Then Jerzy arrived. After a couple more brandies, Jerzy told Kilinski that he would drive him back to the base. The next I heard about Kilinski was when you came to see my husband and said that he was missing. I presumed that Jerzy had taken the bull by the horns and somehow disposed of him. Your finding of the body seemed to confirm this and I am convinced that Jerzy killed Kilinski to protect his family. You may not agree but to me this was an act of nobility. He is dead now, as I shall be in a moment, and I feel the need as we both face our Maker to make a clean breast of it, as you English say."

Merlin passed the letter to Bridges and sat on the edge of the bed staring back at the strangely serene face of its author.

★ ★ ★

"Hello, my dear fellow."

Evans' eyes opened blearily to the sound of the familiar voice. His throat was still affected by the acrid smoke he had breathed in Savile Row and he whispered a greeting. Evans struggled to raise himself up on his pillow.

"Here, let me help you." Anthony Blunt leaned forward and helped Evans to lever himself up on the bed. "There. That's better."

To Evans, there had always been something of Carroll's Mad Hatter as sketched by Tenniel to Blunt's features, with his protruding set of upper teeth. An attractive Mad Hatter though, as far as he was concerned. "How are you, Anthony?" he croaked.

"Fit as a fiddle, but more to the point, how are you, Francis? They tell me you are on the mend."

"A lot of bruises, a cracked rib and a few other odds and sods. I guess I was lucky. I'll survive."

Blunt pulled up a chair and sat down. "Yes, you are a survivor, aren't you? I must commend you on your bravery. I understand from the nurses that you were injured while searching for an ambulance for a police colleague in the midst of a bombing raid. I must admit that physical courage is not a trait I believe I have, though I do believe I have some moral courage."

Evans raised an eyebrow.

"Yes, indeed, Francis, that was somewhat lacking when you suffered your little problem, I concede. I am sorry for my lack of support, although my response was coloured by some anger and jealousy that you could seek gratification with another man."

Evans opened his mouth, but nothing came out.

"Don't trouble yourself to talk, dear chap. I can see it is painful."

"Trubetskoi." Evans managed to spit the word out.

"Ah, yes, Trubetskoi and his senior partner Voronov. I understand from certain friends that they were involved in various nefarious activities and finally came something of a cropper. I apologise if my involving you with him caused you any embarrassment. I just heard that he was looking for someone like you and thought you would appreciate the money. I had some dealings with Voronov over the years. Odd fellows, he and his amanuensis."

Evans waved an admonishing finger.

"Yes, I know, Francis. I shall be careful with whom I deal. Now, I have bought you a present." Blunt produced a slim volume. "This is a monograph I just had published on Poussin's early work. I am sure you will enjoy it." His friend managed a weak smile. "And once you are out of here, you are welcome to come to the country for some recuperation. I intend to make amends, dear fellow, to make amends!"

★ ★ ★

It was just after four and at the Chelsea AFS station Stewart's team were preparing for another night's hazardous duty when Sir Archie Steele strode through the door. "Ah, Jack, there you are, laddie."

Stewart rose to shake Steele's outstretched hand. "And Peter. How do. Where's your young constable?" Johnson gratefully withdrew his hand from Steele's iron grip. "Cole got injured, Sir Archibald. Took a bullet in the shoulder from a looter. He's desperate to get back out there, but the docs say it will be a few days yet."

The three men sat down at the communal table and Elsie poured out tea. Johnson brought Steele up to date with the events at the Burlington Arcade and with Evans' information on the looters. "Maybe they'll be out of the picture now, if this Russian boss of theirs has copped it."

"Plenty more fish in the sea, I should think, Inspector, eh, Jack?" Sir Archibald reached out for the plate of biscuits Elsie had just laid on the table.

"Aye, sir, though I think it should be rats not fish. 'Great rats, small rats, lean rats, brawny rats, brown rats, black rats, grey rats, tawny rats'."

Steele frowned. "I'm not your friend Merlin, you know, Jack. If you want me to name the author, I haven't a clue."

Johnson smiled. "It's Browning. *The Pied Piper of Hamelin*."

Stewart smiled. "Well done, Peter! I can see we'll have to

make a space for you in our competitions. I'll tell Frank next time I see him."

Stewart paused and looked up, thinking he could hear the distant rumble of aircraft. "I was just wondering, sir, if you had any information about the bigger picture?"

"How do you mean, Jack?"

"Well, sir, the intensity of the raids seems to be easing."

Steele pulled out a pipe and tapped it on the table. "The feeling is that if the Germans are to invade, they need to get their skates on as autumn rolls in. The great job our pilots have done may have caught them by surprise. I doubt the air raids are going to stop, but we may well have put off the invasion until next year."

As Steele began to fill his pipe with tobacco, a siren went off. In the back of the room, a phone rang. One of Stewart's men answered it, then shouted out, "Knightsbridge, sir. We're to hook up with the others behind Harrods."

Steele rose to his feet. "Good luck, gentlemen. Take care. There's a long way to go yet in this war, but we shall overcome, no doubt." He lit his pipe and beamed.

★ ★ ★

"Where to, Herr Generalfeldmarschall?"

As the car edged away from the Berlin Reichkanzleri, Hermann Goering, the Fuhrer's right-hand man and Commander-in-Chief of the Luftwaffe, simmered. "Anywhere, Gunther, I don't give a shit. Just drive. No, on second thoughts, drive out into the country. I need to see trees and grass."

Goering loved the countryside. He had several beautiful country homes, adorned in most cases with the heads of the herds of animals he had hunted and shot. Perhaps, he thought, he should go for a few days' hunting to get things out of his system.

He and General von Rundstedt had been summoned to the Fuhrer's office that afternoon. After a long tirade about the incompetence of the Luftwaffe in particular and all his commanders in general, Adolf Hitler had informed them that Operation Sealion, the plan for the invasion of England, was being postponed indefinitely. "You have let me down, Hermann. Your pilots are cowards, are they not? The English are on their last legs, you told me. 'They will not be able to resist our glorious Luftwaffe!' Well, they have resisted, haven't they? With their inferior aeroplanes they have defied the might of Germany – and me!"

"But, mein Fuhrer—"

"Hah! Do not make excuses. It is time to move on. We must turn our attention to the east and that Georgian lout, Stalin. You must both concentrate on that now."

How had the British survived and overcome them? Luftwaffe losses over the weekend had been huge. Goering had never been as dismissive of the British military capabilities as the Fuhrer, but still he had thought his pilots would prevail.

The car had reached the countryside and as the trees and fields flashed by in the growing dusk, the Field Marshall loosened the belt on his uniform and helped himself to a glass of the Macallan Scotch Whisky he kept in the bar compartment in his door. He had looked forward to taking personal possession of some Scottish distilleries after the invasion, but that was not to be, at least not for a while. Perhaps Operation Sealion could be revived in the spring? He sighed and gazed out at a herd of Friesian cattle being chased through a field by some small boys. He drank and felt the warm golden liquid trickle down his throat. He swirled the remainder of the whisky around in the large balloon glass which was engraved on the side with his initials. He closed his eyes and chuckled at the thought of the buxom all-Nordic athlete he had bedded the previous evening. A little more of Greta tonight would help to put the Fuhrer's tirade behind him. Those legs, those eyes…

★ ★ ★

Merlin reached up behind the cuckoo clock where he always kept a medicinal bottle of Bells whisky. Bridges had brought a couple of glasses from the cubby-hole and Merlin poured out a healthy shot in each. Robinson insisted on sticking to her glass of water.

"Cheers." The men clinked glasses.

"Well, it's a relief to have got the Kilinski case tied up, sir."

"So it is, Sam, assuming, that is, that we have got it tied up." Merlin swirled the whisky around in his glass. "Because, I have to say, it all seems a little too neat for me. And there is that niggling little gap."

"Sir?"

"Well, Constable, in her letter, the Countess presumes and indeed is convinced that Jerzy bumped Kilinski off, but she didn't confirm this with him, did she? Do we share her view that Kowalski was up to poisoning a fellow officer?"

"He doesn't appear to have been a very nice man. Look at the way he legged it from the Hampstead shoot-up."

"No, Sergeant, perhaps not a nice man, but a killer?" Merlin finished his drink and shook his head. "Sorry, Sam, you know what I'm like. Never happy with loose ends. But the A.C. is, however, happy with the Countess's presumption of Kowalski's guilt and is delighted to have the case wrapped up, so I'd better stop griping and move on."

He flipped open a folder Bridges had put on the desk and was giving it a cursory glance when the telephone rang. "Oh, yes. He wants to see me? Yes, I think I know who he is. Bring him on up."

★ ★ ★

"And you are?"

"Ryabov. Maksim Ryabov."

"And you were the late Mr Voronov's servant at his Berkeley Square residence where my officers just detained you?"

"Da."

"And would it have been you I saw, amongst others, firing a gun in Hampstead the other day?"

"Da." Maksim was wearing a thick overcoat, which he had taken from Voronov's wardrobe, but was nevertheless shivering.

"You understand that I shall have to arrest you for that?"

"Da. Da. Arrest me. Put me in prison. That is what I want. I want to be away from guns, bombs, loud voices, loud bangs. I need peace."

"We can arrange that. The officer downstairs said you have something to tell me about your dead employer."

Maksim looked around the room nervously. "May I sit down?"

Bridges stood up and offered his seat.

"Thank you, sir. Most kind. Kindness is not something I was accustomed to with Mr Voronov." As he sat down, he looked across appreciatively at Constable Robinson's legs. "You have such nice-looking lady policemen in this country. So unlike Russia."

"I am sure the Constable appreciates the compliment, Mr Ryabov. Now, just a moment, there's something we must do." Merlin signalled to Bridges who cautioned Ryabov and warned him that anything he said might be used against him in court. "Do you understand? Yes? Then if you are happy, what have you to tell us?"

"You know about Mr Voronov and his desire for the gold in Count Tarkowski's possession? Stalin's gold as he called it."

"We do."

"And you know that there was a Polish pilot who got involved with him?"

"Ziggy Kilinski, yes."

"Do you know who killed him?"

"We believe that it was one of his fellow pilots. Jerzy Kowalski."

Maksim smiled to himself. He had stopped shivering now.

286

"It came to Kyril Ivanovitch's attention that Kilinski was paying close attention to the activities of Count Tarkowski. He arranged to meet him. Voronov pumped him for information but Kilinski would not tell everything. Voronov was very angry with him. They met again and Kilinski was more helpful. They shared some more of the things they knew, but Voronov still felt that Kilinski was holding things back about the gold. He decided Kilinski was an irritant who might get in his way. Kyril Ivanovitch did not care for irritants."

Merlin leaned forward over his desk. "Are you saying—?"

"Patience, Chief Inspector. Mr Voronov had many useful friends. He had Kilinski followed. One night, Monday of last week, I believe, Kilinski went to Tarkowski's place. Some hours later, Kilinski was driven away in a car by an air force officer. He was followed to Euston Road. The car stopped, there seemed to be a fight, the officer got knocked down and Kilinski ran off. After a few minutes, the car drove away."

"How do you know all this, by the way?"

"I hear everything in Voronov's house. All is known to me."

"Then what happened?"

"Voronov's follower went over to Kilinski, who had stopped not far from Tarkowski's building, and offered him a drink."

"They knew each other?"

"They had met before, yes. Kilinski was already drunk but he drank some more. In the drink was poison and Kilinski died."

"And who was the follower?"

"Misha Trubetskoi. Since long ago, Misha has always carried a, how do you say, flask that has vodka laced with rat poison. Misha lived a dangerous life with many enemies. He was always well armed. This flask was part of his armour."

"So, put simply, Voronov arranged for Trubetskoi to kill Kilinski?"

"That is so. Trubetskoi even bragged to me about it the

other day, waving his flask, as he often did, in front of my nose. Kilinski was just one in a long list of victims of Kyril Ivanovitch and his cronies."

★ ★ ★

"So there you have the whole sorry story, my darling. We thought we had a Polish killer, then found out it was a Russian. Both, however, are dead and beyond the reach of the law."

They were lying in the warmth of Sonia's bed. She had been fast asleep when Merlin climbed in just before midnight, but had roused at the first touch of his leg. After they had made love, she had nestled into him and insisted on hearing everything before they went back to sleep. "Poor Ziggy." She reached out and hugged him closer.

"Is Jan out of hospital yet?"

"Tomorrow morning apparently. He'll be alright. And how about your constable, Tommy Cole?"

"Bursting to get back on the job with Johnson. Johnson's out with Jack. Doesn't seem to be that busy, though, does it?" They hadn't heard any planes or guns since Merlin had arrived.

"Perhaps the Germans are getting bored with bombing us."

"Perhaps, darling. Oh. Wait. There's something I want to show you." He jumped out of the bed, went over to the chair on which he had hung his jacket and reached into a pocket. "What do you think of this? I should have put in it the Yard strong room before I left tonight, but I forgot." The amulet gleamed in the soft ray of Sonia's bedside lamp. Sonia drew in her breath as Merlin handed it to her. "Try it on, why don't you? It's about 400 years old. First worn by an Aztec emperor, perhaps later by some dark Spanish aristocrat. Whoever wore it before, none will have been as beautiful as you."

Sonia punched Merlin's shoulder. "Idiot!" Merlin winced. "Oh, darling Frank, I am so sorry. I forgot for a moment. Are you alright?"

"I'm fine Sonia. Please, go on."

She raised herself in the bed and was about to put the amulet on when she suddenly stopped. "I think not."

"Why not?"

"Think about all the bad luck this gold brought to the Countess and her family. And to Ziggy."

"Are you superstitious, my dear?"

"All Poles are very superstitious, Frank. No, put it away. Thanks for showing it to me, but you get it back where it belongs."

Merlin looked disappointed. "It has to go back tomorrow, though by all rights it should really be going back to Spain. I thought it would be fun to see it on you one time."

"No, darling. Put it away, please. You will have to make do with me as I am, without gold or other adornment." Sonia smiled shyly before slowly removing the bedcover. Merlin forgot his disappointment.

EPILOGUE

"Ah, Lavrentiy, there you are. Come! Come in." Lavrentiy Beria approached Stalin's desk, a stiff smile planted on his face.

"Sit down, sit down. Please." Stalin waved an imperious hand in which he held some papers. Beria sat in the chair facing the Vozhd across his desk. The chair, as always, was a few inches shorter than that of his boss; an obvious but useful technique for establishing dominance, which Beria himself employed in his own office. "I have just been reading this report from one of our men in Mexico. I know, I've read the details several times and this report contains nothing new, but I do so enjoy the story."

Stalin, as Beria knew, was referring to the assassination of Leon Trotsky, formerly Stalin's partner and then his adversary in the Russian leadership battles after Lenin's death. Trotsky had been killed in the summer by an ice pick in the head, wielded by an agent of Beria's.

Stalin chuckled then set down the report. "Poskrebyshev behaving himself, is he? No ill manners?"

"No, Comrade Stalin. He is as affable as always. He told me a good joke as I was on my way in." Poskrebyshev was Stalin's private secretary and ran his office. The year before, Beria, naturally with his boss' approval, had ordered the arrest of Poskrebyshev's wife, Bronislava, for crimes against the state. She was still languishing in the Lubianka, her fate all but sealed.

"Yes, he always has a new joke to tell." Stalin paused and gazed thoughtfully out of the window, where autumn was already taking a severe toll on the tree leaves in the courtyard. He idly picked up his pipe, which was unlit, and sucked it for a moment before turning his relentless gaze on Beria. "And so, Lavrentiy, we have the gold back now?"

"Yes, indeed, Comrade Stalin. The gold that Grishin found was released by the British authorities to Grishin yesterday. It is in the embassy vault."

"I hope you and Grishin will take more care about its transport back to us than Grishin did in Spain those few years ago."

"Of course, Comrade." Beria could feel the odd bead of perspiration moistening the collar of his tunic.

"And, as I understand it, all the principal criminals in the theft of the gold are now dead?"

"Yes, all."

Stalin reached for his tobacco pouch and started filling the bowl of his pipe. Beria could not stand the smell of Stalin's tobacco and his nostrils twitched involuntarily. Stalin lit a match with a flick of his finger and applied the flame. "Anything wrong, Lavrentiy? Not sickening for anything, I hope?"

"No, Comrade. Just had a heavy day. A very busy time, as you know."

Stalin leaned back in his chair, a deadly twinkle in his eyes, and puffed away. "Busy, yes, busy. You and I are always busy – vigilant as always for the treachery that is ever around us." Stalin abruptly put his pipe down in an ashtray and his elbows on the desk.

"So, there was Alexander Stanislawicki – Sasha, wasn't it?"

Beria nodded.

"So, Sasha stole this gold from under our noses at Odessa. There was some mistake in the paperwork for the gold, which he exploited. With the help of his brother Karol, who in fact turned out to be his nephew, and another nephew…" Stalin briefly consulted a folder on his desk. "Kowalski, the gold was transported to Warsaw."

Beria nodded again.

"Remind me what happened to Sasha after that?"

"Having been attached to the NKVD he fell under suspicion for holding inappropriate Polish nationalist tendencies. He was suspended from his duties and returned to Poland. After the collapse of Poland and our accommodation with Germany, most of the Polish officer corps and intelligentsia were arrested and handed over to us. Sasha was one of those arrested. You will recall that most of those enemies of Russia were liquidated at Katyn in the spring."

"At your suggestion, of course, Beria."

"It was the right thing to do, Comrade." A flash of irritation crossed Beria's face. Fortunately, Stalin had just reached down to spit into a receptacle under the desk. All key members of the Politburo had signed the execution orders, but the Vozhd liked to pretend that he had had nothing to do with the massacre.

"So, this Sasha was killed at Katyn?"

"Yes, Comrade. It is in the report I gave you."

"But at this point you had no suspicions against him regarding the gold?"

"On the contrary, I had identified Sasha as the person in charge of the gold transportation not long after you had charged me with the investigation of the matter. We found out that Sasha had been aware of the documentary discrepancy concerning the shipment and I put two and two together. Unfortunately, by the time I realised that we needed to interrogate Sasha, it was 1939; he had gone back to Poland, Hitler had invaded and we could not easily get hold of him. Then in the confusion of the invasion's aftermath, his arrest and removal to Katyn were not notified to me."

"Excuses never satisfy me, Lavrentiy. You should have got hold of him before the Nazis invaded. Then again, you should have identified him as one of our prisoners."

"With respect, Comrade, although we lost Sasha, I did manage to identify Karol as one of our prisoners and it was through him that we in due course found the gold."

Stalin grunted and spat again. "Very well. And so the two

Stanislawicki boys both perished one way or another, as did the Count and Countess and the nephew Kowalski? And my old friend Voronov, who tried to piss me off one time too many?"

"Yes, Comrade."

"And so this is all the gold we were missing?"

Beria could feel his neck getting wetter. "Not quite, Comrade. There remains a balance lodged in a vault in a London bank, which, pursuant to the Count's will, is credited to the Polish government in exile."

Stalin's face darkened. "Polish government in exile! Ha! What a joke. And how much of the missing gold do they hold?"

"About a third."

"A third." Stalin screamed. "A fucking third! And what are the prospects of its return, Comrade Beria?"

"We have initiated proceedings in the London courts. The lawyers tell us that we have a reasonably strong case. I am hopeful…"

Stalin stood up and strode to the window. He opened it and they could hear the sound of a distant factory whistle.

Beria also rose and stood nervously by his chair.

"I am sure you are hopeful, Lavrentiy. I would be, if I were you."

Beria shuffled his feet and coughed.

"When I understood that all the principal criminals, all those who had connived to deprive me of my gold, were dead, I was not correct, was I?"

"You were, of course, Comrade Stalin."

"What about Grishin?"

"Well, it—"

"It was his negligence that led to the theft in the first place, was it not?"

"Well, yes, I suppose."

"Not suppose, Lavrentiy. It is fact. Recall him and then deal with him as I would expect."

"Yes, sir."

"And what about the other conniver?"

"Who is that, Comrade?"

"You, Lavrentiy, of course. You have connived to deprive me of my gold by your inefficiency."

"But, but, Comrade—"

"But me no buts, Comrade Beria. I remember everything, as you know. And I shall remember this. Now you may go. You are very busy, as you say."

Lavrentiy Beria paused, thinking whether there was anything he could say to his advantage. From long experience, when the Vozhd was in this mood, he knew it was best to withdraw.

As he opened the door, Stalin spoke again, his voice a little mellower. "And Lavrentiy, please arrange some flowers."

"For whom, sir?"

"Why for Voronov's widow, of course. In memory of some good times together. He used to make fun of my Georgian accent, you know." Stalin smiled sweetly at his colleague. "He was not the first, but he was certainly the last!"